NOVELS BY **MERCEDES LACKEY**
available from DAW Books:

THE NOVELS OF VALDEMAR:

THE HERALDS OF VALDEMAR
ARROWS OF THE QUEEN
ARROW'S FLIGHT
ARROW'S FALL

THE LAST HERALD-MAGE
MAGIC'S PAWN
MAGIC'S PROMISE
MAGIC'S PRICE

THE MAGE WINDS
WINDS OF FATE
WINDS OF CHANGE
WINDS OF FURY

THE MAGE STORMS
STORM WARNING
STORM RISING
STORM BREAKING

VOWS AND HONOR
THE OATHBOUND
OATHBREAKERS
OATHBLOOD

THE COLLEGIUM CHRONICLES
FOUNDATION

BY THE SWORD
BRIGHTLY BURNING
TAKE A THIEF
EXILE'S HONOR
EXILE'S VALOR

VALDEMAR ANTHOLOGIES:
SWORD OF ICE
SUN IN GLORY
CROSSROADS
MOVING TARGETS
CHANGING THE WORLD*

Written with **LARRY DIXON:**

THE MAGE WARS
THE BLACK GRYPHON
THE WHITE GRYPHON
THE SILVER GRYPHON

DARIAN'S TALE
OWLFLIGHT
OWLSIGHT
OWLKNIGHT

OTHER NOVELS:

GWENHWYFAR

THE BLACK SWAN

THE DRAGON JOUSTERS
JOUST
ALTA
SANCTUARY
AERIE

THE ELEMENTAL MASTERS
THE SERPENT'S SHADOW
THE GATES OF SLEEP
PHOENIX AND ASHES
THE WIZARD OF LONDON
RESERVED FOR THE CAT

And don't miss:
THE VALDEMAR COMPANION
Edited by John Helfers and Denise Little

*Coming soon from DAW Books

MERCEDES LACKEY

Gwenhwyfar
The White Spirit

DAW BOOKS, INC.

DONALD A. WOLLHEIM, FOUNDER
375 Hudson Street, New York, NY 10014
ELIZABETH R. WOLLHEIM
SHEILA E. GILBERT
PUBLISHERS
http://www.dawbooks.com

First Printing, October 2009
1 2 3 4 5 6 7 8 9

DAW TRADEMARK REGISTERED
U.S. PAT. AND TM. OFF. AND FOREIGN COUNTRIES
—MARCA REGISTRADA
HECHO EN U.S.A.

PRINTED IN THE U.S.A.

Dedicated to Russell Galen,
without whom none of this would be possible.

Gwenhwyfar

The White Spirit

PART ONE

PRINCESS

Chapter One

The talk at the hearth of the high hall of her father's castle was all of magic that wild evening. Harvest-time had come and gone, and Samhain not far off; the old men and women were muttering about a hard winter ahead. Truly, it had turned bitter very quickly, and the harvest, while not scant, was also not bountiful. All that little Gwen knew, though, was that tonight it sounded as if everything cold and evil in the world was trying to get in. She was glad that Castell y Cnwclas was all of stone. Nothing mortal could get past those thick walls and nothing uncanny past the women gathered at the hearth, especially tonight.

Outside, the wind whined around the stone walls, and made the seats farthest from the hearth almost as cold as if the poor fellows relegated to them were sitting out on the walls. They were making up for the cold by drinking plenty of ale and mead. Inside, the drafts made flames of the torches on the walls flatten and dance, and even the huge open fire on the hearth in the center of the hall flickered this way and that, sending streamers of smoke into peoples' faces unpredictably. Gwen was glad she was sitting on the stone floor, a bit of old sheepskin between her and the flags, where she was below the smoke. She hugged her knees to her chest and listened to the women of her mother's circle with the wide eyes of a young owl. Firelight illuminated familiar faces and made them strange with shifting shadows and hectic light.

The Hall was the biggest room in the castle, and served many purposes. By day it was in turn her father's audience chamber, the place where meals were served, and the scene of most domestic work that wasn't done in the kitchen. By night, her father's men and servants slept there. The walls were as thick as Gwen's arm was long, broken only by narrow windows too small for anyone but a child to climb through. Right now, heavy wooden shutters closed off the worst of the winds. The hearth-fire in the center gave most of the heat and light, supplemented by the torches on the walls. The stone floor was covered with rushes—newly changed just two days ago, so the herbs strewn among them were still sweet and the floor beneath still clean. The ceiling was lost in darkness and further obscured by the smoke rising to the louvered hole above the hearth.

It smelled of dampness, of spilled ale, of herbs and cooked meat, of sweaty bodies and wet wool. Faintly, because it had only been two days since it had been swept clean, there was a taint of urine from the dogs and cats that ran free in here. But above all it smelled of smoke.

The women had claimed the hearth itself, sitting about the fire on benches and stools or, like Gwen and her sisters, on the floor, and the men did not challenge them. No sane man challenged a Wise Woman, much less a gaggle of them. Behind them, on the mead-benches, were the men of her father's following. He was Lleudd Ogrfan Gawr, called "The Giant," and unchallenged king of these parts. There were no more Romans to contest his rule. The Romans had come and now gone from here; they mined their tin, lead, and gold no more, and the amphitheater they had built for their so-called games now echoed only to the wail of wild cats at night. And good riddance, said her mother. Her father's words were more pithy and profane.

The good-natured growling and grumbling of the men sounded like a muttering chorus of sleepy bears on the edge of hibernation, fat with autumn berries and nuts, and thinking mostly about sleep. Partly, that was the mead and ale of her mother Eleri's brewing. She put herbs in it—she said to flavor it, but the women all knew it was to make the men calm and sleepy, and that was a secret that would never be breathed to the men, not even to the king her husband. There was little argument on Ogrfan Gawr's mead benches, and no hot-tempered quarrels that could break into blood feud. Eleri the Queen was a Wise Woman in the sense of knowing the ways of herbs as well as of magic, and she reckoned it worth the effort to keep the men from making more grief than there already was in the world. Bronywn, who served as her right hand and the children's nurse, was the keeper of her secrets.

Hunting and fighting and tall tales were the order of business on the mead-benches tonight. With the harvest over, it was hunting that would help keep the men busy until spring, and hunting would be needed to keep the hall fed if the winter was a harsh one. Magic was the subject on the hearthstone; it was the provenance of women— and a very few, very select group of men. The Druids. The bards. The occasional hermit-healer. Eleri had told Gwen that this was because men spent too much time around Cold Iron; wearing it in the form of weapons, crafting it, cherishing it. "Magic shuns Cold Iron," she had said, with a decided nod. "Men might have the Gift, but while they cling to Cold Iron, they'll never have the Power."

Gwen most especially watched her mother, listened to her words, for the Queen was also the chief sorceress here and high in the Councils of the Wise. Eleri had the Power and had it in abundance. Gwen had watched her, by full moon and waning, by Midsummer sun and Midwinter dark, weaving her Power into the spells that were the weapons *she* wielded to defend, protect, and nurture their people. There were two thrones in Lleudd Ogrfan Gawr's High Hall: the one at the mead benches and the one at the hearth. And both were equal. The king guarded the people with his sword. The queen did so with Power.

There were those that said the queen was Fae-touched. Certainly, despite having given birth to Gwen and all her sisters, she often seemed as young as any of the maids at her hearth. There were those that said the two youngest of the brood, Gwen and her younger sister, took after her. But those that said it did so with a touch of pride, not fear; if they were Fae-touched, then, that would be a good thing.

Gwen's sisters sat beside her, watching and listening just as raptly. Gynath who was almost twelve summers, Cataruna who was fourteen, and Gwenhwyfach a mere eight, the sister enough like her to have been Gwen's twin, all listened and remained very, very quiet, lest they be remembered and sent off to bed. All the sisters had much the same look about them; they got their looks from their mother, who was slim and very fair—a rarity among dark people—and not the king, who was burly and, even rarer, had a head of hair like copper wire. They had a visitor this night, who would stay through Samhain to give their rites especial power. Eleri was concerned that the old men and women were right, that this would be a hard winter, and she would do whatever it took to keep her people safe through it.

But it was not talk of the winter to come and the Samhain rites that occupied them now. It was talk of Arthur, the High King, and his court at Celliwig.

". . . and so the High King takes a bride, and the Merlin is making sure the land-rites are performed," the lady visitor was saying; she was very important, a priestess *and* a sorceress, from the great school at the Well of the Cauldron.

"And not afore time, too," muttered old Bronwyn. "Asking for trouble it was, leaving it for so long! It'll be a hard winter, thanks to all this dallying. As the king goes, so goes the land, and that's a fact." She made a sour face as the rest of the women nodded. "If the king be wifeless and childless, how can the land be anything but cold and hard? All very well to say the Merlin could make up for it, but he's only a man, one man, and—"

"Hush," Eleri interrupted, chiding her woman, and the visitor nodded with approval.

"What's done is done; the land hasn't suffered. The land has a long memory and longer patience. One hard winter will not ruin the land, and the Merlin has brought him round to the bride and the rites." The woman sighed. "And now I am here to ask you, has the High King's half-sister been among you?"

"Morgana?" Eleri shook her head. "You surely do not mean Anna Morgause . . . I have not seen her in a year or more. The Orkney clan does not favor us with their attention, much. Why?"

The visitor shrugged, but looked troubled. "It is Anna Morgause I mean. Morgana is hardly more than a child, for all her power, and she heeds the Merlin and the Council of the Wise. But Morgause . . . Anna is a woman grown, with four sons she would fain see raised high. She has the power and the willfulness, and she is wedded to Lot, who speaks the High King fair but watches through his fingers. And Morgause speaks the Council fair, but . . ."

But Eleri shook her head. "Rhianu, be careful of what you say. Have you anything other than gossip and your own suspicions? Has the Cauldron shown a vision of the future?"

The visitor looked away a moment. "No and no," she admitted.

Eleri smiled slightly. "Have done, then, and tell us of the bride. If gossip there will be, let it be of bright things and not dark, truth and not suspicion. Anna of the Orkneys will do as she does, and if the Cauldron gives you no visions, then that is the will of the Goddess."

Gwenhwyfar pondered the visitor. She did not seem like someone who would gossip to make trouble, and normally Eleri would have deferred to her judgment, since she was older and a very powerful Wise Woman indeed, one of the Nine who served the Cauldron of the Goddess. But her mother must know *something* that made her say what she had. Perhaps there was bad blood between Rhianu and Queen Morgause, and perhaps Eleri knew about it.

Rhianu pursed her lips, then seemed to resign herself. "Well, her name is Gwenhwyfar, like your own daughter, and the name suits her, for she is very like to all of you, as fair as a Saxon and slender as a reed. She was not our first choice, but Arthur came to the aid of her father, Leodegrance, saw her firing arrows from the walls, with her fine gown kilted up and fire in her eye." She shrugged. "He was smitten, and she is of the right bloodline and of our teaching. But—"

Eleri raised an eyebrow. "But?"

"She is her father's only child. We question whether his blood grows thin. The Good Goddess knows Uther's line—"

Eleri looked speculative. "Hmm. One child only, Arthur himself—"

"And never a by-blow by leman or lover, and it took the Merlin's magic to quicken Arthur in Ygraine's womb." Eleri nodded. "Still, at least now Arthur has found a woman he *wants,* and all else is suitable. Passion has a magic all its own, and the rites themselves should ensure that there is at least one child."

Rhianu coughed. "We intend to make certain of that," she said, and significant glances were shared among the women.

"That is chancy, meddling in those matters," Eleri murmured softly. "Have a care that your enterprise does not miscarry."

Gwen shivered at that moment, as an icy finger traced itself along her spine.

"Has anyone troubled to scry the results?" Eleri continued, as Gwen shivered again.

"There will be a son born to Arthur, within the proper season," Rhianu replied, with confidence. "At least one."

"Sons!" said the king, cheerfully, coming up behind his wife. "Oh, sons are all very well, but a king's wealth is in his daughters! A son may run off and pledge his service to another man in another crown, but a daughter remembers what is due her sire—what is that old saw, my sweet?" He set both hands on Eleri's shoulders, and she reached up to squeeze one with affection.

"'A son is a son 'till he takes a wife, but a daughter's a daughter for all of her life,'" Eleri responded, tilting her head back to look at him and being rewarded with a kiss.

"There, you see?" the king beamed at their visitor. "And there is my wealth. Fair daughters, strong and comely, and I know they will remember their duty to land and sire. If the High King wants loyal allies, let him have daughters to cement those bonds. If he wants magic to safeguard his kingdom, let him have daughters to spin him spells and speak for him to the gods. And if he is very lucky, he will also have a daughter that is a warrior-woman, for they make the most loyal shield-bearers."

Gwen noticed at that moment, that the queen looked as if she were harboring a pleasant secret.

But she said nothing, only again squeezed the king's hand, and the king chuckled and went back to his men.

"But what of Anna Morgause?" Eleri asked after a moment. "If there is anything about her you should be warning us against, it is your duty to make it plain."

The visitor grimaced with distaste, then looked pointedly down at Gwen and her sisters. Gwen sighed. If she had been just a little off to the side, there was a chance that the visitor would not have noticed her. That happened a lot. Then she tried concentrating very, very hard on not being noticed. Sometimes that worked—more and more as she got the knack of it. But not tonight,

Much to Gwen's dismay, her mother took the hint.

"Off with you," she said in a quiet voice that nevertheless brooked no argument. "Time for bed." The girls didn't even try to dissuade their mother, they just picked up whatever they had been sitting on and trudged off to the private rooms behind the dais.

This was a grand, grand castle indeed. Behind the dais, through a wooden door, was a set of two small rooms where the royal family and their immediate servants slept, away from the tumble of bodies in the Great Hall. A pair of rushlights, one left burning in each room, lit the way just enough that the girls didn't stumble over anything.

The first room was theirs; it was smaller than the second, and it had just enough space for the big bed where they all slept and their clothing chests lining the walls. Mag, the servant woman they all shared, who had been their nursemaid when they were smaller, helped them pull off their outer clothing and fold it neatly, each on top of her own chest. Then they clambered into the big bed, which Mag had warmed with a stone she'd put near to the fire earlier. They had their own particular order for this. The two most restless, Gwen-hwyfar and Gwenhwyfach, on the outside, and Cataruna and Gynath on the inside. The bed, with its woolen blankets woven by Eleri and her women, its fur coverlet from bearskins of the bears killed by their own father, could easily have slept two more. They even had a feather mattress, an immense luxury.

Gwen was the last to climb in, and Mag shut them in with the bed-curtains, leaving them in the close darkness.

Gwen was always the last to climb in, because if she didn't wait, her sister Gwenhwyfach, the baby of the family, would find some sly way to torment her. Poke, prod, pull hair, pinch—they were as alike as twins, everyone said so, and no one could understand why Gwenhwyfach hated her sister so. When Little Gwen was in a fine mood, she was enchantingly beautiful, and she bewitched everyone around her. Her hair, like Gwen's was as light a gold as sunlight, her eyes large and a melting blue when she wanted something. She put Gwen in mind of the tale of the maiden made of flowers sometimes, she was so slender and graceful, even when she was up to mischief. In fact, her real name wasn't Little Gwen at all, but everyone insisted they looked so much alike, the name had stuck and no one even remembered what name she'd been given at birth anymore. Perhaps that was why—perhaps she sorely resented that they were so much alike. It certainly wasn't because Little Gwen was deprived. If anything, being the youngest *and* so pretty, she was spoiled.

Then again, maybe it upset her that there was anyone who could be said to be as pretty as she was, much less that it was her older sister.

Even Gwenhwyfar was at a loss; she didn't remember doing anything that would have warranted this. If their positions had been reversed, had Gwenhwyfar been the youngest, there would be some cause for that resentment. But no, it had been Little Gwen who had usurped the position of "youngest" from her year-older sister, and she'd scarcely begun to toddle when she made her enmity known. From that day, Gwen's life had been a struggle to avoid her clever sister's tiny tortures.

One thing she had learned early on: never strike back. Little Gwen was never caught, at least not by an adult, and retribution on Gwen's part only brought down the wrath of an adult. Gwen was the older; logic said that when there was a quarrel, she was the aggressor, for why would a smaller child bully a larger? When Gwen displayed bruises, she was told that was what she deserved for picking on her younger sibling.

Her older sisters knew what was going on, of course, but protests to an adult only got them told not to take sides.

That was the other reason for having a Gwen on either side of the bed, with two sisters in between. It stopped the fighting.

Well, mostly.

"It's all your fault," Little Gwen whispered in the dark. "You got us sent to bed, Gwenhwyfar. We could still be there if not for you."

"Me? What did I do?" Gwen demanded as both her sisters sighed with exasperation.

"You weren't quiet enough. You made the queen look at you. You were fidgeting. You always fidget." This, from the person that Mag always checked for fleas, since by the nursemaid's way of thinking, anyone who squirmed that much must be harboring a host of fleas.

"Did not!"

"Did so!"

"Did no such thing!"

"Did so!"

"Give over!" snapped Gynath, the eldest of them all. "Gwen did no more fidgeting than you, and she was a deal less obvious about wanting to hear every word about the Queen of the Orkneys. Now go to sleep!"

"I can't," Little Gwen whined. "I'm cold. Gwen stole all the covers."

Since Gwen was barely covered by the drape of the blankets, this was obviously a lie. "Did not!"

"Did so!"

"Couldn't have," Gynath said smugly. "I tucked them under the featherbed on your side. You're a liar, and that just proves you're a changeling. I knew it! The Fair Folk took the real baby and left you in her place! No wonder you're a little horror!"

"Am not!" Little Gwen said, furiously. "And she stole the covers! Ow!"

This last punctuated the thump on the head her older—and much larger—sister gave her.

"Give over," Gynath repeated. "Go to sleep, or I'll tip you out and you can lie on the floor with the dogs all night."

"I'm lying with bitches now," Little Gwen muttered, and Gynath thumped her again for her pains, and, at last, she subsided.

Gwen turned on her side, her back to her sisters, and stared at the place where the curtains met. Stealthily—because if Little Gwen knew what she was doing there would be whining about letting the draft in—she parted the curtains with a finger and peered across the room at the light visible through the gaps between the door and doorframe, straining her ears to make out something besides the indecipherable muttering of voices. She had wanted to hear more too, but not about Anna Morgause.

She wanted to hear about magic and the Power. Hearing about or watching someone working magic always gave her a shivery good feeling. She couldn't wait until she came into her own Power.

She wondered what it would be. Some, like Eleri, could do just about anything in reason. Some were just healers, some could command the weather, or see into the past or the future.

She wanted to be able to do it all, though. Well, who wouldn't? *And* she wanted something else. She wanted to be a chariot-driver, and a warrior. There had to be a way to keep the Power and still wield Cold Iron. Sometimes she felt torn in two, wanting both those things—

But there was no doubt, no doubt at all, that when she came into her Gift, she *would* be sent to the Ladies. The doubt came about whether the King would be willing, no matter what he said, for a daughter to take up weapons. There were not many warrior-women, and most girls who tried the life soon gave it up.

That wasn't the only reason she strained to listen to the talk at the hearth. Besides hearing about magic, she wanted to hear about this new queen with the same name as her.

She wondered what life was like, for this slender, fair young woman. Did her father have a castle like this one? Clearly, if she was a good archer, he let her train with the warriors. Oh, how Gwen wanted to do that, too—

Well, maybe. She would have to be careful that the Power didn't desert her because she handled Cold Iron too much. But there had to be a way! *That* Gwenhwyfar had done it!

But if there isn't . . . which do I want? To be a warrior, or to have the Power?

Did she have sisters? Probably not, and probably not brothers either, if she had been on the walls, shooting arrows at her father's enemies. Brothers were funny about things like that. Gwen had overheard plenty of fights when some of the boys tried to keep their sisters from training with the warriors and the like. No, from the sound of it, she was an only child . . .

Oh yes, Gwen remembered now. Something about the blood being thin and only the one daughter in the line. So there it was.

Gwen envied her. It must be wonderful, to be an only child. No having to share everything. No big sisters who thumped your head nor horrible little teases of younger sisters. She'd have gotten the best of everything; only children got spoiled, everyone knew that. And now, to be marrying the High King, to be his equal in all things . . . she would have her own court; everyone knew that the power of the land went through the queen as well as the king. She was trained by the Ladies, so she would probably be the one in charge of all things having to do with the Power, subject to the Merlin, of course. She would have her own horses to ride and not have to share one elderly pony with three sisters.

And, oh, the clothing. Probably enough to fill chests and chests. She would have new clothing, not things that had been cut down from adult garments and then passed down until by the time Gwen got them, they had lost any color they had once had, and any trimming had long since been pulled off. In fact, with three sisters handing down the same clothing, it was Little Gwen who actually had the best of it, since by the time Gwen was done with what Gynath handed down to her, it was suitable only for padding, patches, and baby's clouts. Little Gwen got true second-hand, just like the eldest of them.

There would be fur linings to that Gwenhwyfar's cloak and hood. There would be embroidered hems to her gowns, and her shifts would be the softest lambswool and linen. She would dress like Eleri did on rare feast days, only she would do so every day, because she was High Queen. All her clothes would be colored, and she'd never have to wear anything faded or plain again. Except her shifts. Her shifts would be linen so blinding white they'd think she was a spirit. In fact . . . in fact, she would have one gown that was that white, too, whiter than snow, whiter than clouds. Everything she wore would be soft, too. No scratchy linens for her, no itchy wool.

And no shoes she had to wear three pairs of stockings with to keep them on. Shoes would be made to fit her feet, and hers alone.

She'd have the best food, too. Whatever she wanted, like as not. The best cuts of meat, the slices from the middle of the loaf, succulent cakes and pies whenever she liked. Goose, oh, lovely goose and the rich fat to dip her bread in. They'd let her have all the sweet mead she wanted. Apples, pears, plums, cherries and berries of every sort.

She would have a stable full of horses, one of every color there was. And a falcon, a real one, not just a little sparrow hawk, a real peregrine or a goshawk. And a coursing hound, with an elegant, long-eared head. She would go hunting whenever she felt like it, and no one would tell her that she couldn't.

There would be a bard all the time in the court, too, and jugglers and gleemen and all sorts of things. She could hear whatever tales she wanted, whenever she wanted, and if she woke up in the middle of the night and wanted to hear one, well, she could.

And she would, of course, have great Power and command the most serious of magic. The High Queen was also the chief of all of the Wise, and at the most important of the rituals of the year, she was the avatar of the Lady for all of the land. Gwen had seen Eleri coming back from the Great Rites, face flushed, eyes shining, exultant, and more alive than at any other time. Gwen wanted to feel like that one day.

Well, one day, she would. Eleri had promised as much. One day she, Gwen, would be leading the rituals, making the magic happen.

Suddenly, though, amidst all her envy, something else occurred to Gwen . . . would it be worth all those wonderful things to have to go far away from home? To never know if you were ever going to see your mother or father again? To have nothing around you but strangers?

Maybe . . . not.

Unable to hear anything meaningful, Gwen let the bed-curtains fall closed and wriggled closer to her sister. The bed was soft, and warmed by the heat of four bodies. They were all safe in here, and tomorrow the bird hunters were going out, and there would, almost certainly, be goose. And then there would be stories and maybe some rough music, and their visitor would talk more about magic.

And Gwen would be able to look up from her place on the hearth, look around her, and know every face in the Hall.

Maybe being High Queen wasn't so wonderful after all.

Chapter Two

Gwen had not meant to overhear her mother and the priestess, indeed she hadn't. It was a cold, bright day, and she had been given sacks of goose and swan feathers to pick over and sort, for the king and his men had gone out bird-hunting and brought back a plentiful catch. Eleri was strict about idleness; there was to be none if there were tasks to be done, and Gwen was deft enough to be trusted with this one. She wouldn't lose a single feather, she wouldn't sort where the wind could carry them off, and she wouldn't leave dirt on any of them. Not even Gynath picked feathers as clean as Gwen could.

She knew better than to sort inside; a chance draft might send the precious feathers into the fire. So she circled the castle and grounds and came to one of her favorite spots, just below the window of her parents' room, on the south wall. This spot got sun all day and was sheltered from the wind; the lush grass made a good place to sit, and no one was likely to disturb her.

So she slowly picked through the feathers. Precious down feathers went into one sack, for making the softest of pillows and featherbeds.

Body feathers went into a second, for featherbeds of lesser quality. Longer feathers went into a third sack, to be used as needed, and the primary and secondary wing feathers went into a fourth, to be used for fletching arrows and very occasionally for quill pens, although there was no one here who could write more than reckonings. Dirty feathers had to be carefully picked clean, but her reward was that she could have any feathers she liked from the third sack. She had already made plans for a feather skirt for her doll and maybe a feather cloak too. It was not hard work, nor difficult to understand, but it was painstaking. Gwen was clever and dexterous, and besides, she loved the silky feeling of the feathers, the subtle plays of grays and whites and browns, so she never complained about getting this chore.

Despite the cold, the sun had baked warmth into the turf and the stones at this spot. She put her back up against the stones and set to work.

She was halfway through the second sack when she heard voices. She quickly recognized Eleri and the visitor, who must have sought out the privacy of the solar in order to keep their words from the ears of the inveterate gossips. She concentrated very hard at that moment, willing them not to look out of the window, even though Eleri knew she was picking feathers and that this was her favorite place to do so.

"Now tell me what you would not say in public about Anna of Orkney," Eleri demanded, in what Gwen thought of as her "queenly" voice. "If there is danger to this realm from her, I want to know about it."

"That is the trouble, the things that I know are as hard to hold to as water," the priestess replied. "The priestesses great and small are not of one mind on this. Some think Anna of Orkney is dangerous, some think her ambition will be held in check by the High King and the Merlin, and some think that nothing will hold her if she reaches beyond her current status. I know that she holds to the Old Ways, and under any other circumstances, I would be inclined to her for that alone. But . . . but . . ." She sighed. "I know that Lot is ambitious. I know that his wife is equally ambitious, and I believe that there is not much either of them would scruple at to advance their ambitions. I know that she has the Power, and I know that she will use it to further her own ends rather than the welfare of the land. But how far she would go? I cannot say with any degree of certainty."

"The High King has a son," said Eleri, sounding irritated. "He has a son by the girl called Lionors. Lorholt, she calls him. Does he need more?"

The priestess made a *tsk*ing sound. "But she was not his wife. And it is only we of the West that still hold to the Old Ways, at least publicly. If your husband had a son by another than you, and he chose to make that son his heir, and you put your blessing upon it, no one here would think it amiss. But in the lands where the Romans once held full sway, The High King must have a son by a true wife, one wedded to him by a Christian priest, as well as promises, and sealed in betrothal. The Old Rites do not signify." Gwen listened to this carefully. This seemed very strange to her. There were plenty of couples among her father's people who had never even seen a Christian priest, nor had any priest or priestess say any words over them whatsoever, and yet no one doubted they were husband and wife. Jumping the fire at Beltane, jumping the broom among friends, that was enough for most. Only those with land, or with some title of honor seemed to need the formality of vows and blessings. Blessings were for babies, who needed every help they could get, and the proof of that was that there were four small graves with other daughters of Eleri in them, who did not live to see the full turn of the seasons.

But the priestess was continuing. "The truth is, young as he is, the High King has many sons, but none of them are . . ." A pause.

"Suitable, to us, to the others. None were sired on a girl to whom he had any true tie, none has he accepted as his heir. None were sired on girls that the servants of the Goddess approve of, girls of the proper bloodline, with the Powers. All are . . ." Again, a pause. "Inferior. They are of no importance. Attempts to see into their futures show nothing of note, not a hint that the Goddess cares for them any more or less than she cares for any other of her daughters. They are toys for the young High King's bed. Their sons will be numbered among his warriors but will never be outstanding. They are ordinary. The High King's heir cannot be ordinary."

Eleri snorted. "So. The High King must breed him a son on a girl acceptable to us and to the followers of the White Christ. A girl with the Powers. A young woman like this Gwenhwyfar he is wedding. So?"

The priestess responded reluctantly. "The scrying bowl shows me nothing I can make sense of. I see a son of Arthur vying for the throne, not one holding it unopposed. And I see the Merlin, and blood, connected with that son, but I cannot make out what that means." She hesitated. "I see the death of many children associated with the birth. And yet I see him surrounded by all the signs that says he has the right to the throne, and I see him as a man of the Powers. I think . . . it would be wise to avoid the wedding."

Eleri sniffed. "We could not go in any case. Arthur has our pledged fealty from his coronation, and he scarcely needs it a second time. That is a very long way to go with winter coming on, and all for a feast that we could as well hold ourselves. Which, to show our loyalty to the king, we shall, with bonfire and all. There will be nothing to complain of in our demonstration of fealty." Suddenly her tone changed. "Do you see Morgause's ambition spreading to these lands?"

"Not directly," the priestess said, though reluctantly, and Eleri breathed a sigh of relief.

"Then hear me out. The magic to make the High King a son will be a powerful one, and I am minded to sip at that same cup," Eleri continued. "My man speaks highly of his daughters, and he loves them true, but—"

"But a man wants a son, and a king wants a son more than most men." The priestess sighed. "To answer your question, that cup will indeed be overflowing, and if you, as the Chief Priestess here, were to open yourself to what is not needed, you likely will find yourself graced with the same gift. But Eleri . . . there is danger there. There may be a reason why the Goddess has seen fit to give you all daughters. It may be because of the Blessing in your blood. We cannot know that, or, if it is true, what that reason is. If you flout Her will in this, there may be consequences."

"The Goddess has seen fit to give me a husband I have come to love, to love enough to give him something he wants and will not ask for." Oh, Gwen knew that tone. The queen was not to be denied. This was what would be, and woe betide whoever stood between her and the goal.

"Then, for what it is worth, my blessing be upon you." The priestess sounded resigned. "In this, I cannot speak for the Goddess."

"You have given me leave, and that is enough," Eleri said firmly. Gwen heard their footsteps leaving.

Gwen continued to pick through and clean the feathers, trying to piece together what this all meant. All that talk of sons and the High King only puzzled her; she couldn't imagine what these Christian priests had to do with who the High King picked as his heir. But then again, that didn't matter. The High King was very far away, and what he did in Celliwig hardly even caused a ripple here. But what Eleri was up to—that troubled her, though she could not have said why. She knew very well where babies came from; her mother was midwife as well as queen, and the Great Hall, where all the rest of the court slept, was open to any sleepless child who would rather go outside than use a chamber pot. Gwen had seen the dogs and cats, the chickens and ducks and geese, her father's famous horses, and no few of her father's men and her mother's maids coupling with pleasurable abandon and no regard for privacy. So she knew where babies came from and what made them, and she had also known most of her life, in that vague sense that put parents in some mental place other than "everyone else," that the king and queen did this same thing in their great bed. Well, they must have, to have produced Gwen and all her sisters.

But this sounded more portentous than that. Magic would be involved. And her mother was going to try to make a son for the king.

Gwen turned that thought over and over in her mind. She wasn't sure she liked this idea, not sure at all. She felt more than a twinge of jealousy. A boy-child would get all the attention, right from the start. He'd be the king one day. He'd be able to order his sisters about in every place but the Circle of the Goddess and the hearth. Her father would take all the attention he now paid his daughters and lavish it on this newcomer.

And why was her mother doing this? Because, she had said, she loved the king. Yes, but didn't she love her daughters? Didn't she realize how they would feel, how they would be made to take second place?

A boy would get a pony as soon as he could walk; she was still waiting for hers, one that she didn't have to share with her sisters. He'd get a real horse as soon as he had mastered the pony. He would get lessons in the sword and the bow without ever having to ask for them, much less beg. When the time came for chores, he would get the interesting ones, not weaving or spinning, picking feathers or sewing. He would get hunting, hawking, mending weapons, fletching arrows, making bowstrings . . .

How could she not be jealous? But also, there was curiosity. Not about the wished-for son but about the magic that would make him.

It was magic for the High King, and Eleri was going to share in it . . . and that did not sound right. Surely that was not right. That magic should go to the High King only, and not someone else, even if that someone was her mother.

It was magic, from the sound of it, that would be made in Circles across the land. The High King might not even be aware this was going to happen, but nevertheless, it was magic that would stretch through every little kingdom that owed allegiance to Arthur. And that . . . it seemed wrong, very wrong, for Eleri to steal some of that away. If it had only been their kingdom, it would have been different, for Eleri was the priestess here, and the magic that was made here should benefit this land and its priestess. But it was not. Eleri had no right to it. Did she?

But this was her mother, the priestess, and the queen. If anyone would know if this was right or not, surely it would be Eleri.

Gwen continued to turn these things over and over in her mind, and finally she sighed and gave up. Besides, the topic had turned to something even more interesting.

"Gynath seems to have little Gift," the priestess was saying. "She should have come into it by now. Cataruna, though, has come on a great deal since I last saw her and should already be serving by you in the rites."

"She is," Eleri replied, with satisfaction. "And that is why I would rather not send her to you. I need her here, and she is not going to be so very powerful that I cannot teach her myself. But Gwen—"

"Already has the signs on her." The priestess's voice was firm with conviction. "And do not think that you are not powerful, for you are; whichever daughter you teach will be as powerful. You must send either Cataruna to us now, or Gwen as soon as she becomes a woman. Either will be suitable."

"That is my intent," the Queen said, then hesitated. "But . . ."

"What?" the priestess asked, sharply.

"Gwen yearns for the Power. But she also yearns for the reins and the sword. And you heard her father, he favors warrior women." The Queen sighed. "I do not know if that is mere words, and I do not know if this is some childish longing, but if there must be a choice, I would rather it was a sure one."

The priestess chuckled. "The king may well not wish to truly see one of his girls going to war. Or if he allows the training, she may tire of it. Even if she began tomorrow, the Power would not leave her overnight in any case, and by the time she is old enough to send, she will be old enough to understand that choice." The priestess's voice took on a shrewd tone. "After all, when a maiden begins to be interested in young men, suddenly all the things of war become much less attractive."

Eleri chuckled. "I bow to your wisdom."

They turned their talk to things in which she had no interest—other kings, other queens, people she didn't know or care about. Gwen went back to concentrating on the feathers.

There were some things she would certainly do. If there was going to be a baby brother, she was going to spend more time begging her father for those things she wanted. She would redouble her efforts to be good. She would do everything she had been asked and some things she hadn't, all so that her father would note what a good and obedient daughter she was. And she would take good care to ask him for those things she wanted—the pony (oh, a pony, she was almost sick with wanting one!), the lessons in sword and bow—at times when he was feeling well content. She would think very hard about convincing arguments why she should have these things, too.

That way, if there was a brother coming, she would have secured her booty before the baby claimed the king's attention.

Making the feather skirt for the doll was easy; just a bit of string to bind the feathers around doll's waist. The feather cloak, however, was proving a bit more problematic. She was old enough to be trusted with a bone needle of her very own, but sewing the feathers to a bit of rag was not working out as well as she had thought. She sat at old Mag's feet with the feathers in her lap, the needle and cloth in her hand, and her tongue in the corner of her mouth as she concentrated, but the feathers just pulled out of the stitches she made. Finally she put the needle back in its keeper and gave up on the idea; the feather skirt was pretty enough. And after a moment of thought, she took the feathers she would have used for the cloak and went to the bedroom. In a corner she found Little Gwen's doll and bound a similar skirt on it. Not out of kindness, out of self-defense. The moment Little Gwen saw the skirt, she would want one for her doll, and if she did not get one—she would hardly trouble to make one for herself—she would ruin Gwen's the first chance she got. It had happened too many times before; Gwen had made flower crowns and skirts for her doll in the spring and summer, and Little Gwen had torn the fragile garments off in a fury when no one would make them for her poppet. Gwen had made a bow and arrow for her doll, and Little Gwen had stepped on them out of spite. Gwen had made a horse out of straw for her doll and Little Gwen had thrown it into the fire. Just for good measure, Gwen braided the yarn hair of Little Gwen's doll and stuck some remaining feathers in the braids. *She* thought it looked ridiculous, but it was something Little Gwen's doll had that Gwen's wouldn't, and that would satisfy her fractious younger sibling.

Wrapping her own doll carefully in a scrap of hide, and putting her away, Gwen considered what she could do to curry favor with her father. What would he like? What would he notice?

Perhaps a nice basket of nuts. She knew of one or two spots that hadn't been picked over yet, mostly because tangled underbrush full of nettles and briars made the trees hard to get to. But she was small and clever about getting into and out of such spots; she got a sack and trudged out into the sunny afternoon.

At the door, she stood considering what she should do, as she watched the horse keepers exercising her father's famous beasts; the old men ran the horses around them in circles on the end of long tethers. She watched them pacing at the end of their leads, their muscles rippling under their rough winter coats, their necks arched, and their eyes bright. Once again, she felt sick with longing for one of them. You didn't ride these horses to exercise them, not if you were old and not as agile as you used to be, or crippled. You needed every bit of your wits and strength to handle them. They were warhorses, trained for war, pulling the dangerous war chariots or charging into the fray, and not for casual riding. All horses were beautiful, all horses were desirable, but these—oh, these—these were kings and queens among horses. When she watched them, all her desire for the Power faded.

Finally she turned away. These horses were not for her, not yet anyway. And if she wasted her time standing there yearning after them, they never would be.

All her father's men and a few of the women were out hunting in this fine weather, for in a few days there would be a great feast, both for Samhain and for the High King's wedding, and a great deal of meat would be needed. Should there be any excess, it would be smoked and salted against the winter. This was also the time when the herd beasts were culled for the winter, but in that case, with the exception of a single ox, it would only be the things that couldn't be preserved that would add to the feast.

You didn't risk the warhorses in that sort of hunting. At least one party had gone out after boar, one had gone fowling, the rest, in pursuit of deer. She hoped there would be a lot of success with the fowling party; just once she would like to be able to eat so much goose that she didn't want any more.

In theory, she wasn't supposed to go out into the forest alone. Well . . . she wouldn't be alone, even though none of her mother's women would care to go scrabbling for nuts. But she wasn't going to take any of the other, older children either.

Instead she marched off to the kennel, and loosed Holdhard, one of the boarhounds. All the dogs loved her, and Holdhard seemed to regard her as his special charge whenever he was let off his rope. With the formidable dog trotting alongside her, she made her way over the hill and down into the valley, where the little copse of hazelnut trees was what she had in mind. Holdhard knew to be quiet when she wanted to slip away; the two of them moved stealthily enough until she was well into the woods.

She avoided the oaks, and not just because they were sacred and dangerous. A thick layer of leaves and acorns carpeted the ground beneath them, and that meant the wild pigs could be feeding in there. Even a young pig could be dangerous to a child, and a grown sow or boar could easily kill a man. Holdhard sniffed at the air and growled as they went past; Gwen called him sharply to her. Whatever he scented had to be dangerous, but it would likely leave the two of them alone if they left it alone. At this time of year, like men, the beasts' priority was to lay up food against the cold. In the case of the beasts, that meant eating everything they could to get fat against the days of starvation.

As a precaution against the nettles she had taken more rags with her; when they reached the nut trees, she wrapped them around her hands and pulled the stinging nettles aside so that Holdhard could worm his way in with her.

Once inside the ring of nettles, thistles, and briars, it was as if she were in a different world. There wasn't a breath of wind; the branches above her were bare and let the sunlight through to warm this place as thoroughly as her little nook against the castle wall. The ground was thickly carpeted with crisp brown leaves that crackled as she sifted through them for the nuts. The air was full of the scent of them, a scent of dying, a little stuffy, with a suggestion of immense age.

It was soporific, and as Gwen felt through the leaves for the hard, round nuts, with the sun on her back, Holdhard flopped down into a sun-dappled spot and began to doze.

Slowly the sack filled. Holdhard snorted and snored and twitched. There was no other sound; there didn't seem to be any birds at all in this part of the woods. The sun didn't seem to move at all, and Gwen worked in a drowsy dream.

And then a snort that did not belong to Holdhard made her look up, and she froze.

Through the screen of nettles, she watched in numb fear as a bear shambled out of the underbrush. He swung his head from side to side, as if he was trying to find something, and finally he reared up on his hind legs to sniff the breeze.

Holdhard continued to sleep. She knew that she did not dare to move, for if she did, she knew that the bear would see or scent her.

The bear dropped down onto all fours and snorted fretfully. Gwen prayed silently to the Goddess, her lips and mouth dry with terror, that the great beast would continue to be oblivious of her presence.

Her fear made everything preternaturally sharp and clear, and she saw in that clarity the gray patches on the bear's muzzle, saw that his eyes were dim rather than bright.

Then those dim eyes brightened, and the bear growled, a deep rumbling that emerged from its chest and filled the air like thunder. Fear turned to horror as Gwen saw what it was that the bear had spotted.

Gliding out of the deepest shadows among the bushes came a serpent.

But this was an impossible creature. It was long, long . . . long enough that if it had its head in the king's bedroom, its tail would still be sticking out the main door of the castle. At the thickest point, its body was as big around as the chest of one of their horses, its wicked wedge-shaped head was as big as a barrel, and its glittering eyes were the size of her fist. It could as easily have swallowed one of the horses as a grass snake swallowed a frog. And it was black, an oily, glistening black, from the tip of its snout to the end of its tail. Even its flickering, forked tongue was black.

The bear reared up on its hind legs and roared at it. Gwen smothered a scream as the serpent raised itself as tall as the bear's head, hissed angrily, and struck.

It sank its fangs into the bear's shoulder; the bear roared with anger and pain and raked its head with terrible claws, laying the flesh open in four long, bleeding furrows. Gwen clapped her hands over her ears as the snake briefly released the bear, then struck again. This time the snake cast two coils around the bear and began to squeeze. Its eyes red with rage, the bear wheezed, but it raked the serpent again and again with vicious swipes of its claws and tore at it with it long white teeth.

As Gwen watched breathlessly, the two combatants rolled and thrashed, tearing up the ground and the underbrush in their struggle. And aside from the sounds of combat, it was a silent struggle; the bear roared no more challenges, and the snake did not utter a single hiss.

Suddenly there was a tremendous *crack;* Gwen jumped and screamed.

For a long moment, serpent and bear were frozen together into a knot of fur and scales and torn flesh and blood.

Then, slowly, the serpent's coils fell away from the bear, dropping limply to the forest floor.

The bear had broken its spine.

But the bear had not escaped unscathed.

It stood there, swaying from side to side for a long, long moment, bleeding from a hundred wounds. Gwen gathered herself to try to creep out of the grove and escape, when the bear looked up and *looked* at her.

She froze. There was something in its eyes. Something . . . desperate. Something with a hint of recognition . . .

The bear held her with its gaze, *looking* at her, making her feel that it was trying, somehow, to tell her something.

Then it moaned once, its legs buckled, and it toppled clumsily to the ground.

There was a roaring in Gwen's ears; little black specks danced before her eyes, then grew, then covered everything with blackness, a darkness that she fell into, and forgot bear and blood and serpent and all . . .

When she opened her eyes again, there was no sign of the bear, nor of the serpent. The forest floor was undamaged, the underbrush rustled undisturbed, and Holdhard snored on, as if nothing whatsoever had happened.

Gwen was silent all through the meal, even when her father petted and praised her for the treat she had brought him. She smiled up at him as Little Gwen seethed, but the smile was only on her lips; her mind was still on that terrible fight in the forest, trying to understand how it could have happened, and then—not happened. She had not been dreaming. She was very sure of that. She had not been asleep.

That meant it could only be one thing: a vision.

She didn't want to tell her mother about it, somehow. She really didn't want to tell *anyone* really, but she had to know what it meant, and if she could not tell her mother, there was only one person she could unburden herself to.

Provided that person would listen to her.

After the meal was over, and the women had gathered at the hearth as the men gathered at the mead benches, instead of sitting at her mother's feet as she usually did, Gwen allowed Little Gwen to usurp her place without a murmur. Instead, she settled away from the warmth of the fire, just in the shadows, and fixed her gaze on the priestess, silently willing the woman to *look* at her. If it worked to will people not to look at her, the opposite should be true too, shouldn't it?

For the longest time, the priestess seemed oblivious to Gwen's gaze. The usual talk went on, of the luck of the hunt that day, of the feast to come on Samhain, of those who were expected to pledge to each other by leaping the fire that night. Of the thickness of the wool, the taste of the wind, speculation on how hard the winter to come might be.

But finally, slowly, the priestess turned her head and looked into Gwen's eyes. Her solemn gaze met Gwen's anxious one, and, finally, she nodded once, then indicated the door with a little inclination of her head.

Gwen got up and headed for the door, as if she were going to relieve herself at the privy. But she lingered beside the door, shivering in the cold with her cloak around her, waiting for the priestess.

She did not have long to wait. The priestess slipped through the door and shut it against the wind, then reached down and gripped Gwen's shoulder.

"Your eyes were burning holes in my back, child," she said, calmly. "What is your trouble? For surely you have one, if you gave up your place at the hearth and hardly smiled at your father's thanks."

"I—I saw something!" Gwen blurted. Then the words came tumbling out of her, like an avalanche of pebbles, as she described the battle of serpent and bear. When she was finished, she waited in silence.

"I do not know what this means," the priestess said, after a long silence, in which the cold wind whipped their cloaks about them. "That it is a vision, and one portentous for you, I have no doubt. But I cannot tell what it means."

"Oh," Gwen said, in a small, and disappointed, voice.

"But I will meditate on this," the priestess continued. "And if the Goddess sends me enlightenment, I will tell you." The hand on Gwen's shoulder relaxed, and the priestess gave her a little pat. "You did well to tell me, Gwenhwyfar. Such visions are rare; your mother has never had one. Should you have another such, do not fear to confide it to a priestess."

"I won't," said Gwen, and that seemed all there was to say. Feeling vaguely cheated, she went back inside and spent the rest of the evening on the edge of the cluster of her sisters, shivering, until the queen sent them all to bed.

Chapter Three

The morning of Samhain dawned as perfect as anyone could have asked for. The sun was warm enough for pleasure but not so warm as to make the old people grumble about summer-out-of-season and bad omens. A cloudless sky and not even a hint of wind meant that the fires would send their smoke straight up, not into anyone's face. A hard frost three days ago had killed the flies, and the hunts had been outstanding; in short, everything was as perfect as one could want to celebrate the High King's wedding, the harvest, and the rites of the Lady of the Fields and the Lord of the Wood.

Gwen and her sisters were rewarded for much hard work in the days before by being given a holiday today. They couldn't stay abed though; the moment the sun was up, so were they, getting their hair braided, putting on their best gowns and shifts. The castle hall was full of people already; folk had been coming for days, and every little space where someone could lay his head had been taken up by someone. There were even tents pitched all about the castle and people sleeping in them.

When the girls left their room, the sleepers had already been cleared from the Great Hall, and trestle tables were set up along the wall, laden with bread and autumn fruit and honey for folk to break their fast on, and ale for drinking. For the girls, however, there was a tastier treat of sops-in-wine and watered wine with honey to sweeten it. All of them helped themselves to apples once they had cleaned their bowls, both figuratively and literally. It was only dawn and a long time to dinner.

Already there was activity everywhere, in the Hall and especially out on the green and about the village. Great cauldrons of soup were cooking, and ovens were fired up with the first baking of the day; the boar's head, the baked meats, fish and fowl, the fruit pies, the cakes and baked vegetables that would be served at dinner. The second baking would be for meat pies for supper and more fish and fowl. There was a whole ox roasting at one fire and a whole wild boar at another. Samhain was not a religious festival, although tonight there would be the Great Working for the High King—it was the Equinox that was the significant date, when the Winter King slew his rival, the Summer King, as the Spring Equinox was when the Young Stag slew the Old. Samhain was the celebration of the end of harvest and the time when those animals who were to be killed for winter meat were culled out. Anything that could not be preserved must be eaten, so why not make a festival out of it? The butchered beasts were already rendered into quarters and in the pickling vats, the smokehouse, or the salt packs. Sausages were already made up and curing. The brewing was done, the ale and mead in their casks.

Still the women were hard at work, tending to the cooking. In-nards and bones, hooves and vegetable scraps had gone into pies and soup, for nothing was wasted. The common folk would get their portion of the ox and the boar—everyone got at least a small share of meat—but mostly they would be eating their fill of the soup. It was the guests of the king who would feast on the choicer stuffs.

So this was mostly celebration for the menfolk. The hard work of farming was over, and the year was about to descend into the dark. Not a bad time of year to handfast, for the sharing of a bed now could mean a fine babe in the summer, and a bed was warmer with two in it. This would be the last time of abundance before the hoarding of winter.

Gwen's father made a point to bring in all his warriors for the days of feasting, organizing contests and games. There were even musicians, and not just the ones from the village.

He was a surprisingly tenderhearted man as well where children were concerned; as this was the time of year when many a lamb grown into a sheep, gosling now big and gray and honking, or pink piglet grown fat went under the knife, he saw to it that there were plenty of things to occupy the children who had made these creatures into pets. So when the former pet became quarters, ham, and sausages hanging in the smokehouse, it was all done when the child was occupied with dancing or gaming or stuffing himself with unaccustomed treats.

As Gwen headed purposefully out with her pockets bulging with apples, she did not follow after her older sisters, who were making straight toward the field where some of the older boys were engaged in wrestling, archery and sling contests, and the hurling of woolsacks.

She also made sure to lose Little Gwen at the moment when her younger sister was distracted by a game of tag. Little Gwen could not bear to be left out of anything that promised attention, and once the child's attention was fully occupied, Gwen took advantage of a couple of geese being chased to get away.

Gwen didn't want to play tag or hoops, to run races for prizes or watch the older boys and men compete at feats of strength. She wasn't interested in the quieter pursuits of playing with poppets or merrils, and she certainly wasn't interested in the mock handfasting that was going on, nor the flirtations of her oldest sister.

She made her way with quiet determination to where the horses had been tethered.

She knew better than to approach them; handling the war-horses was strictly the work of those who were given that privilege— sometimes boys and rarely girls, but mostly fully grown men and the occasional woman. But feast days like these were the only time she ever got to see them do the sorts of things they had been trained to do.

At the moment, they were being readied for the chariot races. The Romans had introduced the chariot to the tribes, and once they had seen chariots in action, there was no stopping the tribes from adopting the vehicle. But unlike the Roman races, which were held in the coliseums on round or oval tracks, and were consequently hideously dangerous for driver and horses alike, these races, like the ridden ones that would come later, were held on the straight. From the line out to some distant spot, then a turn, and back to the start. Horses were too valuable to lose to accidents that could easily be prevented.

The chariots were light wicker affairs, never pulled by more than two horses. The wheels had iron rims and iron fittings, and the wicker cars themselves were open in front, with a curved wall behind. The chariot that their father used for important occasions had seats; these racing chariots did not. Nor did they have the scythes on the wheels that the war chariots had.

The war chariots were fearsome things, and Gwen had never (of course) seen them in use in battle. But these races would demonstrate some of the skill of the charioteers and the warriors who fought with them.

There were four in the first race, which was a very special challenge match; two of them were her father's horses and were driven by his men. The other two belonged to two of his war chiefs. The king was well known to be a generous winner and a gracious loser; no one would hold back for fear of displeasing him. These would be excellent races.

Much as Gwen yearned after the horses like one gone lovesick, there was one pair and their driver that Gwen particularly wanted to watch, and they were not her father's horses. They belonged to Hydd ap Kei, one of the king's oldest friends, and the chariot driver was a woman.

Her name was Braith, and Gwen had watched her race a score of times. She was amazing in the races, and Gwen wondered what she would be like in battle. She seemed to be absolutely fearless, she was known for running out onto the pole, standing on the yoke to help balance for a fast turn, running back to the chariot again. Precious time could be lost in the turns, precious in a race, and, Gwen supposed, precious in a fight, too. Running the pole like that helped in a turn. Gwen had even, once, when the chariot had hit an unseen rock and shattered, seen Braith leap onto the horses' backs and drive them with one foot on each horse, her hair coming loose from its braids and streaming behind her like the horses' tails.

She'd been disqualified, for after all, in a chariot race it is expected that there be a *chariot* behind the horses, but people were still talking about the feat.

Braith was indeed in the first race, and Gwen edged as near as she dared, watching her idol crooning to and soothing her team. They weren't a matched team, like the king's two; the left-hand one was a dark chestnut, the right-hand a dun. Braith combed her fingers through their coarse manes, ran her hands along their stocky necks, and whispered into their short, broad ears, standing between them as if she were a third horse in the traces. Gwen watched her with raw envy, her fingers itching and twitching with longing to touch those soft noses, scratch those warm necks. She wasn't allowed near the warhorses, ever. "Too dangerous," her father said. He didn't mean dangerous for *her*, he meant dangerous for the horses. She might move suddenly, the wrong way, or do something else that would startle them, he said. They could sprain a muscle or make a misstep and hurt themselves some other way.

So Gwen could only watch from afar as the bettors circled the chariots, eyed the great beasts knowingly, and conversed in mutters.

Gwen thought that Braith looked exactly like her team; she was stocky, weather-beaten, rough. Her bright brown eyes peered out from under a kind of forelock of coarse, dark hair that looked as if she had hacked it off with her own knife in a fit of impatience. Her voice had the same intonation as a horse's whinny, and when she laughed, it was loud and sudden and exactly like a neigh. Gwen adored her.

If there was anyone in the world she would have liked to grow up to be, it was Braith. Power? Braith *had* Power! If anyone doubted, all they had to do was see her with her horses! That was Epona's Power, and if Epona was a lesser goddess, well, perhaps she was closer to those who served her.

The race was to begin at the sacred oak grove, and Gwen pressed herself against the bark of one of the great trees, hoping her brown gown would blend in with the bark, and yearned after Braith and her team with a passion she never felt for the gods.

Suddenly those bright brown eyes caught sight of Gwen and locked on her. As if pulled by their reins, her horses turned to look at what Braith was looking at, so now there were three pairs of eyes gazing thoughtfully at her. Slowly, Braith smiled. And Gwen felt a jolt of something that took her breath away.

Then she went back to whispering to her team. But now and again, she looked over at Gwen and smiled.

No one else seemed to notice—or if they noticed, care that Gwen was there. Her ability to be quiet and unobtrusive was working even in this crowd. So she was allowed to watch with the rest as the drivers got into their chariots, as the chariots maneuvered into a roughly straight line, and then, at the shout from the king, reins slapped on backs, whips snapped, and the teams plunged out onto the rough sward for the outward leg of the race.

Gwen would have swarmed up the tree, but she was wearing her one good gown, and she *knew* what her nurse *and* the queen would have to say about it if the garment was ruined before it was even dinner.

So she just ran to stand in front of the shouting, cheering men, who were now so focused on the race that they didn't even notice her.

The hoofbeats didn't sound anything like thunder—more like rocks tumbling down a cliff. Thunder wouldn't make the ground shake; thunder didn't make her heart pound or her throat dry with excitement. Four lines of rising dust followed the teams, but the colors painted on the chariots made it easy to tell which was which. What you could *not* tell, until they turned at the opposite end, was who was in the lead.

That was signaled by the servants at the end, who raised a pole with the owner's pennant on it as soon as the chariot made the turn.

And the first pennant up was for Braith's team. Gwen gave a squeal of glee, and jumped up and down, her hands clasped under her chin. She knew better than to pray to Epona, the goddess of horses, for Braith to win—that was *frivolous* use of prayer, which was important; the queen had made that very clear to all her daughters. If you pestered the gods with petitions all the time, they'd grow tired of hearing from you, and when you needed them to answer, the prayers would be ignored. But she could hope, and she could wish, and she wished with all her might.

But right behind Braith's team was her father's, a pair of handsome grays out of his warhorse herd. If the Romans had still been here, he'd have lost them for certain. The Romans would have whisked them away for tribute before you could say "knife."

The other two teams were lost in the dust, but the king's, and Braith's, were so close that Gwen held her breath; it looked from here as if they were literally one team of four horses. The tension was incredible; she clasped her hands so tightly together that the knuckles hurt.

And then Braith did the unthinkable. She leaped out onto the pole and ran up between her pair, reins wrapped loosely around her wrist, to stand between them, an arm over each neck, shouting encouragement in their ears. Behind her, the empty chariot bounced and bucked; other horses might have shied, but her team paid it no heed. From some depth within them, they found new strength and surged ahead, crossing the finish line a full chariot-and-team length ahead of the King's. The men roared approval at this daring move, even the king whooping and clapping. Gwen's heart was beating so fast she felt faint.

They shot past as Braith ran back to the chariot and began, slowly, to rein her team in and turn them about.

When they pulled up again before the crowd, Gwen hung back to keep from being noticed, but Braith was having none of that. "Young Gwenhwyfar!" she called, beckoning to her. "Come ye here."

Gwen started at the sound of her name, but at her age, she was supposed to obey any adult, and although her father looked surprised to see her there, he didn't forbid it. She eased through the forest of towering men and came to the side of Braith's chariot. The horses steamed, their sides moving strongly, although they were not heaving for breath. "Nah, my beauties have just run themselves to sweat, so what is it we do with them?" Braith asked, looking straight down at her.

"Walk them so they do not founder nor stiffen," Gwen said promptly.

"And water?" Braith prompted.

"Only a mouthful at a time." Gwen knew all this very well; on the rare occasions that the sisters could get their fat pony to work up a sweat, she was the one left to walk him cool. Not that she minded. She just wished he was a horse, but she was fond of him, and a pony, even a shared pony, was better than no horse at all.

"Here ye be then." And to Gwen's astonishment, as well as that of the rest of the crowd (including several adolescent boys who gaped at her with raw envy) Braith put the looped-up reins in her hands. "Be walking them cool, please ye."

Gwen didn't hesitate. She took the reins as the two horses bent to sniff the top of her head. Then, with her heart feeling so full of happiness she thought she would burst, she began walking toward the stream, the team ambling obediently behind her, with the chariot wheels rumbling and swishing through the grass. She let them have the allotted mouthful of water when they reached the stream, then turned and began walking them back. In the distance she could see Braith talking with the king and the rest of the men. The prize was already in her hands, a pair of beautiful bridles with bronze ornaments for the team, a silver torque for her. The team's owner got a drinking horn bound in silver, with silver feet; he seemed well pleased.

Without being prompted, Gwen stopped short of the crowd, reached up under the nearest horse's mane as high as she could, and felt the shoulder. He was still sweaty, so she turned back around and made another trip to the stream. Again, she let the horses have a mouthful of water, and she tried not to feel self-conscious as everyone but Braith seemed to be casting glances at her.

This time when she returned, the horses were cool. It had only been one race, after all; this was nothing to the exertion they would get in a battle. She waited politely until Braith "noticed" her, then held up the reins.

Braith checked the horses herself. "Well done, young Gwenhwyfar," she said, gravely. "Now, will ye be doing me the kindness of stepping into my chariot?"

Now totally astonished, Gwen did as she had been asked.

"And now be running out on the pole and back." Braith did not ask if she *could* do so, she simply acted as if it were just a matter of course that Gwen would be able.

Of course she could; it wasn't as if she hadn't been practicing just such a thing all summer. Not on a chariot with *horses* hitched to it, of course, but on an old one with a broken axle. She flexed her toes and then, fixing her eyes not on the pole but straight ahead, ran out along the limber pole, between the warm sides of the horses and back to the chariot.

"Ah, king," sighed Braith. "It is a pity this is your daughter, for I'd be taking her back with me this day and leaving you the torque in her place."

"And for what purpose, lady?" the King asked, with a chuckle.

"To make a charioteer of her, as I was." Braith turned her head to the side and looked at the king from under her shag of hair. "And I tell you this: Be giving her a horse now, and not a pony, and of her own. A wise old warhorse, too old for battle; let the old horse teach the young rider. And be giving her training; now is the time to do it, while she's fearless. Do that, and you'll have a warrior out of her."

The king pulled at his lip. "And the queen will have a Wise Lady out of her—"

Braith shook her head. "The mark of Epona is on this one; there's two goddesses in this one, but Epona is the stronger. 'Tis a waste to make her go to the Ladies." Braith shrugged. "But if it is your will to send her, still, give her the horse and as much of the training as she can get before she goes; I never heard it said that warrior training did a Lady any harm. She's only nine summers. Maybe, when she is a woman, Epona will let her go. If not, be sure you will know. The Power won't leave her in that time, and I never heard the Ladies say otherwise."

"Nor I," the king agreed, to Gwen's joy and delight. "It will be done as you advise."

She was going to get everything she had wanted! A horse, a real horse and not a pony! Training with bow and knife and sword! Oh, and lance as well, because a charioteer used the lance too! She felt dizzy with happiness, more dizzy than she had the time she'd filched someone's forgotten cup of mead.

In her rush of happiness she did not forget her manners. "Thank you, Father," she said, with a little bow. "And thank you, Warrior." The king beamed down on her, his ruddy hair and beard glowing in the sunlight, his strong shoulders stretching the leather of his tunic, and the gleam of silver at his throat, wrists, and around his head.

She watched the rest of the morning races in a glow of happiness; none of them were as exciting as the first one. Braith won all the ones she cared to enter, but she held back a good deal of the time. The chariot races alternated with ridden races, to give all the horses a chance to rest. The king didn't enter his horses that often either; Gwen had been given tacit approval to stay, so stay she did, at the king's side, but not getting into the way, listening as hard as she ever could as the king and Braith and the king's war leaders discussed the horses and their drivers. They talked not about the race itself but about how the teams might perform on a hill, maneuvering around other chariots, when encountering slippery grass or mud. They talked of the riders, of whether man and horse seemed of one mind, whether a horse was uncertain of his rider, or the rider of his horse; such uncertainty could mean balks and spills on the battlefield. They discussed whether the horses had been seasoned to the sounds of combat. It was then that she realized that these weren't just races for the sake of the holiday; this was the opportunity for the king to see his war chiefs' best drivers and pairs, the best riders and mounts, so that he would know where to put them in a battle.

Perhaps the only race that actually had been nothing but a race had been the one between his team and Braith's. And even then—

"Your pair is steadier than last year," the king said.

Braith nodded. "Last year I'd not have run out on the pole. They'll go through fire and ice for me now. I reckon two more years, maybe three, before they start t' slow, and five or six before I need be training a new pair, then another brace of years before the new pair will be ready." She laughed. "And mebbe then 'twill be me that's out t'pasture."

The King laughed. "You are as ageless as the hills. No pasture for you!"

The rest of the war chiefs laughed and asked Braith's opinion on this or that team. Gwen became aware that not only was Braith *her* hero, her opinion was held in high esteem by all of these men.

I want to be like that, she thought, looking worshipfully up at the woman. *I want people to talk to me like that.*

The sound of a horn warned them all that dinner was ready; this would not be a formal feast of the sort that was held in the Great Hall, but as Gwen knew from earlier years, she and her sisters, her mother and her chief ladies, the king's particular guests and war chiefs, and the king himself would be seated at the trestle tables hauled outside and given the best. Everyone else would help themselves. There would be more than enough; anyone not competing in the afternoon games would probably be stuffed and dozy.

The press of people around the king was too great for her to walk beside him to the tables, and she had an idea that her mother would think it forward of her to do so. She eased herself away, and trotted back toward the open-air "kitchen" where the queen was supervising the last preparations. Before she got even that far, her eldest sister, Cataruna, spotted her, and rounded her up like a straying goose.

"Now you sit here—I put Little Gwen on the other side there, so unless she starts flinging things at you across mother and father, things should be quiet enough—" Her sister paused, and turned her around to look her up and down critically. "—I don't believe it! No dirt, no leaves and grass in your hair, nothing torn—are you a changeling? Did someone make away with the real Gwen?"

Gwen laughed. "I was watching the races."

"And you didn't climb a tree to see them better?" her sister shook her head. "I shall expect a hen to crow, next, and a gander to lay an egg. All right, sit down, and mind your manners."

Gwen had every intention of minding her manners. She was not going to give her father the least little excuse for taking back what he had promised.

Dinner was uneventful, except for Little Gwen trying to command attention at her side of the table, boasting and being self-important. And it was irritating, but most of those around her seemed to find it amusing. Men and boys, particularly, fell under her naughty charm. By contrast, Gwen kept very quiet, didn't grab for the best portions, and didn't even complain when the boys on either side of her and across from her did. She watched wistfully as most of the goose went into those boys, and the juiciest bits of the roast pork, the best baked apples, the center part of the bread. Her reward was the approving nod from her mother. The king didn't notice; what children did or did not do was not something that concerned him when he was busy speaking with his guests.

The boys on either side of Gwen quickly stuffed themselves and as quickly sped off to whatever game or competition had claimed their interest. That was when the queen passed down the remains of the very special dishes that the adults had shared. Little Gwen had also already dashed off on a quest of her own at that point, so Gwen was able to enjoy her feast in peace. And she did, indeed, for the first time in her life, get enough goose that she didn't want any more and enough tasty goose-liver paste to spread on a bread-end.

The king also lingered, when he saw that Gwen was still there, and awkwardly cleared his throat, getting the queen's attention.

"It's Braith's mind that Gwen's ready for a horse and for warrior training," he said, abruptly.

The queen stared at him as if she hadn't quite heard him correctly. She licked her lips and twined the end of one of her braids about her fingers for a moment; she looked, at that moment, very conflicted. "Braith is a very competent trainer and warrior," she said carefully. "And you trust her judgment."

The king nodded. "Braith says it's Epona's hand that's on her. She entrusted her own team to Gwen for cooling down, and I saw it myself. The girl has horse sense. And good sense about horses . . ."

"Pardon, Father, Mother?" Cataruna, Gwen's eldest sister, paused in fetching away the precious silver-rimmed drinking horns for safe-keeping. "Gwen is the one that always takes first care of the pony. And he never kicks or bites her, which is more than I can claim. Ask your horse keeper, he knows."

The Queen sucked her lower lip in a little. "I suppose there's no harm in it. But Little Gwen will want a horse and training too . . ."

The king began to roll his eyes, but then, narrowed them. "Then she shall have them. And when the horse is left neglected and her nurse has to march her down to the stable to tend him, or she cries because he's too tall, and pouts because she got a bruising, or because it stepped on her foot, you shall make her beg you to let her off."

Eleri the queen nodded, then looked past the king at Gwen. "And you will do none of these things," she said to Gwen, who nodded solemnly at what was clearly an order. "Very well then. Let it be as you wish. She has some years before she will go to the Ladies, at any rate, and I suppose no harm ever came of a girl getting warrior training before she went to the Cauldron Keepers."

"Exactly what Braith said," the king replied, with open relief. He sprang to his feet. "Then, by your leave, I'll have her with me for the rest of the races. She can't see too much of them, and perhaps she can make herself useful with the boys."

"Wait—" The queen beckoned to Mag. "Put Gwen into a good tunic and short kirtle, or trews if you can find them to fit her. She's to help with the racers by the king's command."

"I'll help you look!" Gwen exclaimed, her cauldron of happiness overflowing. She pulled up her skirts and ran back to the castle.

Gwen spent the remainder of the day at her father's side, being quiet, obedient, doing exactly what she was told, even though what she *wanted* to do was to poke her nose into everything. She was occasionally allowed to lead horses to cool them as she had for Braith, but most of the time she kept strictly in her father's shadow and said nothing at all unless it was "Aye, sir" or "No, sir." And even though she got hungry and thirsty, she didn't run back to the tables, not even when the wind brought aromas that made her stomach growl. She kept her ears open too, to the opinions of the owners and drivers about various pairs or horse and rider. The races made her forget her growling stomach, even if they weren't as exciting as Braith's were, and she tried to see what it was that others had talked about as the horses thundered down to the turn and back again. As the afternoon went on, the horses pounded the grass on the improvised track to fragments, and raised more and more dust every time they ran. The horses were covered in a fine coat of the stuff, which streaked as they worked up a sweat. The King's grays would have looked a sad sight if they'd still been racing.

There were prizes for every race, but Gwen came to understand that the one that Braith had won was very special and had been arranged far, far ahead of time: the king's two pairs against the two finest pairs of those of his war chiefs who cared to match him. The rest were races among whoever brought a team and cared to challenge.

Finally the ridden races were over, and the best four pairs of all battled for the prize of the day: for the horses, silver bridle and harness ornaments; for the driver, a silver torque like the one Braith had won and a plain silver cloak-brooch; for the owner, if he was not the driver, a cloak-brooch worked in the image of Epona in her White Horse aspect, with a gemstone for an eye. Truly fine prizes, and there were many comments of admiration as they were passed around.

Gwen expected Braith to race for these as well, but to her surprise, the warrior was nowhere to be seen, and her horses must have been taken away for they were no longer at the picket line.

"I am surprised Braith is not here," said one of the war chiefs, echoing Gwen's surprise.

"I asked her not to run," replied Hydd ap Kai, the chief to whom the pair belonged. "It's said there might be trouble on our border before the snows fall, and I'd not have my best pair or driver not at my disposal if there is. This last race is dangerous. Drivers are like to push their pairs because it *is* the last race, and horses are tired."

The king nodded sagely. "That is why my grays are not running," he said. And then laughed. "Besides, I would not have it whispered behind hands for the rest of the year that my pair won only because the other horses were tired!"

All the men laughed at that. "And another good reason for Braith not to run," agreed Hydd. "Whoever takes the prize will know he took it fairly, and those who lose will know they lost it fairly."

The last four teams lined up, and the crowd fell silent. The four drivers leaned forward a little, knees loose, eyes on the turn at the far end of the course. Their teams had all been given a rest and been wiped down. And now it was not just the men who were gathered to watch the race; word had spread that this was the prize race, and the boys and young men had come from the contests, the older women from their cooking and talk, the maidens and the few maiden warriors from their dances and flirtations and contests of their own. They lined the side of the course nearest the camp, leaving the other free so that a team in trouble had a side to pull off to without endangering the spectators. The tension in the air made Gwen's heart race, and her mouth felt as if it were full of dust.

The king solemnly stepped forward; with deliberation, he eyed each of the drivers in turn, then, looking at the sky so that he could not have been said to have cued a driver before time, waited until all was so still that only the distant metallic clatter of the rooks on the castle roof broke the silence, and then he shouted.

The teams shot off, showing no sign of being weary. Without Braith driving, without her father's precious grays at risk, Gwen was able to simply watch them with the same excitement as everyone else.

The cheering started immediately, and did not abate; even if someone had not had a favorite before this race began, he'd picked a favorite by the time the horses were halfway to the grove.

The flags went up and the teams turned; it was a close race, so close that at this point anyone could win.

And then one of the two centermost teams stumbled.

The crowd gasped as one; for a moment the heads of the horses vanished under the dust, and Gwen's heart stopped. Had they fallen? Had one of the horses, Epona forbid, broken a leg? That would be a terrible omen as well as a disaster—and worse still would be if the chariot had gone over, the driver thrown, to break a leg, an arm—a back—his head—

That had happened once a few years ago; she had been too little to be allowed near the course, but she remembered it, the wails of the women, the lamenting around the body, brought back to lie in solemn state on a swiftly cleared table. And that had been a horrible winter too—

But her heart leaped as the horses' heads appeared again, far behind the others but not down—they moved slowly off the course, the off-side one limping, but that was the worst of it, pulled up lame.

She turned her attention back to the remaining teams, who thundered on, until with one tremendous effort, the team that had been farthest behind leaped forward, while the crowd screamed. Gwen shouted; the horses strained, and at the very last moment, they pulled a head-length in front of the team that had been winning.

The three teams pounded past as the drivers slowed them, turning them in a great circle to bring them back to the king and his men. The rest of the company swarmed around the winner as soon as it was safe; they gathered up the driver on their shoulders, and Gwen reckoned that if they could have gathered up the horses as well, they would have.

No one seemed to take thought for the poor loser leading his horses back to the picket line. Gwen's eyes flicked between him and the winner for a moment. Then she ran as fast as her legs would take her for that lonely driver and pair.

"I'll take them and walk them," she called as soon as she was near enough for him to hear. "You find the king's horse leech. He won't watch the races, he's at the ale tuns."

"Epona's blessings on you, little one," the man said gratefully, giving the reins to her. Then, despite his own weariness, he ran.

She led the poor drooping things slowly; it wasn't just the off-side horse that was limping. The stumble must have pulled the other over enough to lame him too. They wanted to stop, but she knew that if she let them, they'd cool too fast, and that might make their hurts worse.

But the driver was back in mere moments with the king's horse healer; not needed now, she handed back the reins and walked away quickly. If it was very bad news . . . she didn't want to be there to hear it or to see the driver's face.

Chapter Four

Supper was what had been left over from the rest of the day for the common folk and baked meat pies and baked fowl for the king's guests. Gwen had thought she had eaten all the goose she could possibly eat. She discovered, to her pleasure, that she was wrong. And this time, the boys, given the option of savory meat pies dripping with rich gravy, merely picked at the goose, leaving most of it to her.

The sun was setting as supper began; it was fully dark and the torches and bonfire had been lit by the time the last of the guests rose from the table, and the servants and Gwen and her sisters (all but Little Gwen, who had disappeared as usual) carried the valuable cups and knives back to their coffers in the castle.

The queen and her women were long gone. No one mentioned this; no one would say anything about it later. *They* had gone off to make magic for the High King to ensure a son from the marriage that had been made this day. That was woman's work, and men were not even supposed to know about it.

Nor were little girls, so Gwen pretended that she didn't and settled down to enjoy the music and dancing. Little Gwen finally put in an appearance; it seemed she had bullied or cajoled some of the village children to make her a Harvest Maiden, and they were parading about with her at the head of them, in a wreath of leaves and vines, with a stalk of weed as a scepter. The real Harvest Maiden chosen by the women was at the Working, of course. And last year, Gwen probably would have been irritated at Little Gwen's showing off. But she was full of goose and the knowledge that she was going to be given a horse and training in a few days and that Little Gwen would surely get her come-uppance if she tried to wheedle and pout and cry her way into the same.

"Be wary of that one," said a voice in her ear. Gwen turned to see Braith settling down next to her, a horn of mead in one hand, and a pottery cup in the other. She handed the cup to Gwen; it held hot cider.

"Why?" Gwen asked, casting a dubious glance after her sister.

"Because there's power in her." Braith nodded at the chain of children. "Look at her. Look at who's following. Boys, mostly. A few girls. Even young as she is, she has that power over the males. Who indulges her? Men and boys. Who persuades women not to punish her? Men and boys. With one like that, there's no reasoning with the menfolk; when she gets older and learns her Power, and make no mistake, she has *Power*, in her presence their eyes will glaze over and their reason fly out the window. The *glamorie*, that's what she's got, a true Power, make no mistake. Anna Morgause has it. I've seen her, and she's but to bend a finger and nine men of ten will come to sniff at her hem. And they say that young Morgana has it too, though more subtle than Anna Morgause. So be wary of her, for once she's woman grown, what she wants, she'll have, and if someone else has it, she'll take it, and the men will stand in line to get it for her."

A strange chill ran up Gwen's back, and she shivered. It seemed absurd to look at Little Gwen lording it among the other small children and talk about her in the same breadth as Lot's queen. And yet . . .

She watched Little Gwen, and despite the absurdity of the crown and the troupe of little boys about her . . . there was no doubt. Her sister was more than just pretty. When you put aside what you knew about her, and just let your eyes follow her, she had something about her that made everything about her a little *more*. Both of them had white-blond hair, but Little Gwen's was glossier, and even when tousled, it looked pretty instead of messy. They both had blue-green eyes, but Little Gwen had a way of looking sideways out of them that made you think she was looking at you in particular. Her cheeks were the pink of wild roses, her chin adorably pointed. And that was now, as a little girl. What would happen when she got to be Cataruna's age?

She sipped her cider and wondered why Braith was telling her all this.

"I tell you this because I had a sister like her. By the time we were twelve and eleven summers, she had the best in the house, and the rest of us got what she didn't want or hadn't a use for. 'Twas a rare good thing for me, she didn't like the horses and they didn't like her; every lad one of us fancied, she took, only to toss aside for the next. M'brothers, m'parents, they fair doted on her." Braith shook her head. "When I got taken up by Chief Hydd's horse tamer, no one even noticed I was going. Never went back, not even t'visit, but I've no doubt she made plenty'f mischief before fever took her. An' she was only a farmer's get. Reckon what mischief yon'll make, bein' the king's." Braith sipped thoughtfully at her mead. "So ... best get ye gone from here, afore there's summat ye hold dear that she comes t'fancy. Or be doin' somethin' she never will."

After that, Braith seemed to have nothing more to say, and they sat in silence. Gwen watched the dancing and listened to the music for a while, then when she looked up again, Braith was gone, leaving as quietly as she had come.

By that time the long day and a full stomach were both catching up with her. She was having trouble keeping her eyes open, and she finally decided that going to bed was a better idea than nodding off and having someone have to put her to bed like an overtired baby.

Besides, the queen and her women had just come back from the Working, and the queen had a strange, wild look about her. Gwen wasn't sure she liked the way her mother looked right now: eyes as bright as someone a-fever, cheeks flushed, looking scarcely old enough to be the mother of one, much less a brood. If you didn't know her, you'd take her for Cataruna's sister, not her mother. And the way her father was looking back at her . . . made her very uncomfortable for reasons she really didn't understand.

So as the queen drew the king into the dancing, taking his hand and pulling him up from his seat as if he was light as a bit of down, then pressing close against him, Gwen picked herself up and turned her back on the fire and her face to the castle.

The Great Hall was full of murmurings in the shadows; she took the straightest path through the middle of it and ignored what was going on; really, the only difference between tonight and every other night was that the Hall was a great deal fuller.

The bed was cold, and she shivered for a while before her body warmed up the hollow; she was almost asleep when half-running footsteps, murmurs, playful growls and breathless giggling heralded the passage of the king and queen into their bedchamber. The sounds made her uncomfortable all over again, but it wasn't just the sounds, and it wasn't just knowing that her mother and father were going to do what all those people in the shadows were doing. It was something else, something she couldn't put a finger on, a feeling that . . . that something was turning wrong that had been right. Like a blight on grain; this wasn't just a matter of her parents, it was bigger than that.

The feeling held her pinned in her bed—

Until she woke suddenly to find that it was dawn, and her sisters were all curled up with her, and, as usual, Little Gwen had stolen the covers.

The king was in a rare good mood; after breakfast he gathered up Gwen—with Little Gwen predictably trailing behind, unasked—and took her down to his horsemaster. "Braith says the lass is ready to be trained and to give her a wise old warhorse to train her," he told the old man. The horsemaster looked down at her critically. Gwen looked him in the eyes. There were scars all over him, at least, everywhere that she could see, and a pair of spectacular knife- or sword-cuts marred a craggy face still further. "I know ye," he said, finally, his voice a low growl. "And a goodly work ye make of the pony. Braith thinks ye ready for a horse now?"

Gwen nodded. "Aye, sir," she said quietly.

"*I* want a horse!" Little Gwen interrupted imperiously. The horsemaster turned to look at her, then Gwen saw him suddenly look up at her father. Something passed between them, and the horsemaster smiled. Gwen got a shiver of pleasure when she saw that smile. It promised that Little Gwen was going to get what she wanted and not like it.

"Well, then, ye'll have a horse," the horsemaster said, "An ye'll follow me?"

Gwen followed obediently at his heels. Little Gwen marched imperiously in front of them all. When they got to the stables, the horsemaster addressed Gwen in a quiet voice while Little Gwen surveyed the horses in the paddock as if she owned all of them.

"And which of these do ye think suits ye," he asked.

Gwen ducked her head deferentially. "You should pick, sir," she said. "Braith said, old and wise. I don't know which are old and wise."

He smiled. "Then pick I shall—" he began, when Little Gwen interrupted.

"I want *that* one!" she declared, pointing at a showy young gray. The king made a choking sound. Gwen caught the horsemaster making a soothing motion with his hand.

"All right," he replied agreeably. "Let's us get him saddled, then."

He ordered the astonished grooms to catch, saddle and bridle the high-tempered beast, and put a lead line on the bridle. Little Gwen was practically bouncing with excitement, but she frowned at the line. "I don't *need* that!" she announced grandly. "I can ride!"

"Indeed," the horsemaster said, but kept the rope clipped to the bridle. "But every rider needs the lead to try the paces." He swung her up onto the saddle, where she perched as if she were on the old pony, legs slack, hands clenched on the reins. The horse reacted poorly to the latter; he tossed his head, and his mane lashed her face, cutting right across her eyes.

She shrieked. The horse reacted to *that* by lurching into a run.

Or trying to. The horsemaster had been ready for that. He kept a tight grip on the lead and pulled inward while pivoting on one heel, which forced the horse to stay in a trot in a tight circle around him. Little Gwen bounced in the saddle in a way that made Gwen wince for what seemed a very long time, her shrieks now coming out as painful *"Ah! Ah! Ah! Ah!"* sounds as she bounced and hit the saddle. Three times she went in a circle around the horsemaster, each time making more and more noise and making the horse try to break into a run. How the horsemaster kept him to a trot, Gwen could not imagine.

It was a relief when she fell off.

She immediately scrambled to her feet, face red with pain and rage. She looked about for something to hit the horse with but fortunately found nothing. The horsemaster pulled up on the lead and soothed the ruffled stallion, but he made no move to soothe Little Gwen.

Interestingly, neither did the king.

Neither man said anything to her as she stared at them in a fury. Gwen prudently backed away from everything and everyone until she had a horse or two between her and her sister. Best to not remind her just who had inspired this desire to have a horse.

Finally, Little Gwen erupted in the tantrum that Gwen knew was inevitable. "I don't *want* your old horses!" she screamed, making every horse in the paddock shy or lay its ears back. "I *hate* horses! You should kill them *all* and make *soup* out of them!"

Then she burst into angry tears and ran off. Gwen slowly emerged from hiding. The king and his horsemaster were both shaking their heads. "She's not hurt, is she?" the king asked.

"Only a bit of bruising." The old man gestured at the straw-strewn paddock. "That be why I kept her on the lead. And I grant ye, I could've made a longer affair of this, picked a horse fit for her, tried to get her to tend it as I know yon girl *will*, an' the end of that'd be more work for *me* when she didn't. So instead, I cut across country, give her what she wanted, and—"

He shrugged. The king laughed ruefully.

She'll find something to take this out on, Gwen thought sourly. But then the horsemaster turned to see her standing there, and she tried to make her expression pleasant. "Nah, Braith's girl, let's find ye a proper horse."

In the end, it came to two, and the horsemaster couldn't make up his mind which. One was a mare, one of the cavalry duns; the other was a stallion of the famous gray line, now almost a pure white, that had been both a chariot horse and a mount. After looking them both over for a long time, the horsemaster sighed and threw up his hands. "Naught for it," he said. "Mun let *them* choose."

He put Gwen at one end of the paddock and turned the two horses loose. "Call 'em, Braith's girl," he told her, and stood away from her so that they would not react to his presence but to hers.

Now alone in the paddock with them, her mouth went a little dry. They were *very* big, twice the size of the pony. She swallowed, licked her lips, and made the little chirruping sounds she made to call the pony to her.

They both looked at her, ears and heads up.

"Come!" she urged. "One of you has to teach me, now, so come!"

The stallion snorted; the mare shook her head. Both of them started forward at the same time, but before they were halfway across the paddock, the dun mare shouldered the stallion aside with a snort of her own and laid-back ears. She picked up her feet in a trot that brought her to Gwen while the stallion slunk sheepishly off to one side.

Gwen held out her hand and the mare nuzzled it, then put her head down and butted Gwen in the chest, blowing hay-scented breath into her tunic, surprising a delighted laugh out of her.

The horsemaster brought saddle and bridle but waited while Gwen put them on, only giving her a hand when something was too far for her to reach. "Ye mun find ways t'be doing this on yer own, Braith's girl," he told her gravely. "I dun help the boys, I shan't help ye."

She nodded. That was reasonable. So taking the hint, once the mare—Adara was her name—was saddled and bridled, on her own she took her over to a stump that had been incorporated into the paddock fence and used that to get herself into the saddle. Once there, she found it not as dissimilar to the pony as she had feared. She was a *lot* higher off the ground, it was true, but the pony was so fat that his girth wasn't a great deal smaller than Adara's. She couldn't imagine why Little Gwen hadn't been able to sit the saddle better, unless it was that her youngest sister really hadn't learned to ride properly. She fitted her feet into the leather stirrups and was relieved that the horsemaster had judged the length right. She was even more pleased when he didn't clip a lead rope to her bridle.

Since he was waiting expectantly, she chirruped to Adara, tightened her legs in the right places, lifted the reins a trifle, and nudged her a little with her heels. Adara moved out in a walk, circling the paddock, then increased her pace from a faster walk into a trot.

Gwen bounced for a few paces before she found her seat again. Adara's ears flicked back and forth and she looked over her shoulder with what *looked* like amusement, and she moved into a canter.

Now this was the fastest she had ever ridden, and it was both thrilling and terrifying. The pony had never gone this fast, not even at a gallop. But the mare had another pace in her, and without Gwen doing anything, she lengthened her stride into a gallop.

The world blurred. All Gwen was conscious of was her own breathlessness, her heart racing, and the horse moving under her. And it was glorious. Like flying.

The mare gave her only a taste of this before slowing, first to the canter, then the trot again, and finally into the walk. She stopped on her own at the side of the horsemaster.

"Ye'll do," was all he said. Then he left her to make sure the mare was walked cool, unsaddled and unbridled, rubbed down, and put up in her stall with her tack with her. Gwen moved in a kind of happy dream. She had thought that yesterday was the best day of her life. But no. Today was.

One of the grooms came to tell her when she was finished that

she was to report to the novice trainer. She thanked him and trotted off to the yard where all the boys, and the odd girl or two, got
their first lessons in warcraft. Or rather, their first lessons in making
their bodies strong enough for weapons; it seemed that handling a
sword or a bow or even a knife was a long way off. Gwen had never
thought of herself as lazy, but after what seemed like an age of lifting
small leather pails of water over and over, of swinging weighted sticks
against a padded pole over and over, and many other similar exercises, she was hot and sore and grateful to be dismissed for the day
to go back to the paddock and commence another round of riding,
this time under the eagle eye of one of the grooms, in the company
of the rest of the beginners. She got no help in saddling and bridling
this time, but neither did the others. No help, that is, from the *groom;*
she was not the only undersized person among the beginners, and
they helped each other reach girths under bellies, pass breastbands
around chests, and persuade the canny old horses to bend their heads
for the bridle. Gwen was especially good at the latter, so no one be-
grudged her the help it took to get a saddle that seemed a hundred
times heavier than it had been this morning onto Adara's back.

Then they lined up, head to tail, along the paddock fence, and
the groom called out what they should do. Oh, not for *their* benefit; it
was very clear to Gwen that she wasn't in control of Adara right now,
and it looked to her as if the rest of the beginners were in a similar
case. No, no. It was the horses who responded to the commands, and
they, the riders, were doing their pitiful best not to fall off, to learn
how to move as one with the horse, and not merely balance there.

Ride in a circle; walk, trot, canter, then drop back to a walk. Wheel
and do the same in the other direction. Repeat until the horses' muscles were sufficiently warmed up. Wheel, so that they were all facing
the same direction. Charge the fence at a trot, pull up, wheel in place
and charge the fence on the other side. Repeat until the young rid-

ers were starting to get the rhythm of things. Go back to riding in a circle. Split into two groups, charge each other, making sure no one collided. Wheel and repeat. Go back to riding in a circle. Trot to the fence and stop, then back. Wheel in place and repeat.

Then the groom ordered them all out of the paddock, and Gwen thought they were going to be allowed to just *ride,* on a jaunt across the grazing meadows, as she used to on the pony—but no. The groom directed them to another part of the training field where there were padded poles set up down the middle, and when Gwen saw them, she knew what they were going to be doing. As she expected, the groom set them to weaving through the poles, down and back, first at a walk, then a trot, then a canter. They didn't go up to a full gallop, but right next to them was another set of poles, around which another set of slightly older warriors-in-training *were* riding at an all-out gallop, and with the reins in their teeth and their hands held out to the side, keeping their seats only through superb balance!

All this was taking an entirely different set of muscles than she used in riding the stolid little pony. She could feel every pull and strain and knew she was going to be very, very sore. And yet—she would not have traded this for *anything.* And no matter how sore she was, it was going to be worth it.

The groom finally led them back to their original paddock, but of course, the work was not over. The horses had to be unsaddled, walked cool, rubbed down, and put in their proper stalls, with saddle arranged on a stand and bridle hung on a peg. Then, and only then, were they allowed to go.

It was sunset, and suppertime, by the time she limped back to the Great Hall. The servants had brought in the kettles of stew and the remains of last night's feast, and people were settling onto the benches and tucking in. The Hall was nowhere near as crowded as it had been last night; at least half the guests had packed up and headed homeward this morning, and the rest would leave tomorrow. Gwen was not altogether sorry to see them go; she was already tired of being polite and always on her good behavior even when some of the boy guests behaved outrageously.

Her father and mother were already seated at the High Table—on the day after a feast, no one really stood on ceremony—when a shriek and a wail arose from the back of the hall where the bedrooms were, and a moment later Gynath and Cataruna came storming out of the room, the one angry, the other lamenting, with ruin in their hands.

"My best slippers!" shouted Cataruna, her cheeks aflame with rage.

"My belt! I just finished embroidering it! I only wore it once!" wept Gynath, consumed with grief.

The pretty leather slippers had, very clearly, been given to the dogs to play with. They were chewed to shapelessness, and the seams had come half unsewn.

As for the belt, someone had taken it out and trodden it into the mud until nothing of the bright colors that Gynath had so painstakingly sewn into beautiful patterns could be seen for the dirt and stains.

A sinking feeling in her stomach, Gwen walked slowly to the bedroom. She dreaded what she would find. Which of *her* possessions had been taken and ruined? Behind her, she could hear her sisters telling their parents how they had found their things—and Cataruna added shrilly that Little Gwen was nowhere to be found.

Little Gwen. Of course it was her. She'd wanted something, gotten it, and didn't like it—so her first thought was to take whatever her sisters took pleasure in and ruin it. Gynath's new belt had been the admiration and envy of the other girls, for Gynath was the best needlewoman in the castle. And Cataruna's slippers had made her feet look very handsome indeed in the dancing; more than one young man had said something about them in ways that had made the blood rise to Cataruna's cheeks last night.

". . . it was no accident, Father!" Cataruna snarled. "The slippers were in my chest, on top of my kirtle, right where I put them last night. She took them and gave them to the dogs, then put them back!"

Gynath was sobbing too hard to be coherent. She had been working on that belt all summer. Gwen didn't blame her for weeping.

But Gwen didn't have to look far to find Little Gwen's revenge on *her*. There in the corner where she had been left was Gwen's poppet. Or rather, what was left of her poppet.

The doll had been torn limb from limb, scalped, and decapitated. Her clothing had been shredded. Mutely, Gwen gathered up the pitiful remains in both hands, and went out into the hall where her mother was trying to soothe a disconsolate Gynath, and her father to placate Cataruna with promises of a new pair of slippers even prettier than the ruined ones. She waited until Gynath's sobs had quieted into sniffs and hiccups, and Cataruna had run out of names to call their sister. That was when the king and queen finally became aware that she was standing there. When their eyes fell on her, she silently held out her hands. It took them a few moments to realize what it was—or had been.

"Oh, no—" It was Gynath who realized it first, and it came out in a moan. "Oh, no, oh, Gwen, your poppet, your poor doll!"

Cataruna's cheeks flamed anew. "That—that—" she spluttered. "Oh! I am going to *shake* that brat until her head falls off and her teeth fall out!"

Eleri's eyes narrowed with anger. The king put up a hand. "You'll not touch her. When she's found, she *will* be whipped, and she'll be living on bread and water for a fortnight, and put to whatever work Bronwyn deems suitable. There will be no playtime for her until the snow flies, and perhaps not even then if I am not convinced of her repentance." He looked to his queen. "I've spoiled and indulged her overmuch, as you said time and again, and this is what comes of it. I am sorry that you, my *good* daughters, have fallen victim to her mischief."

"And her poppet will be yours, Gwen," the Queen began—

"Lady Mother—no," Gwen replied, feeling dimly that if she were given something of *Little Gwen's* rather than just a replacement, her youngest sister would only see it as a reason for more vengeance. She straightened her back, gently piled the pathetic remains of the doll on the table, rubbed the back of her hand across her stinging eyes, and looked up at her mother and father. "I'm a warrior now. Warriors don't need poppets. I won't have time to play with it, anyway."

Her mother gave her a skeptical look, but her father relaxed and beamed his approval. "Well said," was all he replied, but Gwen felt that approval fill her and ease some of the sadness she felt at losing her plaything.

"Bronwyn," Eleri directed, "Take these things and see what, if anything, can be done with them. The belt especially. Then look for Gwenhwyfach, and when you find her, see she is put in the guard-closet to await our pleasure. And let us eat. There is no reason for a nasty child to spoil our supper, nor make us wait until our meat is cold."

Gwen ate slowly, feeling the ache of every overworked muscle, every bruise. She actually didn't mind it; concentrating on that made everything else secondary. And while Eleri consoled Gynath and Cataruna with the most golden-crusted of the pies and the last of the honeycakes, the king directed his server to give Gwen all of the leftover goose and with his own hand poured her cup full, not of cider, but of honey-mead. "You'll be aching, young warrior," he said in an undertone. "This will help you sleep."

The mead was sweet but with a fire under it. It burned its way pleasantly down her throat as she slowly ate slivers of goose, spread a surprise bit of goose liver on some bread, and sopped up the last of the goose fat with the rest of the bread. And it did start to make the aches go off into the distance and give her a warm and soft-edged feeling, as if she were falling asleep. Halfway through dinner, Bronwyn returned and reported that a sulky and unrepentant Gwenhwyfach had been put in the guard-closet, with one of the turnspits as a guard on the door.

The guard-closet was a tiny little windowless niche in the stone walls, with a single hard stone bench in it, that the king used to keep single wrongdoers in while he debated what punishment to mete out to them. From time to time all of the girls had been confined there for mischief, but never had he done what he did now.

"Here," he said, carefully picking out the hardest and most stale piece of trencherbread and a leather cup that he filled with water. He handed both to Bronwyn. "Give her those, and tell her she will be staying in the closet until morning. In the morning, my dogmaster will whip her. And then for the next fortnight, she will sleep in the rushes with the dogs and the scullions. I'll not have her sharing a soft bed that she did nothing to deserve. I'll not have her sleeping comfortable beside the sisters she wronged. When she is repentant and ready to act like a king's daughter instead of a low-born brat, we will see if she may sleep like one."

Gwen's astonishment woke her up from a half-drowse. Eleri nodded approval.

"I put you in charge of her, Bronwyn, to direct her as you like," the king continued. "While she sleeps on the hearth, you will give her work to do so that she learns the evil of idleness. She'll have nothing but bread and water. At the end of that time, she will apologize, and if I am convinced she is repentant, she may go back to the bed and the board."

Bronwyn bowed silently, took the bread and water, and disappeared into the shadows.

Gwen sopped up the last of the fat, ate the last bite of bread, drank the last swallow in the bottom of her cup. She felt the fatigue of the day settle on her like a weight; she begged permission to leave and plodded back to the bedroom.

On the way there she passed the turnspit guarding the door to the guard-closet. There were muffled sobs coming from inside. But they didn't sound repentant, or frightened, or sorrowful.

They sounded angry.

Chapter Five

Winter did not stop the training. Even when conditions were too foul to ride, it was the responsibility of the warriors-in-training to take the horses out to the paddock, turn them loose, clean the stalls, then give their feet a thorough cleaning and put them up again. Normally the grooms did this, but when the horses were confined to the stable, rather than running loose, the stalls fouled that much faster. A horse standing in a fouled stall was in danger of thrush. And a horse with thrush was in danger of having to be put down. As the horsemaster told them all sternly the first time they were set to this task, "Every horse in this stable's worth three of the likes of you, an' ne'er ye forget it."

It was true, too. So foul weather only meant another sort of work with the horses.

As for warrior training . . . well, foul weather meant that some of their "training" involved ax work . . . against the firewood. The trainers had very clever ways of making sure that every stroke accomplished some wood-splitting. Gwen built quite a set of muscles over the winter. And once they could be safely trusted with bows and arrows, they became part of the army of hunters that provided meat for the king's table. And a miss there, against rapidly moving targets, had more serious consequences than a miss at a wand. Gwen learned to appreciate every bite of rabbit pie and to look on goose, duck, venison, and boar with an appreciation she'd never felt before.

After a month of punishment, Little Gwen finally broke down and repented . . . or at least made the motions of repentance. Gwen was expecting some other form of retaliation, but at least where she was concerned, nothing happened. In fact, Little Gwen left her alone for the first time in memory. Perhaps it was nothing more than the fact that from Gwenhwyfach's perspective, Gwen's training regimen was worse than any sort of revenge. It hardly mattered, really; the only time she ever saw her little sister was at meals and bedtime and often not even then. Gwen ate early, rose early and went to bed early, so tired from the physical work that she was dead asleep from the moment she got under the blankets.

But once back in the king's good graces, Little Gwen seemed to be putting most of her effort into becoming his favorite—and to making herself as unlike Gwen as possible. She began walking and talking as daintily as any girl trying to catch the eye of a boy, kept herself fastidiously neat, and for the first time volunteered to do things, as long as they were womanly. The king found this very amusing; as for Eleri, she was too preoccupied with her own matters to pay much attention. And Gwen was just relieved that Little Gwen had finally found something to keep her from plaguing her older sisters.

The winter was not as harsh as everyone had feared, and most took that as a sign that the High King's marriage had had the desired result on the land. Certainly at the Year Turning and Fire Kindling, the Midwinter Solstice, word crept across the kingdoms that the new queen was properly increasing, and that was a good omen indeed.

Someone else was increasing as well, although the queen had

kept it to herself until almost February, revealing it only when her women threatened to tell the king themselves. But again, this had little impact on Gwen's life; now one of the warriors-in-training, she was effectively out of Eleri's household.

Strangely enough, now that she spent less time *within* the household, she came to know more of her older sisters. In many ways, she saw them now through the eyes of the older boys, hearing things from them she would never have guessed. That made her watch them, pay attention to them, in a way she had not before.

All four of the girls were fair, like their mother. This alone set them apart among most of the darker-haired people her father ruled. And now that she came to think about it . . . it was very possible that Eleri's blood was all, or part, Saxon. But if that was true, no one even whispered it; she was the queen and their Wise One, and those two facts eclipsed any mere question of blood.

Or . . . just maybe . . . there was other blood entirely in her. But if that was the case, no one would even whisper about it.

Gwen and Little Gwen were the fairest of the lot, with Gwen's hair now mostly shorn off, and Little Gwen's waist-length locks being tightly braided every morning by old Bronwyn. Cataruna had more than a flavoring of their father's red hair, but she did not have the high temper to go with it. She also had his square face, where Gwen and Little Gwen had inherited their mother's pointed chin and tiny nose, and Gynath had something in between. Cataruna was usually grave and quiet; Gynath was usually merry, and while not a flirt exactly, had discovered that young men were very interesting a year before her older sister did so.

And both of the older girls fitted into the domestic and busy life of the household as Gwen, increasingly, did not.

She found she did not miss it; she did not wish herself back in skirts nor regret trading the chores she used to do for the harder—in the physical sense—labor of the training and the sort of work the boys were expected to do. Even in the worst weather, cleaning the stable, cleaning out her horse's hooves with bare, freezing hands, chopping wood as she practiced her ax swings, she would not have traded this for sitting and learning the making of clothing, how to weave, spin, and embroider, the lore of herbs (other than those needed for battlefield medicine and horse doctoring), the management of a household. No, not even for learning magic.

She found that last growing less and less attractive with every day that her body strengthened, her skills with weapons sharpened, and her ability to understand her horses deepened. Not that magic revolted her, far from it—but where once she had longed to see herself in the rites, taking the part of the Maiden in the Circle beside her mother, learning to control and use the Power . . . now that grew distant. Just as she could look at Little Gwen playing with a lapful of poppets and feel not even a twinge of envy, now she would watch her mother beckon Cataruna off into a conversation with the other Wise Women and no longer even wonder for very long what they were talking about.

Perhaps her mother was right. Perhaps it was being around so much Cold Iron in the form of the swords and axes had blunted her need for magic. Perhaps it had even driven the magic from her.

Or perhaps Braith was right, and she never really was suited for that sort of magic in the first place.

And on the Midwinter Solstice, that change in her position was solidified, when she celebrated the night with the other young would-be warriors and not among the women. She thought her mother looked obscurely disappointed, but the queen had two other daughters both of an age to go to the Ladies. Three, if you counted Little Gwen.

And after Midwinter Solstice, Cataruna's demeanor toward Gwen changed.

Mostly, the eldest of the siblings had ignored Gwen, which was fine. They weren't even close in age, after all. Even before Gwen had gone to the squires, they hadn't had much in common. But now, as if the Solstice had signaled some change in Cataruna's mind, she began to do small kindnesses for her sister. When Gwen came in with half-frozen hands, Cataruna would beckon her over to a pot of warmed water to thaw them. When she went to bed, far earlier than anyone else, all worn out with the work, she found that Cataruna had put a fire-warmed stone in her place. When it was her turn to serve at table, Cataruna saw to it that her portion was kept warm at the fire and kept Little Gwen's greedy fingers off it. Some might have been by Eleri's orders, but not all of it. Gwen found herself exchanging grateful and slightly conspiratorial smiles with her eldest sister, and she got them in return. Cataruna's square face seemed unaccountably happier this winter than Gwen had ever seen it before. Whatever was the reason for it, it made Gwen unaccountably happy too.

While the days lengthened again, and winter lost its grip on the countryside, Gwen found herself outstripping the group of youngsters she'd started with. Not drastically, but enough that by Gwyl Canol Gwenwynol, the Spring Equinox, she was given her second horse.

All warriors had more than one horse. Charioteers needed two, of course, but riders had more than one as well. If your horse was lamed, or killed, or ill, you couldn't count on one of the chariot drivers to be able to take you to the battlefield. The chariot was already considered by some old-fashioned, although Gwen's father used it, and used it well. Many commanders were slowly abandoning it in favor of purely mounted cavalry, following the lead of the High King, who fought Roman fashion. Chariots broke, they needed highly skilled drivers, when accidents occurred they could be terrible and generally involved more than just the driver and his horses. And a single mounted man was always faster than a chariot.

Nevertheless, King Lleudd wanted his cavalry trained in chariot work, and that required two horses. All the more reason for every warrior to have two, or more than two, if he or his lord could afford it. So just before the Equinox, the horsemaster Bran came himself for her and presented her and her mare with the gray stallion that had been one of his two original choices for Gwen.

This time when she called him across the paddock, the mare was at her side. The stallion stepped carefully toward them both and diffidently bowed his head a little at the mare. Adara looked the poor fellow over with thinly veiled arrogance, as was to be expected in a lead mare of the herd, then snorted and perfunctorily touched noses with him. The stallion Dai was to be permitted to partner with Gwen. It was very hard for Gwen to keep a sober face and not laugh out loud at the two of them, but poor Dai had been humiliated once by Adara, and he wasn't going to forget that in a hurry.

So now Gwen would learn chariot driving and the trick of switching from one horse to another when riding. The High King Arthur had made a name for himself with his mounted knights who could move swiftly to any part of the land where trouble was brewing by doing just that—stopping for only the briefest periods, or not at all, by switching from a tiring horse to one that was fresher. Though her father might favor the chariot, he was no fool, and as a good commander he could easily see the advantage this brought him.

This was a well-omened time for her to have such recognition, for along with the rites of the seed blessings, the Spring Equinox was the moment when the young god of Light took up his weapons for the first time, and slew his rival of Darkness, the young Prince of Spring eliminating the killer of his father, ridding the world of the murderous Winter King. As such, Gwen's father generally called for another feast like the one at the Fall Equinox. It was not yet time for planting—the ground was still too cold, and the frosts still too certain for that—which meant that the men were not yet bound up in the sowing and tending. Lambing time was mostly over, and though calving and foaling time was on them, such were the responsibilities of horsemasters and herdsmen, not the warriors. So it was a good time to take stock of what the winter had taken and trade news and rumors.

The women, of course, and the Druids, all had magic to do. So it was a good time for them to gather also. There were the seed blessings . . . and there were other things.

For this feast, Gwen was not required to do any of the hearth chores, although she did, in fact, pitch in. With the other squires, she went to gather fallen wood in the forest. She gathered cress and the young sprouts of the cattail plants, which were delicious when quickly dunked in boiling water. She caught and cleaned fresh fish. There was, of course, little fresh game at this feast—this was the time of year when birds were about to nest and animals were giving birth, and careful custodian of his lands that the king was, he forbade any springtime hunting except for the very old—and those made for tough eating, and required stewing.

But mostly Gwen did the chores that her warrior band did—endless wood chopping for the cook fires and ovens, the hauling of water, which was regarded by their trainers as yet another fine way to build their strength, building temporary paddocks for the visitors' mounts, and a thorough cleaning out of the stables down to the bare earth, which was then sprinkled with lime to sweeten it before sand was brought in to cover the lime, and straw laid down over that.

The castle underwent a thorough cleaning too, with the winters' rushes hauled out, the stone floor scrubbed, and new rushes brought in, but that was mostly the work of the servants.

And Gwen had learned that for her, at least, the time of the celebration itself was going to mean still more work.

Peder ap Duach, Gwen's chief instructor and one of her father's most trusted captains, called all of his particular charges together just before the first visitors were to arrive. "I've assignments for some of ye," he said, shortly, looking them all over with a stern eye. "And no whinging do I want to be hearing. Not all the king's honored guests will be bringin' their own pages and squires, and that'll be the job ye'll be doin'. 'Tis a great honor to be chosen, an' a great trust. So here now. Here'll be the ones that'll be servin.'"

Never in a thousand years would Gwen have thought she'd be picked, but to her astonishment, she heard her name called; she would be serving Hydd ap Kei, Braith's lord.

She didn't question the assignment, however, nor did she complain about being put to work when some of the others were free to enjoy the relative freedom they'd have while the celebrations were afoot. For one thing, it gave her rather a thrill to have been picked over those older than she. For another, well, this was *Braith's* liege lord, which meant that she would almost certainly be spending a lot of time in the company of the real warriors and chariot drivers, without needing an excuse to try to hang about.

So as soon as it was possible to do so, once Hydd had arrived, she presented herself to him as his page. Since the weather was fine, he'd set up a tent, as had many of the lords and captains. She didn't blame them; sleeping conditions in the Great Hall were beyond "crowded." His bodyguard nodded at her and pulled the canvas flap aside for her.

"Lord Hydd, I am to be your page," she said, as the man turned away from something he had been unpacking from a small chest to look at her.

"Peder sent ye?" he asked. She bowed, as was proper, and kept her eyes on her toes, as was also proper. The king's daughter could look boldly into the face of a High Lord and one of the king's favored captains, but a page had to be respectful and show humility. "Then go to the king and give him my compliments, an' ask when he wishes me t' attend him. Bring me back his answer. Is Lord Gwyddian here yet?"

"Aye, milord, I will," she replied immediately. "I don't know about Lord Gwyddian, my lord."

"Then unless the king wants me urgent, go to him and tell him we need to speak about that handfasting at his leisure. Find out about Lord Gwyddian. Then return with the king's word; I'll have more work for ye then."

She bowed again, and ran off at high speed; she suspected sending her to her father was on the order of a test; if she *hadn't* been sent by Peder, and was only trying to find a way to lurk about and eavesdrop on the adults, this would uncover the ruse. But of course, she had been; so she'd pass the test, if test it was.

Her father returned the compliments, as impassively as if she had been anyone but his daughter. There was no urgency, he would gladly receive Hydd at supper. Lord Gwyddian was not yet arrived. She ran back as quickly as she could—without arriving in an unseemly, untidy, and panting condition.

Hydd accepted the answers she brought back without comment, and immediately put her to work in truth. Mostly the work involved a lot of fetching and much more message-taking. In fact, by the time darkness fell she was about run off her feet.

Her duties to Hydd *should* have included serving at his side at table, but she hadn't yet been trained in that, and with a chuckle he dismissed her. "Go and sup with yer family, little page," he told her, kindly. Near starving, she was nothing loathe to obey him.

She found herself seated between the same two boys as at the

Samhain feast, but this time word had mysteriously spread that she was now one of their peers. Instead of ignoring her, they included her in their chatter, and despite the long day, she found herself having a lively conversation with them about tricks they had all learned for managing their horses. Though she was younger than they, she discovered she had great status in their eyes, not because she was the king's daughter but because she was "Braith's girl." And that she could entirely understand. Sometimes the fact that Braith had singled her out made her feel giddy.

She *had* learned how to pour, so when the last of the supper was carried away and the tables set to the side, she stood behind Hydd and saw to it that his flagon was never empty. It was ale, not mead, they were drinking tonight; serious drinking would happen later.

The talk was of nothing particularly serious; that, too, would wait until the morrow, when all the guests would be here. The only thing that Gwen heard of any interest was that Braith would not be racing tomorrow; the best of Hydd's mares were all in foal (the king looked envious), her team included.

Long before the men were prepared to take to their beds, Gwen and the other pages began to droop. She was willing to hold out as long as she had to, or at least to try, but the king took pity on them all and dismissed them. "My own servants can see our cups stay full," he said with a laugh. "And we'll get no work out of these youngsters tomorrow if they cannot keep awake."

As was usual now, Gwen was the first into the big bed. Now she *could* have claimed the choice spot in the center, but she kept to her old place instead. This endeared her to her older sisters, who in their turn saw to it that Gwenhwyfach got not so much as a hope of interfering with her. Little Gwen might have outwardly reformed, but it was clear that Cataruna and Gynath were not convinced of her sincerity,

Nor was Gwen, but since her return to the king's good graces, Little Gwen seemed to have wormed her way back into the position of "indulged baby." Gwen didn't much care, given that she *had* everything she could ever have wanted, but the two older girls were not so happy about it.

And in fact, they woke her up when the three of them came to bed, arguing about it.

". . . Father thinks it's amusing," Gynath was saying, the disapproval so thick in her tone that it surprised Gwen into complete wakefulness. "But it's a disgrace. You shame all of us, acting like that. You're too young to be putting on such a show and old enough to know better."

"But Father likes it," Little Gwen said insolently. "So *you* have nothing to say about it! I'm his favorite, and I can do what I want! You heard him!"

"We heard him," Cataruna said darkly, then laughed. "But you won't be his favorite for much longer, you wicked little changeling. You just wait till harvest. Ha!"

"Why?" Little Gwen's tone was suspicious.

"I'm not going to tell you!" Cataruna taunted. "Because you are so full of yourself that you haven't paid any attention to what's going on right under your nose!"

"Tell me!" Little Gwen demanded. "Tell!"

"Oh, tell her before they hear her out in the Hall and we all get in trouble," Gynath interrupted, crossly. "Oh—never mind. Brat, by the time harvest comes around, Mother will have had a baby, and it's going to be a boy. Which means not only will you not be the youngest anymore, Father won't care a straw about what you want. Not when he has a prince to fuss over. So there! Chew on that a while, and enjoy yourself while you can, because by this time next year you'll be lucky if he even notices you!"

The bed creaked and moved as the two eldest girls got in.

"You're lying!" Little Gwen finally burst out. "I don't believe you!"

"And I don't care. We're going to sleep. You can stand there all night stamping your foot if you want, it's not going to change the truth." The bed bounced and shook a little more as both of the older girls turned their backs on the youngest. Little Gwen stood there for several moments longer, before finally coming to bed herself. But she said nothing, so Gwen fell quickly asleep.

In the morning she was the first awake, and none of the other three even stirred as she slipped out of bed. They must have come to bed much later than she had supposed, and far past their usual bedtime. Could that have been the cause of the quarrel? Or had it been something else?

Well it hardly mattered. Gwen had work to do.

The first thing was to make sure her horses were properly tended for the day. The grooms would ordinarily take care of that, but they would have their hands full with all of the visitors' horses. So Gwen got into her older clothing first and went out to make sure they were fed, watered, groomed, and turned out for the day. Then she returned to the castle, changed into her good clothing, ate quickly, and went to present herself to Lord Hydd.

She spent the rest of the day in a state between anxiety and bliss. Anxiety because she was terrified lest she do something wrong and disgrace herself, or worse, her trainers and her father. Bliss because of the company she was in and all the things she was hearing. She didn't understand more than a quarter of it, as the talk ranged from politics to horse breeding, but she tried to consign as much of it to memory as possible.

Again, at dinner and again at supper, Lord Hydd sent her to sup at the High Table with her family rather than waiting on him. She had assumed that tonight, the night when the women would gather to work the magic that would bless the seeds and the soil, she would be expected to serve as cup bearer. But no, once the remains of supper were cleared away, all the pages were dismissed as her father and his chief lords took themselves to the solar and closeted themselves away from any and all ears, including those of the pages.

Full of nervous energy, for she had keyed herself up to see the night through and not get sent to her bed like a sleepy baby, she was at a loss as to what to do with herself. This not being a great festival like Midsummer or even Beltane, and not being a feast of plenty like the Autumn Equinox, there were no bards, nor even itinerant musicians, only those among her father's men and the villagers who could play a few tunes. That was good enough for dancing, but she had no interest in dancing. Some of her own lot of young warriors were taking advantage of the absence of their elders to dip as heavily into the ale and mead as they could; that held no appeal for her either. Cataruna and Gynath were each enjoying the attentions of several boys, an activity that seemed a pointless waste of time.

Then it occurred to her.

She could spy on the rites.

It wasn't precisely forbidden; she wouldn't have dared such a thought if there was any chance that the gods would take offense at her curiosity—so why not? In a few years she would be old enough to participate anyway, so what was the harm? Even if you weren't one of the Wise Women, there was always a place in the Circle for you.

It certainly wasn't going to be difficult to find them. All rites were held at the stone circle not far from the thicket where she had seen the bear and serpent fight.

She took a quick glance around the hall, and saw no one—no adult at any rate—who was paying much attention to what the youngsters were doing. She got up and walked out as if she had some errand she had been sent on.

No one stopped or questioned her, and once she got out past the tents and the fires, she made a sharp turn towards the stone circle. Once away from the fires, she looked back to make sure she was not being followed, waited for her eyes to adjust to the darkness, then carried on. With all the people about, she was not concerned with wild beasts; all the noise had probably frightened most of them into hiding, and the rest would be very cautious.

She saw the light of the fires within the circle reflecting up on the stones long before she caught sight of the figures within the circle or heard their voices. She knew where there would be a good vantage point, and as silently as a stalking fox, she slipped into it. Her heart raced with excitement; she had never seen any of the rites before, and she was hoping that there would be real magic.

Somewhat to her surprise, for she had thought that only women were permitted at the rites, she saw that there were two men and a boy within the circle. One of the men was cloaked and hooded, and stood well back from the rest. The others seemed to be a bard and his apprentice. The bard was speaking as she moved into place, and she held her breath to listen to him, when her mother answered him, but in a voice full of Power.

Now, she had heard the tale of Gwydion and Arianrhod, of Lleu and of Goronwy, often enough to know within hearing a few words that this was what they were playing out, with Eleri taking the part of Arianrhod and these men the other parts. But then something happened—

The world about her shifted.

She felt incredibly dizzy, hot and cold at the same time, as if she had struck her head in a fall. Everything blurred for a moment.

It was no longer night, but broad day. And she was not on her father's lands near the stone circle; she was on the top of a bluff that fell off abruptly to end in the sea. At least, she thought it was the sea, though she had never seen it herself; there was water to the horizon, an unfamiliar tangy scent in the air, and a roaring sound from the waves coming to shore below her. On top of the bluff was a castle easily five times bigger than Castell y Cnwclas; maybe ten times, it was so big she couldn't rightly judge. And the woman standing before the castle was so beautiful she took Gwen's breath away.

Her hair was a ruddy gold and fell to her feet; her eyes were bluer than the sky, and her face was terrifying in its perfection. She wore a rich gown of some shining, red stuff that Gwen couldn't identify; there was silver at her wrists and her throat, a silver chain served her as a belt, and she wore a silver filet in her air.

Before her was a man as like to her as could be; vaguely Gwen realized that if this was Arianrhod, then he must be Gwydion, her brother. With him was a boy, hovering on the edge of manhood. Both the boy and Gwydion were clothed in rough, churlish clothing with the leather aprons of cobblers.

Arianrhod was angry; but more than angry, she was near tears. And no wonder. This boy was her son, and his birth had been the cause of her shame, for she had been thus exposed by the magic of Math, Gwydion's king, to all as being no longer virgin. It was Gwydion who was the cause of that, so small wonder she was angry at him and angry at his bringing before her the boy, who had until this moment been nameless and whom she had repudiated, abandoned, and denied. "He shall get no name unless he gets it from my own lips, and that will never be!" she had told her brother.

And now he had tricked her again. She had called him "the bright and clever handed," which served very well as a name, so now he was Lleu Llaw Gyffes.

She had just at this moment seen through the deception. "Oh, perfidy!" she cried, and Gwen could see how hard it was for her not to cry. She was so angry with her brother for raising this child, for presenting the source of her shame to her, that she could scarcely form the words. "You have tricked me twice, but there shall come no third time, and this your protégé shall never be a *man*." She all but spat the word. "Hear my will on this! You have got him a name by trickery, but he shall never bear arms unless I give them to him with my own hands! Now go! And find him a fit place among the churls or the women!"

A darkness passed over the scene as Gwen shuddered at the misery in Arianrhod's voice. She sensed how deeply wounded the goddess was, how it wounded her that this beautiful boy, whom she would gladly have cherished, was the cause of the worst experience of her life. And when the darkness faded into light, the scene remained the same, but it was clear some time had passed. Two bards, an old, old man and his apprentice, approached the castle and were welcomed inside. Somehow Gwen found herself in the Great Hall with them, as if she were some sort of bodiless spirit. And while part of her knew that the bard and his companion were, in fact, Gwydion and Lleu in disguise, *she* could not see it and, clearly, neither could Arianrhod.

Gwydion was a famous bard in actuality, something that his sister seemed to have forgotten as he regaled her and her court of mostly women with song and story. But behind the storytelling, there was magic afoot; Gwen felt the Power stirring, could almost see it as Gwydion wove it into the tales of battle and tragedy that he chanted. She felt the Power stretching the very fabric of the air tight, as a drumhead was stretched tight, until at last it took shape from those very same tales just as Gwydion had intended.

The roar of an assaulting army shook the walls of the castle; startled into panic, Arianrhod and her women screamed in fear—as well they might considering how few men were in Arianrhod's retinue. In terror, Arianrhod turned to the "bard," who could be expected to have some idea who might be attacking her all unprovoked and who might well have some strong magic to defend his hostess. "I have given you my hearth and bread!" she cried. "I beg you, help me!"

Gwydion had only been waiting for this, and he thrust Lleu toward the queen. "This fellow is a doughty fighter," he said, "Worth ten of any normal man. Arm him, my lady, and I will strive to make magic in your aid."

Arianrhod called for a sword and armor to be brought, and with her own hands buckled sword and scabbard onto Lleu. In that moment, the clamor from outside ceased, and the seeming dropped from both Lleu and Gwydion, and Arianrhod's fear turned to fury.

"Three times tricked!" she spat. "But this, I swear, will pay for all. *Never*, Lleu Llaw Gyffes, will you have lover or leman or wife that is a mortal woman! Enjoy that sword you got of me, for that is all the bedfellow you shall ever have!"

But Lleu did not care, for now, at last, he had the arms he needed to slay the man who had tried to slay him. His face was alight with a fierce exaltation, so that it outshone the sun, and his eyes burned so brightly that for a moment, Gwen was blinded.

When her sight came back, the scene had changed. A dark but handsome man cowered before Lleu, the treacherous Goronwy, who had plotted with Lleu's faithless wife to slay him.

But now it was Goronwy's turn to be slain. Standing where Lleu had stood, he pleaded for his life. "I have no magic to protect me as you did!" he was begging, as Gwen took in the scene. "Let me at least have a paving stone between us!"

Lleu laughed. "Never let it be said that I was less than fair!" he replied mockingly. "You may have your stone."

Desperately Goronwy pulled up a flat stone and huddled behind it, as if behind a shield. And Lleu stretched his arm back—

As the sun stretches his strength come the Year Turning—

And flung his spear with all his strength—

As the warming spring is flung against the cold and weakening winter—

—and the spear hit the flagstone so hard that it pierced straight through and killed Goronwy in the instant.

Lleu's shout of triumph shattered the world into a thousand, thousand bright splinters.

And with that, Gwen fell back into herself and found herself once again hiding in the shadows of three massive oak trees, watching the rite take place within the circle of standing stones.

Chapter Six

DRIVING a chariot—merely *driving* it, and not doing any of the tricks that the experienced drivers did—was a lot harder than it looked.

To begin with, there were two sets of reins, each set going to a different horse, each of whom had its own ideas about how a good driver handled those reins. Then there was the fact that you were standing on something that was moving, so your balance was constantly shifting, and that caused tugging on the reins if you weren't careful, and *that* gave the horses signals to do things you hadn't intended.

She was just lucky that her pair were so experienced, so steady, so calm. They reacted to bad signals not by obeying them but by stopping dead in their tracks and waiting patiently for her to sort herself (and them) out.

Gwen had never been happier. Braith was right. This was what she had been born to do.

There was so much more to learn! She'd had no idea, not really, when she first started down this path, how much there was to it. She supposed now that it was all a matter of seeing . . . that she'd only re-

ally paid attention to the warriors, who were the end of all the training, and not to the milling lot of half-finished people still in training.
But now that she was in the middle of it all, she had at least a sense of
how much more there was to being a warrior.

And even knowing how much work there would be, how far she
had to go, she still wanted to learn it all.

Today she guided her team carefully around a course laid out by
the horsemaster; they'd been at the walk, then the fast walk, then the
trot. Now he signaled to them to move straight into a full charge. She
slapped the reins on their backs and shouted, bracing herself against
the chariot back as they surged forward in the traces.

The chariot bounced and bucked; she kept her knees flexed as
she had been taught and kept her balance, although it was a fight to
do so. Here is where it was so important for the young warrior to be
"trained" by old, experienced horses. If she fell, she knew she could
count on them to stop *dead,* because they had done just that in the
early stages of her driving training. She got bruised, but she didn't get
as badly hurt as she would have if the team had kept going.

This was far more frightening than riding. Anyone with any
sense would be terrified, with the flying hooves of the horses so close
to you, with the chariot bouncing like the featherweight thing that
it was, and you trying to guide the horses around turns that slung it
sideways as well as sending it bounding into the air.

And for that reason it was all the more exciting and exhilarating.

The horsemaster let them run the course three times before signaling her to slow, then stop. He walked up to them and slid his hand
up the shoulder of the mare under her mane and nodded with satisfaction. She was no warmer than she should be; she showed none of
the signs of fighting with her driver. Without a word, he waved Gwen
off and signaled to the next to come onto the course. She hopped
down out of her chariot, her legs wobbly with fatigue but determined

not to show it, and walked them back to the paddock, where she backed her chariot into its place in line, unhitched them, and led them off to cool. Once they were fit to turn loose, she unharnessed them, gave them a quick rubdown, and let them out into the field. She turned then, to find her mother at the fence, waiting patiently for her to be finished. She looked in her pregnancy like the pregnant Goddess must look: ridiculously young, face glowing and beautiful as the sun.

She was startled to say the least. Not that Eleri was an utter stranger to the stable; she had driven a chariot herself in the past, though she hadn't done so in several years and certainly could not in her current state. She was, perhaps, two moons from giving birth, which made it even odder that she should have come down here to the stables, when her increasing girth made such a long walk uncomfortable. And there was no doubt who she had come to see; Gwen was the only person here at the moment.

She recollected herself quickly. *Here* she was not the queen's daughter; here she was nothing more than a warrior-in-training, and as such, she bowed low and did not raise her eyes. "My lady," she said, and nothing more. It was for Eleri to give an order and for her to obey it without question.

"Gwen, walk with me." The queen's voice made that a command. A gentle one, but nevertheless, a command. Obediently, Gwen went to her mother's side and set her pace to the queen's slower one.

The did not go far, only to a bit of stone outcropping overlooking the chariot course that made a convenient seat. Eleri eased herself down onto it, while Gwen remained standing until her mother patted the stone beside her. Still puzzled, but grateful, Gwen took a seat beside the queen, and Eleri put one arm around her daughter, hugging Gwen close, and with that gesture, Gwen became the princess again, and not the young warrior.

"I'm sending Cataruna to the Ladies," Eleri said, out of nowhere. "I know you wanted that yourself, and perhaps in time we shall send you, but—your mentors tell us that you are doing well. So well that they have urged me not to send you until you are much older, and your training is complete." Gwen turned her head up to look at her mother in astonishment, to see the queen gazing down at her with an anxious look in her eyes. "This kingdom needs as many with the Blessing as powerful as I have been given, as Cataruna has been given, as we can manage to get properly trained. Cataruna leaves today, in fact, in company with two of the village girls who also have the Blessing; the king and I wanted to send her off before she made any serious attachments to a boy, and there are several now with whom she might. I hope you are not upset."

Now Gwen was even more astonished. "No!" she blurted. "Braith was right. This is what I want!"

Eleri sighed, and her face took on an expression of regret. "Your father said that you would say that."

Gwen's brows creased. "Is that bad?"

The queen hugged her again. "Not at all. But you know that the hand of the goddess was strong on you when you were born, and I was sure that there was nothing that you would want more than to take up the Power. Now—" she sighed more deeply "—now you are around Cold Iron so much that the power is fading. I begin to think, as Braith does, that there were two goddesses bestowing their Blessing on you, and one of them was Epona. I cannot fault you at all for choosing her. And I know I will not have to ask you twice; you want this, more than anything."

Gwen nodded solemnly.

"Then my blessing on you, and Cataruna will take your place. There is Cataruna, and perhaps your other sisters." The queen got ponderously to her feet. "I have been watching you at your training, and your mentors are right; your hand was made for the chariot reins, for the bow, and perhaps for the sword. I will sleep well of nights, knowing that you will be a strong guardian to your little brother as he grows."

"I promise!" she said firmly. In fact, she could not think of anything more delightful. She would guard him until he was old enough to take up these first lessons himself, and then she would help to teach him. And when he was a man, she would be one of his chosen Band, and fight at his side.

The queen's hand rested briefly, caressingly, on her head, warm and tender. "Go back to your lessons, young warrior," she said fondly. "Be wise as the salmon, crafty as the fox, valiant as the wolfhound, and fierce as the hawk."

Then she turned, and as she did, Gwen felt something quite peculiar, a sense that something had been loosened between them. Not broken—not at all—but it felt very much as if the queen had opened a door to her and was letting her go through it all on her own, like the first day a young falcon was taken off the creance and allowed to fly free.

She looked up into her mother's eyes. "I will," she repeated, making a pledge of it. "You'll be proud of me."

"I already am," her mother replied, and turned to make the slow journey back to the castle.

Gwen couldn't stand to be indoors that night, sandwiched in the big bed with her sisters. She wanted to be completely alone with her thoughts, she wanted nothing to interrupt, and above all, she did not want Little Gwen to sour everything with poking and prodding—

Little Gwen had an uncanny instinct for when Gwen wanted to think. During the day, of course, Little Gwen didn't come anywhere near her. But during the day, Gwen was too busy to stop to think. That moment when the queen had come to speak to her had been the only pause in the entire day, and Gwen was pretty certain she would not have had that much if it had not been the *queen* who had taken her aside. Gwen's day, like that of her fellows, always began before anyone else but the servants were up, and it was filled with chores, exercises, practices, lessons, and duties. It only ended when the steward, who was the one in charge of Gwen and her fellow squires and pages, said that the day was over.

But she loved it. Not every moment of it, of course—but even in the most tedious parts, the knowledge that *after this, I'll have archery practice* or *we'll be learning to wheel in formation* kept her willing to work through the tedious, or the difficult, or the downright onerous. Or she would be thinking hard about something she was supposed to master, which made the time pass so much faster when she was mucking out, or grooming, or cleaning weapons and armor. And of course, when she served at table, she had to stay on her toes. The Great Hall was a lot more crowded when you were counted among the servitors. Not that all the squires served *every* night, far from it. Most meals were very informal. But they all took it in turn to serve at the High Table to keep in practice. Gwen was never allowed to serve the king—the steward told her from the beginning that a squire was never, ever allowed to serve someone he was closely related to. But at some point or other, she did serve each of the other men at the king's side of the table—his three captains, the steward himself, and any important guests he might have.

That, too, put her out of Little Gwen's reach. And usually she was so tired by the time the Steward dismissed them all that she went straight to bed and was asleep by the time Little Gwen—who was always trying to put off her bedtime—came back to the room. But on those rare occasions when Gwen wasn't exhausted and did want to lie awake thinking for a while, Little Gwen seemed to sense, some-how, that she was feigning sleep and would poke and prod her, "ac-cidentally," or pretend to be tossing and turning, interrupting her thoughts.

So tonight she took a sheared sheepskin rug and a blanket out to that little sheltered corner where she used to pick over the feath-ers. She nodded at the sentry standing guard at the door. "Too hot to sleep inside," she told him, and he grinned and nodded. Of course he wouldn't have grinned and nodded if she had been old enough for boys to be interested, as they were in Cataruna. He would have asked quite sternly if the king knew she intended to sleep out, and if she was sleeping alone, and then he would have made certain that the king *did* know and knew who she was with. Not all her willing him not to see would have stopped him from spotting her if she had been Cataruna's age. Although things were changing elsewhere, it was still the expected thing here that boys and girls, even when the girl was the king's daughter, would make their first fumblings together without there being any formal promises binding them. A swelling belly generally meant a wedding, of course, but Gwen knew vaguely that there were ways of preventing such a thing. If there hadn't been, there would have been a great many more princesses than just four. In the village, at least, the girl that went to her marriage a virgin was a rarity.

Nevertheless, for the king's daughters . . . there were some things expected. You might keep the identity of the boy you were with from your parents if you were an ordinary girl, but the king's daughter—well, there were always going to be complications. That had been carefully explained to them once they were old enough to notice that not all the bodies in the great hall of nights were quiet ones. If you went with a boy, Mother and Father had to know about it, know who he was, and to that end, the king's men would be asking questions if you went slipping out to meet one. And you had better go to your betrothal, if not your wedding, still virginal or at least able to pretend to that state.

But she was still young enough that it didn't matter. He probably thought that he was going to go meet up with some of the squires for an illicit berry feast, perhaps, or some night fishing, or even for the sharing out of too much stolen ale or mead. He still had to know, of course, and he followed her for a bit. But under his watchful eye, she went right where she said she was going, laid the hide down over the grass, rolled up the blanket into a pillow, and laid herself down to stare up at the night sky. Satisfied, he went back to his post.

What the queen had told her still warmed her heart and gave her a thrill of pride. It was one thing to have her father beaming at her— she was doing just what he had hoped one of his children would, she had joined the ranks of the warriors, she was doing well at her duties, and it was only natural that he was proud of her. Perhaps it was a mild surprise that it was Gwen in particular, but Braith was a trusted member of his elite fighting force, and the last thing he would do would be to prevent Gwen from following in the footsteps of such a valued warrior and driver.

But she was doing precisely the opposite of what the queen had planned for her. She'd avoided thinking about it, but underneath everything, she'd been certain that Eleri must be disappointed in her. Maybe angry.

But she wasn't—so not only was Gwen proud and happy, she was relieved. It wasn't often that Eleri changed her mind or her plans; it wasn't often that she needed to. Gwen had felt the weight of Eleri's expectations weighing her spirit down with dread; now that weight was gone, and she felt light enough to fly up to the moon.

Underneath all that was one thing more; the farther her duties took her from the women's side of castle life, the less time she had to spend in Little Gwen's company. That was a relief too. In fact, it was entirely possible that at some point she would be expected to move from that comfortable bed to a pallet in the great hall with the others. Little did they know that she would gladly trade that warm bed and its unruly occupant for relative discomfort and peace!

In the morning Gwen returned to the bedchamber, intending to leave the blanket and rug and go straight out to her duties, only to walk into a storm. And at the center of that storm was Little Gwen.

Cataruna stood with her arms crossed and her lips pressed tightly together as Little Gwen tore through the two packs she had carefully made up, hissing angrily that Cataruna had stolen *her* things. "Where is my comb?" she demanded, her voice getting louder with each moment. "You took it! And my ribbons! And my top!"

Quietly, Gwen edged into the room and dropped her burdens in the corner. She would have liked to edge out again, but by this point, Little Gwen's tantrum was turning into a full-blown tirade when she didn't find any of the things she was claiming were "stolen." Cataruna's belongings were scattered all over the floor as if tossed by a whirlwind, and Bronwyn, awakened by the fuss, appeared at the door curtain—

But at that same moment, someone far more important than Bronwyn appeared at the door to the solar.

It was the king.

Without a word, he strode into the room, picked up Little Gwen by the scruff of her neck, and shook her until her teeth rattled. Shocked into silence, her eyes gone round as river stones, when he let go of her, she fell in an unmoving heap on the floor.

"How *dare* you disturb the queen's rest?" he snarled, staring down at Little Gwen. "How dare you trouble the mother of my son? How *dare* you, miserable changeling? Enough! More than enough!" He turned to Bronwyn. "See to it that *she* repacks all of Cataruna's things with care, while my good Cataruna breaks her fast. Then see to it that when the top and the ribbons are found, they are given to some child of the village who deserves a reward."

He turned his gaze down on Little Gwen again. "I would have thought you had learned your lesson by now, but I see that you have not. Perhaps your hands are too idle. Perhaps you need more work to do."

Little Gwen stared up at the king, her face blank.

Bronwyn compressed her lips tight. "That may be so, my Lord King," she said. "Perhaps some kitchen work?"

Little Gwen made a faint sound of protest. The king ignored her. "Perhaps," he said. "Perhaps she will learn that churlish manners lead to being set among the churls."

Gwen winced. She knew that above all things, Little Gwen was proud. Being put with the lowest servants to do the most menial of tasks would be an agony to her.

The king turned to Cataruna and put gentle hands on her shoulders. "As for you, my daughter, go and break your fast well. We are pleased and proud that you are going to the Ladies; master your Blessing, become wise and true, and return to take your place at the queen's right hand, first among your sisters. I shall be with you anon to bid you farewell."

Cataruna's lower lip trembled a trifle with emotion. "Thank you Father," she said. "I will not fail you—"

The king chuckled slightly, and chucked her under the chin. "Now come, it is no more than a matter of lessons and learning, which we both know you excel at! You are not going off to battle but to something I think you will find a pleasure!" He gave her a gentle push in the direction of the hall. "Now go, for I am sure Bronwyn has managed something special from the cooks for you."

Cataruna ducked her head in a quick curtsy and turned, whisking her skirts as she slipped under the door curtain. Gwen took the opportunity to follow her.

"What was that about?" she asked, as one of the maidservants intercepted Cataruna with a platter heaped with good things, obviously being saved for her.

"I knew there would be a pother last night," Cataruna replied, as Gwen got a wooden platter and took bread and butter, cheese and carved cold meat from last night's dinner. "You know how Little Brat hates it when a fuss is made over anyone but herself, and there was a double fuss after dinner. Mother asked me to sit beside her, and when they weren't all talking about what I could expect to be learning from the Ladies, they were all talking about the baby. I could just see Little Gwen starting to get that look she gets when you know she's going to do something."

Gwen nodded; she knew that look all too well.

Cataruna shrugged. "I expected trouble from her last night, and I think perhaps Bronwyn did too. And maybe Mother. When we went to bed, Bronwyn gave us all possets to drink, and Little Gwen went straight to sleep. Bronwyn and I were able to pack my things in peace."

"If I'd known that, I wouldn't have slept outside," Gwen said ruefully. "I wanted to think a while, and I didn't want the brat poking and prodding at me."

"Well, I wish Bronwyn hadn't done that, because she was awake *far* too early, and the first thing she did was to tear into my packs." Cataruna made a face. "Poor Gynath. You're off with the squires all the time. Pretty soon you'll all be made into a real warband, and you'll all be doing everything together. It could even be that you'll be out in the Great Hall with them, to sleep, and she'll be the one left to deal with the Brat." The eldest of the king's daughters sighed and ate some bread dipped in honey. "I am not going to miss that."

"Are you going to miss any of this?" Gwen asked curiously.

"Truthfully?" Cataruna nibbled pensively on her bread. "I don't think so. I don't make friends the way Gynath does, none of the boys here make me want to kiss them, I *truly* will be glad to see the last of the Brat, and until now there was nothing really special about me except I was the eldest."

Gwen blinked, wondering obscurely if she ought to feel hurt by such a revelation. But she and Cataruna were too far apart in age to have been close—

"Until now, I never really had anything for myself," Cataruna was continuing. "Oh, I had the Blessing, but from what I heard it was never as strong as yours. I'm not pretty, like Gynath and Little Gwen, and I would never want to be a warrior. Up until you got singled out by Braith, I was just—really, nothing special. *You* were the one that was going to the Ladies as soon as you ever could, and if I went, it would be only after you came back. And since everyone expected great things of you, I'd still be coming in your shadow."

Something about Cataruna's tone made Gwen feel obscurely guilty. And even gladder that she'd had Braith to send her in another direction.

"But now—" Cataruna finished the bread with a lift of her head and an air of satisfaction. "Now it's *me* that's going to the Ladies, and it'll be me that will be the Maiden in the Circle when I get back. And the Ladies won't know, or won't care, what great things were expected of you. You've gone the path of Iron, and you'll never be as strong in magic as me now. So when I come back, I'll be me, Cataruna, with my own place and my own path, just as you'll have your own place and your own path." She turned her head to look at Gwen. "I'm really grateful to you, Gwen. That's why I don't think I'll miss home too much. It's not as if I won't be coming back, but when I do, it will be as the Blessed Daughter. You'll be the Warrior Daughter by then, and Gynath—" she chuckled a little "—Gynath will have half the war chiefs wanting her for a bride, and she'll make Father some good alliance, and then she'll make him a grandfather, if she hasn't already by the time I get back. Who knows? Maybe she'll even get a prince."

She didn't say anything about Little Gwen, and Gwen was not inclined to prompt her on that head.

"Did you really want to go to the Ladies that much?" she asked instead.

"As much as you wanted to be a warrior," Cataruna said fiercely.

"Then I'm *glad* you're going." Gwen surprised her sister, and to an extent herself, by fiercely embracing her.

Cataruna returned the embrace. "And I'm glad you're happy where you are." She nodded. "We're lucky."

"We are."

At that moment, Bronwyn made her way across the Great Hall, trailed by a servant with Cataruna's two packs. Cataruna eyed them curiously.

"The king your father thought of several more things you should take with you," Bronwyn said, with a glint in her eye, but her lips set in a severe line. "Little Gwen will be making do with made-over gowns for a time; I trust you will find moments to spare to make yourself suitable garments with the lengths in the bottom of the packs."

Cataruna could not repress a gasp of pleasure; all the girls knew about the lengths of lambs' wool and linen that had been reserved for Little Gwen. Gwen had been indifferent, since gowns were the last thing on her mind at the moment, but she suspected Cataruna and Gynath had suffered a pang or two of envy. "I shall find the time, somewhere," she promised fervently. "Father is most gracious."

Bronwyn looked as if she might say more, but in the end, she only nodded. "Come, it is time. Your escort is waiting."

But it seemed that more than just the escort was waiting. The king himself came to see his daughter off, something else Cataruna had clearly not expected. He lifted her onto the horse himself, after kissing her on both cheeks. "We send nothing but our best to the Ladies," he boomed, in a voice intended to carry. "And we know you will make us all proud."

With her head high, her cheeks glowing, and her eyes shining, Cataruna bowed deeply to her father; then at a word from the king, she and the escort rode off at a brisk walk and were soon over the hill and out of sight.

Bronwyn remained staring after them long after everyone else had gone to their duties, one hand on Gwen's shoulder, preventing her from leaving. When there was no one else within earshot, Bronwyn looked somberly down at her.

"I would not say this in Cataruna's hearing, but it was a spiteful splash of venom from that unnatural child that caused the king to rethink her leave-taking. *Why such a pother over the second best,* she said. And in the next moment, she turned her eyes on the servant and had *him* doing the packing for her!" Bronwyn's lips tightened. "I confess that I am sorely tried by that child. If I had not been the midwife myself, I would suspect her of being a changeling. I think it may be she has some different magic of her own, not out of her mother, of charm or glamorie, that she is only yet vaguely aware of. And this is why I decided to speak to you."

"To me?" Gwen was astonished. "But—"

"If that child does have such a thing, the queen has armored the king against it, as she has armored him against any ill magics—which is why she could not sway his anger. But there are others that will have no such armoring, and they may be those with whom you must deal." Bronwyn shook her graying head. "I wish to tell you to be wary of rousing the child's envy. Try not to come between her and something she wants, at least until I have devised a means to deal with her, or discovered what it is that she has." She looked up again, down the road that Cataruna was traveling. "I am very glad that Cataruna is well away. And Gynath, I think, is safe enough for now. But you have ever had her enmity, and it is best you stay out of her gaze."

Well, that was easy enough to promise. "I will," she said, and Bronwyn let her go.

But it was troubling. This was the second time that someone she trusted had warned her against Little Gwen, and in terms that suggested she was more than just a spiteful little girl.

Chapter Seven

"**G**wen," hissed Madoc. *"Gwen!"*

She ignored him, working hard on her horse's harness with a polishing cloth, a little oil, and talc, trying to get the brass bits to look like gold. The leather was already cleaned and oiled and as supple as a snake. Adara and Dai were groomed within an inch of their lives every day, their hooves oiled, their manes and tails braided and clubbed up to keep them from tangling. Midsummer was barely a week away now, and, as usual, many of her father's war chiefs would be arriving for the festival and the rites. Braith was coming. There would be some abbreviated races—nothing like the ones in the autumn, since some of the mares had foals at heel and you wouldn't race one of those, but there would be a maiden race for the pages and squires, since all of them had horses past breeding age or geldings. Gwen was riding and driving both, and she desperately wanted Braith to be proud of how far she had come. She wasn't really concerned about winning the races— some of the others had horses much younger than hers, three of the boys about her age were, frankly, more skilled. But she *did* want Braith to see that her backing hadn't been misplaced.

So she had gone over her gear twice now, cleaning and polishing, mending not only popped stitches, but stitches that only looked a little weak. The saddle, the harness, all looked new. But the brass bits still weren't *shiny* enough.

"Gwen!"

They weren't supposed to be talking. They were supposed to be tending to their gear. "What?" she growled out of the side of her mouth.

"Is he coming? Here? Is he really coming?" Madoc sounded breathless and nervous. Probably at least as nervous as she was about Braith coming.

"Is *who* coming?" she responded, her irritation growing. Peder glanced over in their direction; he'd clearly heard the hissing, though he hadn't picked out who was talking yet. She bent her head down to her task. With luck, he wouldn't notice. Maybe she had permission to end her chores of women's work, but that didn't mean an end to toil. If he felt she wasn't paying sufficient attention to repairing her harness, he would probably set her to wood chopping, water carrying, paddock building, or even carrying stones for the many hearths abuilding.

"The Merlin!" Madoc asked excitedly. "Is the Merlin really coming?"

The Merlin! Whatever gave him that idea? The Merlin was the High King's man. There was no reason for him to come here, of all places.

It was a title of course, not a name; the Merlin was the chief of all the Druids, as the Wren was chief of all the Bards. And his place was at the side of the High King, advising, working Men's Magic. Not journeying weeks away. Especially not at Midsummer.

"How should I know?" she hissed back, making sure her head was ducked down over her work so Peder couldn't see her mouth moving.

"You're the king's daughter! Don't you hear everything?" Madoc might well have said more, except that Peder had picked out *him* as the chatterer.

"Madoc!" the older warrior snapped.

Madoc leaped to his feet. Gwen kept her head down. "Yes, lord!" he said, faintly.

"It's rare for you to have any thought in your mind at all, much less one so burning a hole in it that you can't leave it until later. Have you something you wish to share with us, Madoc?" Gwen kept her eyes on her work, furiously polishing, but she could hear the mockery in Peder's voice. She also heard his footsteps coming up beside her. He was just behind her, out of her peripheral vision, but she could feel his presence, looming.

"I only wanted to know if the Merlin is coming to the Midsummer feast, my lord!" Madoc replied, his voice breaking a little on the last word.

"Did you now?" There was a long pause. "Well, as it happens, the Merlin *is* going to be one of the king's honored guests. So don't you think you should pay a little more attention to what you are *supposed* to be doing so you don't shame yourself before him?"

"Yes, my lord!" Madoc squeaked.

"Then get back *to* it, boy!"

Madoc dropped back down to his work and began polishing the brass of his horse's harness as furiously as Gwen was polishing hers. She heard Peder's footsteps again and saw his two hairy feet in their old sandals stop beside her. His left big toenail was black, where his horse had stepped on it. She held her breath and continued to polish.

"Acceptable job, squire," was all Peder said. Then he moved on. Gwen breathed again.

But she could feel how the lot of them had come alive with the news of such an important visitor. Some of it was excitement, but more of it was fear. There had been fantastic tales told about the Merlin. That he had narrowly escaped being sacrificed by King Vortigern as a young boy, because he'd Seen the dragon coiled hidden beneath the base of Vortigern's tower—a dragon that subsequently was released to battle another high in the sky above that tower. Some said that he was responsible for the great Stone Circle out on the plain—though that was unlikely for it had been there long before the Romans had come. But certainly, *a* Merlin had built it, which only showed the power that the Merlins held.

It was more likely true that when Arthur's father Uther lusted for Queen Ygraine, he cast illusions over Uther to make Ygraine and her entire household believe that it was King Gorlois returned from war. That, so they said, was how Arthur was conceived in the first place.

Now Ygraine was—or had been—one of the Ladies. And the Blessing was strong in her line, since both Anna Morgause and Morgana were her daughters, and both were noted for their skill at magic. Some even said Ygraine was a generation or two out of Fae blood, which would not have been completely unlikely. There were Sea Fae of great Power who often chose to wed mortal men, and Tintagel was on a coastal cliff, high above the sea. So to deceive her would have taken a great deal of Power—and a great deal of courage as well. The Ladies were not prone to appreciate men, even Druids, even the chief Druid, meddling in the affairs of one of their own.

Of course, Gorlois had been killed that very night. And Uther did not personally have the Orkney king's blood on his hands, since he'd been rather busy with Ygraine. And Ygraine had turned about and wedded him, so no one said much about the wrong or the right of it. Or at least not around Eleri's hearth fire, where, although Anna Morgause was the subject of much headshaking, Queen Ygraine came in for no such censure. Gwen knew better than to ask; she would have been told that the affairs of the very great were of no concern to a mere squire.

But since the Merlin was coming here, it behooved her dig as much as she could manage up out of her memory. The Merlin, it was said, had known that Uther's life was in danger, and he was the one that had spirited infant Arthur away and kept him safe until he could come into his own. Considering the number of rivals there were for the position of High King, that could not have been easy.

And it was certainly the Merlin, this Merlin, Uther's Merlin, that put Arthur in the position to take back the throne that was his, first Uther's own lands, then convincing all the other kings to make him the High King—or beating their armies so they were forced to accept him. There were a lot of stories about how the Merlin had a hand in that, too. Magic swords, mists that sprang up to hide Arthur's movements, and Arthur and his men being in two places at once, two battles on the same day. The Merlin had done the almost unthinkable: he'd turned an unknown stripling, a mere squire, into the High King in three years. And that meant Power. However you looked at it, whether all of the stories were true or not, there was no doubt that the Merlin was a formidable man. And an ancient one, since he must have been a man when Arthur was born, and now Arthur himself was full grown.

Which begged the question: Why was he coming here?

"Gwen."

Gwen's head snapped up, for it was Peder who had spoken her name. She jumped to her feet and bowed. "My lord."

When she looked up, Peder was eyeing her with speculation. "You'll be serving the Merlin."

Her jaw dropped. "M-m-my lord? Me?"

"You're discreet, you're well trained. But most of all, you are the king's daughter. We can't honor the Merlin too highly. The king your father has said this himself; we will show the Merlin that there is only the best for him. You'll be serving him."

She felt her head swimming. "Yes, m-m-my lord," she managed, and then she sat down heavily.

Serve *the Merlin?* Surely not . . . there must be some mistake.

There must be some mistake. . . .

Gwen was still thinking that, as she nervously stroked the front of her tunic, waiting to be presented to the Merlin as his squire. All the squires had been lined up to greet the Merlin; he was too important to just be allowed to turn up and let his servants pitch his pavilion. He'd been watched for over the course of the last few days by outriders from the King's Band, and as soon as he and his entourage were in sight, everyone had lined up to greet him, not just the squires.

Now, however, all of the important people had properly greeted him, and only the squires remained in their stiff rank. The Merlin was talking quietly to the king, while Eleri and her women waited attentively. Like the other two girls among the squires, she was dressed as the boys were, in tunic and trousers, rather than a gown. Not that she looked all that different from a boy—except for her hair, which had grown out again and had been braided up and wrapped around her head, rather than just cut off at her shoulders or shoulder-blades.

At first glance, the Merlin did not look particularly imposing. He was quite an old man, in the usual white Druidic robes, but he had none of the usual talismans or other items of power about his person. Not even a single necklace or torque. His long gray hair had been braided and clubbed like a horse's tail, his beard trimmed short.

But his eyes gave it all away. They didn't look at you, they looked *through* you, as if he were seeing something else entirely even while he took in what you looked like on the outside. They were very pale, those eyes, the same pale gray as his hair.

He had all his teeth too, a rarity in someone that old. It gave him a very fierce look. He had a curiously sharp, clean smell to him, like juniper. And he was lean, but not emaciated. Altogether, he put Gwen in mind of an old gray owl; you trifled with him at your peril, for he still had talons and knew how to use them.

Finally the Merlin's manservant came to tell him that his pavilion was ready. That was the signal for her to be presented.

The king crooked his finger; with her mouth gone dry, she came forward. "My lord," the king said, with the slightest of bows, "This is your squire for as long as you are among us. My daughter, Gwenhwyfar."

"Braith's girl." The Merlin nodded, and Gwen suppressed a start of surprise that he would use that term. "You honor me by sending your blood to serve me." He turned his attention to Gwen, and the force of his regard landed on her like a blow. "Well, by your leave, I shall take mine. I am an old man, and I need my rest."

The king laughed politely but in a way that said without words that he believed none of that. "Then your squire shall show you to your encampment. We look forward to your presence at our right hand at supper."

Gwen thought the Merlin would turn his attention to other things as she guided him to the spot where his encampment had been set up—against the east castle wall, sheltered from wind, shaded from the worst of the heat of the day, but warmed by the rising sun in the morning. And so he did, but not for long. Time and time again, she felt his eyes burning on the back of her neck, and when they reached where his pavilion had been pitched, he stopped her before she could go.

"I have some business I must carry out, and a message I need taken, squire," he told her. "Come." And he motioned for her to step inside the flap his servant held aside for them.

She didn't want to, but what could she do? Reluctantly, she obeyed. He sat down on the stool that had been set ready for him and gestured for her to stand before him. She kept her eyes fastened to her toes. She studied her own feet, studied the wrapped leather shoes she wore, with great care.

"Look at me, squire," the Merlin ordered, sounding impatient. "Look up at me, look me in the eyes."

With even greater reluctance, she raised her eyes to his. The moment their gazes locked, his piercing gray eyes filled her vision, and she could not have looked away if she'd wanted to. She felt dizzy, and yet her knees locked, and she stood as rigid as a statue. As if from far away, she heard him speaking.

"Eleri. The queen, your mother. Was she at Arthur's wedding?" he asked sharply.

What kind of a foolish question was that? "No," she heard herself replying. "She was here, she was the Mother in the rites that night. Everyone saw her there and at the feast before and the fire after. Not even eagle's wings could have got her there and back in that time. Besides, she wanted to be the Mother in the rites, to share the power all the Circles were raising for the High King." She wanted to hesitate, not to say anything more, but the words kept tumbling out. "She wanted to give Father a son, after so many daughters. So she wanted to be sure she could share in that Power."

She heard him mutter to himself. It made no more sense than his question. "Could it be that? The sharing of *that* power and not—the portent said it was his son, but could it have meant the child of his *Power* and not of his blood?"

Gwen strained against the invisible bonds that held her but to no avail. "The child she bears—boy or girl?"

She didn't want to answer, but the answer slipped from her. "A son, as she wanted, the queen says, and so do the signs and all the women."

And again, the Merlin muttered. "—I dare not risk it. I dare not. Better a hundred innocent perish to remove *that* one—"

She felt like a bird in a net. No matter how hard she struggled, she only entangled herself further. The cold hand of fear clutched at her throat. It was impossible to move even a finger.

"Your sister, Cataruna—did she ask to leave because of the new child?" he asked, as her head swam and she found it hard to breathe.

"No, my lord Merlin," she replied truthfully, and she found herself relating word-for-word that last conversation she'd had with her eldest sister.

"And you? Are you jealous of this prince-to-come?" he asked, his eyes burning into hers.

"No!" she gasped, caught unawares by the question. "No! I am going to be his guardian, his protector! And when he grows up, I will be among his war chiefs, like Braith is. I will be his bodyguard and maybe even his advisor! Father is proud of me! He said I would be chief among my brother's warriors! It's all I could want!"

He mumbled something inaudible, then sighed. "Well enough. I will find another means. You will forget all this, Gwenhwyfar. I asked you nothing, I said nothing to you." His eyes grew dark, and she heard a distant roaring in her ears. "You stood beside my seat, I gave you a trifling message to take to my servant who is with my horses, you delivered it and brought back the answer. That is all."

She felt as if she were drowning, felt her lips parting, heard herself whisper, "Aye, sir."

"Very good."

Abruptly she felt herself released from his gaze. She stumbled back a little, disoriented for a moment. Why was she here? Oh, of course. She'd delivered a message for him.

"Do you need anything more from me, my lord?" she asked, diffidently.

He looked up from the wax tablet he was scribing something on. His eyes were distant, unfocused, giving his whole face an absent-minded cast. "Hmm?" he said, then shook his head, smiling. "No, squire, you can go. Oh—but tell the king I will be very interested to meet the rest of his brood at dinner."

She bowed. "Aye, my lord," she replied and quickly left the tent.

But she had two strange sensations as she did so. The first, was relief, as if she had somehow escaped from something very dangerous.

And the other—a sense of unfocused unease—because he wanted to meet her sisters. It made no sense, this unease, but there it was. She wanted of all things to prevent such a meeting, but that was impossible, of course. They would both be there at dinner.

And there was nothing she could do to prevent it.

The smell of baked meats and stewed vegetables, of beer and mead, of the herbs mixed with the rushes, and under that, just a hint that the dogs were not as good about going outside as they could have been, rose about them. So too did the smell of sweat and leather and wool, and over it all, woodsmoke, the eternal scent of the Great Hall with its central hearth. Soon all the meals would be taken outside, for there simply would be no room in the Great Hall for the swarm of guests, but tonight there were few enough that supper was indoors. Gwen stood attentively at the Merlin's left hand, making sure that his cup was never empty, he never wanted for anything his eyes lighted upon. He was the least demanding person she had ever had squire's duty for. He chose plain small beer, not mead nor stronger ale nor cider, and his drinking was moderate. He merely sipped, and throughout the meal she had occasion to refill his cup no more than twice. As for food, once served with his choice of a little rabbit, some greens, boiled turnip and bread, he ate slowly and never indicated he wanted anything else. Every time he moved, that juniper scent wafted from his robes, his hair. It was as if he were always part of the forest somehow. He was . . . strange. A distant thing, like a legend come to sit at the table. Maybe it was the Power about him, more than Eleri had, more than any except the Ladies at Cauldron Well.

While he discussed matters of the High King with her father, his eyes were, for a very long time, on Gynath. With the tables and benches set around the hearth fire, there was plenty of light for him to see whomever he chose to look at very clearly.

Completely unaware of this regard, Gynath exchanged clumsily flirtatious looks with some of the other squires, much to the open amusement of the king and queen. Seeing that the Merlin was watching the girl, the king leaned over to his guest and said in an undertone, "She'll make me a fine alliance one day, there's no doubt."

"Oh?" The Merlin smiled with his lips but not his eyes, which kept their sharp gaze on Gynath. "Her ambition rises no higher than that?"

The king chuckled. "Gynath, Goddess bless her, is a maid meant for a man. Oh, she's a bit clumsy now, but wait a year or two while she learns; the young bucks will be prancing and pawing for her attention."

And with that, the Merlin seemed to completely lose interest in Gynath. He turned his full attention back to the king. With nothing to do, Gwen found herself watching her youngest sister out of the corner of her eye and was glad to be in the shadows, for she blushed at Little Gwen's behavior.

The child was utterly shameless. She filched tasty bits off the plates of others when she was sure they weren't looking and slipped the telltale remains to the dogs under the table; and once, she smuggled a cake with a bite taken out of it onto the plate of the little boy next to her, so that when his father looked for the treat and found it missing, the poor lad got a cuffing and sent off to his bed, whimpering that he hadn't done anything. And Little Gwen watched him go with a smirk. Even when she was full, she continued to steal, hiding nuts and cakes in her pockets.

When she tired of that, she began doing something under the table; what it was, Gwen could not tell, until a dogfight erupted there, and the poor hounds were sent off with kicks by the men. No one else seemed to notice her antics, though, except for the Merlin. Any time anyone cast a glance at her, she was all dimples and sideways glances and got an indulgent smile in return.

It was a relief when the queen rose, signaling the men that it was time to pull the benches together for more serious drinking, while she and the women dealt with the clearing away. Or rather, the women did it under her direction. Little Gwen's smirks turned to scowls as she was set to doing tasks like anyone else, under the sharp eye of her mother. As for Gwen and the other squires, their duty until dismissed was to keep the cups and horns of their appointed guests full, and with that to be done, she had no more time to watch her sisters. Shortly, the women were gone, and the men were left to themselves.

Again, the Merlin was abstemious, paying close attention now to all the men as well as the king. He said little, and when he did speak, he asked intelligent and pointed questions. Gwen was relatively certain that he was probing for weak points in the king's loyalty to the High King and looking for signs of wavering or treachery.

If that was true, he found none of it. Lleudd Ogrfan Gawr was a blunt man, not simpleminded but open in his ways. His loyalty was first to his people, second to his personal allies, and third to the High King.

"It's a good thing to have a strong High King again, and a better to have one who knows his way about a battle," the king said, to the nods of satisfaction of those around him. "Goddess bring blessings to him! For all that he's young, he knows when to fight, and when to talk, and when to send sly men to buy him time."

"And if he calls on you for your levies?" the Merlin probed. "It's a hard thing to have to travel across the width of the land to fight some other man's battles."

"Hard aye, but they won't be some other man's battles, will they?" the king responded. "He's beaten off the Saxons once and the Northerners twice since he was made High King. If we'd had a proper High King when the Romans came, there'd have been no separate peaces, no tearing apart of tribe from tribe. We'd have fought the carlin knaves on the beach, and that'd have been an end to it! Nay, three years he's been High King, and only once has he called for levies, when the cursed Northern men came in force in those dragon ships of theirs. And what happened? We came, and we beat 'em, and they haven't come again!" The men slapped their knees or pounded their feet on the floor in agreement. "If he calls for levies, 'twill be because there's need. And as for other things, 'tis why he has you, Merlin. You're the Merlin. Whatever you tell him, you have to think of the whole land. That's your duty. Aye, men?"

The men pounded their feet again in approval or responded with "aye" in varying tones of enthusiasm and satisfaction.

"So. What Arthur wants from us, by the gods, Arthur will get, unstinting." With a nod, the king dismissed the entire question and moved on to the subject of the tribes in the North and whether or not they were likely to be a trouble this year.

Gwen saw the Merlin's lips curl ever so slightly in a smile. And then he bent his formidable mind to just that question. Gwen let out a little sigh of relief.

The talk turned to lighter subjects when that thorny problem had been dealt with as best it could be. "You have a fine brood of daughters, my host," the Merlin said, with a casualness that immediately set Gwen's senses to alert again.

"Four. My eldest has gone to the Ladies, and a fine Maiden for the Circle she'll return to us. My second you saw—a good girl, a sound girl. But my pride is at your left hand, my lord Merlin." The king cast a glance back at Gwen with a warmth in it that made her stand taller even as she blushed for the praise. "The queen always held that she was strong in the Blessing and should be the one to go in Cataruna's place—but the Goddess clearly had other plans. The Blessing she may have, but it seems it was Epona's, and she was born for the Path of Iron. She takes to weapons as if she were born with a spear in her hand, and as for the horses! Epona herself surely must have smiled on her birth!" The king laughed. "Well, you'll see. Her horses are old veterans, and if she doesn't win, it won't be for lack of skill or heart, and she'll make a good accounting of herself."

"You have great faith in her," the Merlin said, in a neutral tone.

"Oh, she has the heart of a Bouadicca but more good sense. If she can keep her head, as her model Braith does, she'll do well." The king seemed to realize that he was tempting fate with such praise and coughed. "Of course, that's in the hands of the gods. But it's clear enough, for all of that, her place is in the ranks of the warriors, and her love is for horseflesh and the sword."

"And your fourth?" The Merlin's eyes had taken on that hawklike brightness again.

"Oh, Gwenhwyfach." The King shrugged. "A mere chit of a child, given to childish ways and tempers. As unformed as an unlicked bear cub. Too soon to say what she'll be, and it may be we spoiled her a bit too much. But with the new son coming, she'll get over that quick enough or have it beaten out of her. My guess is, the way she queens it among the other children, she'll be another like Gynath, a maid for a man, and make me another alliance. Maybe to Arthur's son, eh? Now, my lord Merlin, on that head, what of the High King's coming son? What birth gift would be best to send? I've a mind to send him my best yearling foal that boy and horse may grow up together."

By the time Gwen was dismissed with the other squires, she was glad enough to crawl into bed with Gynath and Little Gwen. But Little Gwen was still awake, and strangely, for once, she didn't *torment* her sister. Instead, she was as full of questions about the Merlin as any of the boys.

"What did he have you do all day?" Little Gwen demanded.

"Run errands and messages mostly," Gwen replied wearily. "Nothing exciting. I didn't see him work any magic, if that's what you want to know."

"And what did he talk about, with the men at the fire?" The child seemed crazed to know about the old man. "Did he talk about what he's done? What about his magic? Did he tell how he did some of it? How he hid Arthur? How he made Arthur High King? How he helped win battles?"

"Mostly he asked questions." Gwen yawned. "He wanted to know how Father and the men felt about Arthur, I suppose. He didn't talk much about himself, or about Arthur, or the new queen, or anything really. He asked about us, about Mother, as you do for politeness."

"What did Father say about me?" came the sharp reply.

"That you're too young for anyone to tell what you're going to make of yourself. But if you don't go to sleep, you'll look like a thrall that's been beaten, and no one will give you a thought." And with that, Gwen turned her back to her sister.

She half expected a sharp elbow to her ribs, but none came. Instead, there was a pregnant silence, and in that silence, Gwen gratefully fell asleep.

Chapter Eight

The Merlin's own servant was tending to his master's needs, while any errands that needed running would be addressed by one of the king's personal servants. Gwen had leave from her duties for this race, and that was all she was thinking about. Not that there was much attending the honored guest would need during the race; he was with the king, the queen, and both Gynath *and* the king's own squire. He wouldn't be able to lift a finger without someone asking him if he needed something. The king was sparing no effort to make his guest feel just how honored they were to have him here.

Gwen herself was far more concerned with another person among the guests. Braith was here, and Gwen was very anxious that her idol be satisfied with her protégé's progress. She didn't want Braith to think that her trust had been misplaced.

So, in these moments before the race, now that she had gone over every bit of the harness and chariot five times over, she was standing between her two charges, as she had seen Braith do, breathing in their breath and letting them breathe in hers, scratching gently along their jaw lines, whispering nonsense to them. They were old hands at this game, of course, and were far less nervous than she was. They were properly warmed up, and she could sense the readiness of their muscles under her hands when she slid her palms down along their chests. They eyed the other teams nearest them, as if they were measuring their opponents, and then turned their attention back to her.

The starter was an old, scarred fighter from one of the guest contingents; he stopped chatting to a group on the sidelines and stepped up to the starting line. "Drivers!" he barked. "Take your places!"

With a final pat and a whispered word, Gwen left her horses and hopped up into her chariot, taking up the reins. The leather reins felt alive in her hands, as if the horses were speaking to her along them. She saw their haunches bunch as they prepared to leap forward on her command. "Get ready!" the old man shouted, and she flexed her knees, and braced herself for the start.

"*Go!*"

The horses didn't wait for the reins to slap their backs. They were off as soon as they felt her lift them—or maybe they had responded to the starting shout. No matter—they were off. The chariot lurched forward, Gwen bounced a little against the curved back of her vehicle and habit took over as she regained her balance and crouched down even with the rumps of her horses.

She glanced quickly to either side and saw that she was dead even with the chariots on either side of her. Farther than that, she could not see, and she turned her attention back to the course. Beneath her feet, her chariot bounced and rattled; in front of her, the firm haunches of her horses rose and fell, their heads bobbing as they ran, their hooves flashing within a foot of her head. All around her was the thunder of hooves on the hard-packed earth, and the turf flew past in a blur just beyond her feet. Clods thrown off by the horses' hooves pelted the bottom of the chariot.

And for a single moment, there was nothing but sheer terror.

Then, as always, *everything* settled into place. She didn't really have the words to describe it. Calm descended, and she felt as if the reins, the chariot, even the horses were part of her. That she was wheel-to-wheel with the other chariots didn't matter. She *knew* that things were going to happen an instant before they actually did, just enough time to avoid trouble. And she didn't have to think about it, her body reacted before her mind actually registered what was about to happen—

Suddenly she knew that, as they wheeled for the turn, the team on her right was going to veer toward her a little too far and that the only two ways to avoid a collision were to pull back a little or try and get her team to shoot ahead.

And she knew that, as game as the team was, their strength was in endurance, not bursts of speed. They were too old for that sort of burst of speed. So she held them back. They fought her a moment, then yielded and dropped behind the other chariot.

The other team blundered into the space where her horses *would* have been; the driver shot her a look of alarm that blurred into relief, and then they had both made the turn and were on the return leg.

Through the reins, her hands told the team *fast but steady.* Through the reins, the team told her they would give what she asked for. She glanced to either side; the team that had almost collided with hers was ahead by more than a full length, but she recognized them with some satisfaction, for the driver was older than she by several years, and the team younger than hers, about two years into their prime. She was running second; in third, a length behind her, was another team driven by a boy with more experience and younger horses. His horses were laboring; hers were good for much more than just the run to the finish. If this had been a battlefield and not a race, he would be no good after this run.

She could hear the cheers; so could her horses. Their ears pricked forward. *Steady,* her hands told them. *We are,* they told her back. They stretched out their necks, though, determined to make the leader win his prize

And then they were across, and she was pulling them up, as the spectators swarmed the winner. But as she jumped out of the chariot and went to the horses' heads to take their halters and begin walking them to cool them, a smaller group was heading for her in a more leisurely fashion. Braith, Braith's lord, her father, and three of the warriors that were her teachers.

"I told you not to bet against her," Braith was admonishing her lord, as that worthy handed over to the king a fine silver bracelet.

"And you said she wouldn't even place, with horses that old, and young as she is," the king crowed. He pulled Gwen into a hard embrace, laughing. "Well done, daughter! Second place, and your team still ready for another charge! First place isn't everything."

"Not when you bring your team to the finish line heaving and winded, King," said Braith, a broad grin on her brown face. "Someone had better teach that boy in third that he's training for battles, not for sprints."

Gwen said nothing, but she felt as if she were glowing. She'd done it; she'd made Braith *and* her father proud.

"What are the prizes, my lord King?" someone called from the crowd around the winner.

"For first place, a silver brooch!" the king called back. "For third, a fine, fat duck and a flagon of wine from the king's table! And for second—" He looked down at Gwen, his eyes twinkling. "—For second, a tun of ale and the boar meant for the king's table!"

"Then let my prize be served among all the drivers!" she called out, her high voice ringing clearly out before the cheering could start again. "For surely all have earned a share!"

Any grumbling that might have started among the others that the king's daughter had surely had some secret aid was erased in that moment, as the cheering started all over again.

Gwen looked up again at her father, and saw him mouth the words "well done" before he turned back to his guests to escort them to dinner.

But better even than the accolade from her father was the one from Braith, who winked, and mouthed the same.

The tables and benches had been set up outside, around the three hearths where all the cooking had been done. There were so many guests at a Midsummer gathering that the Great Hall would have been stifling hot, and you'd scarcely be able to cram them all in there anyway. There was great rejoicing at the table set aside for the squires who had driven in the race as they squabbled good-naturedly over the best parts of the boar, stuffing themselves with both hands, their faces shiny with the rich fat. Gwen, however, was just as happy back at her place behind the Merlin, serving him. For one thing, she already had the acclaim of the two who mattered to her; for another, her gesture—and her insistence on returning to duty—had favorably impressed her father's guests, the Merlin included. The old man gazed on her for a very long moment as she took her place, and it wasn't the sort of look he gave Gynath, but the sort of measuring he was bestowing on her father's chiefs. It was a look that said *I underestimated you, and you are worth keeping an eye on.*

And anyway, although she liked a slice of good boar as much as the next person, she had overheard her mother telling the chief cook to set aside a quarter of a goose and keep it warm for "our brave Gwen." So she wasn't losing by her generosity.

Once the feast was well underway, however, the Merlin was his usual abstemious self.

But this time he paid special attention to Gwenhwyfach. She was up to her usual tricks, utterly unaware that she was being studied. *First me, then Gynath, now Little Gwen . . .* She wondered what he was thinking.

Then it dawned on her; the High King was about to be the father of an heir. Such a boy was going to need a wife, and as soon as possible. An alliance with her father would give Arthur a near neighbor to the troublesome Orkney crew. And hadn't her father suggested it himself?

Cataruna had gone to the Ladies, and once she came back, the king would not want to give up one with both the Gift and the training. Gynath was, perhaps, a little too old—oh, you could betroth babies in the cradle, but usually they were closer in age than this, and when the boy was old enough to sire a child, Gynath would be twice his age. Besides, if Eleri did not, after all, have a boy, then the king would want to pick a good husband for Gynath, in order to have a male to pass the crown to.

Gwen herself? Possible, but probably still too old. And as long as she was a warrior, she would not only be valuable to her father for those skills but would be much in the company of the men—and without the pressure of being first- or second-born, she might make a match of her own. Or not. Braith never had.

But Little Gwen, now . . . that was different. She was young enough to be reasonably close in age to the High King's son, she was pretty and would likely grow to be even prettier, and she had immense charm. She'd make a good candidate for such an alliance. The king himself had said that there was no telling what she would grow into, so out of his own mouth the Merlin had it that she was not yet seen as a valuable asset. And she was fourth-born. Her father would have every reason to welcome such a betrothal.

So now the Merlin might well be watching her to see if she was trainable. If she *was* betrothed to the High King's heir, they'd want her sent to them. They'd want to be sure she was raised *their* way, with schooling in what *they* thought needful.

And wouldn't that be interesting. Gwen schooled her more malicious thoughts. With the Merlin there, Little Gwen wouldn't be able to use her glamorie, if indeed she had one, to charm people into doing what she wanted. She'd actually have to learn how to behave. Probably how to work, too. The life of a queen was not all fine clothes and goose every day. The queen had charge over the household, and in the king's absence, could be expected even to command the warriors.

It would probably be the best thing that could happen to her.

And Gynath and I would have the bed all to ourselves, she couldn't help but think, wistfully. And then she sighed. The way that Little Gwen was carrying on, the Merlin would probably think she was far too much trouble, even for such a good alliance as with her father. Especially since her father was already clearly loyal.

She lifted the hair from the back of her neck for a moment to let a breeze cool it. She was very glad they weren't stuck in the Great Hall. It was much more pleasant, eating outside, but the king, though he would have scoffed at such a notion, followed the Roman custom of having the family and retainers dining in the Great Hall most times. Sometimes Gwen wondered why, especially on an afternoon like this. It was easier to clean up after everyone was done eating, the sound of talking didn't get bounced about by hard stone walls so that you had to concentrate even to hear a near neighbor, and it didn't smell. As fastidious as Queen Eleri was, there was only so much you could do in a room where cats and dogs did as they willed, rats and mice came out at night, and people dropped food and spilled drink on the floor.

Maybe it was only because in the Great Hall the smoke rose straight up to the roof, and there was no "bad side" for the tables, where wind sent the smoke into your eyes. The people on that side of the hearth fires were looking uncomfortable.

Gwen checked on her charge again. The Merlin was still watching Little Gwen. *Oh, it would be so good if he picked her,* Gwen thought fervently.

Finally, when the last of the food was gone, and the men had settled down to serious drinking and talking, the Merlin's manservant came and tapped Gwen on the shoulder and indicated with a jerk of his thumb that she should go eat.

She went straight to the head cook who had, indeed, saved her a good meal and, wonder of wonders, had carefully put the goose in a clay pot and left it basting in its own juice by the fire so that it didn't congeal in its own fat. Gwen enjoyed every bite, but she felt the need to hurry back, lest she be thought laggard.

By now, the sun had almost set, and the embers of the fire matched the color of the western sky. She took the jar of beer from the Merlin's manservant and quietly replaced him without a fuss. The conversation was about children—the children of the chiefs as well as of the king—betrothals that might be made, daughters gone to the Ladies, second or third sons that might be sent for harder training away from the family. No man would send his heir away of course, but it was thought that other boys would benefit from being away from the shadow of the eldest and the protection of the family. And, of course, *they* might catch the eye of a daughter, and there would be an alliance-marriage out of it.

The Merlin cleared his throat. "I have some interest in your youngest," he said, with great care. "I would like to speak with her at some length over the next day or two."

"Little Gwen?" The King's voice betrayed a touch of confusion. "Why Little Gwen? The conversation of such a child is not like to be entertaining."

"I believe I may have detected another sort of Blessing on her than the one the Ladies look for," the Merlin replied. "Such a thing is elusive, as difficult to follow as a minnow among the reeds, but it is the sort of thing that is useful to the Druids. It may be that as the Ladies have called your Cataruna, the Druids, although we do not usually call females, might be able to train your youngest. We have on occasion great need for maidens. Pure maidens, with special kinds of power to them . . ."

"Aha!" Comprehension dawned on the king. "Virgin foot-holders, as the good Goddess Arianrhod was to Math ap Mathonwy, Lleu's liege lord. Has our High King the need of such, think you?"

"He might. Or I might. If the magic calls for it. There are other Druidic callings for pure maidens, though these rites be more se-cret than those of the Ladies." The Merlin smiled. "I can assure you that if she is indeed endowed with such a Blessing, she and you will be greatly honored for it, protected and guarded—rather better than Arianrhod was. And if she is not, well no harm will come of a little talk with an old man. Hmm? Besides, your trusted Gwenhwyfar will be there." He chuckled deeply. "I assure you, my lord King, I am not such that finds great interest in little girls except as they may grow to power or further the needs of the High King."

"Oh, I had no suspicion of that." The king's ears had turned a little red. "And who am I to deny the Druids what they may need, especially as it may be in the interest of the High King? I shall tell the nursemaid that you are to have custody of the little wench for as long as you require. Or—" he amended with a chuckle "—for as long as you can stand her prattle."

When the manservant again took Gwen's place and she picked her way through the snoring bodies bedded down among the rushes in the Great Hall to the bedchamber, she discovered that once again Little Gwen was wide awake.

She heard the child sit straight up in bed as she lifted the door-curtain. As warm as it was, the bed curtains had been taken down altogether and put away until winter. "Gynath is asleep and said she would beat me with a slipper if I woke her," Little Gwen hissed urgently. "What did they say around the fire? What did the Merlin say? Did he talk about magic?"

"Actually, he talked about you." Gwen figured *that* would shut the little nuisance up, and it did. "He wants to talk to you. He thinks you might have some kind of magic that the Druids can use, and if they can, when you're old enough, they'll want you to come to them like Cataruna went to the Ladies."

"I *knew* it!" Little Gwen squeaked with excitement and gloating.

Gynath rolled over and swatted at her, then rolled back without saying a word. Little Gwen squeaked again, this time with indignation.

"Well, magic or no magic, you had better be on your best behavior, because I am to be there too," Gwen whispered crossly, "You may be sure that Father will ask me about this, and if you act badly, I will tell him."

"I won't—!" Little Gwen began indignantly. Gwen cut her off.

"And if you act like a pigkeeper's brat, or try to lord it over me, the Merlin will take it ill. He holds good manners high, does the Merlin. He treats me like a full warrior, so you had best do the same." Gwen pulled off her sandals and tunic and crawled into the bed. "And you had better let me get some sleep, too, or I'll let the Merlin know that *you* are the reason his squire is clumsy in the morning."

That threat was enough to still the questions—and the gloating—in the child's throat. She laid herself back down, and Gwen curled herself into a ball.

Could Little Gwen have a magic that would be useful to someone besides herself? That glamorie, for instance? Well it might be useful enough if she tamed it and used it wisely. She could lead other children around easily enough; the High King might find it useful if a maid in his court could do the same with adult men.

If the little ferret could be tamed . . .

Thinking that, Gwen fell asleep.

She was up before dawn again and was attending to the Merlin's wants before the old man was even awake. Now well acquainted with his habits, she brought fruit and bread and clear spring water instead of the small beer and meat that the king's other guests would expect. She didn't actually expect Little Gwen to turn up until the sun was high, but to her shock, as soon as the Merlin had broken his fast, she and Bronwyn turned up to wait on the Merlin's pleasure. Gwen's eyes nearly jumped out of her head with shock. Little Gwen had never been up this early on her own, ever!

After Bronwyn had been dismissed, the Merlin also sent away his manservant and sat Little Gwen down on a stool at his feet. Then he looked at Gwen.

And once again, she found herself held prisoner by his eyes. It happened even faster this time, and when the Merlin told her that she would hear and see *nothing* that went on, she nodded vaguely, though her mind battered itself against the fetters he placed around it like a wild thing in a trap.

Then he turned to Little Gwen. And try as she might, Gwen could only make out scraps of what passed between them.

Some things did manage to penetrate the fog that the Merlin had put around Gwen's thoughts. The Merlin asked about the coming heir, and Little Gwen replied with such venom, such hatred, that even Gwen was a bit shocked. And then—

Then the Merlin turned back to her and looked deeply into her eyes. "You fight me, girl," he said with a little admiration and some regret. "But this is not for the honest ears of one such as you. Sleep. And remember nothing."

And that was all she knew—

She came to herself with a start. *I must have been more tired than I thought!* With a touch of alarm, she looked covertly about the tent, but the Merlin did not seem to have noticed her lapse. He was giving Little Gwen a small carved box and smiling with satisfaction. "So, use that as I told you, and your future will be clear," he said.

"But the Druids will call for me?" Little Gwen pleaded, with something like urgency in her tone.

"I pledge you that *someone* will. You have Power, you will have more, and teachers seek such students out." He passed a hand over his eyes, as if he were suddenly weary, then looked up at Gwen. "Escort your sister back to her nurse, then tell your father that this child is indeed Blessed with Power but that the time is not right for her to leave her family."

"Aye, my lord," Gwen replied, feeling disappointed that Little Gwen was not going to be taken off far, far away—at least not for some time. Little Gwen looked even more disappointed, but she allowed herself to be led off, clutching her little box.

"What is that?" Gwen asked, as soon as they had left the tent.

"Something secret," her sister said, a sly look coming over her. "I'm not to tell."

Gwen shrugged. "Then I won't ask any more." Her sister looked disappointed at that response; half of the value she placed in a secret was that she could torment her older siblings with it.

But she didn't have any time to come up with a new tactic, for Bronwyn was waiting for them at the edge of the encampment and looked with curiosity at the box.

"Tis a secret thing between her and the Merlin," Gwen said shortly. "So let her do what he wishes her to do with it."

Bronwyn nodded and took Little Gwen in charge, while Gwen went off to find her father and fulfill the second half of her duty.

Her father seemed a little disappointed as well but said only, "At least we know she *has* a Blessing. But it must not be something the High King needs. Ah, well." He waved Gwen off. "We'll let her age, like mead. Mayhap she'll turn out as sweet with the help of whatever it is the Merlin gave her."

Privately Gwen rather doubted any such miracle could occur, but this was a case when the squire served best by keeping her lips sealed. "Aye, my lord King," she said carefully, bowed, and went back to her duty.

Chapter Nine

The guests were all gone, the Merlin with them, without his making a display of any kind of magic—much to the bitter disappointment of most of the young squires. This time Gwen had not had the slightest wish to spy on the Midsummer Rites. She spent that evening as usual in attendance on the Merlin, and when he retired to join the Rites, she sat quietly with the other squires, on her best behavior. They were all rewarded by a share of mead each, which warmed her belly and made her sleepy. When the Merlin and the women returned, she was surprised, for she had not thought that much time had passed. She was glad when he dismissed her, and she was happy enough to go to bed, even while the young women and men were still leaping the fire, dancing, or making sheep's eyes at each other. Of course, not all of them were confining themselves to that, for it was Midsummer after all, but they were out in the hayfields or the meadows or little bowers under the bushes, and not tumbling and panting in the Great Hall, so she didn't even think of them, but of the soft mattress and how good it would be to get there.

The truth of the matter was, that between serving the Merlin and seeing that her horses were tended perfectly, her gear in good order, and the gear of the older warriors attended to, she fell into the bed and slept like a stone every night, and she simply didn't have the will to sneak out for a clandestine look. Besides, her curiosity the last time had resulted in a vision that, while exciting, was also somewhat frightening. She'd spied upon the gods that night, and she rather hoped that she was below their attention. At least, until she was old enough to start earning some glory in battle.

Little Gwen had finally found something to occupy her besides tormenting her sisters, and for that, Gwen was so profoundly grateful to the Merlin that she would have run twice the number of errands he asked of her. Whatever it was that he had told the child, and given her, kept her captive and quiet in her own thoughts. And meanwhile, now that he was sure of her, the Merlin sent his assigned squire out into the fields and woods to acquire any number of herbs and bits. Mushrooms both poisonous and tasty, baskets of bark, roots, leaves, owl pellets, bones and teeth . . . there seemed no end to the odd things he wanted her to find. It wasn't capricious either; part of the reason he was sending her for these things was that he was graciously sharing his lore of curative things and homely spells with the queen and her women, showing them how he compounded remedies for all manner of injuries, curses, and diseases. The women loved him for this, but of course, this was not the conjuring of dragons or the summoning of demons that the squires hoped to see, so it was all terribly boring to them. In this, Gwen didn't agree; some of the things that the Merlin could cure were downright miraculous.

But at last, everyone was gone, and Gwen was back to duties that seemed light in comparison with the double burden she had carried while the guests were about. Now she knew why the squires had always looked so harried and haggard during festivals and had never had time for games or gamboling. In a time of feasting and leisure, they got none of the latter and only the leftover ends of the former.

It was about a week after the last guest had left that a traveling bard arrived, having spent Midsummer at the festival King Lot of Orkney held. Like all bards, he was as full of news as he was of music, and the women swarmed him to hear his largest burden, that Anna Morgause had been brought to bed of yet another son, her fifth. Four more she had, two older than Arthur—Gwalchmai, Gwalchafed, Gwynfor, and Agrwn. Gwalchmai and Gwalchafed were said to be as alike as she and Little Gwen, and the younger served the elder as a squire. She only hoped Gwalchmai's younger brother had a better temper than her younger sister.

"Thin, small, and sickly looking this one is," the bard said, with a little smirk that made Gwen frown. This man was angling for rewards from Queen Eleri, she thought. But she kept her head down over her task and held her peace. She was not allowed to completely escape the training of a maiden amid all the work of a squire; she still had to mend, if not make, her own clothing.

The king counted on his fingers, and chuckled. "So old Lot made sure of his wife by quickening her *before* he took her to Arthur's wedding. Very wise of him."

"Well, if a man knows he's like to wear the horns," said one of the men with a leer, "That's the best way of knowing he won't be raising another man's brat."

Ribald laughter spread around the benches. Anna Morgause had a reputation that was none too savory. It was said she had even bedded a Northman once, and it was whispered that she did not confine her couplings to humans. And here, far from the reach of her magic, it was safe enough to gossip about it.

"I've half suspected old Lot of being her pander, a'times," said another with a snort. "And she, his."

Queen Eleri was shaking her head as she cradled her belly with one hand. "Four living sons, and what does she need with a fifth?" she wondered aloud. "Well, what's the poor wee thing's name? No matter what kind of mother he has, I'll ask the Lady's blessing on him that he shall thrive. It is hardly his fault what he was born to. And he is the High King's nephew, as she is the High King's half-sister."

"Medraut, gracious Queen," the bard said with a bow. "She calls him Medraut. Her little sister Morgana is much enamored of him."

"Little and sickly, and with the Orkney lot! He'll need Morgana to look after him," old Bronwyn predicted sadly. "If they don't bully him a-purpose, they'll still worry him like a lot of unwhipped pups with a rag they tug between each other."

"Little and sickly, perhaps Anna Morgause will tend to him as she did not her healthy boys. We will hope." Eleri raised her chin, signaling that the subject was concluded. "Did the Merlin come to visit them, as he did us?"

The bard shook his head and went on to other things. Gwen had felt an odd and uneasy interest in the subject of this unknown boy child, but maybe that was only because her mother had taken on an odd expression when she spoke of him. After more gossip concerning Lot, his wife, and their followers, Eleri asked the bard to give them some music, preferably a war song, for there were rumors the Northerners were moving again. Old Bronwyn made a face of disappointment at this; she took a particular delight in the bad behavior of Anna Morgause, to the point where Gwen found herself wondering what the queen of the Orkneys could ever have done to Bronwyn to make her so sour against her.

Little Gwen had been surprisingly good, although she looked as disappointed as Bronwyn when the queen changed the subject away from the Orkney clan. Gwen was relieved. Perhaps all the attention she had gotten from the Merlin had done her good. She certainly had been on excellent behavior this evening, fetching the queen anything she asked for and not even trying her coy little tricks on the bard. It was rather too bad in a way that Eleri *had* changed the subject; the bard was not very good, and Gwen found her interest straying away from the war song that was less *song* and more toneless chanting, mostly in praise of a nebulous leader who, she supposed, was intended to resemble her father. That was often the way with these bards; trying to flatter their hosts in hopes of a rich present, rather than earning the rich present by honestly performing to the best of their ability. Sadly, her father didn't seem to see the ploy for what it was; he nodded to the monotonous strumming and looked as if he were going to interject an approving grunt on the chorus, when suddenly Eleri clutched her swollen belly and screamed out in pain.

It was not just a "cry"—this was a sound that Gwen had never heard from her mother, and from the look of it, neither had any of the other women, not even Bronwyn, who had been with her through all of the births of her children. The look of startled alarm on Bronwyn's face, made a stab of fear go right through Gwen. Swiftly, Eleri's women surrounded her and half-carried her into the royal chamber, as the king tried to make light of the situation.

"You see, Bard, your song has roused my son, and now he wants to come forth and do battle!" He stripped off a bracelet—only bronze, to the bard's swiftly covered disappointment—and tossed it to the man, looking distractedly at the entrance to the chambers, now covered by the curtain. "Let us drink to him and to the safe delivery of the queen! And let us take our drinking outside, so that we do not disturb the women at their work!"

The rest of the men were nothing loath to do so, taking up their cups and moving with unseemly haste to the fire outside. And Gwen had to go with them, in her capacity as a page.

And of course, even though they were all outside and the cries were muffled, when the screaming began, everyone knew that something was going horribly wrong. It was bad enough that this was far too early for the baby to be coming. Two weeks more, better still, a month—not now. But the awful sounds that Eleri was making—she didn't sound human anymore, she sounded like an animal in pain. The men all raised their voices and gabbled about nothing at all to try to cover it, but the king was pale and sweating, and Gwen wanted nothing more than to run away, far away, and curl up in a ball with her hands over her ears.

It was worse when the terrible screaming stopped, and a cold silence took its place.

They came to get her, two of Eleri's women, sobbing. Gwen didn't want to go with them, but they took her hands and pulled her along into the room that smelled of stale sweat, and blood, and something else, something sweetly sickening. *Poison,* she would have said, if they had asked, but no one actually asked her anything. Gynath was already there, sobbing as she wrapped something small in long bands of white cloth. They made her go to the side of the bed, but the thing in the bed with the twisted, agonized face was not her mother, could not have been her mother. Eleri had never looked like that.

But, like Gynath, she cried as she did what she was told to do. Eleri's women did most of the work, washing, dressing, and laying out the body, trying to smooth that tortured face, carrying her and the wrapped infant that had never breathed to the bier in the Great Hall. Gwen and Gynath gathered flowers, herbs, boughs of sacred oak and ash to make the bier. Once, Peder stopped her as she was gathering meadowsweet and made her look up into his face. "You are a warrior," he said. "You must grow used to death."

That only made her burst into tears again, and he awkwardly

patted her head. "You must," he said, then, after a moment, his own voice choked. "But you never do."

After that, Peder kept her with him except when she was fetched by one of the women. He gave her hard things to do, things that forced her to concentrate, like splitting a wand with an arrow, or braiding a horsehair halter in an intricate pattern for a foal. Then he would give her things that exhausted her body, like carrying water and chopping wood. For the most part, though, she seemed to exist in a haze of disbelief, interrupted by the same anguish that caused Gynath and Bronwyn and some of the other women to kneel beside the bier and howl.

That was not for her, though. She couldn't let herself do that.

But it made her feel torn into a thousand pieces to see her father sitting there beside the bier, eyes dull, hands dangling, face almost gray.

It seemed a hundred years. It seemed no time at all. It seemed as if she had thrown herself down, exhausted with weeping and work and woke to find herself at the side of a barrow. The king's barrow, of course. She knew it; she visited it dutifully and left offerings of fruit and flowers and thought no more about it. Now there was a hole in the earth beside it, and at the bottom of the hole was Eleri. She had been draped with a linen cloth so fine that her features could be seen through it, and in her arms was the son she had died trying to give the king.

Gwen stared down at her, numb. There was no Lady here now, and they could not wait for one, so Bronwyn said the words for the women, and the bard, who had stayed, shaken, but there was some bravery in him to have stayed, said the words for the men.

Gwen wanted to run away as they all began, handful by handful, to throw dirt and flowers into the grave. She wanted to scream, to throw herself down there and beg her mother to return, to do anything but what she was doing—tossing in the meadowsweet and angelica she had picked, watching Gynath crumple to the ground, seeing her father look as if he were going to collapse at any moment.

All her anguish centered, at last, on that tiny bundle in Eleri's arms. The cause of all this grief. The brother she had intended to serve.

She didn't hate him. How could she? She had loved him for months. It wasn't his fault this had happened.

But with a stab of grief so deep it felt as if her heart had been ripped from her body, she swore a silent vow to Epona.

I will never, never, never have a baby just to please a man.

Even when they were putting Eleri in the ground, Gwen couldn't believe she was dead. And now that the wake was long past, and there were even little pinpricks of green poking through the brown earth mounded over the queen's grave, Gwen still couldn't make herself believe it.

She felt numb, and her thoughts were muffled by a thick fog of grief and disbelief. She kept thinking that it was all some sort of nightmare, and she would wake up, and everything would be normal again. But she didn't, and it wasn't. Nothing would ever be normal and right again.

The rest of the family was no help. Gynath was utterly inconsolable; she and Bronwyn spent most of their time collapsed in each others' arms.

The king looked . . . shrunken. And old. He'd aged a dozen years in a night, it seemed. He still went through his day, doing all the things that a king had to do, but there was neither life nor light in what he did. He was a king, and he acted as a king, because it was his duty to be a king, although the man in the king wanted only to mourn.

Little Gwen was as mute as a stone; her face had a closed look about it, and she hadn't shed a single tear. She just went about, doing what people told her to do without saying three words in the entire day, like a little ghost girl.

The night it had happened, Gwen had stumbled over the box that the Merlin had given her little sister, open, cast aside, and empty. Gwen had numbly picked it up and put it on Little Gwen's chest; when she looked again, it was gone. For the first time ever, she felt sorry for Gwenhwyfach. Whatever charm the Merlin had given her, Little Gwen must have tried to use to bring their mother back, and it had failed. Not even the strongest magic could bring back the dead, of course, but Little Gwen wouldn't have believed that until she tried it for herself. Probably her faith in the Merlin and his promise had been discarded in the moment, like the box.

Gwen herself spoke only when she was spoken to, and she spent as much time as she could in the company of Dai and Adara, weeping into their manes.

Nor was the king allowed to grieve in relative peace. No, first the lords and the chieftains, then the messengers had descended. And now, here were come the Queen of the Orkneys and her brood. Supposedly to tender condolences and help, but . . . something in Gwen roused angrily at the look in Anna Morgause's eyes. There was a satisfaction there, a kind of gloating, that was ugly.

She came with an entourage, but without King Lot or any of her older boys. Gwen had to admit, the only word for her was "enchanting." Her lush figure would have been the pride of a much younger woman, her raven hair must have stretched out on the ground when it was unbraided, for the single plait that stretched down her back brushed her heels, and was as thick as a strong man's wrist. Her little face reminded Gwen of a fox. Her clothing would have aroused immediate envy in every woman there, if they had not all been so wrapped in grief.

When she was handed from her cart as she first arrived to be greeted by the king, she looked as if she had just stepped out of her own chamber rather than been traveling for a fortnight. And every man's gaze was riveted on her. Eleri had always looked far, far younger than she was. Anna Morgause looked ageless.

She had brought with her a wet nurse and Medraut, her new son, and Gwen hated him at first sight. He was long, thin, and pale, with a strange head of thick, black hair, and he didn't act as a baby should. He never uttered a sound, not even when he was hungry, and he stared at people out of round, black eyes like shiny pebbles, not the blue eyes of most babies. She hated having his eyes follow her, she hated that he looked like a changeling, and she hated most of all that this *thing* was alive when her own brother, and her mother, were both dead. Vaguely, she felt that this was wrong; she was ten years older than this infant, she shouldn't feel so threatened by a baby. But she did.

With the queen had come her younger sister, Morgana. Gwen hated her, too. She was poised and controlled, and although she did not have the level of enchantment Anna Morgause had, she still made the young men's eyes follow her. Her hair was the same raven black, but her face was more catlike than foxlike, and her green eyes glittered with secrets.

When they were presented to the king, Anna Morgause said all the right things, but Gwen heard what was under the words. Silken, soft murmurs of condolence covered piercing blue eyes that looked everywhere for signs of weakness. And when she presented Morgana, there was more calculation. Gwen was proud of her father, though; he might be bleeding inside, but he gave no sign; instead he was gra-

cious, hospitable, and offered his and his daughters' own bedcham-
bers to the visitors.

"I would not like it that you should take your rest in a rude pavilion," the king said. "My chamber for you, your son, and his nurse,
and Morgana can sleep in the chamber beyond."

"You are most gracious, my lord. Morgana can share it with your
daughters," Anna Morgause replied, smoothly. Gwen immediately
decided that it was time she began sleeping with the squires. Or out
of doors. Anything other than sleeping next to the cat and waiting
to see if she scratched you in the night. She made the best excuse
she could think of, that she came to bed early, smelling of horse, and
arose before dawn and would not for the world think of inflicting her
coarse and boyish ways on a lady like Morgana. Her excuse seemed
to pass muster with the guests, for they exchanged an amused look,
but they said nothing at all when she took a rug and a blanket and
went to sleep elsewhere.

For the first two days, Gwen did her best not to leave her father's
side, and it was the purest of good fortune that it was her turn to
act as his squire and page. She had an idea that Anna Morgause had
brought her sister with the idea of getting her wedded to the king.
She remembered what had been told her, of how Eleri had armored
him against enchantments, and from almost the moment she set eyes
on the pair, she was horribly afraid of what might happen.

And Morgana? As the queen? Lording it over Gynath, and her?
The thought made her sick.

It appeared, however, that the same thought had occurred to
some of the other women—and was just as revolting to them as it was
to Gwen. After the first night, Bronwyn, under the excuse (inspired
no doubt by Gwen) of keeping Morgana from being disturbed when

Gynath arose for her morning work, took Gynath to sleep with her among Eleri's women.

By the third night, when Gwen was lying wakeful, restless under the double burdens of a bright full moon and a heart full of anxiety and mourning, she heard the sounds of several people slipping away from the castle. She left her rug and blanket, pulled on her shoes, and followed the shadowy figures as far as the Stones.

And that was when she was seized from behind by a pair of strong hands. A third hand was clapped over her mouth, smothering her yelp.

"Go back to sleep, Gwen," Bronwyn hissed in her ear. "We are armoring the king against the enchantments of that trollop and her sister. This is a women's war, and not magic for you. Keep yourself and your power as Epona would have you."

In the moonlight, one of the figures huddled about the altar stone turned her face toward Gwen. It was Gynath, and it seemed to Gwen that it was more than the moonlight that made her seem pale. The other woman let Gwen go as Bronwyn took her hand away, and with a shiver, Gwen crept back to her rug and a restless sort of sleep.

Whatever they did, it left Gynath listless and dull the next day, but it seemed to have worked. The king was courteous but distant, and Anna Morgause's eyes held an annoyance and bafflement that heartened Gwen.

Then it was Anna Morgause's turn to make some sort of trial.

Now, in all this time, both the queen and her sister had made a great pet out of Little Gwen, begging the king to release her from her ordinary work to play page for them, complimenting her, even praising her "charming manners" at meals. Gwen truly thought that they would use Little Gwen as their next means to get at the king, pointing out that she needed a mother, and how much she and Morgana doted on each other. That was a fearful thought, for Gwen couldn't see how Bronwyn and the others could armor her father against that.

But instead, Gwen woke with a start on the first night of the waning moon. At first, she couldn't think what would have woken her—especially not feeling as if a terrible storm were about to break. The sky was utterly cloudless, there was no hint of disturbance, and yet the longer she lay there, staring at nothing at all, the more certain she became that there was a disaster building, some horrific deed about to happen. She had made her bed, as usual, near the wall of the castle, and without thinking much about it, not far from the window of the solar where the king and queen had slept. But it was when she heard whisperings that sent chills up her back coming from that slit of a window, she knew *that* must have been what awakened her. It sounded like two women whispering to each other. The queen and her sister, surely.

Those whispers were—not right. Not clean. She couldn't make out the words at all, but the very tone made her feel ill.

And when she heard the scream of a rabbit from *inside* that room, her blood froze in her veins.

The whole castle seemed frozen, plunged into an unhealthy sleep. And there were no normal night sounds at all: no insects, no owls, not even a bat overhead. There were night noises in the far, far distance, but nothing *near.*

The whispering grew more urgent, and there were definitely two voices in it. Then one made a wordless cry of triumph, which was mingled by the squall of a cat, swiftly cut off in a gurgle—

And suddenly, Gwen found she could move.

She snatched up her blanket and rug and ran, without thinking, blindly, and in pure panic. She didn't know where she was going, and she didn't even know how she got there when she came to herself again in Dai's stall, with the stallion sleepily whuffling her hair.

She cast her rug and blanket down and huddled in them, still shaking with fear, and remained there until morning. At some point she must have fallen asleep, for after a timeless age of mindless terror, she found herself awakened by the sound of ordinary voices.

She was roused by the other squires coming to feed their charges; no one commented on her sleeping in Dai's stall, but it was not unusual for squires to do so, if a horse was restless or acting a little "off." So she shook the straw out of her clothing, attended to Adara and Dai, and then shuffled back to the castle, still feeling horribly ill. Bronwyn immediately intercepted her at the door.

To her shock, *Bronwyn* looked just as ill as she felt—but there was an air of triumph about her. "Drink this," the old woman commanded, shoving a beaker at her. It was something pungently herbal and very nasty, but it immediately made her feel better. When she gave the beaker back to Bronwyn, the old woman grasped her chin and made her look up, into her eyes.

"Aye, you felt it," she declared grimly. "There was dark magic last night, and this morn, there's a black cock missing from the hen roost, a black rabbit from the hutch, and a black kitten from the stable. But look yon—" she jerked her chin at the high table, where Gwen saw with astonishment that Anna Morgause and Morgana were picking at breakfast. Astonishment because they looked—common. There was nothing of the enchanting queen and her bewitching sister about them this morning.

The Queen of the Orkneys was wan, her cheeks sallow and waxen, her hair and eyes dull. Morgana was *plain,* and she could hardly even manage to nibble at a bit of bread and honey.

"It was them, for nought else would have rebounded on our protections on the king. What they did came back on them," Bronwyn said with angry triumph. "Let this be a lesson in magic to you—what you try can be cast back on you, and you'll suffer for it if it does."

Gwen nodded and rubbed her head. It still ached a bit, but it looked as if the Orkney pair had heads that ached much worse.

"I've told your masters that you're ill and got you leave to sleep off what I gave you," Bronwyn continued, and gave her a little push toward the huddle on the women's side of the hall, where she could see Gynath's blonde hair among the sleeping women, several others, at rough count.

"Why—" Gwen began. She meant to ask, *why did you know I would be ill?* But she never got that far.

"I reckoned, given all in all, you'd be sick too." Bronwyn did not explain herself, and after another moment, Gwen felt a heavy lassitude creep over her that smothered all curiosity. She stumbled toward a pallet, pulled a corner of blanket over her head, and slept till nightfall.

And when she woke, she learned that the queen and her sister had taken to their beds to be nursed, struck down by the "mysterious" illness that seemed to have struck so many of the women. The men did not ask about it—but then, that was hardly surprising.

". . . we will be grieved to see you go, my lady," the king said politely, but in tones of indifference that brought that flash of annoyance into Anna Morgause's eyes before she swiftly covered it. She and Morgana were long back to their enchanting selves, and whatever safer ploys they had tried to bewitch the king had also failed so much that he was not even sorry to hear that they intended to be gone.

"And I shall be grieved to part from you," she replied with false sorrow. "Your company, and that of your family, is so wonderful to me. I wish that I could take some part of you with me when I return to my home. My home is so lonely and remote, my husband so often gone, and my boys—are boys, and of little companionship to a poor woman and her sister—" She sighed theatrically, then snapped her fingers. "But I have it! I can help you and ease my own loneliness at the same time, my lord!"

The king looked at her as if she was mad. "Of course, my lady, but—"

She bestowed a dazzling smile on him as Little Gwen looked up with a sharp and avid alertness that made Gwen wary. Whatever was going on, Gwenhwyfach was in it up to her chin. "Oh, King, let me take your youngest to foster with me. A child that young needs a mother, and I so long for a pretty little daughter." The emphasis she put on the word *pretty* made Little Gwen preen and Gynath flush and frown. "Only think! Coming to live with us, the child will grow up with my boys, and there are five of them—surely one of them will come to like her, and from liking cleave to her, and then we shall have an alliance of blood as well as borders! And even if that great good does not come to pass, I can teach her as her mother would have, in the maidenly, womanly things she must learn to be a King's daughter. She will not run wild with me, as she might if she is left to grow without a woman's hand to guide her. What say you?"

Now there was subtle insult in that, for Gwen, for Bronwyn, for Gynath—but it wasn't something that a man would note, and it was nothing they could take exception to, though Gwen felt her cheeks growing hot, and Bronwyn looked like thunder. The king looked bewildered, and Little Gwen took advantage of his hesitation. She flung herself down on her knees beside him and clasped her hands around his wrist. "Please, Father! Please!"

This was all leaving Gwen speechless with astonishment, and it seemed the king was just as surprised and unable to think, for the first thing from his mouth were the words, "Well, I suppose—"

Little Gwen flung herself on his neck. "Oh, *thank you*, Father!" she squealed.

And at that point, of course, there was nothing to do but agree.

Chapter Ten

It had been two full moons since Queen Eleri died and one since Little Gwen had gone off to foster with Queen Morgause. In some ways, nothing had changed. The farmers still toiled in the fields, the herds still needed tending, all the work of the kingdom went on as it had no matter who the king and queen were. Gwen continued to toil at her lessons and chores: the cutting of wood and hauling of water to build strength, practice with bow and wooden sword and blunted spear, with staff and bare hands to make her a warrior, on horseback and in chariot to make her one of the fighting elite, a knight. She added new lessons: tracking and scouting—how to read signs, how to slip undetected across the face of the land, how to spy and not be seen. She was especially good at this last.

And in many ways, everything had changed. The king had emerged from his stupor of grief, but he seldom smiled and never laughed. It was Gynath who supposedly was "The Lady" of the kingdom, though in reality it was Bronwyn who made all the decisions and advised Gynath what orders to give. The evenings in the castle were quiet times, with the king withdrawing immediately after dinner to discuss whatever needed to be discussed with his chiefs and then going to bed. There were no more long evenings of drinking and tale spinning at the king's hearth. Gwen knew, of course, that such things were still going on, but it was at an improvised hearth, between the stables and the practice grounds. She had not been set to serve there at first; her teachers had let others take her place, but she supposed that now they thought enough time had passed, and it was time for her to do her duties again. And it wasn't as if there were anything happening there in the evenings that the king needed to be concerned about. Even the carefully "spiced" mead and ale would continue to be the same; it wasn't as if the secret of the brewing died with Eleri, for Bronwyn was well aware of the recipe and the same "spices" were going into the batches being made now.

No, it was nothing more than the same sort of talk and laughter that she had heard all her life; in a way, it gave her both comfort and melancholy. Comfort because it was so familiar. Melancholy because . . . she felt guilty. It seemed wrong not to go on mourning all the time, somehow disloyal.

And then, as the summer turned heavy and the first of the harvests began . . . the messenger from the High King arrived.

He brought with him news that the queen who shared Gwen's name had given the High King not one, but *two* sons. Fortunately for his own safety, he had heard on his journey of Queen Eleri's death, so the first words from him were not of Arthur's good fortune but of condolence. Only after he had delivered a long—and to Gwen's mind, suspiciously fulsome—speech on Arthur's sorrow at hearing of this, did he deliver himself of his real purpose.

The king merely shook his head after a long moment of silence. "I wish the High King and his new sons well," he said at last, not troubling to hide his bitterness. "All health and long life to them. I do not have rejoicing in me—but I wish them all well." Then he dismissed the messenger with a small gift.

Bronwyn came and took him away to the women to be fed, and it was from Bronwyn that Gwen heard the thing that was both shocking and scandalous and almost not to be believed.

Bronwyn had made a habit since Eleri's death and the departure of Little Gwen of making sops-in-wine for Gynath and Gwen before they went to bed. This was especially welcome to both of them, because both of them were laboring far longer than they had used to. Gwen found herself pouring for her father and then being summoned to the men's fire to pour for one or another of her father's chiefs until the last of them went to their beds. And Gynath was taking on the task of being the chief of the women far earlier than anyone had reckoned she would need to. Of course, it was Bronwyn that actually made most of the decisions, but Bronwyn was very careful to make it seem as if Gynath were the one doing so. Under Bronwyn's eye and unobtrusive coaching, Gynath was doing almost everything that Eleri had.

Which meant both Gwen and Gynath were up at dawn and working long, long past sundown. They needed those sops-in-wine.

They also needed to hear what Bronwyn gleaned over the course of the day, carefully winnowing news and important details from mere gossip and speculation. Gwen had had no idea that Bronwyn had performed this service for Eleri until Bronwyn herself told them, over that first bowl of toasted bread covered with sweetened, spiced wine.

And she looked grim this night as she handed them the thick pottery bowls. "This is for no ears but yours," she said quietly, as they settled down on their bed—a bed luxurious to the point of decadence now that only two of them shared it. "I would not have the king your father hear of this, or his loyalty to the High King might well be tested to breaking. But you should know."

The bite Gwen was swallowing all but lodged in her throat; she swallowed it down with difficulty. Her stomach knotted with anxiety.

"This messenger was sent to spy on us," Bronwyn continued, her jaw tight. "He sidled about and put his questions mingled in with other things a-plenty but I could tell what was important to him, and it was about babies. Who'd given birth of late, who had sons, and when? Strange thing for a King's Messenger to be asking, I thought. And I liked it not at all. So I made sure to keep his cup full, and nothing loath was he to drink it. And that was when I heard the tale—"

She shook her head. Gwen waited, spoon resting in the bowl, no longer with any appetite.

"I don't have the gift the queen had, the knowing, that she could say when a man was telling true, telling false, or telling nothing more than wild rumor. But . . . well here it is." Bronwyn looked them both in the eyes, each in turn. "He said that once his sons were born, on the Merlin's advice, every boy child born in those parts within a week on either side of their birthing date was taken from his mother and smothered."

"*What?*" gasped Gynath.

Gwen could only sit there, half frozen, as memories she didn't think she was *supposed* to have came flooding back. Of the Merlin's questions. Of what he had mumbled.

"There were not, thank the good Goddess, many of them," she continued. "But . . ." She shook her head again. "The way he said it, made me think it must be true. And so cold-blooded—"

"Perhaps . . ." Gynath began, in a whisper, her face gone pale. "Perhaps it was meant as . . . a sacrifice."

They all three exchanged sober glances. Even as young as she was, Gwen knew that there were sacrifices. From time to time one of her father's treasured white horses went off and never came back.

There were sacrifices at all the Great Rites. Mostly fruit and flowers and grain, of course; among other things, you didn't waste the life of an animal that could breed more of its kind unless you needed something really badly from the gods. But animals were sacrificed and—sometimes people as well.

That was mostly in the hands of the Druids. Mostly. Though sometimes there had to be a Year King . . . only in dark times though.

But the Merlin was the Chief Druid. And he was the one who had advised Arthur to do this terrible thing. Was he playing the Substitute King with the High King's new twins, sacrificing other boy children like them so that they would be spared? If he was, well, that was just wrong. Even Gwen knew it didn't work like that. The Year King had to go to the sacrifice willingly, had to know what he was doing, and do it for the Land and the people, and how could a baby do that?

But if they were sacrifices, what were the sacrifices *for*?

It was baffling, and somehow, that made it even more horrifying.

"This is something I thought you should know," Bronwyn concluded. "And it will go no further than the three of us. But you, Gynath, may well be queen here one day. And you, Gwen, will likely serve her as you would have served your brother, had he lived. And you must both know about things like this and keep a sharp watch on the High King's doings." She bit her lip, and the flickering flame from their rushlight made her look even older and more drawn. "It may be he has done this for the Land and the Folk. Unless the Ladies bring the word to us, we cannot know. But on the face of it, these are dark doings, and the High King is besmirched by their foulness. If these are dark doings, there is one thing you may be sure of."

"What's that, Bronwyn?" asked Gynath in a whisper.

"That they will come back at him when he least expects and be his ruin," the old woman said, grimly. "Blood will have blood, and innocent blood calls more strongly than any other."

The messenger went on his way. The season turned, summer to harvest, and the rites and the festival. Poor Gynath was at her wits end trying to arrange all, even with the help of Bronwyn and all the women, but out of respect for the king, few guests replied that they would come, and only the king's closest friends arrived. For the villagers, it was no different from any other Harvest festival. There was food and music, dancing and gaming, drinking and more drinking, coupling and handfasting, and all the usual doings in their season. And if the gathering at the king's hearth was a subdued one, if there were no races this year, well, at least there was, at last, a gathering at the king's hearth, and when the guests were gone again, there was no more going out to another hearth and leaving the king to mourn alone over the ashes. In part that was just plain sense, for there was no other place big enough to hold them all when the winter winds began to blow, but in part it was because the king was taking an interest in life again.

A few women made attempts to draw him out, but by Midwinter it was clear that there would be no queen taking Eleri's place.

As for Gwen . . . her instructors were keeping her too occupied to brood and had been for moons, so that when Midwinter arrived, it came to her one night as she served as her father's page that the terrible ache of grief, the chasm that had been inside her, was—not gone, never that, but—changed to something that was somewhat easier to bear. And looking at her father's face, it seemed he felt the same. He took an interest in things that he had not even at Harvest. Still not in women, but much the same, if somewhat grimmer, interest in the small affairs of his people and his kingdom and the greater affairs of what was going on outside that kingdom.

Perhaps it helped that there was, without a doubt, going to be fighting in the spring. The High King had sent out his messengers again, just before the snow flew, to warn that the seafaring chiefs, the Northerners, too disorganized to be called "kings," were uniting for what Arthur thought was another push to oust him and overrun them all.

It gave her father something to think about besides his own pain.

So at Midwinter, the talk was all of war and the preparations for war.

Gwen paid great attention to all this talk, for this was to be her business. There might not be a brother to guard now, but there were two sisters, one of whom would surely wed someone that their father would name as his heir. Whoever that was would need someone he could trust.

When the guests were all gone, Gwen and the rest found their hands being turned to those preparations that had been discussed. The nasty, barbed war arrows that would tear a man's flesh on being pulled out needed to be made. That was a matter of several steps, some of which could be entrusted to the squires. War chariots, spears, armor, bows, harness . . . all needed to be checked and put in good order. Much could be put in the squires' hands, and much was.

Gwen worked feverishly, and the work did much to help her set aside her troubled thoughts. There were no further ill tales, though more messengers came from the High King, traveling with great difficulty across the winter landscape, bringing with them the questions of levies and what could be supplied in lieu of or in addition to the levies. Now Gwen was glad that her father had not heard the tales, that Bronwyn had kept them to herself, for he threw himself into this work with a whole heart.

As might have been expected, there were other rumors coming out of the west, that King Lot had demurred, saying that mere rumors were no cause for raising levies, and that in any case, the Northerners might well lose interest before spring. "He intends to send nothing, or as little as possible," Gwen's father spat one night in disgust.

"There would be no loot in it for him," pointed out one of the chiefs. "Even if we drive them far back into their own lands and seize what we drive them off of, it is not on Lot's border, and he would get no share of it. If we only drive them back, well, what will we win? Arms and horses, both the worse for war." He shook his head. "And Lot is far enough from Celliwig that there is little the High King can do at this stage to enforce his will. Lot will find some excuse, a plague of flux or weather washing out the roads, and if he arrives, it will be too late to be of service."

"All the more reason for us to act with honor." The king set his chin firmly, and Gwen silently cheered. She felt better for seeing him so alive again and more like his old self.

The talk around the hearth was lively enough to satisfy anyone, and Gwen wished with all her heart that she would be allowed to go along with the levies. But she wouldn't be; none of the squires her age were going. Only the seasoned warriors, neither too old nor too young, would be sent. Even the king himself would remain behind, and that was on the orders of the High King himself. Her father grumbled at that, but he agreed that it was a sound decision, once he heard the reasoning.

"The High King is concerned that this might be a trick." The messenger that brought them this news was no mere mouthpiece; it was one of Arthur's handpicked warriors, part of his personal band. "He fears that either the Northerners themselves, or someone who has been scheming with them, is arranging for it to look as if they are preparing for a war when in fact they have no intention of facing us in the field. Instead, once the levies are committed, it is possible that the Northerners will retreat, drawing us after them—and then the real attack will happen somewhere else."

No need to ask where else. "The Saxons," her father spat in disgust. The messenger nodded. "So we need you, ready with a second force, to hold them back if they do push forward."

With Gwen watching and listening, committing everything to memory even though she didn't understand more than half of what she heard, the messenger outlined the possible strategies. Rough maps were sketched out in charcoal on the stones; the best of those were transferred with great labor onto tanned hide with a quill and walnut-hull ink. By the time the messenger left, Gwen's father had nothing but praise for the wisdom of the young Arthur.

There did not seem to be enough hours of daylight for all the preparations, and the warmer the weather became and the longer the days, the more the sense of urgency increased. Now it was Gwen who was up at dawn and hard at it until she almost fell asleep with her work in her hands; Gynath had a great deal to do, yes, but not nearly as much. Eleri had always kept ample supplies of healing herbs and so forth on hand, and there had not been much call for such things in the last year. "Always be prepared for warfare," had been her admonition to her women, and so they always were.

It was about lambing time, when it was possible to move freely about the countryside, and the storms of winter were past and boats could sail, that messengers again galloped among the High King's allies. The High King had been brought word from his spies. The Northerners were indeed massing ships, as if to make a great raid. The levies were called up and marched off to join the High King. King Lleudd made a great show of sending them off and advised the men he sent to make double fires at night, and drag brushes behind them to make it seem that their numbers were larger. Then he told those he had kept in reserve to be ready and to keep their weapons to hand, as Arthur had warned him.

And Arthur was right.

Near sunset, very near Beltane, a messenger on a winded horse rode across the southern border of Lleudd's kingdom of Pwyll, having already come through Pengwen, Calchfynelld, and Caer Celemion. The Saxons of the south were, indeed, massing for war and marching. And Lot of Orkney was about to have a rude surprise, for the Northerners were making straight for the shores of Lothian, not further south. Perhaps it was just as well he had delayed in sending his levies, for they would not have far to march to meet the enemy. Doubtless, he would claim that his wife and Morgana had had some manner of magical warning this was to be so. And doubtless, for the sake of peace, Arthur would accept this, whether he believed it or not.

So said Bronwyn as she and the women methodically passed the readied saddlebags to the squires, who put them on the horses they had already harnessed. The king had planned this to a nicety, so that the warriors could move out on a moment's warning, and the moment there was light, every man, woman, and child was up and putting his preparations into action. The cavalry would go first, followed by the chariots. There would be no men afoot; Arthur would supply the foot soldiers, for Lleudd's levies that had gone north consisted primarily of foot. Arthur had begged him to reserve the troops that could move faster for the Saxons.

The king himself would lead them. And this alone showed how grave the threat was. If he fell, that would leave Pwyll in the hands of three girls, none of them wed.

But he would not fall. Gwen willed it, fiercely. Besides, he would be in his chariot, and his chariot driver was second only to Braith in skill. He would be guarded by his sworn band, who also were well aware of what would happen if he fell.

By the time the sun was three fingers above the horizon, they were ready to depart. Gwen, to her sorrow but not her surprise, was not going. She was not being slighted; no one her age was being allowed to go.

She stood by the king's chariot, looking up at him. Around them, horses stirred restively. Gynath held her hand tightly, but of the two of them, it was Gwen who was the calmer.

"I rely on you, my daughters," the king said, his voice stronger and firmer than it had been since Eleri's death. Gwen could only marvel at how war had made him come alive again. For that, she could actually feel *glad* about it. "I do not know how long we will be in the field, but come what may, the lands have to be tilled, the flocks tended, the harvest brought in, and the rites celebrated. You must see to it that these things are done, and done well."

Gynath looked up at the king, her eyes bright with tears, so it was Gwen who answered. "We will, my lord."

He nodded. "Now hear me well. I expect to return, in triumph. I *plan* to return. I have every intention of coming back loaded with Saxon wealth, carried on good Saxon horses. But the gods mayhap have other plans. Should the very worst befall, I have left certain orders. Gynath, and you, Gwen, and those who choose to flee are to take shelter with the King of Gwynedd. He is my oldest friend, for we fostered together and swore an oath of brotherhood. I will make no orders other than that. If affairs have gone that badly, let each man act on his own conscience."

He had spoken loudly enough that his voice carried over the crowd, and though there were some murmurs, there was much nodding. Gynath sobbed. Gwen had a terrible lump in her throat . . . but also a strange certainty. King Lleudd would return. There would be others who would not, and she somehow knew there would be great grief for her, but her father would return and, as he hoped, in triumph.

Gynath had no such feeling of certainty; that much was clear from her look of despair. But she had courage. She swallowed back her tears, stood up straight, and despite red eyes and trembling voice, replied, "Yes, my lord Father."

He bent down and embraced them both, kissing the tops of their heads, then released them. As soon as he had, Gwen could tell that his spirit was elsewhere, already down the road, eager to face battle. Fiercely she wished she could go too—

But her fate was already written, and she had to step back and watch as her father took the reins from his chariot driver, and the horses, already impatient, lurched out at a trot.

And then they were gone.

Then came the worst part: the waiting. Gwen was too young to re-member much about the last time the levies of Pwyll went to war, but Gynath was not, and Bronwyn certainly was not. Gynath collapsed in an orgy of grief and despair; Bronwyn allowed her two days to wallow in it, then roused her roughly, took her down to the brook, stripped her bare and ducked her in the freezing cold water. Gwen had no idea this was going to happen and only happened to look up from the bowstring she was plaiting to see Bronwyn hauling the weakly protesting girl in that direction.

There is such a thing as curiosity that can't be suppressed. Gwen pinned the string down and followed, just in time to see Bronwyn strip Gynath to the skin and shove her into the spring-fed pond.

The water was ice cold, and Gynath shrieked and flailed her arms wildly trying to keep from falling in.

She failed, of course.

The water was only waist deep, but she came up gasping and spluttering, only to be hauled onto the bank just as roughly, rubbed down with a drying cloth, and have her clothing shoved at her.

"Wh-wh-what d-d-did you d-d-do that for?" Gynath cried indignantly, between the chattering of her teeth. Gwen ran the last few steps to help her get into her shift and gown.

"You've had your wallow. Two days of baaing like a lamb taken from its mum is enough," Bronwyn said, her jaw set. "Your father is very much alive, and you have an example to set. What if every woman in this kingdom went bawling and blethering as if her man was already dead? Straighten your back, go to your duty, and remember that from the time you leave your bed to the time you take to it, you are being watched."

Gynath looked furious—but furious was probably better than weeping. Certainly Bronwyn seemed to think so. She nodded and pointed back toward the castle. With her head erect and her eyes practically flashing, Gynath stormed off. She didn't look back.

Bronwyn simply followed, without acknowledging Gwen's presence. After a moment, Gwen went back to her bowstring.

It was not that long after that Gynath went briskly past, followed by one of the servants, both of them with their arms full of bundles of something. Clearly, Bronwyn's ploy had worked, though it might take Gynath a while to forgive her.

Gynath was present at dinner, very much present, and sitting in their father's place. It actually made Gwen proud of her, to see her sitting there, dry-eyed and talking as their mother had talked when the king was not in the high seat. And when dinner was over, she invited the remaining men to stay at the hearth, picked the most senior of the warriors to take the king's seat, and directed Gwen to tend his cup, before taking the women aside.

"That was well done, tonight, sister," Gwen whispered when she came to bed. She didn't know if Gynath was still awake, but as it happened, she was.

"It was hard," Gynath replied, with a little break in her voice. "And Bronwyn was horrid."

Gwen debated a moment before saying anything. "Bronwyn was right," she ventured.

"Which made her all the more horrid." There was silence on the other side of the bed for a moment, then a sigh. "I wish one of us could See what was happening with Father. At least then I would know."

Gwen pondered this for a moment. "Why don't *you* try?" she asked.

"Because I—" Gynath began. And stopped.

"What would the worst be?" Gwen continued. "That you don't See anything. You would be no worse off than now, and you'd know you tried."

"I'll . . . have to ask Bronwyn. For help. I've never tried scrying." Gynath plucked at the blanket covering both of them nervously.

"Cataruna went to the Ladies. I'm on the Warrior Path. That leaves you," Gwen pointed out. "You might as well try. You might be stronger in the Blessings than you think. Mother's blood runs strong in all of us." *Even in the brat, Little Gwen.*

She wasn't sure where those words were coming from, but they seemed to do Gynath a lot of good. "I might as well," Gynath replied, and the tight sound in her voice was gone.

❧❧❧❧❧❧❧

Gwen, somewhat to her own bemusement, had a real talent for braiding bowstrings and working with the fletcher, so that was what Peder set her to do. The work was exacting enough that it took her mind

off her worries and fears, without being so demanding that she felt
as if she were being pulled in too many directions at once. The men
had taken almost every arrow and spare string with them, for there
would be no time to make more on the march, nor when they closed
on the Saxons; but that meant that just to have the means to hunt, a
lot of work was ahead of those with the skill.

And now that she had rudimentary abilities in fighting—and now
that all the older boys were gone—Peder had turned all his concen-
tration on her and the rest of the young squires. This was not a bad
thing at all. Such individualized attention meant that instead of being
trained as a herd in the same things, Peder was taking the time to as-
sess them, and decide what they might be best suited for. He might
not have had that time until they were a year or more older, if it were
not for the war. And if they were going to be the last line of defense
against the Saxons, or a rear guard on an escape to Gwynnedd, they
had better be doing what they were best at.

For some, the choice was obvious. Tall, meaty boys with a lot
of sheer brute strength already were clearly made for fighting afoot.
To them, Peder now assigned training with the staff, the cudgel, the
hammer, the ax. Those with the best eye—Gwen among them—got
extra training with bow and spear. Those who clearly were not doing
well with their horses either had their difficulties sorted out or were
(to their profound relief) dismissed from the chariot and cavalry altogether. Peder spent all of a day studying them, measuring them,
looking at their parents, and consulting with the oldest folk in the
village about their grandparents, in order to try to determine what
they might grow to be like.

And that was when Gwen's own abilities became apparent. "Ye'll
never be a giant," was Peder's shrewd assessment. "They tell me for
size ye be the spit image of yer grammar and granther on king's side.
Except the hair. Otherwise, small and fast and sleekit, not tall, like

the queen. Braith was right. Epona put her stamp on ye. And the best place for ye, bodyguard to yer kin and scout. Cavalry or chariot an' ye *must,* but I'd sooner see ye scoutin'. Ye've got the way of movin' quiet and not being seen that it bain't possible to teach. That's not be from the king's blood."

Now this was a revelation to Gwen, but it occurred to her immediately that this was true: She *did* have a knack for getting around without people noticing her when she didn't want to be noticed. It had worried her that she was so little and would have to go up against much larger and stronger men. But Peder had found the right place for her, and it was something no one else would have been as well suited to, and she felt suddenly as if everything was *right.*

Meanwhile, Gynath had made up with Bronwyn, and part of her day was spent in learning more of Women's Magic, so that she could try scrying as soon as Bronwyn thought she had the strength for it. In fact, Bronwyn heartily approved of the planned attempt. None of the other women had so much magic in them, and the mere fact that Gynath was going to at least try to see what was happening with their men made them all encourage her and look to her.

On the afternoon when Gynath was going to make her first attempt, Gwen found herself at a variation of her old chore taking goose feathers that she herself must have cleaned and carefully stripping the vanes, so that the fletcher could use them to feather his arrows. Of all of those who were left, she was the best at it, perhaps because she had cleaned so many and knew how to handle them. She spoiled very few; most were so perfect that the fletcher had very little to do but trim them to fit and glue them in place.

Her thoughts drifted to Gynath, wondering if she had begun . . . wondering what it felt like to be the center of a circle of Power . . . and that was when the feathers vanished from her hands, and she found herself . . . elsewhere.

On the top of a mountain? It seemed so, but this was not like standing on any real mountain, for she could see everything below her as clearly as if she stood within arm's length. A battle was about to begin.

A battle not between men but between two armies of animals.

On the one side, boars, an army of boars. Huge, brutish creatures, with greedy eyes and long, vicious tusks, with ravens circling above them. Leading them, a white dragon.

On the other side, another army, of mixed beasts: hounds, stags, keen-eyed wolves, with falcons on-watch above, and a great bear leading. Beside the bear, a noble white stallion.

She had only time enough to take this all in before the two forces leaped at each others' throats.

She had no experience of human wars, to know if this was more or less bloody, noisy, confusing, and chaotic. She wanted to look away, sickened by the slaughter, but she could not.

It seemed to go on forever. And then, at last, the boars began to lose. The mixed army drove them back over a field slick with blood and thick with fallen bodies. The white dragon turned tail and ran, leaving the boars alone.

Then it happened; pressing eagerly ahead, the white stallion stumbled over the corpse of a boar. Another, its tusks dripping with the blood of its victims, saw the chance, and leaped for him. Other animals saw what was happening but were too far away; they would never reach him in time to save him—

All but one.

With a high, thin cry, a falcon dove out of the sky, talons slashing at the boar's eyes. The boar roared with pain, reared, and snapped, catching the falcon before she could escape, killing her instantly. But that was enough time for the stallion to scramble to his feet and rejoin the army, which rushed on the boar and slew it before it could even drop the poor, mangled corpse in its mouth.

And then—she was back, dazed, feathers still in her hands. But this time, this time she knew what she had seen. The boars were the Saxon army, for boars were sacred to them. The bear must have been the High King Arthur, the stallion, her own father. And the falcon— the falcon could only have been Braith.

And she had just seen how Braith had died . . .

Heedless of the feathers, she buried her face in her hands, and wept.

PART TWO

WARRIOR

Chapter Eleven

Gwen's breath steamed in the frozen air as she looked down on the encampment of Saxon raiders, settling in for the night. She was in a tree at the edge of a natural meadow; they were camped just inside the trees, where the smoke from their fire would be broken up by the branches so that it wouldn't betray them. It was an orderly camp; that argued for a group that fought together regularly, with one man commander over the rest. They traveled lightly, no animals, one pack each, and their weapons. They camped properly, arranged around the fire, pine boughs and bracken over the boughs laid out to keep them off the snow. The fire had been well made in a scrape, so that melting snow didn't overwhelm it and put it out. They thought they were alone in the wilderness, roasting their stolen sheep, counting over their loot. Which was, all things considered, not much; they'd managed to find one poor peddler and had raided a single farmstead. It scarcely seemed worth the effort. They were bold, or desperate, to be making raids on her father's lands this deep in winter.

Unless, of course, they were scouts for a larger force. And if that was the case, they were looking to see what defenses were here once the snow fell and hoping to drive well into enemy territory before any organized defense could move in. The more she considered them, the likelier that seemed. Probably they were counting on the fact that her father was known, still, for his skilled charioteers, and chariots did not travel in snow at all.

But Gwen was not her father, she was her father's guard and right hand, and she had been schooled in a generation that was coming to rely on horsemen. More and more, the king was listening to her recommendations. And at her urging, he had gradually increased the strength of his cavalry over the past several years. His own near-escape in the battle where Braith had fallen had shown him that chariots were of limited use and even an actual hazard on broken ground. Now his chariots were mostly used for massed charges and rescues over good flat land. This year, for the first time, horsemen in his ranks had outnumbered chariot drivers by two to one. Even the High King was taking notice of his tactics.

She had a good idea what the Saxon leader was probably thinking, if that was a scouting force below her. Even if someone saw them and reported their presence back to King Lleudd, the winter would keep him and his warriors bound to their holdings. Meanwhile, the Saxon scouts could roam with impunity and bring back intelligence to the army in time for them to drive deep into this kingdom. Once there, it would be costly to dislodge them. This land was less populous than the area to the east; easier to take, easier to hold, and the Saxons actually tended to be decent to farmers who didn't resist them. If you could stay hidden until the worst of the fighting and looting was over, you'd likely survive. Saxon fighters didn't till the land, and they needed to eat; there was no point in killing the hands that would feed them, so farmers were generally safe. If they could take this country, they might have a better chance of holding it than the lands the High King was pushing them out of.

Ah, but horsemen could go anywhere, regardless of the weather, so long as food for the horses could be found. And all villages within her father's lands were required to put in hay and keep it for the use of the cavalry in winter. That had been another of Gwen's suggestions, and she was unreasonably proud of it. It meant that the cavalry could get anywhere quickly, even in winter, unburdened by the need to bring fodder with them.

The villages were not doing badly by the policy. King Lleudd permitted the unused hay to be fed to local animals as soon as the snows melted, and until this year, that was what had generally happened. Gwen wondered, as she crouched on her tree branch, if the pressure that High King Arthur was putting on the Saxons in the east was making them concentrate on him, and they were not even taking her father's reputation into consideration. Perhaps in concentrating on Arthur, they underestimated a "lesser" king, one who was old enough to be a grandfather to boot.

The tree Gwen was in, though leafless, hid her perfectly. Not that they ever looked up. But she, in her white furs and gray clothing, merely blended into the snow-covered branches and the haze of leafless twigs. She had mastered the art of holding absolutely still for as long as she needed to. And there was, of course, that subtle magic that was all her own, the ability to will herself unseen.

The ironic thing was that Arthur, by all accounts, would have been perfectly ready to accept the Saxon surrender and alliance, would honor their rulers and their customs as he honored those of his other allies, like Gwen's father, and Lot of Orkney and Lothian, and the King of Gwynnedd. But they would have none of this. And so they fought him, lost, slunk back behind their shrinking borders, recovered, and fought him again. In more than fifteen years since her father had sent out his levies, they still had not learned that lesson.

This tree was not in the familiar hills that she had trained in and run over in her first years as a warrior. Over the last several years, Pengwen, Calchfynelld, and Caer Celemion had come into her father's hands, and all peacefully.

First had been Pengwen; when those levies of so long ago had come home amid mingled rejoicing and grief, the young—very young—ruler of Pengwen had come with them, had seen Gynath, and within a day even a fool would have known that the lad had lost his heart. From that moment, the conclusion had been forgone. And because he was so young, his father fallen in that last battle, with the agreement of his own chiefs, he had given over governorship of his land to King Lleudd.

He could have taken his throne by now, but he was not the least interested in having it back. Quarrels among the chiefs bewildered and upset him as a youngling, and as an adult, they bewildered and exasperated him. He hated fighting, he hated having to judge men, and above all, he hated being *looked* to for answers. He was happier by far doing the work of a steward; he deeply understood the land and the farmers and herdsmen. He had an instinct for what would be a good year, and what would be a poor one; those who followed his advice prospered. And so, instead of ruling, he served as steward and seneschal for what had once been four kingdoms, adored his wife and his children, and was a blessing on King Lleudd's house.

As for Calchfynelld, and Caer Celemion, the entire ruling household of the former had been taken by a rheumy plague one winter, and the latter's king died within an hour of his son on yet another battlefield against the Saxons. Seeing how well and justly her father had dealt with Pengwen, the assembled chiefs of both lands had come to him and begged him to accept their fealty. From the time of Gwen's second year in warrior training to now, the little Kingdom of Pywll had quadrupled in size.

Which was why Gwen was perched in a tree in the winter, just inside the border of what had been Caer Celemion, looking down on the evening camp of a band of Saxon raiders. She had no mind to move just yet; not until it got darker. She was as at home up a tree as under it, as cozy under a snow covered bush as any rabbit, and so quiet and near-invisible in her ghostings about that the men of her troop all said she truly was a "white spirit."

In fact . . . that was what the Saxons called her as well, except that they were sure she was a spirit in truth.

I should think about that, she reflected, as the odor of burned mutton came to her nose. *That could be very useful. There must be some way to encourage them to believe I really am some vengeful phantom.*

Peder had been right. And so had Braith. She was Epona-touched; there wasn't a horse in all her father's herds that she couldn't ride. She took to weapons work with the same ease that Gynath danced or Cataruna sang. Clearly, she had been born to walk this path, and Peder's careful weighing of her talents and physical abilities, his selective training, had made her the best scout in King Lleudd's entire army.

Her father was not just indulging her; she was of great value to him doing what she was. And it was not as if he lacked for heirs, for Gynath and her beloved Caradoc had already given him five living grandchildren. If that were not enough, Cataruna had graced him with two more. Four years ago she had returned from the Ladies of the Well not only a Lady full trained but with a bard husband who just happened to be one of the King of Gwynnedd's younger sons and well schooled to be Forest Lord to her Lady of the Fields in all the rites.

Which left Gwen free to do as she pleased, and what she pleased was to serve in peace as her father's right hand, and in war as his eyes and ears, and the eyes and ears of his army.

She bent her ear to the rough talk about the fire; she had schooled herself in the Saxon tongue this past year and more, reckoning it would be useful both in questioning prisoners and in understanding things she was not meant to overhear. It was an ugly speech, harsh and guttural, having none of the lilting beauty of her own, the song of that used down in Cornwall, the poetry of the Gaels, the measured grace of the languages of the east, or even the logic and cadence of the Latin it was said that the High King spoke. Cataruna's husband, Ifan, was the one who taught her all these tongues, and perhaps he had worked some special magic to put them into her head, for surely they came to her as easily as breathing.

An overcast sky meant no sunset; the darkness thickened as the Saxons huddled closer to their fire, hacking chunks of mutton from the carcass spitted over the fire with their knives. They were going short for drink, it seemed, melting snow in a battered pot rather than seeking out a stream. And they were not happy about this thin drink, either; there were muttered complaints and unhappy looks cast at the man Gwen judged to be their leader. He was probably what passed for a lord among the Saxons, and one's lord was expected to furnish good food and plenty of it, along with presents and loot.

There was not much to distinguish him from the rest save for the wolfskin cloak he sported. He might be a little older, but all of them had much the same in the way of arms and armor. Shield, spear, long-knife, and a heavy leather jerkin; two had bows, the rest, slings. But the leader had a sword; in fact, from the look of it, Gwen judged it was a Roman sword, probably looted and possibly passed through several generations of owners. She liked the look of it; it was a proper Roman blade, so it was short by the standards of those her father's smiths made. That made it the perfect length for her.

I should not mind being that sword's next owner.

Then she chided herself. She must keep her mind on those men below, not on their possessions.

The conversation around the fire was remarkably uninformative. The men seemed to be taciturn by nature, conversed mostly in grunts, and were uninterested in discussing the reason why they were here. The best solution would be to take one or more of them alive and beat the answers out of them. She'd learned all she could from them at this point.

She needed to time when she ghosted out of the tree very carefully. There had to be enough light to see her way through this part of the forest and back to her troop, but not so much that the Saxons would see movement.

"You think King Bear has aught men about?" one of them asked suddenly, looking around, as if he had sensed her eyes on him. She froze.

The leader laughed. *"Nay. He be a-casting himself on grave of the she-bear and her cubs and weeping senseless. Mayhap he'll find his man-parts again come spring, but he's throwin' of his apron o'er his head now."*

The others laughed as well, and the first speaker shook his shaggy blond head and went back to gnawing his mutton.

So that was why they chose now. It made perfect sense—though she was more than a bit put out that these Saxons had better intelligence of what was going on at the High King's seat than she did. Word *had* come, just before they'd heard rumors of skulkers on the border, that Arthur's twin sons had died, and his queen had perished of grief for them. The details had been confused and muddied; some said they'd been killed in a boar hunt, some that they had been murdered, and one grisly tale swore it was the High King's own foster brother, now his seneschal, Kai, who had murdered them out of jealousy and in secret, That is, the tale ran, it was meant to be secret, but the head of the fairest had been sent in a box that only the murderer could open, and Kai, all unknowing, had opened it before the whole court.

A boar hunt, well, that made some sense. They were *just* of an age to participate in such a dangerous pastime. And murder, well that was possible, though less likely. But Arthur had a temper, and if it had been Kai, foster brother or no, there would have been a fourth grave and a new seneschal. On the whole, she was inclined to think it was a boar hunt after all, since one of the few details of that version said that Arthur's favorite hound, Cabal, had died defending them.

But there had been nothing more before Gwen and her troop had gone south and east as fast as their horses could take them. This was fresher news than she had, and she was heartily annoyed.

But . . . there was a certain feeling of grim satisfaction in hearing it, too. So the High King was prostrate with grief was he? Well, perhaps the carrion crows he had set to fly when he'd had all those tiny babies killed had come home to roost in the royal bower. Now he tasted the grief he had given to so many. And if it was the Merlin that had given him that evil advice, well, it was too bad the Merlin couldn't sip from that same cup of gall.

She could not help but think of her father, and her mother, and the little brother who never got a chance to draw a breath . . .

But that thought softened her bitterness. It had been said for many years now that this between Arthur and his Queen was not only a marriage of state but a love match. And she thought of her father sitting hollow-eyed in his hall and thought of the High King doing the same, and her heart turned to pity him.

But only for a moment; more movement below in the thickening dusk alerted her. All the men (except the leader) were settling onto their beds of bracken, their cloaks wrapped tightly about them. The leader had taken a seat with his back to the fire, scanning the open meadow. And, as if the gods of the place had decided to favor her entirely, thick snowflakes began to drift down out of the blue-gray sky.

She began to flex and stretch all of her muscles, from fingers to toes, warming them and getting ready to move. And when she judged she was ready, she moved as slowly and deliberately as a tortoise, backing her way down the branch and then the trunk, making absolutely sure of every hand- and foothold before committing her weight to it. It was the sort of climb that took great patience and a lot more strength than most might think. But she got quietly to the ground without the Saxon leader having even the faintest idea of her presence.

She blessed the snowfall; she had been planning to pull off her gray wolfskin cloak and drag it fur-side down on the ground behind her for a while to muddy her tracks. Now she would not have to. There would still *be* tracks leading away from the tree, but it would not be possible to tell what had made them. And if she had more luck, at least one of the men would blunder about in there, looking for wood, and further churn up the snow.

At this point, however, night was all but upon her. Now she had to turn to her other trick to find her way. With her left hand, she reached for the trunk of the next tree just at shoulder-height; even though she had good night-vision, she could barely make it out, dark against the white snow. She ran her fingers along the bark, and found the little cut she had put there, pointing the way she should go.

Step by slow and careful step, making sure to make as little noise as possible, she made her way from tree to tree, following her marks. She counted each tree that she passed, and when she had gone far enough, she took a deep breath and called like an owl, three times.

The answer came back. Three calls, then a count to five, then four calls. She followed the sound, pausing now and again, to repeat her call and follow the reply.

She had done this so many times in the past that she had schooled herself to patience. It only *seemed* as if it took forever to make her way through the snow-filled darkness.

But, at last, she did. She hooted and heard the answer right beside her, and she felt Aeron grip her elbow with one hand. She reached around and clapped him on the back, and the two of them made their way to the carefully concealed camp.

She didn't speak until she squatted down beside the fire and accepted a fire-warmed stone to cradle in her hands. "Small raiding party of six," she began, and made a succinct summary of everything she had seen and heard. "I think we're going to have to take them," she finished. "And get one alive to tell us what they're up to."

The others nodded. "Try to ambush them in the morning?" asked Aeron. "Or see if we can find a better place to bring them down?"

"Morning would be best. They don't think there're any fighters out here, just the odd farmer. They're good enough not to let their guard down, but they're also not as alert as they could be." She let the heat from the stone soak into her. "I want to hit them before they have any inkling we could be here." She looked around her troop; four, counting herself, but that should be enough. Aeron and Meical were the best of the archers. So they would be best put as first and last watch, so they had solid, unbroken sleep. "Aeron, first watch, I'll take second, Owain, third, Meical, last. Meical, wake us all at first light. We'll take them from the forest, and I only need one living."

The other three nodded. Aeron wrapped his cloak tightly around himself and ghosted off into the night. They set a proper watch, regardless of conditions, with the sentry making irregular rounds outside the camp. She smiled to herself. She could not have asked for better men.

The rest of them took heated stones from beside the fire and curled up around them to sleep. Like the Saxons, they had made beds of bracken to keep them off the snow. Tolerably comfortable, actually, especially situated as they were in the heart of a thicket, screened from wind and most of the falling snowflakes.

Sleep when you can. Eat when you can. Reminded of that second of the warrior's rules of the field, she rummaged out a lump of cheese and some cold rabbit from the common food pack. That was the one good thing about a winter campaign. Food didn't go bad; you didn't have to subsist on rock-hard journey bread and dried meat. If you had it in camp, you could take it with you for a good wholesome meal. She ate quickly and neatly, licked her fingers clean, then ate a handful of clean snow for a "drink," curled up around her own rock, and went straight to sleep.

Luck was with them. When the troop eased up toward the Saxon camp, five of the men were still asleep, and the sixth was nodding over his ax, his back warming at the fire. Gwen signaled all of them to leave the rightmost man alive. They nodded and spread out a bit, to get a better field of fire. Her shot would be the signal to the other three.

She lined up six arrows point-down into the snow, then put a seventh on the string. Seven. Always her lucky number. She pulled back her arrow, sighted carefully on the lookout, and let fly.

The first missed, lodging in his shoulder. But before he could shout, her second took him in the throat. Her third and fourth went into one of the sleepers, as two more arrows hit the sentry before he could slump to the ground, her fifth and sixth went into the next sleeper, and her seventh into a third. By that time, all of the men but the one she had designated as the one to save were feathered with four to six shafts, all without any of them uttering a sound. The last one woke by being kicked over by Aeron, to find three swords pointed at his throat.

He tried to get up and fight anyway. That didn't last long. He was lying down, and although his ax was at his hand, there wasn't much he could do before a vicious slash to his arm opened it up from wrist to elbow. Aeron was the best of them at sword work; he managed to keep from cutting the man open so badly he would bleed to death before they got any information from him.

Gwen had stayed well out of his line of sight, letting the men disarm him and tie him up. She had an idea; she didn't much like the results she had been getting from beating information out of prisoners—it tended to be wrong as often as right, and there was no way of knowing which. She'd talked this over with the troop this morning; they had agreed with her on that point and decided to let her try something different.

One of the things in her kit was powdered chalk; she dusted her hands with it when she was going to attempt a difficult climb or when she was unsure of her grip on a weapon. While the other two kept the prisoner busy, Aeron came over and helped her dust it all over her face. She held her breath to keep from inhaling any of it, then did the same with her bare hands. Then she took off her cloak, and unbound her hair, and approached the prisoner from behind, naked sword in her white hands.

Owain wrenched him around when she was in place and forced him to his knees so that he gaped up at the white-faced, white-haired, gray-clad virago glaring down at him.

His eyes registered his shock. She smiled.

"Do you know what I am?" she whispered in Saxon. She had reckoned that whispering would be more impressive than speaking.

His mouth worked for some time before any words came out. "Th-th-th-the White Ghost!" he stammered, sweat starting all over his greasy brow.

She leaned down slightly. "Yes," she breathed. "And I eat men's souls. The bodies I leave for my black chickens."

As if on cue, several ravens, attracted by the red blood soaking into the white snow and made bold by winter hunger, alighted in the tree branches above her, calling. She did not bother to keep the glee from her face. This could not have been timed better if she had planned it.

His face had been white with pain and fear, but now every vestige of blood drained from it. She leaned forward a little more. "I have feasted upon the spirits of your companions," she said, narrowing her eyes and smiling as if sated. "And I am inclined to let you live—if you tell me what I wish to know."

She straightened, and allowed the smile to slip from her face. "You might as well," she added. "I will have it from you anyway."

By the time the man fainted, he had told her everything he knew. Not a great deal, but it was enough. Indeed, this group had been advance scouts to test the borders of Pywll, moving ahead of the Saxon army. As she had suspected, they were making a push here, but not only because of the pressure that High King Arthur was putting on the Saxon kingdoms in the east; they hoped to flank him by spring, and when his army rode out again, to cut it off from his lands and supplies.

As her men looted the bodies—and she made a good trade with Owain, to whom the short sword had fallen, her longer blade for the Roman gladius—they discussed this. She glanced over at the unconscious prisoner, belting on the new blade.

"I have an idea in mind," she said, finally, as the other three debated the merits of trying to haul him back with them or killing him outright. The men broke off the discussion, which was getting a little heated, and gave her silence. "I'm thinking we should take off his thumb so he's spoiled as a warrior and turn him loose to make his way back to his lines."

They stared at her in utter astonishment. "But—why?" Aeron asked, finally.

But Meical had the answer already. "He thinks you be a thing un-canny, lady," the eldest of them said, slowly. "And you be wanting him to take that back with him. That King Lleudd has some terrible spirit bound to his service. Ghost, fae, witch, any or all. It doesn't matter, the tale will grow in the telling."

She nodded, and looked to the other two. "What say you?"

Aeron grinned broadly and spread his hands. "Peder'll be proud, girl. He'll wreak more havoc on his own with his tales than we could with a hundred men."

Owain finally chuckled. "Aye. Aye. I'm for it."

She wiped the chalk off her face with the fur of her cloak. "Right then. Take the thumb so he can't use an ax or any other weapon. I'll not send another fighter back to them. Cauterize the stump and that wound in his arm, and leave him with food and water enough to get back to his lines. He'll leave a trail a blind man could follow. Aeron, you and Owain ghost after him, make sure he actually *gets* there, and come back to our lines when you see the Saxon army so we know where they are. Meical and I will get back to our people and report."

Aeron gave the old Roman fist-to-shoulder salute some of the men, particularly those that had served with the High King, still used. It was the first time, however, that anyone had ever given it to *her,* and she felt warm inside. "As you will it, lady. 'Tis a privilege to serve you."

That warmth stayed with her for the long miles back to the main camp, better far than any heated stone.

Chapter Twelve

"Meᴅʀᴀᴜᴛ ɪs ʜᴇʀᴇ."
Those were the first words to greet Gwen as she and her troop rode into the camp of the small force her father had sent with her. Aeron and Owain had caught up with her easily enough; she and Meical had been taking their time, and Aeron and Owain had made sure to harry their Saxon along by making uncanny noises at night. The wound to his arm and the loss of his thumb were both painful of course, but in the winter after being cauterized, they were unlikely to fester and were not going to slow down a seasoned fighter significantly. These Saxons were tough, and a seasoned fighter would have survived other, more serious wounds than that.

According to the men, he hadn't even stopped to make camps; he'd make himself a warm nest with whatever he could find when it was too dark to keep going, sleep till dawn, and move on as if demons were after him. *"Or as if you were,"* the men had joked. He had stumbled into his own army within three days, and that was when Aeron and Owain turned back and put on all speed. The weather had remained good, and the snow was not too deep; her father's sturdy horses made good time in it.

So they knew now where the Saxon army was and that it was waiting for word from the scouting parties—for the ones they had come across were surely not the only ones. And Gwen had done something that, she hoped, would make the night a hell of fear for any more small groups the Saxons would send out. The White Phantom was hunting them, the Fair Apparition knew them, and being unsure if she was mortal magician or fae or even some bloody-handed goddess, they would be looking for her in every shadow. It gave her great satisfaction to imagine them so. And she knew men on campaign; they were greater gossips than any girls. The tales would only grow in the telling. If the commanders were foolish enough to forbid their men to speak of the White Phantom, it would only inflame them further.

Gwen and her men rode in to the camp on a bright, crisp, sunny afternoon having made all speed with their news, and she knew thanks to her work that a messenger sent to her father would have a substantial force here in plenty of time to give the Saxons second thoughts about invading. Her spirits were high, and with good luck she would see some fighting.

Above them was a sky of cloudless perfection. Before them was the camp, laid out in ordered rows. "Roman style," was what Peder said, though he would never, ever have used those words to her father. But Gwen now knew exactly what he meant. The Romans had perfected the art of making a defensible camp, and High King Arthur was not above using that art. King Lleudd's war chiefs and captains had learned it from him, found it good, and adopted it.

Such a camp could be made in much less than half a day in summer; in winter, it was oddly much easier. Square in shape, and surrounded by a ditch and wall system, it was possible to make snow walls higher and faster than dirt or brush walls, and in place of a ditch, simply making a fast fire of brush, allowing the snow to melt and freeze into ice served the same purpose. There was an entrance to the camp in the middle of each of the four walls, guarded night and day; the tents and pavilions inside were arranged in orderly rows, every tent was always in the same place in every camp, and if those tents were not as uniform as the ones that the Roman army had once had, at least it was possible to know exactly where everyone was in the camp. In the event of an attack, that was vital.

This wasn't a huge force or a huge encampment, not like the big Roman ones, which had held tens of thousands. Only a couple of hundred—just enough to for hit-and-run delaying tactics in case there *had* been a Saxon army actually marching across the border. It looked very peaceful, with the horses picketed neatly, the stacks of hay brought from the nearby village, each man with his cook fire going. Almost like a village in itself. But peace was not what they were here for, and she knew the others were chafing for some fighting just as much as she was. Strange thing about winter—some people nearly went mad with inactivity, and some just contentedly drowsed the dark days away. She, it seemed, was one of the former. The ambush of the scouting party had only whetted her appetite for more.

But her good humor came plummeting down when the first person she met—aside from the sentry who challenged them—was Peder, who greeted her with those warning words.

Medraut. Son of Lot of Orkney, now eighteen years old. The only person she wanted to see less than Medraut was the woman he had married, her sister Gwenhwyfach.

Which, of course, utterly ruined her mood. She pulled her horse up; he was not happy about being halted so close to his picket and that lovely, lovely hay, and he curveted restlessly despite his weariness. Peder stepped back from him; this was her warhorse, Rhys, one of her father's famed grays; it was not safe to be too near those hooves and teeth if a mood was on him. "What is *he* doing here?" she demanded sharply. There was no need to mince words with Peder; her old mentor knew exactly how she felt about the little pest. She had good reason for her dislike.

It had all begun five years after Anna Morgause had taken Little Gwen off to foster. The Queen of Lothian and the Orkneys had been making a state visit to the High King, which was a politic thing to do every so often, and had made sure to include in the journey a long pause at Castell y Cnwclas so that Little Gwen "could be with her family." And it had been unpleasant enough to have Gwenhwyfach swanning about, trying to lord it over Gynath, doing not a bit of work but making plenty. But that was not the end of the unpleasantness, for Anna Morgause had brought Medraut with her.

Now, when this planned visit had been announced, Gwen had thought that her worst difficulty was going to be with the queen herself again and attempts to work magic on King Lleudd. After all, this visit might just have been another excuse to lure her father into marrying Morgana again. Morgana was five years older now and still unwed; Pywll was four times the size it had been. King Lleudd had been a tempting prize before; now he was a brilliant one.

But she made no attempt to work magic, and old Bronwyn was watching her like a cat at a mousehole. Not only Bronwyn but also Gynath and just about every other woman that had been involved in thwarting the queen the last time.

It was not Anna Morgause that caused any difficulty; it was Gwenhwyfach, and that was merely petty. Gwen managed to avoid everything but feelings of irritation, and if had only been that, the visit might have been inconsequential enough.

Except for Medraut. It was absurd that a five-year-old child should trouble Gwen—yet trouble her he did.

Gwen had disliked him as an infant, and in her opinion, five years had not improved him. He was simply nothing like a normal child. He was thin, preternaturally agile; he looked more like an adult who had somehow been shrunk to a miniature size than like a child. He didn't play with other children. He didn't play at all. He was either somewhere doing secret things or . . . well, not underfoot exactly, but always there, nonetheless. His mother seemed to allow him to go where he wished and do as he pleased without supervision. And for some reason, he decided that what he wanted was to attach himself to Gwen.

He followed her about as much as he could, always watching her; he'd have followed her *everywhere* if she hadn't figured out that there were places he wasn't welcome, like the stable and the practice grounds. Horses disliked him, as did dogs, and a small child was forbidden from being on the practice grounds; it was too dangerous. There, at least, she could escape him.

She could not account for how he made her feel, since no one else seemed to have that strong a reaction to him. She couldn't help herself. With his smooth cap of black hair, his thin little face, and those flat gray eyes that seemed to be looking for secrets, he made her skin crawl.

She couldn't escape him at meals, though, nor any other place where he knew she was supposed to be serving as page or squire. He never said anything to her, never interrupted her. He would simply be there, tucked into a corner, staying out of the way. And he just kept staring at her.

That is, that was what he did right up to the point where the queen's party was due to leave. That night, as she was serving the men and had gone to refill her ale jug, she felt a grip on her elbow and looked down into his flat gray eyes.

"I am going to marry you," he announced. A command. A

princely command, from a prince to a servant. It was not the way a
normal child would have said such a thing, with the silly baby-love
some little boys got with a pretty woman, or in the manner of a joke,
or even as if it were something he had overheard his mother discussing and was parroting. It was . . . imperious. It sounded as if it was
something he had decided for himself without any coaching from
Anna Morgause. And he spoke the words as if he, and they, were
very, very certain. It made her skin crawl.

She stared at him, then laughed uneasily. She decided that the
best way to deal with him was to treat him as . . . well . . . a child. Even
if he wasn't acting like one. "Go away, infant," she replied, with a lift of
her lip. "Or I will tell your mama that you have gotten into the mead,
and you are making up lies and silly tales. You are too young to think
of marriage, and even if you were not, I am not for your marrying."

She pushed past him and went back to her serving . . . but she
could not help the strange chill that went up her back. The relief she
felt when they were all gone on their way was so intense it seemed to
brighten everything around her for days.

The next time she saw him, he was ten, and the years had not
changed him, except to make him taller and even more uncanny. At
ten, he was a full two heads taller than any other child his age—and
he seemed more like a miniature man than a boy. He was Gwenhwyfach's great pet and Anna Morgause's pride. By this time, Cataruna
was back, established as the Lady of Lleudd's lands, and the queen
sought her out on all possible occasions in order to discuss matters
of magic. For the most part, Gwen had very little to do with that, but
it was impossible to avoid some of it. Anna Morgause expected great
things from her youngest child, and she went on at great length about
how powerful, magically, the boy was.

"If I have no daughters, the gods have chosen to give me a son as
gifted as any girl," she asserted. And Cataruna (somewhat reluctantly,

Gwen thought) agreed. At the time, Gwen wondered if that was what made her so uneasy around him. Men's Magic was that of the Druids, who did have to do with the warriors . . . maybe it was that unpredictable vision of hers that was trying to tell her that the child was strong in such things.

But after only a day, she knew it was not that. It was that Medraut was obsessed, unnaturally obsessed, with her.

At least this time he did not follow her about, but every time she was near him, she was acutely conscious of his eyes on her. More than once, she suspected he was trying to work some sort of magic on her—as mad as it would have been in anyone else, she had more than a suspicion that he had not given up his idea of marrying her. But if he was trying to bespell her in anyway, it didn't work.

Horses still disliked him, and she had every reason to be with her horses now. She was training her new warhorses, two of the best grays from her father's herd—Rhys and Pryderi. They were her sole care at the moment, for she was about to join the ranks of the real fighters and would need her warhorses.

Anna Morgause was there for more than just a familial visit. This time, however, her designs were not on King Lleudd, and Morgana had not come with her. No, she had other plans entirely, although they did involve marriage within the king's family. By the time she left, Gwenhwyfach had been handfasted to the repellent boy; they would be formally betrothed in a year and married when he was fourteen, and Gwen had strong hopes she would never have to see him again. After all, Orkney was far from Pywll, the boy was anything but a warrior, and he was to be married to her sister, which *should* put an end to his uncomfortable obsession with her.

No such luck, it seemed.

And once she reported in, it seemed her luck was out even further. "Prince Medraut wishes to have speech of you," she was told by the war chief, in a tone of voice that said *and you had best go see him now*. Evidently, Prince Medraut was considered a Personage of Importance now. Reluctantly, she made her bow to her commander, and went to find him.

It wasn't hard. All she had to do was look for the showiest pavilion. It stood out in the encampment, with its decorations of red and black leather, its banners, and its utter new perfection. No one else had such things. The tents here had weathered many campaigns in all conditions and seasons, and they showed it.

And, of course, there he was. He was wearing all black: black cloak, black trews, black boots, black tunic. The only relief to the black was the silver penannular brooch holding the cloak closed at his throat. It was expensive, all that black. Black faded and needed to be redyed often. His was perfect. He was making sure he would be noticed. He invited her in, as his bodyguards stood one on either side of the tent entrance. The very idea of going into his tent made her want to turn and find her horse and ride as far away from him as she could. She demurred, politely, though. He was a Prince of Lothian and the Orkney Isles, and she was a Princess of Pywll. "I would not inflict my person on you at this moment. I'm straight from the field, and I stink of horse, Prince Medraut. And blood," she added, though she was rather sure that it wasn't the blood that would bother him.

Sure enough. "You do smell of horse, a bit," he said, wrinkling his nose. "I wanted to tell you of the news from my court in a more private surrounding, but . . ." His flat gray eyes did not warm with humor, or with anything else. "Well, everyone will learn this soon enough, from my servants if nothing else, so no harm if we're overheard, I suppose. First of all, my mother is dead."

He announced this in the same matter-of-fact tone that she would have associated with "I've killed a deer," or "one of the watchdogs died," so for a moment, she was so utterly taken aback that it took her a while to stammer out, "My condolences, Prince—"

"Oh, don't bother, the cow got what she deserved," he said, his eyes finally glinting with cruelty, which took her so by surprise that she actually lost her breath. "Two of my brothers, Gwalchmai and Agrwn, found her with a lover. Somehow, they were all too thick to realize she's had more lovers than a queen bee, but this time they caught her in the middle of making the two-backed beast. They killed her and him." He shrugged. "He was the son of one of the High King's allies, so there will be trouble over it, I expect. But it was the price of stupidity, and she was getting more stupid every year. Eventually someone was going to catch her, and if it had not been my brothers, it would have been someone else that King Lot could not ignore. Even if it was him that was her pander more than half the time. She had the appetite of a cat in season. My Aunt Morgana has more sense than the lot of them put together."

Gwen was so shocked, all she could do was stare at him.

"But that's not why I'm here," he continued. "I'm going to my father's court to present myself to him now that she's gone, and you should hear that from me."

She blinked, unable to understand. "Haven't you just come from there?"

He curled his lip again, and gave her a look of disgust. "Not Lot's court. My father's court. My blood father." When she failed to understand, he heaved an exaggerated sigh. "Arthur."

Her jaw dropped. "Arthur?" she repeated, stupidly.

He nodded with some satisfaction at her shock. "And now that there're no little princes in the way, I expect my dear blood father will be pleased to see me. He has no obvious heir, after all. His other sons also seem to have had tragically short lives. So I need you to promise me some things. Morgana gave me some good advice, and I am going to take it. First, I don't want Arthur to know I'm wedded to your sister. At least, not just yet."

Not that she was going to get anywhere near the High King to tell him, but—"Why not?" she managed.

"I'm trying to replace his sons. I'd rather he thought of me as a helpless little lad whose mother has just been rent from him. Someone in need of pity, comfort, and guidance from someone other than King Lot." Somehow, in that moment, Medraut . . . changed. In an instant, his face seemed to grow rounder and softer, his eyes larger and brighter and infinitely sad. His lower lip quivered ever so slightly.

In the next moment, he was back to his normal self, as always, looking like a man far older than his years, with eyes that belonged in the hardened face of someone like Peder. If Peder had no conscience at all.

"You can see how being married would interfere with that," he pointed out.

She nodded, finding herself agreeing with him, although she really did not want to.

"Second, don't tell anyone I have the Gifts." His eyes bored into hers. "That's something no one at the court needs to know. Ever. I don't want the Merlin to know, nor the Ladies. I've had good training at Morgana's hands, she has promised me more as I need it, and I don't feel as if I need to undergo it all over again."

Again, she nodded.

"Good. Thank you, fair sister." He smirked. "Fair indeed. I hear they have taken to calling you 'White Ghost.' That you frighten the Saxons. That they think you are some uncanny creature out of the spirit world or the realms of the elves."

She had felt so proud of that, but it felt so . . . foolish when she heard him say it. "There's no accounting for what soldiers will say," she replied harshly. "The Saxons don't believe that a woman can be a warrior, so they have to have some foolish explanation about why and how I can best them. It doesn't matter to me what they think I am. I do my job, and I am good at it."

"So you are," he replied, somehow making it sound as if he meant the opposite. "And, of course, there is nothing magical about you at all. Now remember. Keep my secrets."

"I will," she replied, and he turned and went rudely back into his pavilion, dismissing her as if she had been a churl and he—

Well, he was a prince. Rather more than just any prince, if he hadn't been lying. Arthur's son . . .

She didn't put it past him to lie . . . but somehow she didn't think he had this time. She turned *her* back on his tent and went off to her own tent and the single camp servant she shared with her troop, intending to get something to eat. Most of the men did their own cooking over their own fires; she had always found it better to forego some of the duties her servant would have done in order to make sure that everyone under her command was properly fed. And it was only as she was sitting with her troop, alternating bites of hard camp bread soaked in the gravy of the ever-present stew with bites of the stew itself, that many things she had already known suddenly fell together into a pattern.

That Medraut, as a baby, had looked as if he had been born before his time because he *was* born before his time. That he should have been born at the same time as the High King's twin sons.

At the same time as Eleri's son . . . she thought, and hastily shoved the thought away.

But . . . that meant he had been conceived at the time of the Great Rite. At the very wedding, the celebration that Lot and Anna Morgause had traveled to in order to pledge their fealty.

And that was when the world went to white about her, as it had not for many, many years. The bowl and bread fell from her nerveless fingers, and she heard, as if from a great distance, Owain and Aeron shouting, and felt hands catching her. But that was of no matter, because of what she was seeing . . .

Anna Morgause, alone in a luxurious tent, lit by a dozen candles, and much younger than when Gwen had last seen her, working . . . well, magic.

Some sort of magic.

Impossible to mistake it when the whole tent glowed with power, when there was a knife of white bone in her left hand and one of black flint in her right. When there was a tiny cauldron steaming over a charcoal brazier at her feet, and when there was a litter of small objects around that cauldron. Most of what she was doing was hidden by the woman's body. The woman's nude body. But when she turned, Gwen could see that she was written all over with signs and symbols in what could only be the blood of the black cat that lay dead on the floor of the tent beside her. And she had turned because a man had come into her tent.

He was tall, handsome, with a warrior's body. He was somewhere between dark and fair, with a young man's beard. He moved as if he was walking in his sleep. Anna Morgause smiled and drew him to her. The High King. It must be he, though Gwen had never seen him.

Then there was a moment of darkness. When it cleared, it was Anna Morgause surrounded by women, now in a stone-walled room, another brazier burning brightly, crying out in the throes of giving birth. And at the same time, overlaid onto Anna Morgause, Gwen saw another woman, a second woman, in another stone-walled room, fair-haired as Gwen herself, and even in the middle of her travail, beautiful, also giving birth . . .

Darkness passed across her eyes again. Again it cleared.

And then . . . she saw a new scene, a single bright space in the midst of the darkness. In the center of that, the same enormous serpent she had seen fighting the bear, striking at two handsome young man-boys, who must have been Medraut's age. They fell dead without a cry.

And then she found herself lying on the snow with men around her, anxiously looking her over for some sign of sickness or a hidden wound, patting her face, putting snow to her forehead. It was Aeron who saw the sense in her eyes.

"Thank the gods, you're back with us!" he exclaimed. And before he could say anything else or try to prevent it, she struggled herself into a sitting position.

"I won't say I'm all right, but I'm not ill, and I'm not injured," she assured them. "This is just—it's part of Epona's touch on me, I think. I See things. Not often, this is the first time in—in years. It's harmless enough—" She let Peder chaff her hands in his, because she was cold from lying in the snow. And she considered what she might say. "It was something Prince Medraut said to me, the bloody news he brings to the High King. His mother's been kin-slain by his brothers. Anna Morgause is dead. I Saw it happen; I suppose Epona wished me to act as a sort of witness to such a terrible deed, in case a witness was needed."

That was enough to shock them all into silence and take their minds off her for long enough for her to get to her feet. "Let me get some drink and food into me, since I've managed to drop what I had."

Peder came out of his shock first. "Aye, lady, and I'll have someone put a hot stone in your bedroll, and when you've done with the food, you'll be going there. I know a little about these matters; when your sister does a Seeing, she needs rest after. You're no different, and you should do the same. Your father would have all our heads if summat was to happen to you. Do I need to find a Lady?" He looked so worried over her, she wanted to pat his head and tell him kindly not to be such an old hen. But she didn't. For one thing, she knew that, like her sisters, like Queen Eleri, she looked absurdly young, a fact that caused her much irritation when those who did not know her treated her as if she was merely Medraut's age and barely more than a squire. For another, her head really was still swimming, and for once, it was nice to be cosseted.

She shook her head. "This will be something they already know, I think," she said truthfully. The Ladies had ways of seeing these things that were more reliable than her own unpredictable visions. "And I'll be fine. I just need to sleep."

"Sleep you'll have. I'll make it right with our commander," Peder promised. And then, when she had eaten what she could, he escorted her to her little tent himself and saw to it she was rolled up in the now-warmed furs and blankets. As she settled in, another unpleasant thought occurred to her. Those infants that Arthur—or the Merlin, through Arthur—had ordered murdered. What if the reason he had done such a terrible thing was that he had been trying to be rid of Medraut?

She could almost . . . almost . . . forgive him, if that was the case. Medraut as a child made her want to shove him down a well. Medraut as a boy-man made her want to run to some land where he could never, ever go. Or . . . shove him down a well and fill the well in after him. What would he be like as a man grown?

As the High King's son?

Well, it wouldn't matter. He was married to Little Gwen. He wouldn't bother her any more.

She honestly could not remember what she had felt like the first two times this had happened to her, but she had a killing headache now. It made it hard to think. She reached for the skin of mead that Gynath had insisted she take, not to drink for pleasure, but as medicine at need; it was her mother's special recipe, and Gwen reckoned that if it calmed anger, it might just calm a headache too.

She gulped down a good tankard full, and after a while the headache did ease, and she felt muzzy-headed and sleepy, and then, she slept, dreamlessly.

Chapter Thirteen

The scouts, Gwen's troop among them, had been ghost-ing about the Saxon army camp for a week. "Ghosting" was the right word, too, because it had soon become clear that Gwen's trick with the Saxon they'd let go was bearing fruit past all expectations. No one ventured outside the bounds of the camp at night. Even by day, no one went alone. Three spies had been sent in under the guise of selling the Saxons grain; they came back out again with a cart full of loot that had been traded for the food and a much richer store of camp rumors.

As a consequence, all the scouts had taken to doing what they could to add to the rumors of the White Phantom. Cries and screams in the middle of the night, for instance—not too often, or the Saxons would get used to them. And nothing that was obviously masculine either. But there were a couple of lads whose voices hadn't broken yet who could manage a very convincing female laugh or sob, and young as they were, they were carefully shepherded to the edge of the Saxon lines to give their little serenades.

When Gwen herself got involved, the nights got even more interesting. Since she knew Saxon—and seemed to have exceptionally keen ears—she would linger around a particular section until she had picked up on someone's name. Then, in the middle of the night, she would utter a blood-curdling wail, ending in the words, "Horsa"—or Ordulf, or Sidric, or whoever's name she had picked up—"Tomorrow I come for *you*."

She tried to pick very common names, the better to give Fate a hand in giving her a victim. And more often than not, Fate gave her one. Where there were armed and edgy men, there were always accidents and quarrels. Where there were armed, edgy, men convinced that a supernatural agency was after them, the accidents and fights were fatal or near-fatal as often as not. A man who is sure he is going to die will do so even from a minor wound. By the time the king's full force arrived, it was a full moon again, and Gwen had been emboldened enough to show herself.

Never for long. There was no point in risking a lucky bowshot. But by now she and her scouts knew every inch of land around the Saxon camp, and they could, in the shifting clouds and moonlight, make miraculous appearances and disappearances. So at one moment, a hilltop would be empty of all but moonlight, then suddenly a sentry would shout in fear, for the White Phantom was there, silver rider on silver horse, staring down at the camp. Then a cloud would obscure the moon, and when the Saxons looked again, she was gone.

It was very effective.

And by now there were desertions, not many, but enough to make the commanders angry, and angry commanders faced with desertions often make poor decisions regarding the treatment of their men. When you added to that the fact that those same men were not eating as well as they expected, had not had much loot, and their lords were running out of presents . . .

So it was that once King Lleudd's men were rested and ready to deal with the Saxons, the Saxons were not nearly in as good a condition to deal with them.

The night had been an active one for Gwen and her troop; with a good moon and intermittent clouds, they had taken full advantage of the circumstances to bedevil the Saxons almost until dawn. There had been little sleep in that camp, and the lot of them had take to their bedrolls with weary satisfaction. A few more nights like this one, and the Saxons would be falling asleep on the battlefield.

She woke to hear a great commotion in the camp, and she was on her feet with her sword in her hand and her blankets cast aside before she realized that this was not the sound of an attack. Men shouted orders, but not in the tone of voice that indicated trouble; horses were clearly being brought in and picketed. It sounded as if a substantial addition to King Lleudd's troops had arrived.

Well, any additions are welcome. She couldn't for the moment think who would have been able to muster out winter fighters, but it didn't matter. She would find out soon enough, since she had best pull on a good tunic and present herself to welcome them. She might not be a general, and her actual rank was low among the officers, but she *was* King Lleudd's daughter, and as such, it would be an insult not to greet and thank the new arrivals.

Her servant was of the same mind, for even before she had started to shiver, he came diffidently into the small tent, prepared to wake her if need be, with her best leather trews and embroidered wool tunic in his hands. She laughed at his relief—she was not known for waking gracefully—and pulled the clothing out of his grip. "Go wake the others," she ordered, "I'll be ready quickly."

She normally kept her hair tightly braided and clubbed like a horse's tail, so it was tidy enough not to need combing out and re-braiding. She cast aside what she had been wearing, smelling of horse and sweat as it probably was. The gray wool trews and leather tunic could use a good beating and cleaning in snow, and the linen shirt could stand a boiling. She hopped from one foot to the other, shivering as the cold air bit at her, dressed again from the skin out in good clean linen and woolen hose, then pulled on the trews and wriggled into the tunic. She reflected wryly as she did so that among the captains, war chiefs and generals she was going to stand out as much as that pest Medraut had; the trews were white doeskin, and the tunic, unlike the festal garb of most of her father's folk, was *not* a checkerboard of bright colors, with contrasting bands of embroidery at hems and neck. Her best tunic was light gray, with silver and white bands. Somehow, she realized, she had come to have most of her clothing made in these colors, as if she were trying to live up to her name. And, thank the gods, it was so stark as to give her too-youthful face a more serious cast. There was nothing she could do about the fact that her cheeks were not scarred, browned by the sun, weathered by the wind. Nor could she change that she had not so much as a sign that she was more than old enough to be a mother six times over by now—twenty-five, and she looked sixteen at best! But at least she could look as serious and remote as a vengeful spirit.

Bah, it is more that I am trying to look as unlike Gwenhwyfach as possible, she thought, a little crossly. Her sister, the last time she had seen the chit, was as profligate in her love of opulent, showy dress as Medraut was—except she did so in colors rather than stark black.

Well, no matter. All things went to serve a purpose, and she would stand out, which was good, but not in an ostentatious way or as if she were trying to, which was also good. And the clothing had been laid up in lavender and meadowsweet, so she would smell less of horse than usual. She opened the small chest that held her few jewels, bound the silver fillet around her brow, got out her silver torque with the horsehead finials, and put it on and fastened her cloak, not with her old bronze brooch, but with the silver Epona brooch that had been the latest gift from her father. Stamping her feet to settle them in her soft boots, she pushed aside the tent-flap and headed in the direction of the tent of War Chief Urien, who was the chief of all her father's generals. That was where newcomers of importance would be taken.

It was the largest tent in the encampment, and that was needful, since outside the hours of sleep, it had to house the table where the maps were laid and strategy made, and in the hours of sleep had to hold Urien's entire personal band of companions, some twenty men in all. Companions of this sort were men who did nothing other than hold themselves ready to fight; they held no lands, and they got all their substance from their chief. This was a Saxon custom not often found among Lleudd's folk or the other tribes north of where the Saxons held sway. But Arthur had adopted the practice, making the sons of his underkings into his band of companions and setting them, it was said, about a round table that had neither head nor foot, as a sign that there were no "greater" or "lesser" men among them, that all were equal. Shrewd, that was. Supposedly he had got the curious table, which must have been enormous, as part of his queen's dower.

His now-dead queen . . .

To think I envied her as a child.

At any rate, Urien followed the High King's example, and Lleudd saw no harm in his doing so, though he himself did nothing of the sort. Having to haul around so large an expanse of canvas and hide was a nuisance, but Gwen was glad of the shelter and relative warmth in this winter campaign.

Outside the tent was all astir with men coming and going with purposeful looks and brisk paces. She winced a little at the bright light; being out so much at night . . . she smiled to herself, thinking she was as sensitive to the sun as the spirits she was imitating, now. She did not have to push her way through the crowd, even though she was a good head shorter than most of them. Those that did not personally know her made way for her anyway. After all, there were not that many woman warriors in this camp, the fact that Lleudd's daughter was the head of the scouts was widely known, and dressed as she was, there was no mistaking who she was. She pulled aside the tent-flap and entered unannounced.

Inside the great table had been set up and the hide maps that she and her scouts had drawn up laid over it. All of the war chiefs and generals had gathered about this table, and all of them were listening with rapt attention to a young man not much older than she.

He had plainly come straight off his horse and into this meeting; there was horsehair no servant had yet brushed off clinging to his cloak, and his dark hair was all sweaty and askew from the helmet he had taken off and set aside. He was still in armor too, chestnut-colored leather breast- and back-plate over softly gleaming chain mail that she immediately craved in a way that she had never craved fine gowns. He was not handsome, his face being too craggy for beauty, but it was full of intelligence and character, and his voice was as worth listening to as that of any bard.

". . . and obviously, as I am sure you have already seen, we want to find a way to force them up this slope," he was saying, as he arrayed handfuls of wooden counters representing the Saxons onto the map. "It's not so steep they'll even think twice about charging it, but every time we force them to charge, they'll be laboring against not only the snow but also the slope. We'll tire them further."

"The trick will be to get our men to hold and not answer their taunts," Urien replied with a frown. He was a big man, looming over the newcomer, and yet his posture bespoke willing subservience. Whoever the young man was, Urien was giving him pride of place without in the least resenting it. As dark as Urien was, and as bearded, he looked like a great bear in his fur cloak. "The good gods know I favor Roman tactics, but our men are not Roman soldiers . . ." He looked up, spotted Gwen standing diffidently in the door, and motioned to her to come forward. "Lancelin, this is Princess Gwenhwyfar, daughter of King Lleudd."

The young man looked up, and Gwen found herself the focus of a pair of the bluest eyes she had ever seen in her life. He had the direct gaze of a hawk, with a challenge in it that melted away when he smiled.

"My lady." He came from around the table, and bowed to her. "Your reputation precedes you."

She flushed, but she did not look down as a "maidenly" girl would; no point in giving him any reason at all to discount her. "Your courtesy seems equaled by your grasp of strategy, sir," she replied, with an enquiring look at Urien. "If you can hold War Chief Urien's full attention, you must be cunning indeed."

"Gwen, this is Lancelin, the High King's *best* strategist," Urien replied in immediate answer to that look. He beamed. Gwen blinked a bit in surprise. Urien must feel that the young man's mere presence was a kind of honor.

"Arthur sent me, in place of himself," Lancelin added. A shadow of something—disapproval? Uncertainty? Passed over his face. "And as many of his cavalry as could be mounted and sent in haste. This is an unprecedented push, and the High King wants a decisive blow struck against the Saxons, one that they will not forget soon. Arthur himself . . ." he trailed off. It was Urien who laughed coarsely and completed what Lancelin would not say.

"Arthur is trying to replace his heirs, having already replaced his queen," Urien said with just the hint of a leer. "Another Gwenhwyfar, can you believe it? Gwenhwyfar, daughter of Gwythyr son of Greidiawl. I suppose having had such luck as to get twins with one Fair Apparition, he decided to try another."

The rest of the men chuckled as well, and Gwen made an amused and wry face. They had long since ceased to treat her as anything other than a fellow warrior, and as such, she shared in their jibes and bawdy jests—and again, an unmaidenly reaction merely helped to reinforce a position she had to fight to hold in their eyes. Only Lancelin seemed abashed. "There are many rites that the priests of the White Christ are demanding," he said, looking uncomfortable. "Arthur must conform to them before they will let him have his new queen. Greidiawl, King Gwythyr's father, was a great patron of those priests, and all his household was brought up in that service. Greidiawl brought to the last battle with the Saxons a banner that was said to be holy, and it is true that the Saxons broke and ran when it was brought on the field. When the queen died of grief, Gwenhwyfar the Golden, who was one of her ladies, strove to comfort the High King—"

"Oh, aye, *comfort*," Urien chuckled, and the other men roared with laughter. Lancelin squirmed.

"There's fine comfort to be had between a pair of white legs," someone said loud enough to be heard, and even Gwen had to chuckle at that, shaking her head.

When the laughter faded, Urien came around to where Lancelin stood and slapped him on the back, staggering him a little. "We mean no harm, lad, and no disrespect to the High King either. The old queen followed her boys to the Summer Country, and alas for that, but she was a follower of the Good Goddess and knew as well as any that Arthur could not mourn her forever. Better he find himself a new queen quickly, before the thaw, in time for the seedling time. As the king, so goes the land. He was mateless for too long, and the land suffered for it. There is not a man here that begrudges him a new queen, nor looks through his fingers at the notion that you are here instead of he."

Lancelin coughed a little. "I make no excuses—"

"Nor need you. Look you, he sent with you full eighty of the best of the best of his cavalry." Urien nodded his shaggy head. "And I've been on the Saxon campaigns; I'd as lief have you here as Arthur. The companions may be all equals, but in strategy you have no peer."

Now Lancelin flushed, but he held his head high, as a warrior should. "By your leave then, sir, lady? Since the lady has seen and scouted the ground herself with her men, I've need of her counsel and memory."

She hid her relief. The battle had been won again. He took her seriously. Now they all gathered around the map table, while Lancelin examined the maps, asked Gwen highly intelligent and detailed questions about the terrain, asked the others equally intelligent and detailed questions about the temper and skills of their men, and he and Urien moved counters about.

And now Gwen saw exactly why Urien valued him so highly. There were two reasons. The first was that while this was Roman strategy indeed, it was Roman strategy adapted to the much more volatile men of the tribes. If a war chief or general said that he did not believe his men could do such-and-so, Lancelin immediately changed the strategy to something they *could* do. Some could, and would, hold the "Roman Square." They had fought under Arthur, they understood how the thing worked, and they would overcome their own battle spirit to stand and not respond to the Saxon taunts. Some would not. Those, Lancelin appointed to places in the lines where it would do no harm, and much good, for them to follow the standard battle practice of running up by ones and twos, casting their spears at Saxons who had done the same, and perhaps engage in single combat.

And as for the cavalry . . .

"I know what my men will do," he said with confidence. "They will be here, and here, and at my signal, they will close in around the rear of the Saxons and harry them onto the spears and javelins and archers of the Square."

In his hand were the few counters that represented Gwen and her scouts. He juggled them, looking from the map to her and back again. She answered the unspoken, and very awkward, question.

"My men are like me, small, light of limb. We are horse archers, mainly. But we have King Lleudd's finest and fastest warhorses; I would reckon they could be at the finish of a race while your men were halfway down the course—and be ready to take you all over again," she said with pride.

He brightened. "Fast, agile, and deadly. Good! There are two tasks for you and yours, lady. The first is to sting the Saxon boar, but precisely; I want you here, beside the Square, to run out in relays, find a leader, try to take him and no other, and race back to our lines."

She sucked on her lower lip. "Not likely we can hit more than once in a dozen shots," she replied honestly. "When we fight, we generally shoot at the mass of men, and try to arc over the shields. Generally we hit something because they are so close-packed."

He nodded. "But deliberately choosing a leader—that will goad them, even if you do not hit. His companions will have had their honor touched, and they must defend him. *That* is what I want; I want them enraged, I want them charging up that hill and onto the Square without a second thought. And the second task is this: After they charge, you all retreat behind the Square, and when they break, and they will, you come out again to sting them a second time." He smiled. "This terrain, this weather, can all play in our favor. We can wear them down, saving ourselves, in case they have more than one force out there."

Now that had not occurred to her, and from their faces, it also had not occurred to Urien and his men. Lancelin shrugged. "The Saxons fight like maddened boars," he said. "That does not mean they cannot be cunning. We must be more cunning."

"And fight like *men!*" Urien roared, slapping Lancelin's back again. The others shouted their approval.

Lancelin was still looking at her, and she realized belatedly that he was waiting for her assent, as he had for the other chiefs. "That we can do," she replied, nodding. "We all have changes of horses too; we can keep both at the lines and make sure we always have fresh mounts."

He didn't smile as she had half expected, but his look of satisfaction was the same he had given to the other chiefs and generals. "Then by your leave, my lords, I will take these plans back to my men, and you take them to yours. One day for my men and horses to rest, and then we will show these Saxon pigs that it is ill done to covet the acorns beneath the High King's oaks."

She took her leave while Urien was still speaking to the young man and returned to her troop. They had been awakened and were sleepily devouring their stew and bread. Over food, she laid out what was to be expected of them, while they listened thoughtfully. Although this seemed a fine battle plan to her, she half expected that there would be some discussion, if not objection, but there was nothing of the sort.

"Clever," said Owain after a long silence.

"Aye, but not too clever." Peder came to sit down to join them. Gwen made space for him beside her on a log. He accepted a bowl of stew from her servant. "If the High King and the Merlin have a fault, it's the making of plans that are a bit too clever, so no one understands what's to happen but them. I like this Lancelin."

"Come to steal our food again, old man?" asked Meical with a laugh.

"Aye." Peder cuffed him; or rather, cuffed at him. Meical ducked out of the way. "I'll not poison myself before a battle with my own cooking."

"Arthur's Companions do the same," said Aeron suddenly.

"What, poison themselves?" The others laughed, and Aeron wrinkled up his nose.

"No fools, have a common store and a common cook pot. Like we do. No man starves because he didn't want to burden himself, no man carries too much. Food is always waiting, and they never go into a battle or to bed hungry."

"Another Roman thing?" Owain asked, curiously.

Aeron shook his dark head. "Nay. This was Arthur's idea."

Gwen ate another bite of stew. Someone must have been hunting, for there was rabbit and maybe some duck in this along with the usual dried mutton, turnips, parsnips, and pease. "The Romans did as we do, except that there was a grain wagon a man got his bread ration from," she offered. "I can see the advantage, but what happens when the enemy fires your provision wagon or carries it off? And it would slow you down."

"No slower than foot soldiers," Peder pointed out.

"True." She savored the smoky taste of the broth, but she wished for a little thyme. "Something to think about."

When the men had finished, and Peder had wandered back to his own tent, she sat beside the fire, thinking. There was enough afternoon sun on her back to warm her; between the fire and the sunlight, she was, for once, nicely warm. So Arthur was not so grief-stricken that he had not filled his bed again . . . that was interesting. She could not imagine her father doing the same . . .

. . . unless . . .

She scratched the back of her head, absently, staring into the fire. There might have been more to this than just a man not wanting a cold bed, and a woman willing to sleep her way to a crown. Anna Morgause was not the only woman in the world to employ the magics of *glamorie.*

But this Gwenhwyfar is a follower of the White Christ! Don't they shun magic?

Maybe. But Anna Morgause had—supposedly—been one of the Ladies. And the Ladies would not have approved of what Gwen had seen in her vision. You did not use Gift of the Goddess to lure a man that was not yours to your bed. You did not steal the magic meant for the High King and his Queen to put a babe in your own loins so you could use him later as a tool to manipulate the High King himself.

She had no doubt that was what Anna Morgause had intended for Medraut.

She brooded into the flames, listening with half her attention to the buzz of the camp life about her, and tried to think this through, as the daughter of a king should do.

The priests of the White Christ had been angling at the High King for a very long time. His father, Uther, had toyed with them, although he had not actually committed to their faith; but he had given them shelter and leave to build their churches. Even one very near to the Isle of Glass, where the Ladies taught.

It was hard to imagine these men and what they were trying to do. She had never actually met one. The notion of converting a man to another spiritual path was foreign, even a little alien to Gwen, but it was one of the chief pursuits of these people, it seemed. So much so that it appeared they would do almost anything to bring a man into their ranks.

So maybe they allow—or forgive—magic, if it brings them another man. And if that man were the High King?

Probably anything short of murder would be forgiven.

Well, the High King was far away. And he would never repudiate the Merlin, nor would he do anything to drive away his allies, who were not Christ-men. *Glamorie* could do only so much; it would not turn a man against a friend or make a friend out of an enemy. The most that this Gwenhwyfar could accomplish would be to grant the Christ priests more tolerance, to put their rites on equal footing, at least at court, with the Old Ways. Probably.

Gwen considered what others had said about these men, these priests, how they pushed themselves and their god forward. Was it possible that Arthur would neglect the Old Ways in favor of the ones his queen followed, if he were infatuated enough?

Well. Yes. Anything is possible. After all, the gods had done nothing to preserve his sons. He might even be persuaded that his sons had died *because* he did not favor this new god.

She made a face at the fire.

Well, the High King was not here. And by his own decree, the customs of a kingdom held of him were to continue. She was certain that he would not dare to offend his allies by demanding that they give over their rites and gods and take up with this new one. If he did, he would soon find himself without allies altogether.

Fine. Let the Christ-men have him. The Romans brought their emperor and their Mithras, and look where they are now! Tumbled in the dust.

Then something else occurred to her. Medraut was still on his way to the court, fully expecting to find a distraught Arthur who would welcome this unlooked-for, undreamed of son—

—this son of his own half-sister—

Oh, that will put the cat among the pigeons.

Even among the followers of the Old Ways, people would look a little askance at that. They would accept it, if Arthur did, and find excuses for him. Tell themselves he could not have known Anna Morgause was his half-sister. Or that he was under her spell so deeply that he did not know who she was. Those things might even be true. But still . . . there would be some looks askance, and if harvests were bad, or winters long, people would ask themselves if this was the fault of the High King's dalliance.

But Medraut would not find a father in mourning and an empty throne. He would find a father infatuated with a new love, a queen who looked to supply him with more heirs, and one who followed the Christ to boot, whose priests most certainly would *not* look kindly on the love child not only conceived out of wedding bonds, not only sired on a Lady-trained sorceress and a follower of the Goddess, not only begotten on someone else's wife, but the love child of a man and his half-sister.

She almost laughed aloud to think of it.

Arthur certainly could not acknowledge Medraut now, even if he was not beglamored, even if he was not inclining to these new priests. How could he? He had a queen with whom he expected to produce true heirs. The last thing he wanted was to set up a rival to them.

The new queen was hardly going to welcome him, either. He would always be a rival to her own children. And if this same queen actually was given Gifts and the use of magic . . .

I think they will eat each other alive.

She went to her bed, chuckling at the thought.

Chapter Fourteen

If Lancelin had not been so modest and self-effacing away from the war table, Gwen would have been hard put to restrain her jealousy of his instant prominence among the war chiefs. He had overleaped her and the position she had spent seasons, *years,* achieving, and he had done so overnight.

But he was, in fact, a quiet and astonishingly modest man outside of the tent, and when she was honest with herself, she had to acknowledge that *he* must have spent just as long a period among Arthur's Companions to get that same position. So jealousy was not what she was really feeling. It was envy. And she had to admit that he was a genius at strategy.

Every man in the oddly assorted army fielded by her father was perfectly placed to take advantage of his strengths—or, at the very least, to take advantage of what he *would* do no matter what had been planned.

Those who were going to charge no matter the orders had been put in the front lines of the flanks, so at least when they charged, it would be across the hill rather than down it. After that initial planning session, Lancelin had made a round of the fires, using charm, honesty, or, occasionally, a skin of strong mead to find out what each commander knew of his mens' behavior in battle and what he thought the others would do. Then he had revised his plans to account for what he learned.

When he spoke to Gwen, it had been with respect and honesty. She and her scouts—for the scouts had seen much more of how the others fought—answered him with the same frank candor. The result was that their disposition remained the same: to sting the Saxons until they charged, then hold back and harry the outliers, watching for an effort to flank.

She sat her horse easily, looking down the shallow slope to the Saxon army spread out in their rough battle line at the bottom.

There was a great deal of noise: challenges being shouted on both sides, weapons beaten on shields, insults, catcalls. It didn't matter that most of them didn't understand each other's language; the tone made the content clear enough. And if they had been fighting with traditional tactics, eventually one man or another would break from the lines, run forward, and throw a spear into the enemy nearest him. Unless he was extraordinarily strong or lucky, the spear would glance off the shield, fall short, break, or bury itself in the wooden shield. Then the man attacked would wrench it out, pick it up or take his own spear, run forward, and return the favor. Then the two would fight, one on one, while the rest of the armies cheered them on. The victor would taunt the enemy, return to his own lines, or remain for someone else to challenge him. Perhaps another fighter from his own side would join him. This would continue, with the number of single combats increasing until the tension broke and one side or the other would charge.

Of course, that was not going to happen here. Gwen would have thought that by this time the Saxons would have realized, the moment they saw forces forming the Square, that they were facing another force using the High King's Roman tactics.

Perhaps they think it is a ruse. Or perhaps they are confident that this time they can induce us to fight their sort of battle.

The noise was making her horse dance and fidget in place; if this had been summer, she would have soothed him to keep him from wearing himself out. But it was winter, not summer, and all the prancing and stamping was keeping his muscles warm. This was all to the good.

She watched her men out of the corner of her eye. Their horses were as restive as hers, and they sat them as easily. They looked calm. She hoped she did. This would be her first major battle, the first where the armies of more than her father had joined together to face the foe.

There had only been one point of conflict between her and Lancelin. She had wanted to lead the scouts on their stinging attacks on the Saxon line. He had insisted that she ride somewhere in the middle of the skein. "You are almost the only woman in the army, lady," he had pointed out. "It will not be hard to identify you as the White Phantom. This will make you a tempting target for all archers if you ride first. But if you are in the middle, the confusion you and your men will cause will ensure they do not even realize you are a woman."

She didn't like it, not at all, but she had to admit he was right. What was the point of creating the legend of the White Phantom if the feared creature went down under the first volley of arrows? Still. She didn't have to like it, that he was right.

She watched the front line of the Square. It was Urien, not Lancelin, who would give the signal for her group to begin their assault. At least they would be *doing* something, not standing there chafing against the inactivity like the steady fellows who had formed the Square.

The noise rose and fell like the sound of waves on the rocks at Tintagel. The sun burned down on the white hillside, soon to be churned into an expanse of blood and mud. Things always grew well on a battlefield . . . as if the gods were saying, "Out of death comes life." If the local farmers were not eager to plow and plant this expanse come spring, they would surely not hesitate to scythe down the lush grass that would spring from the blood that watered this land. It would only last a season, but that season would be a good one.

From the center of the Square, a pennon on the tip of a lance shot up. Urien's forces released their pent impatience in a roar as Peder spurred his horse, leading the scouts in their gadfly charge.

She was third and had forsaken her usual gray clothing for ordinary leather armor with metal plates riveted inside, protecting breast and back. It obscured her shape, and her sex was further concealed by a half-helmet. All of the scouts looked reasonably alike, except for Gwen's long braid of white-blonde flailing her back. She had tried coiling it up under the helm, but it wouldn't stay. She needed a new and better helm.

Peder's horse labored a little, galloping through the snow. This pass would be the hardest; as the horses tired, at least the snow would be easier to get through. The others pounded in his wake, snow clots flung up by their hooves. The Saxons watched them in astonishment. Evidently, they had not expected this.

It was not easy firing a bow from the back of a moving horse, and even Gwen's men, who had practiced this with her against the day when they might be surprised and have to flee pursuit, were not what anyone would call *good* at it. But then, when the idea was to discourage pursuit, you didn't need to be accurate. You only needed the appearance of accuracy.

Gwen, however, was good. After all, she had reasoned, if Braith and some of the warriors she led could hit a man from a moving chariot with a spear, enough practice and a horse you could guide with your knees should make such a thing possible for a rider with a bow. Peder and the man following him more or less marked their target, a big Saxon with a russet shield. It was fairly obvious who they were shooting at, as two men near him screamed or went down. Gwen shoved her reins in her mouth, guided the horse in daringly close to the line, aimed quickly, and fired.

It was all luck, of course. She was aiming for the broader target of his chest, since he'd dropped his shield to gawp. She got him in the eye.

She kneed her horse, heeling him over to follow in Peder's wake, taking control of the reins again. A shout of rage followed her from the Saxon lines.

She didn't look back.

They gathered again at their first position, and only then did she wheel her horse to see the results of the attack.

"Well, they are not charging yet," Peder observed.

"Aye. But they aren't happy."

In truth, that was an understatement. The Saxons were outraged. Gwen smirked as she made out some of what they were saying. "They are calling us dogs without honor," she said. Peder laughed.

"They're welcome to chase us," he suggested. Gwen's smile turned into a smirk. The scouts were not mutton-headed bull-men whose idea of "honor" overrode the need to win battles. They couldn't be. All of them were small and wiry, and to stand and bash at one of those Saxon boars would have been suicide, and from the time they had gotten their full growth, it was very clear that they would never be the sort of fighters that won champions' battles and got songs written about them. While this turned some away from the warrior's path, this lot had become pragmatic. Let other men worry about gaining honor and glory. They would become clever and invaluable. And if no one sang about them, well, the war chiefs knew their value, and they were well rewarded with gifts and loot.

"Well, the cursed Saxons can throw whatever names about they care to. We might get a song out of this from our side," Gwen observed.

But Peder was already setting his horse for another part of the line, and a moment later, the second run began.

It took four before the Saxons' temper broke. Gwen was never again lucky enough to take her man down, but she forced the leaders to duck behind shields like nervous maidens, and that infuriated them. Finally one of Gwen's targets had enough. His face purple with anger, he waved his sword over his head and charged after her, roaring.

That was her signal to send her tiring horse not for the side, but uphill, straight for the Square.

The front line of the Square opened up to let her and the men behind her through, then closed behind them. She pulled up her horse to a trot and joined Peder, waiting for the rest. She didn't look back; the clash of arms and the shouts and screams from the front of the Square said everything that needed to be said.

With every nerve afire now with excitement, once the rest were gathered up, she made a chopping motion with her hand and pointed to either side of the Square. They split into two groups, one led by her, and one by Peder, trotting off to either side, first to scout for any hidden reinforcements, then to harry the Saxon flanks and rear.

They already knew the likeliest places to look, and on horseback, even in the snow, Gwen and her group moved swiftly across the landscape, finding nothing. She could see from their faces that they were as impatient to return to the battle as she was. It was with relief that she sent her horse homing for the noise in the middle distance. As they pushed over the last hill, the smoke from a dozen fires rose blackly to their left. Gwen laughed when she saw it. Peder's men had fired the Saxon camp. Victorious or defeated, there would be nothing for them to come back to. No food, no shelter, no carts, no oxen or mules to pull them.

Not the time to think about it, however. They were coming up fast on stragglers, either left behind or fleeing the battle. Gwen drew her Roman sword, a fine piece of steel that she'd put a good edge on. Reins in her left, blade in her right, she charged down on the man in her path.

The Roman sword was meant for thrusting, but she used it to slash instead, cutting viciously at the man's face as he looked up at her in shock. He gurgled out a kind of scream, there was blood, and then she was on to the next, her heart pounding, shrieking herself, afire with excitement, full of sick nausea, driven with a cold anger and a hatred of these men who had dared try to invade *her* land, enthrall *her* people.

She slashed at men in her path until the edge of her blade grew dull and she used it like a club. At one point there was a spear sticking up out of the bloody snow in front of her; she snatched it up in passing and ran it through the next man to be in her path. It was only when her horse stumbled with weariness that she reined in her emotions and nudged the poor fellow over to the side, off the field, and under the trees where her servant, Gavin, waited, with their remounts, hidden. She was the first in.

She dismounted, handed the gelding's reins to Gavin, and mounted the mare, noting absently that her sword arm was blood-soaked.

That was when the nausea hit her like a club.

She doubled over in the saddle. It was always like this. When battle fever wore off, sickness would overwhelm her for a moment. Her stomach knotted, cramped, and heaved; she swallowed bile that burned in her throat and fought it down. Gavin handed her a water-skin; she took it and gulped down several mouthfuls, pushing them past the lump of sickness in her gullet. Then it passed; she straightened and handed the skin back to Gavin as one of the others rode in, spattered from head to toe with blood and mud.

When they were all gathered—*all*, which anxiety had been part of her sickness, worry for them—she led them at a trot for a good place to get a quick reconnoiter.

The battle had degenerated into knots of combat. One was centered around Urien; one around Lancelin. These were not Gwen's concern, although she wasted a moment admiring Lancelin's fighting. He was ahorse—all of Arthur's chosen Companions were horsemen and fought mounted—and though there were a dozen men around him trying to pull him down, he and his stallion fought like a single lethal entity.

Mentally she scolded herself for losing even a moment and turned to her men. There was still no way of knowing how this battle would turn, "Scout again," she ordered. "Then it's bow work."

They nodded. Once again the group divided, and they pounded off to make sure there were no reinforcements coming in.

The Saxons had committed everything. Gwen led her group as far as was reasonable and then scattered them. They came back to her to report—nothing. *If* there were reinforcements, provided that Urien won this battle, it would be too late for them to do anything.

They galloped back to the battle lines. They were all riding mares; less speed, but more stamina.

They saw the deserters before they heard the battle. As one they pulled out their bows and strung them.

Shooting from the back of a running horse was hard. Shooting from the back of a standing horse wasn't.

It was over.

That is, it was over for *most* of the army.

There was loot to be had, of course, and here the mounted had an advantage over those on foot, although those on foot would be where the chieftains and war chiefs had fallen, in the thick of the battle. Still, not all of those chieftains had fought to the last, and Gwen's scouts had taken down enough of them that all of her men wore weary, satisfied smiles as they packed their takings on their horses.

And once they'd all mustered back at camp, eaten some food, and made at least an attempt at cleaning themselves and their gear, Urien called them to inspection, sent out the least exhausted to patrol, and ordered the rest to their beds. Neither Urien nor Lancelin were taking chances.

Gwen herself reported to the commanders with tally sticks of everything (well, mostly, you couldn't prevent the men from cheating a little) her scouts had taken. In theory, half of that should have gone to Urien and her father. In practice, there had been so much that Urien simply waved the tallies off. "Your men fought bravely and deserve what they took." In the corner of the tent, Lancelin was winding a bandage around his wrist—not because he had been struck but because, unbelievably, he had sprained it, he had cut down so many of the enemy.

Some stragglers might have escaped, but Gwen didn't think there were many of them. The snow had hampered escape and had made it easy to see escapees. And for those who *had* gotten away, without food, without shelter, with no real knowledge of the land, possibly injured . . . the night was going to be very cruel. And if a storm came, which it very well might . . .

So far as the Saxons were concerned, their army would have vanished utterly into the winter.

Lancelin looked up and caught her eyes. "I think enough messages got back to the Saxon leaders of the dread White Spirit that they will probably blame this defeat on her," he said, with a wry smile.

She blinked at him in surprise. "I wasn't even thinking of that," she replied.

"I was." He finished winding the bandage and tucked the end in, then flexed his hand experimentally.

She flushed. "I'm sorry to have spoiled your victory for you then."

"No, you aren't." His smile remained.

"I'm not what?"

"Sorry." He stood up. "And you shouldn't be. That was very clever. I will advise the High King to make use of what you began."

Urien laughed. "Your High King's new queen cannot be half as clever as our princess," he said with unconcealed satisfaction.

"Not in the same way, nor at the same things, no." Lancelin lost his smile. "Queen Gwenhwyfar turns her mind to a different path than the princess."

And it is one you don't approve of, Gwen thought with some surprise. That was when she wondered if she should warn Lancelin about Medraut. She had sworn to tell no one but . . .

The moment passed. He bowed to her and left. She spoke a little more with Urien about the disposition of her men, but weariness had begun to fog her thinking, and it showed. The war chief sent her off with a laugh.

Still, it nagged at her. Someone should know about Medraut. Was there any way she could tell Lancelin without actually *saying* anything?

She decided to wait until morning. Sometimes things came clearer in the night.

In the morning nothing was clearer, but by midafternoon the last patrol reported that there was still no sign of any reinforcements. And ravens, both two-legged and winged, had come to scavenge on the bodies.

When pickings on a battlefield were lean, the winners generally stripped the bodies of the dead bare before burning them. But from all appearances, either the Saxon war chiefs had anticipated trouble from their men because of the difficulty of a winter campaign and had come laden with many gifts to keep them contented, or they had been forced to send back to their holdings for rich gifts in order to retain them after Gwen began her "haunting." In any case, the bodies beginning to freeze in the churned-up bloody snow were still mostly, or at least partly, clothed, though good fur cloaks, fine shirts and trews had gone into packs and on backs.

Out of nowhere, the last of the battlefield gleaners had arrived; the local villagers and hunters who had hidden during the battle and hoped that the conquerors were not the Saxons. Urien sent out men to meet each little group as it arrived and struck a bargain. Now they were cleaning up the battlefield, stripping the corpses of the least rags, piling them up for burning. This, of course, would disappoint the ravens, who were gorging themselves and berating the humans for stealing their food from under their beaks. If it had not been that they were Saxons, the bodies would have been given at least a modicum of dignity. It had not been so long ago that the tribes here, the little kingdoms had been constantly skirmishing with one another, for the death of Uther, the High King's father, had had them all vying for ascendancy.

"I pity them," said Lancelin, as he walked up to stand beside her. "I do. It seems so unfair, to have followed their chieftains so far in the dead of winter, on the promise of land and more, to end like this."

She shrugged. "I don't think about it. I think about our people, who had to hide in the forest, who would have suffered greatly had the Saxons gotten this far, who did nothing to deserve an army come to make them thralls. If they did not think about ending like this, these Saxons, then they were fools. And if they did and came anyway, then they were doubly fools." She turned to look at him, a strand of hair blowing across her eyes until she moved it impatiently out of the way. "They will not come here again, I think, or at least not for a long time. And since they know that the High King himself is not here, they will know that it does not require the High King's presence on the field of battle to be defeated."

"True enough," Lancelin replied. They had all managed to clean themselves of the filth of battle by now, and she noticed that his hair had a touch of gold in it. A little Saxon blood? That might account for the pity. "That is a good thing, but I do not think it will keep them quiet for long. They are growing desperate. Arthur is pressing them hard."

"Was, you mean." She shrugged. "He has a new bride. That will keep him home a season or two. The Saxons said as much around their fires. They may be less desperate if they are left alone. I think the queen is like to wish to keep him at her side, and he is like to stay there until he has himself an heir again, at least."

Lancelin made a sour face. "And the new bride may keep me from court for longer than that. She does not like me, nor does she like my faith. I cannot say I care for her, nor hers."

Gwen did not ask why there should be dislike, and he did not offer. She only replied, "The High King, I have heard, is accustomed to keeping his Companions close. A man might abide by the crochets of a lady for a time, but he grows impatient for his old comrades. I do not think that any woman will change that for long."

Again, he made a wry face. "Perhaps. This one also has the Christ priests hiding behind her skirts. Thus, it is difficult to predict. Arthur wishes these men to support him; their followers grow more numerous with every year."

She wanted to ask why, but she refrained. Instead, she shrugged, because this gave her an opening to drop some hints about Medraut without actually telling what she had pledged to stay silent about. "Then Prince Medraut will find himself unwelcome, I think. He is the son of a sorceress, and the Druids are more welcome at Lot's court than the Christ-men. The High King may find himself poised between pleasing the queen's priests and pleasing the prince, and I think that he will choose in her favor in that."

"I had heard the prince had come and gone before my arrival." Lancelin eyed her with speculation. "Why did he not remain to fight?"

A hundred answers danced on the tip of her tongue; she chose the most polite. "Business more urgent sent him to the court." She explained about the murder of Anna Morgause by her own sons. Lancelin stared at her in horrified fascination.

"I know Gwalchmai well. His temper has often been his bane, but this . . . it seems impossible. Is this widely known?" he asked after a moment.

"I think not," was her reply. "I think Medraut intends to tell the King only that she is dead and not at whose hands. After all, the ones who murdered her are Arthur's Companions. This would put him in a difficult position."

Lancelin looked pained. "He should always choose justice over . . ."

"Convenience?" she suggested. "Friendship? Expediency?" She snorted. "And I think King Lot would not be pleased to have his sons haled up to answer for their mother's murder, since he has not pursued this himself."

"Walk with me, warrior?" Lancelin replied, looking about for a moment to see if there was anyone near.

Warrior? And not lady . . . There was a brief tinge of regret in her,

that he had named her the former and not the latter. This was not the
first time that a young man had regarded her so. It seemed that she
could be one or the other . . . but not both. Like women's magic, the
more she took up the sword, the farther she went from the path her
sisters had taken. The twinge went deeper for a moment, almost a
stab of pain, as if something had been cut from her. Then she squared
her shoulders and accepted it. So be it. This must have been the same
choice Braith had made, and it was not a bad one. And at least he
treated her as the seasoned warrior she was and not as the stripling
she resembled. She was listened to with attention and respect by the
war chiefs. Her ruse in this latest campaign had brought her praise.
It was very likely that when her father went to the Summer Country
and Cataruna's husband took the throne, she would be his favored
war chief and advisor. She did not want a throne, but she did want
respect. And freedom.

Perhaps giving up the notion of a lover, and womanly things, was
not so great a thing to sacrifice for freedom.

"Surely, Companion," she replied, and the two of them walked
slowly away from the charnel field, facing away from the piles of naked bodies and the feasting ravens, moving slowly and obliquely in
the direction of the camp.

"You seem more familiar than most with Lot of Orkney and his
brood."

She nodded, being careful where she stepped, both literally and
metaphorically. "My youngest sister went to foster with Anna Morgause when my mother died. That was about the time of the birth of
the High King's sons."

She turned her head slightly and saw him make a calculation.
"There is often a handfasting in such cases," he said cautiously.

"And there is in this one." She said nothing more. He was intelligent. She would see how intelligent.

"Ah." He waited some time for her to elaborate, and when she did not, he nodded thoughtfully. "You are fond of her, this sister?"

"There is no love between us," she said, the words coming from her mouth before she could stop them. *Curse it. Ah, well. I shall never make a courtier.*

He nodded again. "In that case . . . I would be in your debt if you can tell me what you *can* of the Orkney brood. For while I hold Gwalchmai my friend, and there is no sweeter-natured man than Gwynfor, I have never met Medraut, Gwalchafed is as hot-tempered as Gwalchmai with none of his brother's virtues, and as for Agrwn, the less said the better."

Gwen pondered this for a moment. "Well," she said carefully, "I had very little to do with any of the brothers but Medraut. He is crafty, cunning, and exceedingly intelligent. He can convincingly feign whatever he thinks will bring him the most advantage. He is much like his mother in that he will use any craft or guile to get what he wants. And there is only one person I have ever seen him exert himself to benefit."

"That would be Medraut himself, I think?" Lancelin's face was quiet, and thoughtful. "I think he will find himself very much at odds with the queen." He nodded decisively. "Thank you, warrior. You have given me a great deal to consider."

With that, they reached the camp and separated. She did not envy Lancelin, returning to a court that evidently contained a queen with an uncertain temper, and Medraut, as well as whatever other factions were simmering.

Not in the least.

Chapter Fifteen

Gwen returned to a life of work and solitude.

There was absolutely no doubt in her mind that she was needed. There was no doubt in her mind that she was, as she had always wanted to be, respected. Her father's men were accustomed to her now, and they took no more thought of her being female and looking strangely young than they did of her father's gray hairs. It was only when they were among strangers that they seemed to realize it again; now that they were home again, everything went back to normal

Which meant that Gwen sent her scouts out to patrol the borders, keeping their skills sharp. Any that had good reasons to bide, she found other work for and replaced them. And she herself served as Caradoc's personal bodyguard when he went out to look over the lands or stood behind her father when he welcomed strangers. When she was not doing that, she was hunting, and when she was not hunting, she was training.

On the whole, she preferred to wake early, work to exhaustion, and fall into bed at night. So long as she did that, she did not think too much about how narrow and solitary that bed was, nor how she had no fast friend among the men or the women either in whom she could confide.

Rarely, very rarely, she would watch Cataruna and Gynath with their heads together over something and wonder what it would have been like if Little Gwen had been her friend instead of her enemy . . . after all, there was really no reason why they should have been rivals. They didn't want the same things and really never had. But then she would shake that off and go on about her business; she had neither the time nor the energy to waste on fantasies. And the more she could put Little Gwen out of her mind, the happier she was. Presumably she was queening it at Lot's table, since rumor put Morgana somewhere about Celliwig, and she would be the only woman of rank there now. With luck, that would be enough for her.

Spring came and went with no sign of the Saxons making any more trouble, which was just as well since there was more than enough trouble in the South to make eyebrows rise.

King March of Kerrow . . .

It seemed that the Saxons were not the only ones who were interested in the High King's obsession with his new wife (one could scarcely call her a "bride" at this point). Now, Lot was a sly snake and not to be trusted, but March was an entirely different cut altogether. If you were the sort—like King Lleudd—who held that fidelity to one's oaths was of the highest importance, then March was as treacherous as they came. Not only did he seem to regard his oaths to the High King as of importance only so long as they were of benefit to him, he seemed to regard all oaths in the same light.

Add to that, so far as Gwen could tell from the reports of others, the man was mad.

He had a temper that he did not even try to govern. Not only had he slain messengers and even the High King's Companions when a rage was on him, he had killed dozens of his own warriors.

And now, for reasons best known only to him—or out of sheer insane spite—he had raised an army and was marching on Arthur. The fact that he was going to have to cross either lands holding fealty to Lleudd (who was not going to allow it) or Saxon holdings did not seem to matter to him.

Gwen studied the maps alongside her father and his war chiefs. "I had rather that March wore himself out against the Saxons," Lleudd growled. "A pox on the man! And a pox on whatever demon sired him! No sane man would act as he does."

Much to Gwen's pleasure, on the other side of the table was Arthur's Companion Lancelin. True to his prediction, he was staying far from the High King's court at Celliwig to escape the jealous regard of the queen. Lleudd had welcomed him with his knowledge of warfare with pleasure, and his self-effacing nature ensured that the other war chiefs were not made to feel that they had been put aside. She regarded him with pleasure not only because she enjoyed his company but also because his respect for her reinforced her own position among even those who knew her. Perhaps she was finally overcoming those too youthful looks.

Though without a doubt, wherever she was, Little Gwen was taking every advantage of the apparent youth they shared.

"If that is truly what you want, my lord King," Lancelin ventured, "I do not think that March can win against your men and especially not against your chariots. There are plenty of places along the way where the ground would be ideal for them."

"But the loss of a single man to that fool is one man too many," Lleudd replied. "Be sure the Saxons are watching this with greedy pig eyes, still smarting from the last defeat we handed them. If we engage March, they will be on us when the battle is past and we are spent and exhausted." He looked around the table, and his other war chiefs nodded.

"He probably will not fight the Saxons," Lancelin said, after staring at the maps a while longer. "He will probably bribe them to let him pass. It is what I would do."

Gwen smirked. She couldn't help herself. "Perhaps we can find a way to trigger that famous temper," she suggested. "Even if the Saxons accepted reparation rather than killing him themselves, they might ruin him with weregild."

The idea of March finding himself forced to pay a heavy weregild in addition to a bribe made the other war chiefs chuckle a little. But Gwen had more to say at this point.

"I have a thought about keeping him from trying to cross our lands," she continued. "Look here—" she pointed at the map. "This is where he will have to make the decision whether to bring his army through our land or to treat with the Saxons. We need to make the choice easier for him, but by not opposing him at all."

Lancelin looked at her quizzically. "Why would you say that?" he asked.

She smirked. "Because March is—" She *almost* said "a man" but quickly modified it to "—like to a bull. Wave a red rag at it in the form of armed opposition, and he *will* rush at it. We have a choice ourselves; we can send him across Saxon lands, save *our* men and join *our* force with the High King's, and the two will crush him. Or we can take the chance that he will defeat us, pillage our lands, then attack Arthur. So we do not present him with visible opposition but rather make it unprofitable for him to try to cross our land."

"Unprofitable?" Lleudd looked at his daughter in puzzlement.

"See here?" She pointed at an area of flat land. "My dear brother-by-marriage is a bard and a Priest, and Cataruna is a trained Lady. I think that between them they can persuade the waters to rise here and make that a marsh for as long as we need it to be so. Faced with a swamp, I think March will take the Saxon road."

They all stared at the map. "It seems the coward's way . . ." Peder said, doubtfully.

"Not if, when we are sure of him, *our* army joins that of Arthur," her father replied, decisively. "It is merely postponing the fight and choosing our ground. Only a fool fights a battle going up a hill."

Gwen nodded, grateful that he had thrown his support behind her.

Lancelin studied the map, rubbing his chin, but he said nothing, neither for nor against the plan. That disappointed her a little, but in the end it was King Lleudd's decision and no one else's.

Which meant, since this was her idea, she needed to have speech with Cataruna.

Ifan and Cataruna had their own room, as did Gynath and Caradoc; two new rooms had been made by the simple expedient of partitioning off two spaces side by side at the end of the Great Hall where the entrance to the king's solar and the room they had all shared as girls was. Now you passed through Gynath's room to get to the door that led to what had been the girls' room, which now belonged to Cataruna. Gwen had the smaller space, not much bigger than the bed, but she didn't need much space. Cataruna often sought privacy in that sanctuary while Bronwyn watched her children. But it was in the Great Hall that Gwen found her sister and brother-by-marriage .

Cataruna was sewing, and when Gwen explained what she had in mind, her sister pinched the bridge of her nose between thumb and forefinger and made a face. "I mislike meddling with the land—"

"I mislike having King March's men come across it, love," said Ifan, as he put aside the tuning pegs he was carving. "I mislike seeing herds slaughtered and farms laid waste. March is unpredictable and not entirely sane. There is no telling what the King of Kerrow is like to do."

Cataruna's brows furrowed for a moment, then her face cleared. "As Lady of the Fields, if I hear the Lord of the Forest urging protection for our people, I think it would be wise of me to heed his words." They beamed at one another, and Gwen felt a twinge of envy as well as of relief.

"But can you do this?" Gwen wanted to know. She hesitated. "The place is often marshy and soft. But—"

"Alone, no, but with Ifan, Bronwyn, and Gynath, yes." Cataruna smiled at her. "Well, find us some swift horses, and I'll find Bronwyn. We will need them to get there before March's army does."

Gwen grinned at Ifan. "I thought bards lived for epic battles to make songs about."

Ifan snorted but did not comment. Gwen left them making preparations and headed for the paddock.

She would not be using Rhys or Pryderi. Both of them were ideal for scouting, with great endurance, agility, and intelligence, but not much speed. To get to the right place before King March and his army did, they needed only speed and endurance.

They needed five horses out of the king's herd used by his messengers. They were ugly as mongrel dogs, stupid as stones, and uncomfortable to ride; you would *never* dare to leave one unattended or it would run or wander off, and no few of them were as skittish as ferrets, but they had a ground-eating lope that they could hold from dawn to dusk with minimal rest.

She picked out five with relatively even tempers and ordered them saddled and bridled, speeding things up by taking care of the fifth one herself.

Ifan shook his head in dismay as he brought a small pack and traveling harp to the paddock where the five horses were tied up to the fence. "My back will curse you for this, Gwenhwyfar."

"Your back isn't the part of you that I am worried about," Gwen replied without thinking and then blushed as he roared out a laugh. "I meant your *hands*, brother!"

"I'm sure you did." He was still snickering when Cataruna and Bronwyn arrived, both looking resigned when they saw the horses awaiting them. Then he sobered. "However my back will complain, I will endure it."

It was not only Ifan's back—and rump—that were complaining when they reached their goal. It was worth it, though. March's army was not in sight. After a few hours of rest, Gwen took it on herself, while Ifan, Cataruna, and Bronwyn made their preparations, to ride out as fast and hard as she could to the west, taking two of their mounts with her in order to change them out and keep them all relatively fresh. March's army was not within a day's hard ride, which meant they were not within three to four days' of the border yet.

She and the horses were weary when she rode back to the campsite. She had carefully chosen a spot hidden away from casual view, like her old favorite nutting spot, in a copse tangled with nettles and raspberry bushes, and she had instructed Ifan on how to further conceal the camp. He had done a fairly good job—not nearly as good as she would shortly but not at all bad for someone who had only made hunting camps before this. If she had not known they were there, she probably would not have spotted them.

There was just enough room in there for the horses, but since she now knew that March's army was quite far off, it would be safe to move them and hobble them where they could browse. Her three were tired enough that they would probably not cause any trouble, at least, not for a while.

She whistled the signal that they had all agreed on and was rewarded with the sight of Ifan popping out into the clear and waving at her.

"How far?" he asked, when she was in hearing distance.

"Far enough that we can finish the work and be gone," she replied, dismounting with a wince. How the messengers weren't crippled, riding these boneracks, she could not imagine. "How near are you three to being ready?"

Ifan grinned and ran his hand over the top of his head. Gwen was struck, once again, by what an odd sort of fellow he was. He looked as if he had been put together from the gods' leftovers. His hands seemed to be too long for the rest of him, and they were very graceful, which was at odds with the rest of his body, which was gangly and awkward, like an adolescent's. His chin stuck out like the prow of a boat, his brow was almost too broad, his hair was so coarse and perpetually tangled it could have come from the mane of a wild pony, and even his eyes were strange, one blue, one brown. Yet those hands could charm the most amazing music from any instrument he picked up, and as for his ability to tell a tale or create a song, well, it left his listeners spellbound.

"Cataruna can do anything if she puts her mind to it," he said with admiration. "Of course, you chose the right place, she tells me." He waggled his eyebrows at her. "Mind you, we're going to be right miserable before she is finished."

Gwen was not certain she wanted to hear the rest, but Ifan told her anyway.

"She's calling the rains. They should be here soon. And now that you are here," he added with a smirk, "We can call the waters."

Cataruna had spent the time while Gwen was gone in preparing her ground, creating a ritual circle by cutting into the turf and peeling it up, setting in a stone for an altar, and four more at cardinal points.

As directed, Gwen took her place at the southernmost stone; Ifan and Cataruna took west and east respectively, leaving Bronwyn with the north. And from that moment on, once Cataruna cast the boundaries of the circle itself to seal the power in, it was unlike any ceremony Gwen had ever taken part in before.

While Ifan played a small hand-drum, he and Cataruna chanted in a language that was nothing like anything that Gwen knew. The words sounded as if she *ought* to recognize them, but she didn't; she did, however, get the sense that she knew the gist of what they were chanting without knowing the words.

It was vaguely disconcerting. After a while, she decided that they must be using one of the secret languages of the Druids, a tongue much older than the one Gwen knew.

As for the sense of what they were chanting—

They were begging the waters to rise to the surface and cover the land here. Begging the gods to allow this to take place, and asking the waters to remain this way for two fortnights.

This was not an exercise of power as such. This was more like going to an ally and asking for help.

At least that was how it felt to Gwen.

She began to lose herself in the chanting, and although it was broad daylight, she began to feel as if she were walking in a dream. A silvery mist crept over the valley, seeming to form from nothing and, in defiance of the bright sunlight, growing thicker by the moment. Soon it had closed in around them and rose to obscure the sky and the sun. Tiny sparks of glittering color hung suspended in it, winking gold and green. Each time she blinked, she got glimpses of . . . something else scuttling through the mist, just out of view. Something, or rather multiple things, just out of the corner of her eye, that vanished when she turned to look fully at them. She didn't get enough of a look at any of these things to have said successfully what they were, but she did know that they weren't, and had never been, human.

And she started to feel things from them; not all of them were particularly friendly. They weren't inimical to the four of *them*, but as Gwen listened to the chanting, she understood that Ifan and Cataruna were striking a bargain with these creatures: For as long as the waters stood above the ground here, they were being given leave to do what they willed with any human (save the four of them) who tried to cross that they could catch and hold.

She shuddered a little; at first there was no acknowledgment from the creatures, but then, between one moment and the next, the circle was surrounded by them.

Their shapes faded in and out, ghostly and transparent at one moment, solid in the next. Nearest were the Gwragedd Annwn, the Ladies of the Lake, golden-haired and so fair of face that Gwen felt utterly coltish and rough hewn in their presence. Small wonder that they came; they were the guards and guardians of the Ladies at the Cauldron Well and were surely on speaking terms with Cataruna. They were tall, as tall as Ifan, and looking on them, Gwen suddenly wondered if the white-gold hair she shared with her sisters and Eleri had come not from Saxon blood but from these creatures. There were more of the Ladies than there were men of their kind, and bards were full of tales of love and marriages between their race and that of mortal men. They were said to live in their own villages at the bottoms of lakes and ponds, guarding some of the entrance points between the world of mortals and Annwn, the Otherworld. One of the High King's two famous swords was said to have been given to him by them . . . though Eleri had always said, no, it was not the sword that had been given but the sheath, which was by far the more important of the two. The sword Caliburn signified only because it had been Uther's, and been driven into a stone by the Merlin—only the lawful heir to Uther could pull it out. But the sheath—Caliburn's sheath— was said to be able to heal any wound. And it would make a great deal of sense for such a thing to have come from the hand of one of the Gwragedd Annwn.

Their faces were solemn, a little stern, and all their attention was on Cataruna and Ifan. Gwen was just as pleased. She did not want the attention of the Folk of any kind. Yet she could not help it, feeling an odd kinship with these creatures that only grew the more she was in their presence. If they felt it as well—

One of them cast a sidelong glance at Gwen, who felt warmed and chilled at the same time. Then she returned her gaze to Cata- · runa. Cataruna, who shared Eleri's blood. Blood that, Gwen was now sure, was shared also with these ladies of the Fae. It was to this blood, it must be, that she, her mother, and Little Gwen, owed their curi- ously youthful looks . . .

And it was Cataruna's blood they had answered to, not whatever she and Ifan had chanted.

Equally lovely were the Swan Maids and Men, who flocked close beside them. Again, there were a half dozen of the Maids and only two of the Men; among the Folk of Annwn, there were often such disproportionate numbers. They were silent and stayed farther back in the mist, their golden eyes glittering and betraying their difference from humanity.

But near to Gwen were a pair of the Ceffyl Dwr, the Water Horses, who were more mischievous than nasty. Initially appearing as a pair of tangle-maned black stallions, they caught her looking at them, and in a blink she found herself staring at youths who initially seemed very handsome and who both winked at her as if they knew her. Looking closer at them, she noted their water-weed-entangled hair and hooves instead of feet.

They grinned at her, and one of them made slight, but suggestive movements with his hips. She flushed a little, and looked away, and heard them laugh.

Deeper in the mist, she also got glimpses of what might have been Nykers, although it was hard to tell. There was something out there, dark and ugly and hunched over, with a hunger about it and a malevolence. It might have been Nykers or it might have been Groac'h, the females of the same sort: ugly, evil creatures who made a habit of snatching folks and drowning them. Some said they were the spirits of the drowned themselves, others that they were the dark cousins of the Gwragedd Annwn.

Even the Gwragedd Annwn, for all their beauty, were known for being chancy to bargain with. But they would at least stop to bargain with you; the others would pull you under before you even knew they were there.

And so they came, flocking thicker and thicker about, as Ifan and Cataruna chanted, only staring, never answering, until at last one of the Lake Ladies *did* step forward and reply in the same tongue, in a voice like a nightingale.

Ifan and Cataruna stopped chanting, listened, and then Cataruna replied.

The Lady spread her arms wide and sang again. Ifan looked startled. Cataruna, speculative.

The Lady repeated herself. Gwen concentrated as hard as she could, trying to pull sense from the words. When the Lady was done, she stared across the circle at Cataruna. "She wants to make a marsh of this place *permanently?*" Gwen spoke in hushed tones, as the cold mist collected around them, chilling her.

Cataruna nodded, but it was Ifan who replied. "She says that we mortals have pressed the water peoples hard. She wants a grant of this land and the right for the water folk to do as they will here for as long as Eleri's blood flows in our people." Cataruna took a deep breath. "I told her that I have not the right to make such a bargain, for I am not a war chief, only the Lady of our land. But I told her that you can."

Gwen considered that, as all of them, mortal and fae, watched her expectantly. "I'm not likely to give land away, for all that Father's given me the right to. I'll be having a bargain of this." Inside, she shook at her own temerity, daring to bargain with the Other Folk. But they didn't respect anyone who didn't bargain, at least, not in the tales. Cataruna repeated her words in the language of Annwn. The Lady nodded, as if she had expected this.

Gwen considered every possible way in which she could phrase her bargain. The good part was that this area hadn't been claimed for farming, and any herders who were using it could come to King Lleudd for other grazing lands. But the point was, if she closed this— treaty, she supposed it must be—she'd be opening this place to who knew what sorts of dangerous creatures. And even if, as some claimed, the beings of Annwn were not fae at all, but just mortals with a great deal of the Gift and the Power and some ugly odd shapes . . . well, that made them all the more dangerous.

"Tell the Lady . . ." She faced the speaker squarely and looked into her cold eyes, the color of lake water before a storm, and she did not, not for a single moment, doubt that the Folk of Annwn were not of the world she knew. "Lady, this is the bargain I will be having. By the right my father, King Lleudd, gave to me as a war chief and able to make grant of land, I give you and yours this valley, to be covered with water and made your own. In return I will be having this: No creature that lives here is ever to *take* a child, a youngling, a maiden, or a woman. No creature that lives here is ever to *take* a man that comes in peace, with no ill will toward my people or those of Annwn, nor those that pledge to the High King."

There was muttering behind her, discontent from those dark shapes that would not let themselves be seen. Anger, even, of a sort that put the hair up on the back of her neck. Nevertheless, she continued. "But for those that would trouble my people, and those that will not pledge to the High King, or those that are oathbreakers of that pledge, whether they are an army bringing upon them war and sorrow or merely thieves and rogues who would bring them loss and grief, should they put so much as one toe in your waters, they are yours. Take them, drown them in deep waters, harry them across the marsh, drive them mad with fear and despair. That is my bargain. Take it, or not."

Cataruna repeated all she had said, but the Lady had already nodded as if she understood it all, and turned back to the others.

Gwen waited patiently, feeling colder by the moment, as the otherworldly creatures conferred. The mist roiled darkly around all of them now, and the sounds of their voices rose and fell. Both Cataruna and Ifan looked a little bewildered, as if they had not truly expected this to happen.

Well, and I cannot blame them. Who would? She had never seen these beings even once in her life before—though both of them surely would have, the Ladies, at least. But the others? Who did she know had ever confessed to seeing a Swan Maid or a Water Horse? And to see so many of them . . .

And then to have the temerity to bargain with them?

She reminded herself of who she was doing this for. And why.

Finally, the muttering stopped. The Lady turned back to them and sang. Gwen did not need Cataruna's translation. It was a bargain.

She stooped, seized a handful of the soil at her feet, and took a little knife from a sheath in her boot—not iron or steel, which was anathema to these folk, but a flint knife she used for skinning game, for it was easier to keep at a razor edge. She cut her thumb across and bled onto the handful of dirt, squeezing it tight. "My blood upon it," she said, binding the bargain.

The Lady stepped to the edge of the circle, cut her own thumb with a knife very like Gwen's, and added her blood to the handful of soil. Gwen noted absently that her blood was as red as any mortal's, and not blue, or green, or starshine.

Gwen stooped down again and patted the handful of soil into place, opening the circle. The Lady clapped her hands, the mist swirled around them so thickly that for a moment Gwen could not see anything at all—

And then they were gone.

And her boots were beginning to get very damp. She looked down, and saw that water was rising around them.

Fast.

"Back to camp!" Ifan said, as the mist thinned, but only in the direction of their campsite. Gwen had no wish to argue with him, for the water was already at her instep and rapidly rising to her ankle. All four of them ran up the way that had opened in the mist and did not stop until they were well out of it.

Only then did they pause and look back down at the valley.

For as far as the eye could see, it was covered in that thick mist, which the setting sun was now turning to gold. There were things moving in it. She shivered. She pitied March's men if they did try to cross here.

Cataruna and Ifan looked at each other, numbly. Bronwyn shook her head. "There's more moving here than we reckoned on," the old woman said.

That night, the storm Ifan and Cataruna had called broke, and Gwen had cause to regret that she had not put some form of provision against *that* in her bargain.

Not that there was any way of knowing whether a bargain with water spirits would have any effect on a storm.

They had done their best to prepare the camp for the onslaught, but there was only so much shelter that branches and stacked bracken could give against the sort of storm that eventually arrived. This was not a country for caves, and they had been traveling too light even for a bit of canvas.

When the storm hit, it did so as a full tempest. Torrential rain, lightning, thunder, wind . . . it would have been impressive within the walls of Castell y Cnwclas. It was a nightmare out in the open.

They had gotten the four horses into the little clearing, and because Cataruna had a foreboding, they had tied and hobbled them so that they could scarcely move, then made crude blinders and tied them over the horses' heads. It was a good thing they had done so, or they would have been kicked to bits, trampled, and, had they survived that, found themselves without mounts the next day. As it was, the poor beasts whimpered and moaned and fought the hobbles until they were exhausted. Based on Cataruna's foreboding, Gwen had opted for "sturdy" over "space" when it came to the shelter. It was a lean-to made of branches and many layers of bracken, and the four of them could barely squeeze into it.

They had been sitting around their fire, gnawing the last of the meat off the bones of the rabbits Gwen had shot, when they heard the storm coming. As it approached from the southwest, the steady growling of thunder was like a great beast in the distance. The closer it came, the more the horizon lit up with so many lightning strikes it looked as if it were crawling on dozens of legs toward them.

Down in the valley, the mist still had not lifted, and there were strange, dim lights moving in it. Those lights actually brightened in response to the coming storm. And strangest of all, as a wind sprang up, strengthening until their cloaks were blowing straight away from their bodies, the mist remained, unchanged, and unmoving.

At that point, with the branches of the trees tossing wildly, the horses fighting their bonds, the fire actually blew out. That was when they all scrambled into the tiny shelter and wrapped their cloaks tightly around themselves. Gwen and Ifan put themselves on the outside corners and grabbed the branches, determined to hold onto the thing no matter what.

Then the storm hit.

Rain pounded down onto them quite as if someone had emptied a river on their heads. The wind was terrible, and it was a good thing that Ifan and Gwen were holding to the shelter, or it would have blown away. There was so much thunder, and the wind was roaring so, it would not have been possible to hear a shout in your ear. All Gwen could do was duck her head, keep a good grip on the pitiful lean-to, and hope they would not all be struck by lightning.

The gods themselves must have concocted such a storm. Surely she heard the Wild Hunt out there, the hooves of their monster steeds pounding anything that got in the way as flat as cloth. They were all soaked within moments even with the shelter. All it accomplished was to keep the worst of the rain and wind off.

Before long, the pounding and howling and cold numbed her into a state of unthinking endurance. She couldn't manage to put a single coherent thought together, and all that mattered was the slightly warmer place where all their bodies met. How long that went on, she could not have even guessed.

Then, at some point, the storm passed. The wind dropped. And although they could not have managed to separate their tangled limbs to attempt a fire, the warmth of their combined bodies finally dried out their cloaks enough that they began to doze.

Gwen woke with the birdsong of false dawn. Trying not to wake the others, she got herself loose to check on the horses. She was too tired to really think clearly, but she would not have been in the least surprised to have found them dead.

The poor things were in a sad state, but they were not dead. The crude head coverings had been blown away, and they had all fought their bonds so hard that they were now in a state of head-hanging exhaustion. She released some of their hobbles, gave them each a couple of handfuls of grain from the saddlebags, which they lipped up dispiritedly, and felt their legs to see if they had damaged themselves.

She could feel that the muscles had been strained, enough that it would be a good idea to give them a couple days of rest, but there were no sprains. With a sigh of disbelief at their luck, she crawled out of the open center of the brush-tangled copse to see what the rest of the world looked like.

And gaped at what she found.

Where there had been a flat valley, there was now a marsh. Not just *water;* she had expected water. No, this was a marsh, one that looked as if it had been there for generations.

Huge reed beds separated by stretches of open water spread out before her, out to the horizon. Here and there a was a hummock where a few trees and bushes hung on; the reeds and marsh plants in most places were as high or higher than a man's head. Mist threaded its way along the water, hung in banks in other places. Ten feet in, and you would be lost and disoriented. If fog closed in so you couldn't see the stars or the sun, you would never even know what direction you were going. It was a place that warned you, just by the look of it, that it would be full of sucking mires and unexpected sinkholes. You'd never find a secure, dry place for more than a couple of men to sleep. You'd never find the wood to make fires, or a place to make them. And that was all aside from the supernatural dangers hiding in those mists. It would be insane to take an army across that.

Of course, King March *was* insane, and he might try.

He wouldn't get far, though. The border here was safe from him.

Gwen set about finding deadfall for a fire, then when she had piled up enough at the entrance to their little copse that the others could remake the camp while she was gone, she went hunting for some breakfast.

There was a great advantage to suddenly being on the edge of a marsh. There were fish in it, and they all seemed hungry. She fashioned a fish spear from an arrow, scattered some crumbs over the surface, and set to work. By the time the sun was a thumb's breadth above the horizon, she had enough to satisfy the most ravenous of appetites. And she had the shrewd idea that she had been "helped" in this, for she thought she had caught a glimpse of amused eyes among the reeds.

She wasn't going to argue about it. Given the size of this marsh, the water spirits were going to have plenty of room for some time to come. It was a good thing that Ifan was a bard, though. He would know to be careful of coming down here, even avoid it altogether. The Lake Ladies were a mixed sort, and there were those who would not hesitate to steal a bard from his lawful wife and take him down to their dwelling beneath the waters.

She brought the fish back up to a camp of people already packing to leave, though a fire had been started and twigs prepared to spit whatever she brought. She raised an eyebrow.

"I had thought to stay and rest the horses," she offered.

Ifan took the fish from her, and he and Bronwyn began cleaning and gutting them, as Cataruna shook her head. "We can walk them if we need to, and make our way slowly back home, but I think we should put some distance between us and—that," she said, thought-fully. "Yes, they are feeling well-inclined towards us now, but—"

"Besides, we have raised a great deal more power than either of us expected to," added Ifan, with a frown, as he set a fish to cook over the fire. "One could liken it to setting down a chest of gold and silver and spilling it open in the village square. Some will come to admire, but word will spread."

She blinked. She had not considered that. "And what comes to look will not be bound by the bargain I made with the water spirits," she said, slowly. "Which could be equally bad for March *and* for us." She straightened her back. "On the whole . . . I think a slow walk back for a day or two would be of great benefit to all of us."

"Healthier than remaining here," said Bronwyn.

Chapter Sixteen

Lleudd's war chiefs and captains sat around his hearth fire in varying states of relaxation. Gwen had already recounted what she had done to Peder and her father privately and had gotten praise for her quick thinking. Now she had been asked to tell the tale at the hearth for the rest, who were all relaxing because there was no longer an immediate threat from March. Relaxing because of what she had done.

Supper was over, the mead was being poured out by the young squires, and Gwen had to hide a smile when she realized from the taste that Eleri's special recipe had survived intact. The fire smoked just enough to drive the insects away and imparted just enough warmth to be comfortable. This was an occasion for a more . . . bardic retelling.

So she obliged, as best she could. At the end, King Lleudd roared with laughter. "Well, my war chief daughter, I hope that you are content with *your* lands being the ones under water!"

That elicited laughter from the rest. "Will you be farming eels and frogs?" one of the others asked, straight faced. "I hear the Romans thought frogs right tasty, and I am partial to an eel pie."

"When you plant eels, do you plant 'em head first or tail first?" asked another.

Gwen smiled ruefully. War chiefs were expected to offer gifts, of course. And up until now she had mostly given things like ornaments, horses, or weapons. But land was always an option, and as Lleudd's daughter, she was entitled to a certain amount to hold for herself or give as rewards as long as it had not been granted to another.

"I am content with awarding the new guardians of that border with the land they are guarding, my lord King," she replied dryly. "If they prefer it being under water, well so do I."

The king laughed again, as did the rest of his chiefs. "Well said. And, yes, I approve, most heartily, of your decision." He looked around the fire at the men on his benches. They were all nodding too, even if one or two of them were doing so reluctantly.

"Also . . . if I were to give advice on this," she added cautiously, "I would say it were best to simply stay away from that marsh. While Cataruna thinks they are bound, and well bound, by the oaths they gave . . . the less traffic with the Folk of Annwn the better." *With the Folk of Annwn. With my mother's people? Does Father guess?* "I certainly have no plans to return there. Not even to see what March makes of the situation. He cannot pass there, that is all we need to know. That will force him through Saxon lands."

Now no one nodded reluctantly.

She realized, and not for the first time, that she was, always had been, and always would be one apart from the rest. Even those who had come up with her as pages and squires; she shared a level of camaraderie with them that never went farther than the battlefield and the camp. Though Lleudd had never shown any favoritism to her, she had still always been the king's daughter. Some had been jealous of that, some had been resentful, and even when she proved herself over and over, there had still been that distance of rank between them.

Even the handful of girls that had begun training with her had kept a wary distance, a distance that had only increased as most of them had decided to give up and try some other path. The only two who were left were chariot drivers, and she saw nothing of them.

Well, it was what it was.

The remainder of the talk centered on what to do when March moved toward the Saxon-held lands. Gwen listened but did not comment; this was not where she had any level of expertise. Everyone was agreed that he would at least try to buy his way to free passage. Some thought he might well try to ally with them.

"He would be very foolish not to try," Lancelin said, his big hands absently rubbing the silver band on his drinking horn. "And they would be equally foolish to fight him or reject such an alliance. Neither of them can afford a battle on two fronts, and the Saxons are somewhat weakened from the losses they took this winter." Lancelin's suggestions were very astute, however, and she found herself admiring his knowledge and skill all over again.

And . . . truth to tell . . . admiring him for himself. He was not a beautiful man, but she had never cared that much for beauty in a man. A quick mind, however, a good and even temper, a sense of humor—those were things she cherished and admired.

She was not the only female to find him attractive; he, however, did not seem to notice any of the women casting glances at him. Or if he did, he was feigning not to notice. She wondered if he had a love elsewhere.

If he did, she could not imagine that it would be at Arthur's court. No one she knew would be kept from the side of a lover just because the queen misliked his presence.

She regarded him across the hearth fire, and decided that he was probably heart whole. He didn't act as if he were pining for a love. If anything, he seemed relatively content with being here as Lleudd's

advisor and liaison. The only time she had heard him voice any discontent, it was because he was missing the fighting at Arthur's side.

*As for that fighting—pay attention. You are in charge of the scouts,
now.* That was the reward her father had given her. She, and no one
else, would be the one commanding all of the scouts, the saboteurs,
and outliers for whatever force was sent to aid the High King.

As she listened, she began to formulate some ideas. A few were
based around her ruse of "The White Apparition," but she had plenty
of others. March might very well know that "Gwenhwyfar" was a very
real, mortal human creature; she would have to determine that, first,
before she tried such tricks on his forces. But he would be fresh from
dealing with her "allies" of the Folk of Annwn; there were other ways
she could invoke "supernatural" terror among his men. The Saxons,
of course, knew about the White Lady; she would find herself a few
more of the woman warriors and recruit them to impersonate her. If
one White Phantom was terrifying, what if there were many haunting the dark?

And spies, of course. She needed spies. People in March's camp,
people in the Saxon camp.

*I wonder how much it would take to buy the ears of washerwomen
and camp whores?* If she could succeed in convincing them that when
this was over, they'd have a place, protectors, on the High King's
side . . .

More than that, she'd have to find places. And each one would
probably be different. There would be women who had gone to the
life because they had no other options, women who were captives
or near captives, women who liked the life, or at least, liked the sex
when they weren't afraid of being abused or beaten . . .

*I should talk to Bronwyn. Maybe Cataruna, too. Don't the Ladies
need servants, helpers?* It couldn't be impossible. *Bah. If I have to, I'll
make them my own retainers. And if they're the sort that are hot as cats*

*in heat, I'll get them money enough to go to a town and set themselves
up as courtesans.*

It would also enrage the Christ priests, she suspected, if they
found out about it. Well, that was not her problem, and she would
not make it the problem of the women. If she dealt with this properly,
no one would ever know who her spies were. But she really liked the
idea of the women as spies; women had the potential to go anywhere
and listen to anything in the camp. She was probably not the first person to think of doing this, but it was a new idea to *her,* which meant
it was likely to be a new idea to their enemies as well.

As for sabotage . . . well, she would think on that, as well.

Meanwhile, as the other war chiefs continued to talk, she was
making mental notes. Nothing was decided tonight, of course. They
would have to discover what March was doing. The High King would
have to decide what *he* was going to do. Then he would have to ask
for levies through Lancelin.

Would he ask Lot? Probably. And Lot would say "yes" and actually do nothing. But now all four of Lot's sons were with the High
King; whatever Medraut had told Arthur about how Anna Morgause had been murdered, all of it had been smoothed over somehow, for Lancelin had several times said that Gwalchmai, Agrwn,
and Gwynfor were still Arthur's Companions, and Gwalchafed was
absent only because he had wedded recently and taken up life in his
lady's lands.

And Medraut is still at court as well. Gwen pondered that, as she
pondered how the firelight made shadows on Lancelin's face. From all
that Lancelin had said, Medraut had made himself welcome there—
although, like Lancelin himself, Medraut was no favorite of Arthur's
queen. *Hardly surprising. She would be no favorite of Medraut's either.*
Lancelin had said nothing about Medraut being Arthur's son . . . perhaps Medraut himself had not made that openly known. But Arthur

had made him one of the Companions, and from the little Lancelin said, he was giving a good account of himself among them.

Was it possible he could have . . . reformed, somehow?

A nice dream. A viper does not cease to be a viper because it smiles.

In the absence of concrete information, the talk had devolved to mere man-gossip. The mead had made them mellow and sleepy; even Lancelin, who had drunk but sparingly of it, looked heavy lidded. She slipped away.

Only to have her arm seized once she was away from the benches.

It was Bronwyn.

"You are not thinking of using the Folk of Annwn—" she whispered urgently, drawing Gwen into the shadows. Gwen was startled.

"No!" She shook her head. "No, I had rather stay well clear of them. They are unchancy. And unreliable as well, if you listen to the tales that Ifan sings. Too often those in stories call upon them only to be unanswered or not answered in time. Too often they flit off elsewhere or turn on you because you gave them some unintended slight. No. Let them dwell in the new marsh and leave us be, and I will be content."

Bronwyn let out a deep sigh of relief. "I saw that you had that thinking look and—what were you thinking, then, that you did not tell the other chiefs?"

She was glad that the shadows hid her blushes, for she did not want to say that at least half the time she had been thinking about Lancelin. Instead, she explained her idea of using the camp followers among the Saxons and March's army as spies. Bronwyn heard her out.

"It could work," she said at last, "But better that we find some women among our people willing to go."

Gwen blinked. That had not occurred to her. "But—would—I thought—"

"Leave that to me," the old woman told her. "There are those we took from the Saxons who would dearly love a taste of revenge. There are those of the western lands who are shamed that March is rebelling against the High King. The Ladies favor the High King; there would be some among them, mayhap. And . . ." She chuckled. "I can think of one or two who would gladly do this for the sake of the means to set themselves up in luxury in a city. Not everyone thinks the height of all good things is a sheepcot, a flock, and a shepherd who cannot put two words together without 'baa' in them."

Gwen giggled a little. "I leave it in your hands, then," she said and was about to go to the room she now shared with no one when Bronwyn tugged again on her arm. "My girl, that Companion—I would give you good, sound advice."

She froze.

"There are men, a very few, who could look on a warrior, see the woman within, and remember the warrior. He is not one." Bronwyn's voice was steady. "He will see you as a warrior and a comrade or as a woman. Never both. It will be up to you to choose which he sees. And when you make that choice, remember, he will treat you as you have chosen."

Gwen went cold inside for a moment. Bronwyn was right. She knew that Bronwyn was right. It made her angry—at herself and at him. It made her sad with disappointment. It made her embarrassed. But that did not make it any less true.

She could go to her chest and dig out one of her gowns, let her hair loose, and go and act as Gynath had, back when they were younger. Make big eyes at him, hang on his words—yes, she could do all of that. And, yes, he would see her as a woman, and he might even find her attractive. And so he would treat her as a woman.

Even in her armor with her hair clubbed up, he would treat her as a woman.

And so would the other war chiefs.

All that she had worked for, all that she had built, would be gone. Her father would lose the war chief that she was becoming. Her sister would lose the steady guard and guardian for her own children. Caradoc would lose the captain she would be for him. And for what? So that she could play the fool over a man.

Or she could keep things as they were, and she would have the friendship and high regard of a man whose company she enjoyed. They would speak and act as equals. He would listen to her ideas with respect, criticize them if it was needed, teach her more of the ways of war.

It was only years of schooling herself, training herself, controlling herself, that kept her from raging, weeping or both. She knew that outside the tiny group of her family and Bronwyn, she was thought to be cold, unfeeling, and in no small part that was because she meant them to think of her in that way. In that first year of her training, when some of the older boys had bullied or snubbed her, and even some of the younger had sometimes tried to sabotage her with dirty tricks and things meant to put blame on her, she had pretended that there was no hurt, no loneliness, that nothing would mar the armor of her control. Now that was habit.

"I see," she was able to say, slowly. "Thank you for the warning, Bronwyn. You are . . . entirely right."

"I have lived a very long time, my dear," Bronwyn said, a little sadly. "I have seen many a girl throw over what she held dear for the sake of a trifle."

She patted Bronwyn's arm, glad that the old woman could not see the expression on her face. "This one will not," she said.

Then she went to her bed. She lay, staring into the darkness, an-

gry at fate for making her female, angry at herself for being so foolish, grateful to Bronwyn for seeing what she had been blind to, yet
angry with her too. There were bitter tears in the back of her throat
that she would not shed. Not now. Not ever. After all, what was she
weeping for? Nothing more important than that poppet that Gwenhwyfach had torn to bits all those years ago.

Gwenhwyfach—and what would *she* have done?

Put on the gown of, course, and thrown herself at Lancelin—

But she was not Gwenhwyfach, nor did she ever want to be. She
was herself. And even if that was a cold and lonely thing, it was what
she had wanted to be. Not "someone's wife." Not "someone's mother."
Herself, with her own honor, her own place, and her own path. She
owed nothing to anyone, save duty to her father.

It was comfort, if cold comfort.

She turned on her side and stared at the wall, sternly telling her
eyes that they must dry. Or rather, she stared at where the wall should
have been.

For at that moment, she felt that dizziness come upon her once
again, and where the wall was, there was dim light instead, light that
grew, and warmed, until she found herself staring into a fire-lit room,
and at the backs of two women.

One had white-blonde hair that streamed down her back to her
ankles. The other had raven locks that pooled on the floor. Both were
wearing nothing more than their hair.

They bent over what at first she took for a table; then she realized
that it was an altar, not a table. What there was upon it, she never got
a chance to see, for the blonde suddenly raised her head.

"Morgana," said Gwenhwyfach, in a voice so like her own that
Gwenhwyfar felt her breath catch. "we are overlooked."

The second also raised her head and turned slightly, staring straight into Gwen's eyes. And now Gwen felt her breath freezing in her throat.

"Well," Morgana said, her tone even and measured. "Blood will tell. Even untrained and on the Path of Iron, look who has found her way to our working."

Now Little Gwen turned. Her naked body was astonishingly beautiful, even overwritten as it was with runes painted in blood. And her face was Gwen's own, but contorted with a sneer.

"Spying, sister?" The sneer turned into a snarl. "Well, that will never happen again. And you will forget what you have seen,"

And something hot and red flashed between them, struck Gwen like a thunderbolt, and sent her tumbling down into darkness, her memories slipping between her fingers and running away like water.

***

Despite a near-crippling headache the next day, Gwen went grimly to work on her plans. Bronwyn found women as she had promised, and they were a varied lot. One had been a Saxon thrall and had lost her family to them and wanted nothing more than revenge. Two were very poor indeed and honest about their wish to be amply rewarded. "As well be swived by a mort'o lads an' come to a saft bed after as be swived by one an' come to a mud hut," was the calm and logical response of one. One was sent by the Ladies and remained silent about her reasons; since Cataruna vouched for her, Gwen accepted her without comment. What all of them had in common was that they were attractive, under no illusions as to what would happen to them as camp followers, and were as fierce in their desire that March and the Saxons be beaten as any of Arthur's Companions.

They did not need to remain in the camps long, much to Gwen's relief. She felt enough guilt about sending them in there in the first place.

"And you have no guilt about sending your scouts out to spy?" was Bronwyn's dry question, when she fretted aloud one day.

"Of course I do!" Gwen snapped. "But . . . this is different!"

Bronwyn raised an eyebrow. "So you see them as women and not as warriors."

Gwen opened her mouth to protest and shut it again. Because, yes, she did. And she felt great irritation that she did so. And yet— they were women. They were not warriors. They had not been trained as warriors.

But she was glad enough when they got what she needed and made their way back to her—the sure information that March had allied with the Saxons, rather than buying his way across their lands, and the combined forces intended to attack Arthur together.

Now she could concentrate on her real duties with a whole heart—or so she thought.

Gwen had not chopped wood like this since she had been a mere squire, but she needed to take out her temper on *something,* and splitting wood was less damaging than hurling pots against a wall and more satisfying than perforating a target with arrows. She swung the ax against her hapless targets with accuracy and fury. Every blow split a log. At this rate, the squires would not need to chop wood for a week.

The squires who had been assigned to this task had all taken one look at her face and fled. Everyone else had already heard the news and wisely were avoiding anywhere she was even rumored to be. The pile of neatly split logs grew, and her temper was eased not in the least. She was in a self-imposed circle of silence in which there was only the wood, the ax, herself, and her anger.

Finally the king himself came down to the yard, and sat on a stump, and waited. She could not remember him *ever* coming here before. But she knew herself well enough not to trust herself to speak right now, so she pretended that she had not noticed him there.

The ax handle was a comfort in her hand, and the steady *chunk* as it cleft each log was just as much of a comfort. This, at least, she could control. She had chosen to do this. No one had said "you must," or "you must not." No one had come to say "So-and-so would do this better, go tend to your horses." Yet it took her quite some time before she was able to get anything like words past the tightness in her chest and throat.

"It's not *fair*," she managed at last, the final word punctuated by the blow of the ax. She tried not to wail. She tried not to sound as if she was accusing Lleudd, whom she did not in the least blame.

"Indeed, it is not," King Lleudd agreed. "Very unfair. You have spent long days training your scouts. You work as an effective group, and without you, they will be less effective. They trust you; they will not trust another leader so much. You have proven yourself in battle. You should have been the one to lead and command them."

The ax thudded into another log. The two halves fell to either side of the chopping block. "Whoever this 'Kai' is, he cannot possibly know what they can do! I am not even sure he knows how to properly use scouts, much less my men!"

"He is the High King's foster brother, and no, he cannot know what they can do, nor do I think from what I have heard of him that he is a particularly good war chief." Lleudd sighed. "He is usually in charge of the squires and the court. He is not terrible . . . but he is not particularly good, either. At least they will not be misused. The High King fights with Roman tactics, and your men do not charge into battle like Saxons with no strategy. They will be just one more scouting troop among another dozen."

"But they will get no chance to use all the things we have worked out together," she said angrily. "They will get no chance to harry the Saxons as we did this winter."

"No, because Kai will think such things unnecessary. But at least, because you trained them, they will know to be clever. They will know how to fight with the Roman style that the High King uses." Lleudd sighed again, heavily. "I am sorry, my daughter. I am sorry that their command has been taken from you. But the High King prefers to use his own commanders."

"And the High King does not trust a female warrior," she said, bitterly. "He does not think such a one as I can command anything. Younger *men* than me have been put in command. Younger *men* than me are his warleaders." *Thunk.* The ax split another log. "He thinks that I am only a chief because I am your daughter, and he does not trust my ability."

"Probably not," King Lleudd agreed.

"And Lancelin did not see fit to argue for me." *Thunk.* That was another sore point. He spoke with her as if they were equals. He seemed to consider her a friend. He knew she was intelligent. And he had not spoken up for her.

"Possibly not. I cannot say. Possibly he did. Possibly he did not try because he did not want to remind the queen of his presence." Lleudd shifted his weight on the stump. "I do not know, because I was not there. It is hard for a young man when he is caught between a man and his wife."

She finally stopped and turned to face her father.

"Which makes him a coward?" she asked, angrily. "I had not thought him a coward."

"It makes him . . ." The King sighed. "It makes him a man torn. On the one hand, he knows what you can do, even if he did not consider himself your friend. Which, I believe, he does. He knows you are not only a good leader, he knows that you know your men as no one else, and you are always thinking of the best way to use them with the best outcome. And as your friend, he would desire to advance you. On the other hand, the one thing he desires above all else is to serve his lord, his king, and his friend. Someone he has known far longer than you. You have seen that with your own eyes."

Reluctantly, she nodded. She could tell; every moment he had been here, his heart had been with his king. She had been wrong in thinking him heart whole. He was a man driven by duty, and protective of his friends. He mistrusted the queen. There was nothing else that would have so great a part in his life. Not even, maybe, a lover.

"Perhaps, perhaps, there is also a touch of wariness there," Lleudd continued. "You bargained with the Folk of Annwn. You are being served by them, in a sense. You are known to be subject to the Sight at times. Most warriors are uneasy in the presence of magic. And, yes, the Merlin has served the High King for longer than Lancelin, but the Merlin has ever been secretive about his magic. Few have ever seen him actually use it."

Slowly, slowly, the king's calm reason overcame her fury. Tears started into her eyes, and she dashed them angrily away. "You are not uneasy in the presence of magic!"

"I was wedded to Eleri," he pointed out dryly. "I have a Lady for a daughter, a bard for a son-by-marriage. Even so, I have never seen the Folk of Annwn. No one I know has, until now. This is more than mere magic, my daughter. This is meddling with the Spirit Realms."

And this was her fault, how? "I didn't know they would come! I only wanted to make a swamp to last for a fortnight or two!" Her eyes burned, her stomach tightened. "They wanted to treat with *me*, not the other way around!"

"I know that." The king pointedly ignored her reddening eyes. "But . . . you are like your mother. You look much younger than your years. You are fair, and most of them are dark. And now this; it makes people wonder if you have the blood of Annwn in your veins yourself. Now, this is unfair. It is unjust. But it could have been predicted, I think."

She stared in unhappy outrage—and some guilt, for had she not thought these very things herself? "What can I do?" she asked, controlling herself with an effort. Again, she tried not to wail.

"First, we do not speak of the Folk of Annwn in your swamp. Your bargain means that they will not harry our people; likely will not show themselves."

She nodded. That was good sense. "You think maybe people will forget?"

He shook his head. "But we can put it about that it was Ifan they treated with, and I will say I granted *him* the lands you gave them. Only my war chiefs know the truth. Ifan is a bard. Everyone knows that the Folk of Annwn favor bards."

Again she nodded. "And—"

"And as for the rest, this will be hard, but you have done harder things." He smiled at her. "The High King has never had a female among his warriors. And if you are to break past that, you must remember that you are a warrior first, last, and always. That you are a woman is merely . . . an inconvenience. Do you understand?"

She was very glad that the other war chiefs were not here to see her fighting to hold back tears. The last thing she needed at this moment was to seem weak. Womanly. Her father was right, very right, and he was only reminding her of what she had known herself.

"Yes, my King," she replied, straightening her back.

"Good." He smiled. "Now, any warrior thus supplanted could be expected to be angry. I have seen many of my own chiefs in a rage over such an insult. Chopping wood is a good way to relieve that anger. Is your anger relieved?"

She took several deep breaths and blinked her eyes dry. "Yes, my King."

"And since the High King has seen fit to leave one of my *ablest* strategists behind, I expect War Chief Captain Gwenhwyfar to take command of all of my men that have been left to me." He waited a moment for the meaning of what he had just said to come home to her. And the moment it did, her eyes widened in shock.

"But—I—"

"My remaining chiefs do not think as quickly as you do. For that matter, your king and father does not think as quickly as you do." He gave her a look of warm approval. "You have a knack for solutions where others see only that there must be fighting. You dealt with March on our border in a way that cost us only a little land and no men. Should March double back, or the Saxons desert him to attack here, we will have to defend our lands with less than half the men we *should* have. All of my chiefs agree that you are the fittest to lead in that case. Now. Make me a defensive strategy." He stood up. "In fact, make me several. Think like that madman. Think like a Saxon. Find a way to make ten men fight like forty."

She gave him the fist-to-shoulder salute of the Romans. "Yes, my King."

"That is my war chief." He patted her shoulder with approval. "That is Eleri's daughter. You fight with your head. My chiefs only know how to fight with their swords. Now come." He beckoned to her. "Let us go back to the maps. Arthur is my High King and possibly the greatest leader I have ever seen, but no one has ever said he was incapable of being a fool. Though in this case . . . *I* am not the loser by his foolishness." He laid one hand on her shoulder. "In fact, he has done me a great favor, in leaving me the finest sword still in my armory."

And that was enough to take most of the sting out of the insult.

Chapter Seventeen

N**o one ever** *said Arthur was incapable of being a fool.* Never had Gwen thought that those words would come back to haunt all of them. But they had. Arthur's current actions had brought them all to a stalemate.

A chill mist hung knee-high above the ground around a lake and billowed higher above it. It was very quiet; a little splashing somewhere out there in the mist and an occasional call of a loon or some other water bird only made the silence deeper. For some reason, even the frogs were quiet. Gwen glanced uneasily at the great tor that loomed over them all in the predawn light. There was Yniswitrin, the Isle of Glass, rising above that mist that always hung over the lake that surrounded it. At the top, if you knew what to look for, you could see a squat stone tower. That was the abode—or at least, the visible part of the abode—of Gwyn ap Nudd, one of the Kings of the Folk of Annwn, so it was said. Either there beneath that tower, or beneath the waters of the lake, or both, were entrances to Annwn, the Otherworld, itself. On the shores of the lake were two more poles of power. On the one side, a church and abbey of the priests of the White Christ that was over three hundred years old. And on the other, the Cauldron Well, hidden, secret, guarded by the Ladies who had their school here, where it had stood for far, far longer than the church. The three formed a triad of balancing powers, and managed a sort of uneasy truce.

But that was not why they were all here, this army of the High King's allies. Before them, also on the island, was *that* reason. Built into the side of the tor, its top barely visible above the mist, was a stronghold made of stone. The fortress of Melwas of the Summer Country, a man who had once been one of Arthur's Companions, whose blood was at least as old as Arthur's, and who *might* have a touch of the Folk of Annwn about him.

A man, and a king. A man and a king who had taken Queen Gwenhwyfar when Arthur was off skirmishing with the Saxons, carried her off to this fortress and was using her as his claim to supplant Arthur as High King. He had every intention of wedding her, according to all the sources, and using the claim of his old blood and hers to take the throne.

And there was rumor about the camp that Gwenhwyfar might not have gone unwillingly.

Gwen rubbed her aching head; this was all a hideous tangle, and it was only getting worse. Arthur had tried to get across the lake any number of times and had not even landed more than a handful of his men at the base of the stronghold. The mist would come up and bewilder them all, the boats would land anywhere but where they should, once a storm nearly drowned them all by all accounts, and the one time he did get some men at the foot of the castle, they'd been successfully repulsed.

She had not actually seen the High King in person, but she could well imagine the tone of his temper.

And what had happened to the Merlin did not help matters at all.

Oh, the Merlin . . . if there was anyone who might have been able to find a way to get Arthur's men onto the island, it was he. He had purportedly worked greater feats of magic in the past. He could probably have disguised Arthur as Melwas and gotten him into the fortress that way, or somehow built a bridge to the island out of the mist itself. There was only one small problem.

The Merlin was no longer in a position to conjure anything.

Though rumors were flying throughout the camp about just what, exactly, had happened to him—the wildest of which featured him being locked inside a cave, a rock, or most improbably, an oak tree, by the Lady Nineve—one of Ladies had come to Gwen as soon as she had made camp and told her precisely what had befallen the Merlin.

"He was elf-shot," the woman had said. "Though whether it was a curse, or some cruel weapon bought of the fae by Melwas, we cannot say. But as Melwas was fleeing, with Queen Gwenhwyfar as his captive, the Merlin was looked for in vain. He was found at last on the floor of his room, taken with a fit. And now he lies as one made of oak, with Nineve tending him. He cannot speak, and only his eyes seem alive."

She could not help but wonder, although she did not say, if this was the punishment for all those innocent infants he had ordered killed so long ago. Certainly now he was as helpless as an infant, as trapped within an unworking body as if he had in truth been encased in a tree.

So much for the Merlin. The Ladies, of course, did not have any sort of magic that could be used to solve Arthur's problem. And if Gwyn ap Nudd was inclined to help, well, he had not even so much as showed a light in his tower.

Gwen had turned up at the head of King Lleudd's contribution to the army; she shortly thereafter discovered that in some ways, her arrival had made things even more complicated. To begin with, there was her name. It had caused rumors to fly through the camp when she first arrived, that Arthur's queen had escaped, that she had arrived at the head of her own warriors, that she was, in fact, the ghost of Arthur's *first* queen come from beyond the grave to help him. It seemed that everyone and his dog needed to come look at her to be sure that she was only herself, Lleudd Ogrfan Gawr's daughter. It had gotten to the point by sunset that she simply left her own encampment and with a small escort made a tour of Arthur's entire forces, introducing herself to all the war chiefs and making sure that everyone got a good long look at her.

That solved one problem, anyway, though now scarcely anyone called her by name. "The Giant's Daughter," they mostly called her. That was maddening, but understandable. What else were they going to do? Two Gwenhwyfars was one too many in this situation. And it wasn't as if she had yet earned one of those clever descriptive names some warriors got.

More vexing was the unspoken assumption that Gwyn ap Nudd was simply going to appear and declare himself for Arthur just because *she* had turned up.

And oh . . . what a mixed set of expectations *that* was. Because not everyone here wanted a King of Annwn to turn up and make himself an ally. First and foremost of those that would object were the Christ priests.

With the abbey so near at hand, it was not surprising that there were monks wandering about the camp; and since the abducted queen was a follower of the White Christ . . .

Well, she supposed they were finding it necessary to make it clear that they favored Arthur. If the queen had, indeed, turned her coat, then they certainly would want to show by their presence that they still favored Arthur. Although, of course, there was a further complication because Melwas himself was Christian.

Gwen felt, rather cynically, that it was possible these priests were trying to play both sides; although they were praying ostentatiously for the return of the queen, if Melwas won out, they would also be right here to be the first to proclaim him the new High King.

Whatever was on their minds, they did *not* approve of anyone who consorted with "demons" as she was said to do—and evidently, a "demon," in their eyes, was any creature that was not mortal and not an "angel."

The monks, therefore, did not like her, and the rumors that Queen Gwenhwyfar was not an unwilling captive were making them uneasy. And that made them even more unhappy with *her* presence. She was a living reminder of everything the queen wasn't—including, it seemed, loyal to the High King.

Then there were the followers of the Old Ways, who evidently expected her to conjure up Gwyn ap Nudd, who would then divide the waters of the lake, or build a bridge of rainbows across it, or fly the entire army through the air to take it to the fortress where the queen was. And then, of course, more magic would breech the walls, and in the conquering army would go, stopping only for enough combat to make them all heroes.

After all, hadn't she won allies of the Folk of Annwn already?

Oh, it was irritating; here she had foregone the credit for striking that bargain in her marsh, only to have everyone turn right round about and decide that of course she *had* done it after all.

It made her head hurt. And she wanted to swat them all for being so foolish.

Well, she had gotten another summons, this time from Lancelin, to meet with him, some of the Companions, and some other, unspecified, leaders. And where once she would have been excited to meet with these warriors who were famed from the Channel to the Western Sea, now—

Well, she just hoped they weren't expecting any magic out of her.

She nearly jumped out of her skin when the first person she saw as she entered the fire-circle was Medraut. She restrained herself however, and by the time he turned away from the person he was talking to, a huge, broad-shouldered man who looked just about as angry as if he had strapped on a helmet full of hornets, she had composed herself.

Lancelin had spotted her by then and welcomed her, giving her a seat between himself and the angry man, who turned out to be Gwalchmai. Gwalchmai actually *was* as angry as if he had strapped on a helmet full of hornets, and with good cause. He had been out in a boat trying to find a place to land; Melwas mocked him from the battlements.

And so did Gwenhwyfar.

Now, according to Lancelin, at best Gwalchmai had what might, at the kindest, be charitably described as a prejudice against women.

Of course, given his relationship with Anna Morgause . . .

But this was a great deal more insult than a warrior and one of Arthur's Companions could be expected to bear with an unruffled temper, even if that warrior was the next thing to a statue. Gwalchmai had, by all accounts, a nature so hot that he got into quarrels merely because he thought someone had looked at him oddly.

He glared at her as she sat down. She gave him the most sympathetic look she could muster.

His glare turned to suspicion. She shrugged and put on a rueful expression, trying to convey that she not only sympathized with him, she had no sympathy whatsoever for the queen. She caught Medraut watching them with veiled amusement.

This meeting turned out to be mostly Arthur's chief Companions. Lancelin, of course. Gwalchmai, Kai, Bors, Peredur, Geraint, Bedwyr, Trystan, Medraut, Caradoc, Dinadan. The firelight made moving shadows on their faces, these famous men, Arthur's closest comrades. Square and narrow, bearded and beardless, dark-haired, most of them, a few lighter. She supposed she should have felt intimidated by them, but they looked no different, really, from the men she had fought with and beside for all these many years. Experienced, yes, but so was she. Kai looked petulant, as if he forever labored under a grievance. Bors seemed weary, as did Bedwyr. Trystan, the nephew of March—oh, now that one gave her a chill. There was a look of doom about him, and a melancholy, as if he felt it too. Dinadan was impatient: clearly a man of action and few words. Caradoc was sardonic, and Geraint looked as if he considered everything something of a joke.

They were men, like any others. No matter that she had spent years listening to tales of their deeds. Braith had been just as courageous and deserved just as many tales. The only two that gave her pause, really, were Trystan and . . . Medraut. Of course. It was always Medraut.

There were three of the allied war chiefs she had not met yet, the chief men of three of the allied kings, sent, as Gwen herself had been sent, at the head of their forces. There was a Druid, Aled ap Meical, who seemed to be taking the Merlin's place, although he did not have the title and looked ill-at-ease in the position. And there was a Christian priest, Gildas, who glared at the Druid and Gwen with equal impartiality; clearly he hated them both.

"I asked you all here," said Lancelin, carefully, "Because of something that happened to Gwalchmai today. I do not believe this should be bandied about the camp yet, but we need, I think, to discuss this. Old friend?"

Gwalchmai got heavily to his feet. "This afternoon, I took a squire and a boat and went to look at that bastard's walls," he rumbled. His shaggy red brows furrowed together. He was a bear of a man, and he gave the impression he could easily snap an ordinary man in half with his bare hands. "I bethought the mist would keep me hidden, but I should have known my cursed luck would make sure that whatever I wanted, the opposite would happen. The mist blew off, and there I was, and there was Melwas on the tower, and if I'd had but a knife or even a stone to throw, we'd not be sitting together having this meeting, because I'd have killed him on the spot."

The last was growled with an air of frustration, and Gwen didn't blame him.

"At any rate, he commenced to flinging insults instead, and I did the same. And then, after a bit of this pleasantry, someone comes to join him. Gwenhwyfar."

Those who were not yet aware of this news exchanged uneasy looks and murmured to one another.

"If his tongue's sour, hers is like a whip," Gwalchmai continued, flushing a deep red with anger. "I'll not repeat what she said to me, though there wasn't much of it before she ended it with, 'Let us leave the loons to paddle back to their nests,' and drew Melwas away. But she looked nor sounded not like any captive."

And with that, he cast a glare at Gildas, who was plainly taken much aback.

"I came and told this straightaway to the High King and to Lancelin, and Lancelin called you here." Gwalchmai sat down again.

"This is ill hearing," Kai muttered, staring at his clasped hands. "But I cannot think what we are to do about it."

"Well, I will tell you what you are to do about it."

All their heads came up as a voice like the sound of a hunting horn cut across the silence. And one strode into their fire-circle as if he owned it and immediately caused all the hair on the back of Gwen's head to stand straight up.

He was beautiful and gold and white, with golden hair, pale skin, gold-embroidered white tunic, trews and boots. He could easily have been the brother to one of the Lake Maidens, and he was as beautiful as they were. Inhumanly so.

"Inhuman" was a very good word for him. Having seen one of the Folk of Annwn once, Gwen was not likely to forget their look again.

This one wore a thin gold circlet about his brow and a torque of gold with orm-headed finals, so there was only one person that he was likely to be.

And she was the first of them to recover her wits and realize it. She leaped to her feet and bowed deeply; she made sure that they saw her offer the ultimate respect before the others, who might not have the eyes to see what and who he was, offered him an insult.

"Greetings to the noble and generous Gwyn ap Nudd, King of the Folk of Annwn," she said, as she straightened again. "Welcome to our Council. I know that the High King counts you as a friend and one of his Companions, as well as ally."

Those who had recognized him, had also gotten to their feet and likewise bowed, a bit later than she had. Those who had not, looked stunned for a moment.

Then one by one they recovered their wits and their manners and, as Gwyn ap Nudd looked them over with amusement, scrambled to follow their example.

"Greetings, my fair cousin, fair of speech as you are of face," he replied genially. "I regret that I did not seek out the High King before this, but I had hoped that this situation would sort itself out without my intervention." He lifted one long brow at Gildas. "My meddling is not always considered welcome."

Gildas looked uneasy.

"And I have a solution to this knotty problem. If—" now he turned an ironic expression on Gildas "—if the honored and holy Abbot Gildas is prepared to follow up on the—*assertion,* for of course no priest would boast!—that I know that he made to his fellow monks."

Gildas went red, then white, then red again, and back to white. He was caught, and he knew it. Whatever it was he had boasted that he could do, or at least attempt, he had done so in the hearing of Gwyn. And now he had two choices. Either try it, whatever it was, with Gwyn's help—the help of a pagan thing, perhaps a demon, certainly a creature with whom the good Christians were not supposed to consort. Or back out of whatever he had said, and be held up to ridicule by, yes, that pagan thing, that possible demon, who would no doubt find a way to mock the religion as well as the man.

The latter, clearly, was not a choice for him. He straightened, still white. "I said that I would try to bargain a settlement between Melwas and Arthur if only I could get into the fortress," Gildas said bravely. "And so I shall."

"And I shall get you in. I weary of this Melwas, who calls himself King of the Summer Country, which is one of *my* titles that he usurps." The blue-green eyes turned nearly black, although that was the only sign of the King of the Annwn's anger. "I weary of him setting himself up on my island. I weary even more of the presence on my island of Arthur's queen. This quarrel stirs up my people, your iron and steel bring them discomfort, and the peace of my island has been disrupted. I want them gone from my shore. But he is—supposedly—a follower of your Christ. So, man of Christ, as I and mine have not troubled you in all the years of your presence, perhaps you can repay that peace by making him come to see reason."

Gildas swallowed. "I hope I may. And if you can take me to him—"

Gwyn ap Nudd laughed softly. "Nothing easier." Before Gildas could move, or even flinch, the king had seized him by the arm.

Even Gwen could not rightly have told what happened then. To her, it looked as if Gwyn had stepped through a door, drawing Gildas after him. But there was no door there. They were there . . . and then two steps later, they were gone.

Gwen blinked and rubbed her eyes.

"Well," said Medraut into the silence. "That was curiously satisfying. I was wondering if there was anything that could silence that pompous prig."

There was clearly nothing more to be done that night, so the council broke up, with Lancelin and Kai volunteering to tell the High King what had just transpired. The awkwardness was palpable, as no one really knew what to say or do. Gwen wondered, though, just what sort of magic they had seen before—after all, the Merlin had been an integral part of the High King's entourage since the beginning. Had he simply never done anything in their presence?

Or maybe the awkwardness was partly due to the queen's defection and partly due to the fact that Gwyn ap Nudd had just appeared and trumped them all. Whatever plans they'd had in mind would have involved more siege, more fighting. Gwyn had aborted all of those, carrying off Gildas to try and end this thing without further warfare. At the moment, they were all so taken aback that they couldn't think.

Well, if they couldn't think, they could certainly *talk,* but she realized immediately that as she was not one of the inner circle, they were not going to do any frank talking around her. Wryly, she decided that sleep was her best option, so she bid them all farewell and started back to her encampment.

She had gotten just out of the reach of the firelight when she realized that she was not alone. And the figure that was keeping pace with her was not one that she welcomed.

"'Fair cousin,' is it?" said Medraut, in a tone that sounded perfectly pleasant if you didn't know him and realize there was certainly some other motivation behind his question than the wish to be conversational. "Are there folk of Annwn in your bloodline, then?"

"Not that I know of," she replied, throttling down her revulsion and replying with the same surface pleasantry. There it was again. And he was married to her sister; wouldn't he *know* by now if there was fae blood in them? Or—maybe he wasn't as strong in magic as he liked to believe. "I'm sure someone would have mentioned it before this if there were. I believe that the King of the Isle of Glass was merely acknowledging that technically I am the overlord to some of his people now. Of course, he could have had some other motive; it's impossible to tell with the Folk."

"Ah, yes. Your little bargain." Medraut stalked alongside her, and with his longer legs, there was no way she could outdistance him without running. Damn him. He was the last person she wanted to talk to. You had to be at your cleverest to exchange more than a few words with him, if you didn't want him to ferret more out of you than you wanted him to know. "That was cleverly done, by the way. I salute you. I had no idea you had enough power in you to call up the Folk."

"I don't." Actually, she didn't want Medraut to think she had any magic at all. "I gave all that up when I took the warrior's path. It wasn't me that summoned them, it was Cataruna and Ifan, and even then, I think it was entirely accidental that they did so. We only summoned the waters to make a swamp, so King March would have to take his forces across Saxon lands rather than ours. I actually think that the Folk came by themselves."

"Still clever. You saw an opportunity and took advantage of it. It was a good bargain; you lost nothing but a bit of land and got some formidable guards in exchange. Morgana was annoyed that it had not occurred to her to do the same. By the way, you may congratulate *me*. I have a son." There was a flash of teeth, catching the light of a campfire as they passed. "And before you ask, no, Arthur is still unaware that your sister and I are wed."

Which meant, of course, that he didn't want Arthur to know and was reminding her of her promise. "I see. Well, congratulations. You are now ahead of the High King in that game. And the queen remains childless." Unspoken was the depth of Medraut's ambition. Unspoken, too, that although Medraut was not only a bastard but the product of incest, when presented with a grown man, a proven warrior, with his own heirs, if Arthur died it was likely that the irregularities of Medraut's birth would be . . . overlooked. No one wanted to go through the chaos that had followed Uther's death.

"I know. I live in hope." There was another flash of teeth. "Meanwhile, I find that I quite enjoy being one of the Companions. It is a strange thing that I find get along better with my brothers now than I did at home. Gwalchmai has been a particular boon friend; he seems to appreciate my wisdom, and I certainly appreciate his muscles. Perhaps he wishes to make up for pummeling me so much as a child."

That was easy to read. Medraut was finally able to manipulate the rather dim eldest of the Orkney clan and possibly the others as well. "This is the first I have encountered any of them but you. Well, again, I give you congratulations on siring a son. Where are you keeping him and your wife?" she asked. "Surely not with Lot—"

"Oh, Morgana has her. They get along famously. " He waved a hand airily. "Like sisters, really. It's quite affecting, to see them together."

Now what did that mean? That Morgana and Gwenhwyfach

hated each other as cordially as Little Gwen hated her real sisters? Or was this to mock her with; implying that Morgana and Little Gwen were alike? Surely if Morgana hated Little Gwen, she would not have her in her own castle, no matter how much she wanted to oblige Medraut. Gwen had heard stories about Morgana, who was supposedly an even more powerful sorceress than her sister, Anna Morgause. She seemed to spend half her time helping Arthur, and the other half being a thorn in his side.

But then—stories. They were only that. Men were uneasy enough around a woman with power of any sort. It would not be surprising that they made up tales about one who was powerful and refused to tie herself to any man to boot.

For just a moment, something too faint to be called a memory drifted past in her thoughts. An image, a glimpse, of Morgana and Little Gwen, side by side—but it was gone before she could grasp it.

She decided that she had better say something; she had been silent a little too long. "So long as I can assure Father she is content, that is all that matters," Gwen replied untruthfully. The reality was, somewhere down inside, she was sickened. Gwenhwyfach by herself was bad enough. Gwenhwyfach tutored by Anna Morgause was worse. And Gwenhwyfach working hand in hand with Morgana? Gwen pitied anyone foolish enough to cross them.

"Yes, well, you can tell King Lleudd anything you like," Medraut replied, stopping suddenly. That was when Gwen realized that they were at the edge of her encampment. "Just as long as you keep the oaths you swore. I have many plans in motion, and I would be very vexed if they were to be disrupted." His eyes glittered in the darkness. "Morgana and my wife would be even more disappointed than I."

That was easy to read, too. *Keep my secrets, or there will be a price to pay.* Morgana had always struck Gwen as the sort of person who liked being the hidden power and preferred to do nothing overtly.

Morgana was also, by all measures, someone who never staked all of her ambitions on one plan, or one candidate. If Medraut lost his bid for Arthur's seat, she would have a dozen more directions she could go. But Gwenhwyfach? Without a doubt, she was already, in her mind, measuring her brow for the High Queen's crown. Cataruna could probably handle Morgana and her magic if Gwen were to tell what she knew. But Gwenhwyfach, or the two of them together? Oh, no. Gwen was not minded to cross her little sister.

"And I have no plans except to serve my father and his heirs," she replied honestly. "I am a plain warrior, cousin. I have no head for grand schemes."

"Sometimes it is a good thing to have no ambition." The flash of teeth, the glitter of eyes in the dark, put her in mind of something feral. "And on that, I bid you good night. It has been a most fascinating evening, with great potential for amusement to come. We will see what the morning brings."

She was only too happy to leave him there and retreat to the safety of those she trusted.

She gave her own chiefs a brief explanation of what had happened, omitting only Gwalchmai's report of the behavior of the queen, the strange way in which Gwyn ap Nudd and Gildas had vanished—and that the King of Yniswitrin had called her "fair cousin." If the word of the queen's treachery was to be spread about the camps, she did not want it to come from *her* people. And as for Gwyn ap Nudd, well, she intended to publicly distance herself from the Folk of Annwn and from magic as much as possible. Especially with Medraut snooping about. The less he thought about her, the better.

They accepted the news with astonishment. Then she left them to mull it over themselves. It was always better to let the men talk themselves out without her there to overhear them. It let them know that she trusted them; it also allowed them to air whatever foolishness came into their heads without the risk of looking foolish in front of *her.*

As mother once said; men are worse gossips than women ever were.

In the morning, nothing much had changed, except for the rumors flying about the camp. As she had expected, a garbled version of Gwalchmai's narrative was all over the encampment, and the stories of how Gwyn ap Nudd had made off with Abbot Gildas were even more incredible than what had actually happened. In some, he vanished in a flash of lightning, in others, he grew great wings and carried Gildas off, and in some . . . good lack, it was *Gildas* who sprouted wings and flew to the Island.

At least she could, with great virtue, make the assertion that none of that had originated with *her* men.

In the meantime, the orders from the High King were to wait. So, wait they did. Morning became midday, and still there was no sign of anything going on, either on the mainland or on the island. The mist did not lift; if anything, it thickened. An overcast day meant everything was shrouded in gloom, and it was easy to imagine strange shapes in the mist. Most men stuck close to camp, save for hers. King Lleudd's force, emboldened perhaps by her connection to the Folk of Annwn, went out hunting and fishing. Gwen thought about trying to pay a visit to the Ladies and the Cauldron Well, then thought better of it. With all these strangers here, they had probably hidden the entrance to their school and stronghold, as they often did when times were uneasy, and although they would probably let her in, it might take her a while to get their attention. Besides, she had little or no magic these days. She would not be there as a fellow Lady, but rather as one who comes to see the sights . . . not entirely welcome under the circumstances. No, they knew she was here. If they wanted to see her, they would send a messenger, and if they did not send one, it was because mere visitors were not, at the moment, welcome.

The High King had not summoned her though he had sent courteous, if overly formal, greetings and thanks to her and her father and further thanks for the gift of the two of her father's famous gray cavalry horses that she had brought. Until she was summoned, it was poor manners to intrude on him and his councils, and really, there was not much more she could add. Nothing about this situation answered to either Roman tactics or anything she was good at. Add to that—her name. It would not be easy, hearing the name of his runaway wife attached to someone else.

But there was not much more she could do here at the camp, except add to gossip. She saw to her gear, but she had been so thorough that there was nothing left that she needed to attend to; Rhys and Pryderi were not much inclined to go riding out in the mist and gloom and showed their reluctance clearly. She didn't blame them and couldn't think of a reason why she needed to risk their legs and necks to an accident. After a good long while of staring blankly at the fire, it occurred to her that there was one foot of the power triangle here she could visit after all. After mulling it over, deciding against it, then deciding she was being a coward, she went to have a look at the church and abbey of the Christ priests.

It was not very imposing; the abbey was about the size of the village at Castell y Cnwclas; it was not a single building but a bevy of little wattle huts inside an enclosure, with the church, a more substantial timber structure, at the center. The huts looked like chicks surrounding a hen, and the church was about half the size of her father's castle. But one thing struck her almost forcibly when she ventured inside the dark, incense-scented building; as small as it was, within those four walls she encountered a sense of deep peace the like of which she had not felt outside of a Sacred Circle. And that—was astonishing.

When she left the church, she was accosted by a swarm of the inhabitants. The monks that lived at the abbey were all in a state, not quite panic but certainly great anxiety about the well-being of Gildas. She got the sense that he was greatly admired, and even loved, here. And far from being made to feel unwelcome, when they made sure of who she was, she had a group of tonsured men in plain brown and black robes surrounding her, pressing fresh, hot bread and butter and a mug of small beer into her hands, asking her anxious questions. Was this Gwyn ap Nudd truly an evil creature? Was he honorable? Could he be trusted? Would he use some sort of magic on Gildas to corrupt him? Would the Abbot come back to them safely?

"Wait, wait," she said, as they clustered around her. "I will answer any question I can, but I must be able to hear them!" She got them to stop talking all at once, finally, and sat down on a stone bench in the abbey herb garden where they had gathered around her. "I'll tell you everything I know about the Folk of Annwn and Gwyn in particular," she said, calmly, reassuringly. "But first of all, Gwyn ap Nudd is a friend to the High King, and, so I was told this morning, counted among the King's Companions of the Round Table even if he seldom comes to court." She waited for them to take that in. "If he comes to the Round Table, he has already passed the many tests that the High King sets his men. Yes?"

They looked at each other, then nodded.

"Now, among the Folk of Annwn, vows are taken as seriously as—" she looked about her, and although she *did* see a few faces showing suspicion or fear, she didn't see any she would have thought dishonest "—as seriously as among you. Vows are sacred. Gwyn will have taken the same vows to the High King that all the Companions have, and one of those is to protect those who do not bear arms."

"'That is true," murmured the fellow who had insisted she have some of his beer. "Women, children, and men of the cloth . . ."

"Furthermore, among the Folk of Annwn, the person of an envoy is held in the highest esteem. Their lives are sacred. Their words are to be listened to with courtesy, and they are not to be threatened nor harmed just because one side does not like what they have to say. Abbot Gildas is an envoy. Gwyn will defend him to the death and would not allow harm to come to him even at the hand of his own lady or son. I would lay my *own* life on that or that of my father, whom I hold dearer than myself."

There was a collective sigh of relief at that, and a little of the tension eased. "Now, as to the Folk of Annwn . . . no, they are not mortal as we are. But they are not demons, either. They are just . . . other." She shook her head. "It is hard to explain, but I think I can pledge to you that Gwyn of the Annwn would have no more difficulty in being within the walls of your church, there, than I did."

"A demon cannot abide within church walls," said someone else. "Nor stand on consecrated ground."

She had to smile a little. "I daresay that if you looked closely at some of those who have come once or twice to your rites, you would find that more than one of them are of the Folk, for they are a curious set of peoples, and you are their near neighbors. They dwell in the Other World, not here on the middle earth, nor heaven, nor hell, but as if it were *sideways* to the lands we know. The doors to their lands are few; two are here, which is why Gwyn's stronghold is here."

"I heard a tale once," one of the fellows faltered. When the others made encouraging murmurs, he got up courage and went on. "It was said that when Lucifer revolted and made war in heaven, there were some spirits that would take neither God's side nor the Devil's. And so, when the battle was over, and Lucifer and his minions cast into Hell, these other spirits were also driven from Heaven. Because they had not taken God's side, they could not remain. But because they had not taken Lucifer's either, they were not sent to Hell. And so they came to live beside, but not among, mortals, in a state that was half of spirit and half of the world . . ." His voice trailed off, uncertainly.

She shrugged. "I had not heard that tale before, but it is as likely as any other explanation. They are as many and varied as mortals and all the mortal creatures. There are good, bad, and middling ones. Many are tricksters. Some are evil, but Gwyn will keep *those* firmly under control here. They are quick to anger, slow to forget. A gift places a debt of obligation on them, and the freer and more genuine the gift, the greater the obligation. They will always hold by the letter of a bargain, but you must be careful, because if they feel they are being coerced into it in any way, they will try to find a way out of it. As I said, they hold the person of an envoy sacred. The best thing you can do if ever you see one is to offer it a gift, however small; by making a gift you will bind them not to harm you, and they will not rest until they feel they have discharged their obligation. Bread is always a good gift." She thought some. "Would you continue to live in peace with Gwyn's folk?"

"We had rather convert them and save their souls, if souls they have," said a dry voice from the rear of the group. "As our brothers in Eire saved the souls of the Daughters of Lyr. But yes, if we can buy peace of them—"

"Then make a gift of bread at the water's edge, once a week, say, if you have it to spare." She smiled. "Most of them live beneath the Lake, and it is a little difficult to bake bread at the bottom of a lake. Mark it with one of your crosses, so that they will know from whom it comes, and nothing evil will be able to touch it."

There were murmurs, but nods. She found herself smiling even more; she had not expected to like these men and certainly had not expected them to be asking advice of her.

They asked her a few more questions, which she answered as honestly as she could, and she left burdened with bread, butter, and honey for her men, for the abbey's cattle and bees were evidently famous. One of the monks came with her, there was so much to carry.

She returned to the encampment burdened as much by thought as by the gifts. She had expected acute disapproval, even hatred. While some of those men clearly disapproved of her, more simply accepted her as her own people accepted her. And there was no hatred. Mostly they seemed to be grateful that she was taking the time to explain things and reassure them. Even those who seemed to disapprove of her had listened to her words.

So she found again, when she had seen that the food was properly distributed. As the monk said farewell and began to leave, he suddenly turned back to her.

"You are a great and kind lady, to have spent so much time explaining matters," he said, shyly. "I hope you do not mind that I brought the brothers to speak with you."

She grinned a little. "So it was your doing?"

He flushed. "Aye. When I saw you in the chapel, as fair as Our Lady is said to be, and with such a look of peace upon you, I knew that you had a good heart, even though your soul is pagan. I knew that you would tell us the truth and not put us off, as lord Kai has done. And I knew that because you are a woman that knows the hearts of your men, you would see us as a kind of warrior too and serve us the truth, instead of seeing us as womanly, as the Companions do, and serve us empty assurances."

She was so taken aback that all she could do was blink and blush. He didn't seem to mind; he just took her hand and wrung it a little.

"I know that goodness and beauty do not always go hand in hand," he finished, simply, "But in you, White Spirit, I think they are united. God's blessing on you. I will pray for you."

He trotted off back to his duties and his brothers, leaving her staring dumbfounded after him.

Chapter Eighteen

O n the third day after Gwyn vanished with Gildas, a parley flag appeared on the tower of Melwas' stronghold. After much discussion, Arthur sent his foster-brother Kai out in a boat to hear what was to be said.

They watched as Kai was taken into the stronghold. And then there was more waiting. As the time passed, the tension grew greater, and it was with tremendous relief that they all saw Kai come back out again.

This time, he was not alone. Two more men were with him; in the shifting mists, it was hard to make out more than Kai's red tunic and the vague shapes of the other two, but—

"No, fair cousin, one of them is not me," said Gwyn right into her ear. She jumped, and he laughed as she spun to face him. She was standing a little apart from the rest of her men, and they didn't seem to have noticed that Gwyn had simply—well, probably, he had pulled the same trick as he had the last time, stepping out of nowhere to end up beside her.

"Gildas is a stiff-necked fellow, but honest and fair, and once I saw that he was going to make good on his boast, I left him to it," Gwyn told her. "Let him have all the fame, if fame comes from this, for reconciling Melwas with your High King." He chuckled a little. "In truth, cousin, I think that Melwas was getting mightily weary of the company of his prize, confined as he was to one small island, and not all of that."

"And will he still be calling himself 'King of the Summer Country'. . . cousin?" she asked.

His smile grew teeth. "I think not. He has seen that it is not wise to usurp what is another's, whether it be a wife or a title. And by the way, I thank you for calming his flock of little brown chicks." The smile softened. "That was courteously done."

She flushed a little. "That hadn't been my intention when I went to look over their hennery," she said, with a slight laugh. "But they clucked and fussed so, it moved me to pity. Besides, it was no great effort, I only had to tell them the truth."

"As fair-spoken as you are fair of face," he laughed. "It is as well that I have me a lady who holds my heart fast—and *you* have your duties to your father. Elsewise I would steal you away as Melwas stole that fool of a Gwenhwyfar to the true Summer Country." He lifted an elegant brow and gave her a thoughtful look. "I think you have great things in you, cousin. I do not yet know what they are, but surely the hand of a goddess is on you."

She was a little flustered now, although she was determined not to show it. That was twice, now, that men had called her attractive. She was not at all sure what to make of this . . .

Then again . . . the two men who had found her lovely were the King of the Annwn and a monk. Neither were "men" in the ordinary sense. She ought not to place too much importance on this.

"Have you any notion of what Gildas brought about?" she asked instead.

"Some. He'll turn over the queen, of course. And for taking her, there will be some Christian punishment or other. I think he'll be giving over his stronghold to Gildas, though what the monks will do with it, I've no notion." He shrugged. "They do not trouble me, I do not trouble them. They will bring no weapons of iron and steel to my door, and that is all I care for."

She pondered this. "Well . . . if ever the Saxons overrun this place, the stronghold will make a safe place for them to go."

Gwyn nodded, his eyes on the nearing figures. "And this is no bad thing. Blood spilled so near my door would bring the sort of the Folk that I do not care for. The sort that only look for more blood, and finding it not, goes hunting for it. That is always bad. You mortals are not so discriminating when it comes to my kind and are like to punish all for the faults of a few."

She could find no reason to dispute that claim and sighed. "I wish it were not so. But if wishes were horses, my father would have no need for stallions."

"Well said." He bowed a little to her. "With that, fair cousin, I take my leave. The Folk still owe you something of a debt. You may feel free to claim it of me at your will."

And then, he stepped . . . away . . . again. A single pace to the side, and he was gone, just as the boat touched the shore.

And so there was more waiting.

Not with the tension that there had been, however. Her men, grateful for the fresh bread, something all too seldom seen by warriors in the field, went out hunting and fishing again, and they shared their catch with the monks, who in turn supplied another round of bread and honey. An interesting spirit of camaraderie sprang up between them; a spirit she encouraged. In the rest of the encampment, the sense of relief was palpable. It was one thing to go to war against the Saxons; they were the enemy. It was quite another to go to war against someone whose men you had recently fought beside.

There was no doubt that Gildas was going to do well out of this. He did not much care for Arthur, or so it was said by a few of the monks, but he cared even less for Christian to be fighting Christian. And he would likely exact some sort of price from Arthur as well as from Melwas for his services. Gwen could not fault him for any of this; actually, it only seemed fair. When he had agreed to negotiate, *he* knew nothing of Gwyn ap Nudd, had no assurances that Melwas would not kill him out of hand, nor that Gwyn himself could be trusted. Gwen might not like Gildas, but she could admire his courage.

Finally, just before sunset, the word came at last.

And shortly after the word, the lady who was the cause of it all.

A breeze—no doubt engineered by Gwyn ap Nudd—blew the mists off the lake as she came, rowed over in another boat. The setting sun touched her golden hair and made of it a crown and gilded her linen gown. She sat upright and proud in the stern of the boat, with no sign that she felt any guilt.

Gwen was not sure what her feelings were. Mostly relief that all of this was over. Some contempt, perhaps. And puzzlement, that the woman would be so foolish as to desert a man who engendered such passionate loyalty. It should have been obvious that very few of his allies would desert him and that the ruse that she had been carried off against her will could not have held up for very long.

Lust? Love? Ambition?

Not that it mattered in the long run.

When she alighted, she was surrounded immediately; the bodies of Companions and monks hid her from view, so it was impossible to tell if she was led off, taken off as a prisoner, or went under her own power and will. But off she went, heading for the High King's tent, where Arthur and Gildas awaited. Melwas was gone. The queen would face her judgment alone.

Gwen shook her head and decided that today might be a good day to go hunting.

She returned, empty-handed, which didn't really surprise her; with so many men hunting the same fields, the game was probably hunted out by now. And perhaps because of that very thing, she returned to find many of the allies already packing up to leave.

"Have we been dismissed?" she asked Afon ap Macsen, her second in command.

"Not yet. But there is no real reason to hold us here," he pointed out, and looked uncomfortable. "A good fight, that's one thing. But this—it isn't the sort of thing a man likes to have witnesses to."

Well, she could see that. The High King had been made a cuckold of in front of his allies, and his queen hadn't looked in the least repentant. She wondered what Arthur would do.

It wouldn't have been a question if he had been a follower of the Old Ways, as her father was. King Lleudd would have had an easy choice, since a woman, particularly a queen and a Lady, *did* have one irrefutable excuse for something like this.

It was done for the Land.

Arthur was still childless and looked to remain so. And while he was still in fighting trim, his queen, if she had been a Lady, would have been bound to show herself fertile. And . . . well . . . this was his way to *prove* he was still worthy to represent the Land. If the Old Stag could not drive off or slay the Young Stag, then it was more than time for the Young to supplant the Old.

Even time for the Old Stag to shed his blood to renew the Land.

Now, that had not yet happened with her father, in no small part because neither Ifan nor Caradoc were minded to make the challenge to King Lleudd. Besides, Cataruna was firmly Pywll's Lady, and the vigorous and very, very virile Ifan was Lord to her Lady. There was no need for King Lleudd to be the Land King, for Cataruna had a consort, and all was well.

But Arthur—

Well, the Old Stag had conquered the Young, so no one would be pressing for him to be supplanted yet. And it was through no fault of his own that he had no heirs but Medraut.

Gwen sighed. "Tell the men to be ready to move out. You are right. I have no wish for the High King to have us present for this."

The queen was a follower of the Christ, and there were no excuses for her behavior in their creed. She would have no allies there. Not even Gildas would support her now.

Gwen tried to think of what options were open to Arthur. This was treason, of course. But would he put her to death? Could he put her away by Christian law? If he tried to put her away from him, she was still going to be a source of contention for his throne. She could still attract another like Melwas, maybe more. She could still be a source of trouble.

It was a situation fraught with ugliness and difficulty, and one she was deeply grateful that she was not involved in.

There was one thing she might do, though; it would remind Arthur that the followers of the Old Ways had not wavered in their loyalty, and it would reflect well on her father.

She had come here with a gift of horses for himself and his Companions, but in anticipation of fighting, all of King Lleudd's men had come with extra mounts. She herself had brought six—Rhys and Pryderi of course, but also four more, just in case something happened to her two main mounts. Now she pulled those four extras from the picket line, found a squire, and sent them off to the High

King with the simple message that the horses were from King Lleudd Ogrfan Gawr.

The camp was uneasy that night and unsettled. This did not taste like victory, even though Arthur had won.

Talk around the fires was subdued, and no one had much appetite. Gwen was thinking very strongly of making use of that mead Cataruna had sent along to help her to sleep early, when she looked up to see one of Gildas' monks peering around the circle of warriors at her fire. He finally whispered to the one nearest him, and to Gwen's further surprise, the man stood up and conducted the monk courteously to her.

"If you would be so kind," the monk said, diffidently, once he had given her the bow of respect, "Abbot Gildas would like to speak with you."

She stood up immediately. "I would be honored," she said honestly. Whatever the abbot wanted her for, he was clearly an important man. He was also a beloved man; however disagreeable he had seemed to *her*, he had to have earned that regard.

So, she would give him the courtesy that she hoped he would show her, and see what happened.

The monk conducted her quickly to the Abbey, and it was quite clear that the subdued mood in her camp was shared across the entire encampment.

Gildas was waiting for her at another fire, and he rose to greet her without the disagreeable expression he had worn before. She gave him the same bow of respect that she would have given the Merlin.

"Lady . . . I wish to thank you," Gildas said awkwardly. "You were very kind to reassure my people."

"Abbot Gildas, your people were extremely worried for you, and they deserved to have someone treat them with courtesy," she replied. "The High King's Companions would have done so if they themselves knew what I did about the Folk of Annwn. Since they did not, and what I knew could ease the hearts of your people and allow them to devote their attention to—to—"

"To prayer and their devotions," Gildas supplied, with a little smile. "Yes. And again, I thank you. I also wish to apologize to you. Without knowing anything of you, I harbored ill thoughts of you. You, in turn, rather than doing the same to me, have given me a lesson in what should have been *Christian* charity. For this lesson, too, I thank you. I want you to know that despite our differences in belief, you may count me as a friend."

She was for a moment taken aback, but she quickly recovered. "I am honored, and I would be more honored if you will accept the same from me."

"I know that you are all curious as to what is to happen to the queen." He sighed. "I should prefer, as you seem to not be prone to exaggeration, if you were to make it known that the High King and the queen will remain here for a time while I strive to make peace between them."

She winced. "I do not envy you that task. This was . . . a sad and bitter thing."

"I wish that I had hope of success." A shadow passed over Gildas' face. "But that will be as God wills it. I shall do my best. Arthur is a great man. I would that he were more a man of peace and less of war . . . for one of my brothers rebelled against him, you know, and met his death at Arthur's hands."

Well, that explains a great deal . . .

"Still I have forgiven him. And I know him to be a great, and great-hearted, man. And a good leader, of the sort that this land needs. He has a vision of this part of the world being united and strong, as the old empire of the Romans was. I hope that this does not harden his heart and make something terrible out of a good man."

Something terrible . . . like the sort of man who could order the deaths of infants? She said nothing, however, only nodded. She and Gildas exchanged a little more conversation, then he pleaded exhaustion, and she took her leave—making sure to stop with several war chiefs on the way back to her encampment to relate what Gildas had tacitly asked her to pass on.

And then she and her men followed the example of the rest, packed up, and returned, thankfully, to their homes.

Nevertheless, she was somehow not at all surprised to learn, about a month after their return, that Queen Gwenhwyfar had caught an unexpected chill, sickened, and died, and was buried on the grounds of the Abbey.

PART THREE

QUEEN

Chapter Nineteen

It **was just** cool enough for a fire at the king's hearth, but the light it cast gave very little aid in reading facial features. Gwen could not believe what she had just heard, and stared at their visitor in total disbelief. "If this is a jest, it is in very poor taste," she finally managed.

But her father looked completely serious, as did the visitor, the Lady Aeronwen. "Lady" in the sense of "one of the Ladies." The Lady looked outwardly no different from any other woman, and Gwen was not Gifted enough to sense the Power in her; her clothing was unusual only in that it was of plain, undyed white linen and wool, and her hair was unbound, signifying she was not a married woman. There was nothing whatsoever to mark her as a person of any importance at all, but she had been sent directly here from the great School, and Cataruna, who bowed to almost no one, practically groveled to her.

She did have the most piercing dark eyes that Gwen had ever seen; eyes that definitely looked far beneath the surface of everything around her. Her speech was clipped, her manners rather severe. That, of course, was probably very effective against the young women sent to the School, but it cowed Gwen not at all.

And her proposal was . . . well, on the surface of it, sheer insanity. Why in the name of every god and goddess should *she* become the High King's third wife? She had never even laid eyes on him to her certain knowledge, and she doubted he had ever seen her. And she was twenty-seven. Even if she did look eighteen. Surely he would want a younger bride.

If he does, he'll reject this whole scheme out of hand.

"The High King *must* have a queen. He dallied not at all after the death of his first, and there is no reason to wait this time, either. He drew up a pathetically short list of names that he indicated would be acceptable to himself and one or another of his advisors. The only other candidate that we will accept is Morgana," said Aeronwen flatly, her eyes hard. "And leaving aside the little problem that she is also the High King's half-sister, she is completely out of the question, because she is completely uncontrollable."

"Oh. And you can control me," Gwen replied dryly, raising one eyebrow. The tiny, dark woman flushed, disconcerted. Gwen sensed that she did not often find herself contradicted or her will thwarted.

"That is not what I mean, Gwenhwyfar." The Lady's glare could have put ice on a pond in summer. "I mean that you will work for the good of the land, for the good of the followers of the Old Ways, to protect the Folk of Annwn. You will think first of the good of others, not yourself. You have proven that, as a warrior. Morgana will work only on her own behalf, or Medraut's."

"And leaving aside whether or not Arthur will be remotely interested in a bride who has followed the warrior's path, just how do you propose to get the High King to accept a third wife with the name 'Gwenhwyfar'?" she asked. "I should think at this point he will regard that as very ill-omened."

"Or he will hold by the common notion that the third time pays for all," the Lady countered, and shrugged. "I confess, I am not in his confidence. I do not know what he will think, I only know that, like you, he considers first the good of his people. He needs an heir, the land needs a queen, and all else is secondary. He is getting no younger. He has no time to waste. We who have counseled him have made very, very sure that he understands this."

"There is another factor; the High King wants my horses," her father rumbled, nodding. "To get them, he will take you. It is a good bargain, as you know I do not part with them easily."

Her cheeks flamed with suppressed anger. "So *that* is what this is about. I'm now the unwanted part of a horse trade!"

"Unwanted by the High King perhaps, but greatly desired by us!" the Lady snapped. "The King's second wife did us great damage with her adherence to the Christ priests. The High King grows old; in the back of his mind, I suspect, is the fact that the Young Stag supplants the Old, and Lleu slays Goronwy. The land is not suffering—yet— but if it does, his age may be blamed, and the followers of the Old Ways may look for a Young Stag. The Christ priests do not demand that the High King sacrifice himself—ever. Except metaphorically, of course."

"And do you?" she asked, pointedly.

The Lady shrugged. "It has been our experience that the gods take that in hand before we need to. The Merlin is useless to us now, and the King has decided to forget that his old mentor was a Druid before he was the King's man. Even though you have not the Gifts, Gwen-hwyfar, you can undo some of that. You are called 'cousin' by Gwyn ap Nudd, and you are accepted by Abbot Gildas. You can turn some of the rancor of the Christ priests away from us. You can bring Arthur back to us. And perhaps you can supply an heir to the throne."

Gwen felt like a rabbit in a snare. All of this did make very good sense. She probably *was* the best candidate to be the High King's new wife. And she *could* do much. Unlike many of the followers of the Old Ways—the Ladies being prime examples of that—now that she had actually met with some of them, she didn't think all that badly of the followers of the White Christ.

But this was not what she wanted to do! This had nothing to do with *her* dreams!

But I am a king's daughter. And kings' daughters know that duty comes before desire. Kings' daughters know that they will be called upon to sacrifice much. I have had my dream for years. Now . . .

Now it was time to pay for having had that dream in her hands.

And it felt horrible. As if something she loved was dying before her eyes.

It's me that's dying. It's the Gwen that is the war chief, the only Gwen I've been for all of my life. And something I don't recognize is going to take her place.

And . . . it wasn't Arthur she wanted to wed . . .

"Am I really the only one?" she asked, in a small voice.

"Would I be here if you were not?" Aeronwen shrugged. "At least the High King is not in love with you. He was in love with the last Gwenhwyfar, and that did not end well. His wedding to the first Gwenhwyfar was far more arranged than the tales would make it seem; he wanted her father as an ally in the days when he had far fewer. Trust me, he is no stranger to marrying for expedience. For his second wife, he pleased himself; deluded himself, perhaps, but he did not think first of his people, or the Land, and the result was almost a disaster."

Gwen wanted to ask how the second queen had really died, but—no. It was probably better not to have an answer to that question. Whatever had happened was in the hands and judgment of the gods. Whichever gods those were.

It was ironic, when she thought back to her childhood and how when she had heard that the first queen had her name, she had wished she too could be a queen and have goose every day and gowns that were not made-over. Now all she could think was how it meant the end of her freedom, that not all the fine food and handsome gowns in the world would make up for that loss. She had not been willing to give that up for one she truly wished for—and now she was being asked to give it up and for what?

Duty.

Finally she hung her head in defeat. "If I must . . ." she said reluctantly.

"The alternative is Medraut on the throne," replied the Lady, her voice showing that she very clearly cared no more for Medraut than Gwen did. "You know Medraut as well as any of us. You know your sister, who was trained by Anna Morgause, just as Morgana was. You know what will come of that."

That was no alternative at all.

"Very well. I accept," she sighed. *And I will find some way to have at least a part of my dream, too.*

But first, as she had feared, she found that to be made into a queen, she must be unmade.

This was a strange world that she reentered. It was not that she had abandoned womanly things so much as that she had made a choice that left no room for them. But now, suddenly, there was a veritable flood of womanliness that had swept her up and was carrying her off, and she watched the banks of simple practicality rushing past, out of reach, as Cataruna and Gynath and all the women of Lleudd's court descended on her, determined to "make her over."

She understood that this was needful. She could not turn up at the High King's stronghold in her armor and tunic and trews. And if she did not *act* like a queen she would have ridicule for her portion. If she did not *look* like one, well . . . not only ridicule, but perhaps even scorn.

She hated it. But she threw herself into it with a will. There was no turning back now, and hard as this was, it had been far more difficult to become a warrior. She had discipline, and she applied it as firmly as she had ever applied herself to learning a weapon, or to ride.

The women began with her hair, which seemed a logical way to start.

She had not chopped hers off short, as Braith had, because it tended to behave itself if properly braided, and what was as important, it made a good padding under a helm. But now it was unbraided and brushed until her head was sore, and washed first in lime-water to make it even paler than it had been, then in rainwater. Then she had to lie with it spread out while it dried. They did all this several times over the course of a week. She got very tired of it by the second round.

With all this came several sorts of baths. Now, as a whole, she enjoyed baths. But she did not really enjoy *being* bathed, then oiled, then bathed again, then oiled again, then bathed for a third time and rubbed down with perfumes while there was a woman on each hand and each foot, tsking and fussing over the toes and fingers.

When they were done with the bathing, and her hair was finally pale and silky enough to make them happy, it was time for the final step in the process. It was braided up, but no, not in her sensible single plait. Now it was braided in two, hanging down on either side of her face, braided with gold cord, which seemed a shocking waste of gold to her, then the bottom third of the braids were wrapped in a bit of fine cloth, and that, in turn, was held in place by a criss-cross of more gold cord. The braids hung heavily from her temples and made her head ache.

Why couldn't she just keep it loose, like every other maiden she'd seen?

Evidently because that wasn't what a king's daughter did.

She liked to keep her breasts bound—not flat, and not tight, but enough so that they didn't get in the way or move about and cause problems.

Well, that, it seemed, was completely out of the question. Her breasts were to be . . . prominent, and she found herself with braids *and* breasts encumbering her and making it impossible to move quickly.

Then there was the new clothing to get used to.

Oh, she was not averse to wearing a gown now and again, provided it was one that was comfortable, easy to move in.

Well.

First, a whole new wardrobe had to be constructed. The women did this at breakneck speed, while her hair and body were being scrubbed like a fish being descaled. The new wardrobe began with the linen chemise, of which she had three. They were fine; they were quite comfortable and very soft and lovely on her almost-raw skin. She would have enjoyed them except that they gave no support to her breasts whatsoever. Then came the undergowns, with tight sleeves— so tight she could never have drawn a bow or swung a sword or an ax in the wretched things. That was not fine. It didn't at all matter that they were of a perfectly lovely linen and wool mixed, as soft as the chemise. It didn't matter that they had grand bands of embroidery of a sort she could never do herself. It didn't even matter that every woman who looked at them sighed with naked longing. Because they were an absolute horror to wear.

Nor was it fine that they dragged on the ground behind, making them exceedingly impractical anywhere outside. Still, she could kirtle them up . . .

But then there were the overgowns, with wider, shorter sleeves and more bands of heavy embroidery on them. They were just wide enough that she had to try to keep the edges of the sleeves from drooping into things and getting filthy.

And last of all came the wide, embroidered belt, that she was supposed to tie as tightly as possible to show off her small waist and push up her breasts (though it gave them no support at all), from which dangled keys, a knife for eating, pouches for this and that—

On top of all this there was the mantle, which was not a practical cloak, oh no, but a great awkward rectangle of fabric that she was supposed to drape becomingly about her waist, and arms, and sometimes over her head.

Finally, as a last insult, a fur-lined overmantle she was supposed to pin at the shoulders over this entire mess of cloth; it didn't even close properly at the front, so she would stew at the back and freeze at the front.

So there were all these swaths of cloth to manage, and the tight arms of the undergown, and the dangling bits on the belt, and it seemed as if she was catching some part of the outfit on something whenever she moved. She had never felt so sorry for other women in her life. She felt even sorrier for herself.

Nevertheless, she was a king's daughter and a war chief, and she was not going to allow herself to be defeated by mere fabric.

So she did what anyone with sense would do. She put it all on and practiced. Practiced walking, walking quickly, moving about indoors and out, maneuvering around furniture, eating, carrying things—she couldn't possibly do most of the household chores that other women did in this stuff, but, then, she wouldn't have to. Cooking, cleaning, all that would be done for her. The High King's queen did not even have the duties that Queen Eleri had had (and Queen Eleri had dressed much more simply, with one chemise, an overgown, and in the cold, a good heavy cloak). She even practiced some dancing, and riding—and with some teeth gritting, being carried pillion behind a rider. And the others, anxious for her success, helped her. They had some little time; although the High King wanted her father's horses a great deal, he was less anxious to leap into a third marriage, and so the negotiations and bargaining went on through the autumn, and only concluded when the first snow fell. So she would go to the High King as his new bride a bare four months after the death of his second.

And by then she was the master, or perhaps mistress, of her own clothing. She moved as gracefully in it as Cataruna, if not more so. She had managed to contrive a breast-binding that at least made her chest stop aching. It might not be the height of fashion, but she didn't care. It was one comfort she *would* have.

By then, too, she had learned how to carry on a conversation that did not involve two or three ways to kill a man, nor how to track game, nor the three best remedies for horse colic. Her childhood skill with a needle had come back to her, though she was never going to be able to embroider with any level of competence. She had learned a great many songs that did not involve any marching cadences nor randy bed frolics. In one thing at least, her warrior training stood her in good stead: She could concoct a medicine and bind up a wound with greater skill than any of the others save Cataruna, who was Lady-trained.

And then, far too soon, it was time to be off to her fate. It was with mixed relief—for she was finally able to put on her warrior gear—and regret that she mounted Rhys; and with a guard of her own warriors, the escort sent by Arthur, and a half dozen horse keepers, she set off with the herd of grays for the stronghold of the High King at Celliwig.

The land lay barren before them, not yet covered with a sheltering blanket of snow, the trees bare, the grasses sere, the sky for the most part sad and gray. The only birds were rooks, crows, ravens, and now and again a wood dove. There was nothing festive about their group, either. They might as well have been riding to a parlay or a possible battle as to a wedding. Or perhaps to a funeral.

At night, she kept very quiet, quieter even than her usual habits, and listened to the men talking. That was how she learned that it was not only the Merlin who had been struck down, but that the senior Druids were dying, getting ill, or outright vanishing.

This was the first she had heard of such a thing, and it rather took her aback. But when she asked one of the escort, a fellow named Neirin, what he made of it, the man just shrugged.

"They're all old, lady," he pointed out. "There's nothing mysterious about old men dying."

She certainly couldn't refute his logic, although there was still something about it that bothered her. But surely if something was wrong, the Druids themselves would be falling all over themselves to get to the bottom of the matter . . .

They passed within a few miles of the Isle of Glass, and she was tempted to detour to pay a visit—but there was no guarantee that Gwyn would come out to see her, she had already had just about as much of the Ladies as she could stand, and Gildas was, in fact, waiting at Arthur's Castle to wed them by the Christian rites, along with Aeronwen to bind them by the Old Ways.

She was just as tempted to detour to the great Henge, but again, there was not much there to see. She did not have the Gift to see the Power in the Stones outside of the time of a major ceremony. There was no School or Convocation of Druids permanently in residence there as there was at the Cauldron Well. Other than marveling over the construction itself, there really was nothing to "see."

So in the end, she bypassed both places and kept on the straight road.

The nights were the hardest. Not because they were cold, though they were, but because she knew that every time she slept, she was that much closer to the end of her former life. But rather than feeling desperation, she felt only a deepening melancholy.

Until, finally, it was over. The road finally brought them within sight of Celliwig and the hill on which Arthur's castle stood.

At first, she was not at all impressed. There was a hill; on top of it, the walls of the more permanent version of the Roman-style fortification she was altogether familiar with, and just barely visible above that, roofs that appeared to be tiled. It was disappointing, actually. She had expected, from all the tales, to come upon some enormous artificial mountain of stonework, looming high above the plain below.

It did seem odd that there were no men patrolling the top of the walls, however.

It wasn't until she saw small dots moving atop the walls that she realized her mistake. It wasn't small. It was enormous—not in height, but in size. Probably the individual buildings were no taller than Castell y Cnwclas, but they were *each* just as large, if not larger. And there were as many of them, at least, as there were huts in the village. Clustered at the foot of the hill were houses and huts, indeed, enough to make up twenty villages the size of the one she had known.

Now she was very glad that she had fought in so many big engagements; if she hadn't, the sheer number of people would have been daunting.

Before they even reached the city of Celliwig—for it was a city, not just a village—she caught sight of what looked like a cluster of tents and pavilions at the side of the road. As they drew near to them, she saw the High King's red dragon banner flying above them, and she thought for a moment that Arthur had come ahead to inspect his . . . bargain.

But no, as they reached the tents, the party split into two; the horses and their keepers went on, while her escort halted, and one of her chests was taken out of the cart that held all her belongings. That was when she knew, with a stab of pain, that this was truly where she was leaving her old life behind . . .

Without a word, she dismounted, and went straight for the most elaborate of the pavilions. Before she even reached it, the flaps were opened by a pair of servant girls; two more took her by the elbows, exclaiming with distaste over her travel-worn and "manly" garb. Numbly, she gave herself over to them.

They couldn't manage a bath out here, but they did strip her down, warm some water at a brazier, and scrub her down and perfume her. Stubbornly, she did *not* allow them to take her comfortable breast bindings, but other than that, she submitted herself tamely to dressing, braiding, fussing, and bejeweling. And she submitted to being picked up and placed on a pillion pad behind the oldest of her escort. She hated it, and so did Rhys; he was tied to the saddle and following behind, and he eyed her with confusion and resentment. He didn't like being hauled along like a pack mule.

Well, she didn't like being baggage, either.

But she put a good, brave face on it. And when they reached the outskirts of the city, with people crowding around the road to the stronghold, cheering and peering, she continued to put a brave face on it, waving and smiling, nodding, and acting as if this was the culmination of her greatest dream.

Even though at that moment, if she'd been given an honorable way out of it, she'd have bolted like a rabbit.

Through the city, up the hill, through the gate in the wall, and then . . .

The entire cavalcade, which had, by now, acquired quite a long tail, stopped in front of the largest of the buildings. It was of stone and white-plastered timber, with roofs of red tile. Dead center was a grand entrance with tall white columns, and beneath the triangular pediment that surmounted them was a group of richly dressed men. She recognized Lancelin, Kai, Gwalchmai . . .

. . . Medraut . . . looking outwardly happy enough, although she very much doubted he was pleased with all of this.

And in the center of them, the man who could only be the High King.

Bearded, the red in his hair going to gray, he looked . . . worn and tired. His gold crown seemed to weigh him down. Over his fine red tunic he wore armor, breastplate and greaves in the Roman style; under it he wore sensible trews and boots. His red mantle was lined with ermine and was easily large enough to serve as a bedcovering. His expression was resigned.

As for his Companions, many of whom had met her already, their expressions were far more gratifying. Kai looked astonished; Gwalchmai grinned with great appreciation, as did many of the others. These were expressions she was not used to seeing on the faces of men when they looked at her, and at first, she had to stop herself from looking about to see what lovely woman they were staring at.

Am I really . . . pretty? she wondered. Practicality asserted itself. It was only the contrast, of course. They had seen her streaked with soot and dirt, in clothing that made everyone look the same, equally sexless. They were just surprised that she *was* a woman and that she had turned up looking like one.

But then she saw Lancelin's face.

He looked utterly stunned. And when his eyes met hers, her breath caught in her throat, and for a moment, her resignation turned to something else. A sorrow that stabbed her, as if he had pulled out his knife and driven it into her heart.

If only he were the High King . . .

The thought was repressed, instantly. It did not matter. The High King could be a bear in a crown and it still would not matter. It was her duty to wed him. So wed him she would.

A servant brought a tall stool with three steps and placed it beside the horse. Gracefully, as she had practiced, she gathered up her garments and alighted, one foot outstretched, as if she were a goddess slipping down from the sky. Gracefully she descended the three steps and waited for Arthur to come to her, dropping her garments to fall about her in the most becoming folds. He took her hand and bowed over it.

"Welcome, Lady Gwenhwyfar," he said, without any hesitation when he said her name. "We rejoice at your coming."

And that was when she felt it. The sheer force of his personality, which crashed over her like wave. It was not meant for her—not meant for anyone in particular—it was merely what he *was*. You felt that, the power in him—felt his wisdom, his care for his people, his strength—and all you could think was that it was not a duty to serve him but a privilege.

It was a glamorie, of course. But it was all the more powerful because beneath it, the strength, the wisdom, were real.

But when she felt it, she fought against it. She was here from duty. She would fulfill her obligations. But she was not going to be seduced into liking it by magic.

"And I to be here at last, my King," she replied, with a slight inclination of her head.

And he led her into his palace. Which felt, as the walls closed about her, altogether too much like a prison.

Chapter Twenty

With a cloth on her lap protecting a fine gown she would rather not have protected at all, Gwen carefully laid in the feathering on another arrow. Much to the horror of her ladies, who were all gathered about her with their fine sewing and bands of embroidery.

She was beyond caring how scandalized they were. She had already horrified them by laying aside the woolen mantle and tying back the sleeves of her overgown. They shivered in the occasional draft. She was too warm by far. These rooms were heated by means of something they called a hypocaust, a contained fire that sent warm air under the floor. It was as warm as spring in here, although these fragile flowers seemed to think there would be icicles hanging from their noses at any moment. This device was Roman, of course. Arthur was . . . extremely fond . . . of all things Roman.

She laid in another line of glue from the pot on the brazier beside her and quickly laid down the line of fletching.

She was working on arrows because these charming ladies had made it painfully obvious that there was nothing she could sew that they would not have to undo and resew again. She simply was not allowed in the still-room to make medicines. That was the job of a single servant. This exhausted her repertoire of "womanly" tasks. She wasn't going to sit there with her hands in her lap and listen to them giggle and gossip.

So she was, by the gods, doing something she *could* do, and do well. She was making arrows.

With both sets of vanes in, she took fine thread and bound them at the nock and the end of the vanes, laid the arrow aside to dry, and picked up a new one.

Inwardly, she seethed. Another thing that Arthur seemed very fond of. Roman customs. Such as the custom that confined women to a single section of this villa and kept them, for the most part, from mingling too much with men. Kai was in charge of the household. Not her. He set the menu for the day's meals, he oversaw the chief servants, the housekeeper and the cook, and kept track of and dispensed the stores. She had never seen the cook. The housekeeper pretended not to understand her and went about ordering things in the way *she* pleased. Gwen was expected to remain here, in the queen's chambers, until called for. Men were not supposed to come here unless they were servants or entertainers or came with Arthur. *She* was not supposed to mingle with the Companions, except under very supervised conditions, like meals or celebrations.

She was only at those meals perhaps once every three days, and such meals were as structured as a magic rite. She and her ladies entered the hall after the men; she was seated beside Arthur. There was music, to which Arthur paid careful attention, so that she did not get much conversation from him—but she got contradictory glimpses of both the tired old man and the charismatic leader. She heard maddeningly brief bits that hinted at ideas that were truly visionary. Most of all, she saw how the Companions all virtually worshiped him, and they did so in a way that told her that he had earned that worship, that it was not the result of some trick of attraction. And then, when the meal was over, they all rose, and she and her ladies went back to the maddening confines of her "bower." The only man that was allowed to come and go as he pleased there was Arthur.

Which he did, precisely, every night. And then went away again to sleep somewhere else.

She knew very well what lovemaking was all about. She hadn't been afraid of it. But she certainly hadn't expected it to be like . . .

. . . like a household chore. Something tedious, to be gotten over with as quickly and efficiently as possible.

Not that he was unkind, and not that he hurt her, except for the first time, and then it was nothing near as bad as some of the milder injuries she'd gotten in training. And for a while she had tried to be at least *pleasant* to him. Tried her best to look attractive where she waited for him, made sure that she smelled sweetly, that her breath was good. It was all to no purpose. She was nothing but a not-so-prize mare to him; he just wanted her breeding, so he need not visit her anymore. The Arthur that came to her room was neither the tired old man nor the vividly alive leader that she saw glimpses of at the table now and then. He was . . . like a horse trainer who had no vested interest in the horse he was training.

Making arrows was soothing. She felt in grave need of some soothing.

Was this why the other Gwenhwyfar had run off with Melwas? Because she was so bored she finally could not stand it any longer? At the moment, Gwen could not find it in her heart to blame her.

But that Gwenhwyfar should have been raised and trained to appreciate this life. She should have found the too warm rooms, the endless hours of sewing, the gossip, the idleness appealing. And Gwen had to admit that this villa was wildly luxurious by her standards.

There were no dirt floors anywhere, nor floors covered with rushes. Even the floors in the servants' quarters were tiled, and the ones here were covered with jewel-like mosaics. Her quarters included her own bedroom, her own dining room, rooms for her ladies, this room, which *they* called a solar, just for receiving visitors and spending the day with her ladies, and hearing the reports of Kai, the housekeeper, and a few other important servants. Not that she was expected to *do* anything about those reports . . .

There was even a bathing room just for her and her ladies. And all these rooms surrounded a colonnaded courtyard, in which, she presumed, she would be "allowed" to stroll on the perfectly manicured grass in fine weather. All she had to do was produce an heir and look, if not beautiful, at least queenly.

It was driving her mad.

The only relief she'd had from this cage was when Gildas had come to talk with her. Presumably, being a Christ priest, he had been "safe." He and Aeronwen had presided over a pair of marriage ceremonies with civility and calm, if not liking. Aeronwen had made her immediate departure. He, however, had stayed for another fortnight, for the weather had turned foul as soon as Aeronwen was gone. She wondered if he suspected the Lady had something to do with that; certainly Gwen did.

Gildas did not care for Arthur; that was hardly surprising, since Arthur had slain his rebellious brother. But for some reason he had taken to Gwen. He had spent many hours in this solar, asking her intense questions about her beliefs, inviting questions from her about his. Arguing cordially with each other. She came to see what it was that made his monks so intensely loyal to him. Under that dour expression was a remarkably sweet temper, and if he was stern, he was also able to forgive readily, even eagerly.

"I think that you will never convince me to leave my path," she told him, finally, "But I am becoming more certain after listening to you that our paths are so near one another as to be identical in many places."

He had looked at her with a raised eyebrow. Opened his mouth. Closed it again.

"There are things that the Ladies cleave to that I find . . . wrong," she admitted. "I will never believe that the gods and the land require blood be spilled so that both can prosper. Think of all the blood spilled in war—if it were merely blood that was required, the lands that were battlefields should forever be waist deep in lush grasses and yielding four times the corn of others for all eternity. Yet I have never seen that. The first year after a battle, yes, but that is just logic, since you could get as goodly a harvest spreading manure. But not after."

"And neither have I!" he began, eagerly.

"Wait," she had said, holding up a hand to forestall him from yet another attempt to persuade her to his way of belief. "Aside from that, now I must look to the followers of both our gods. Your own god has said that one knows the tree by the fruit it bears. Those people that heed the Druids and the Ladies, I see to be not much different from those that follow Christ. There are liars and thieves among both, kindly, honorable and wise among both, virtuous and vile in equal measure. Can you refute that?"

He had looked as if he would have liked to, but he admitted that he could not.

"So our peoples are not so very different. Their hearts are not so different. So—" she shrugged. "Since it is the gods that rule men's hearts, it follows that your gods and mine are not so different. It seems to me that the faces we put on them have more to do with ourselves than with them."

He had looked at her with such astonishment on his face that she'd had to laugh. Eventually so did he, and gracefully he had turned the talk to more questions about the Folk of Annwn, about whom he was as curious as an eager child.

But now he was gone, and there was nothing to make one day different from the next. She rose after sunrise. She ate. She heard what the cook would be making. She approved it. She came to the solar, to be surrounded by these fatuous women, and tried not to die of boredom. She ate. Then back to the solar. Or every other day, a bath.

And not the efficient sort of bath she was used to, no indeed. This was a bath that took up an entire afternoon. First, she was ushered into an even warmer room, a bath in the Roman style but reserved for her and her women. This was, she was told, almost atop the furnaces that put warmth beneath the floors, and it was full of steam. There she put up with being washed with soap and cloths—as if she could not even wash herself!—and rinsed with jugs of warm water, which ran away into a drain in the floor. Then her hair was pinned up on the top of her head, and she was led like a dotard into a second room, where there was a pool—a pool!—of steaming hot water. All the ladies soaked in it together, occasionally going to a tub of cooler water, only to return to the hot one. And there they would gossip, gossip, gossip and talk of nothing but trivialities. She heard nothing of what was going on in the greater world, only endless details of dresses and love affairs. The few times she actually heard anything that *did* sound worth listening to, it turned out to be so distorted as to be incredible. Then, when she was sure she was going to fall asleep from boredom or the heat, came the drying, the massaging with lotions and scented oils, and at last, dressing and going to dinner. Dinner was generally in the company of the King and his Companions, but *they* never discussed anything worth listening to either! Oh, no, it was all pretty compliments and talk of hunts and weather—not a word of the Saxons, or King March, or anything else actually worth hearing about.

The whole tedious business happened every other day. And she was certain that at least some of her ladies would do this *every* day if they could.

This was not a bath day, so there would be no dinner with the King either. And finally fed up past bearing with the boredom, today she had ordered a servant to bring her the fletching materials from the armory. He hadn't wanted to, but there was no reason why he shouldn't, so at last she bullied him into it.

At least she was getting something constructive done. She had not seen one single arrow in Arthur's forces that was any better than hers. None of these women had ever seen fletching done, much less put feathers to arrows themselves, so there would be no undoing what she had done.

Arthur finally had something to say to her besides a curt greeting when he turned up that night and the doors closed behind him. He looked at her, as she was waiting patiently in the far-too-luxurious bed, and frowned slightly. The bedroom was—like everything else— in the Roman style. It was long and narrow, with the bed under a vaulted ceiling at the far end. The floors were warm enough to go barefooted on them, but the alcove with the bed was a little drafty, and she pulled the fur up around her shoulders. Every night her women put her naked into this bed; every night the King turned up to perform like a bored stallion and depart.

"I heard an odd thing from Kai, my lady," he said, carefully, making no move to disrobe, although she was already naked beneath the covers. "This afternoon, he said, you ordered certain materials brought to you. You were . . . fletching?"

She nodded and wondered how much of her expression he could read in the light from the single oil lamp at the bedside. "I was."

He paused. "I should like to know why. It seems . . . an odd occupation."

"Because—" she took a deep breath. "Because it was better to make arrows than to pick up small objects and begin flinging them at the heads of those vacuous, simpering, gossiping idiots that I am supposed to be polite to."

His mouth dropped open, and he looked at her in astonishment.

"Husband, I am *not* one of these women!" she exclaimed passionately. "I was not made, nor trained, for idleness! I am a warrior, trained from childhood to be a warrior. I have not one thing in common with them. I do not believe that any of them has done a single piece of simple, practical work in all her life! They have no thoughts beyond dress and gossip. I do not find gossip to be entertaining! *I am a warrior!* And being caged up in these rooms, hour after hour, day after day, doing nothing with any meaning to it, hearing nothing but trivialities discussed as if they were matters of the realm, is driving me mad!"

"I—see—" he said. Finally he walked heavily to the bedside and sat down on the foot of it.

"Husband, I am stifled. I cannot breathe here. My clothing weighs upon me, heavier than any armor; the rooms are too warm, the food so rich it makes me ill. I feel that if I do not see the sun and feel the wind, I will lose the few wits I have left to me." She looked at him with pleading. "Surely you can see now what is wrong."

And then she saw understanding dawn on him, and he smiled a little. "Yes, wife, I do see!" He picked up her hand and squeezed it. "I understand. I shall leave orders I think will please you, and I expect after such a stressful day, you will want some sleep. I shall leave you to your rest."

And with no other words than that, he left her. This time, *without* the . . . the "servicing" that was so automatic that it felt like nothing more than a tedious chore for both of them.

Relief suffused her like the warmth from the floor. Finally, he realized what kind of a person he had taken to wife. And he was truly as good and kind a man as she had seen him be with others. She blew out the lamp and pulled the covers about her, thinking happily of the hunting she would do tomorrow and of being, at last, part of his councils.

She awoke to silence.

Her first thought was gleeful. He had sent those awful chattering women away! Or at least, told them to take their unwelcome company elsewhere. The servant that slept in the chamber attached to hers woke up as soon as she heard Gwen moving about and tried to put her into those maddening drapes, but Gwen sternly ordered her to find her old clothing, the tunic and trews and good sturdy boots, and though the servant protested, she obeyed. A glance while she was dressing at the light coming from the tiny window up near the top of the ceiling—after waving the servant away—told her that she had slept well past midmorning. Another sign that the gaggle of ninnies was elsewhere! She quickly tied on her boots with a happy heart.

Silently thanking the goddesses, Epona in particular, Gwen strode cheerfully into her solar and headed for the doorway to the outer corridor, intent on getting to the stables and finding Rhys. She hadn't seen either of her horses since she had arrived here, and of the two, Rhys was the one most inclined to be lazy when he got the chance. *Probably stuffing himself on hay and congratulating himself on escaping exercise, the slothful beast,* she thought happily. *Time to wake him—*

She pushed open the door, and at once was stopped by a bar to her exit. "Halt!" the guard at the door said, "Boy! What are you—"

"Boy?" Gwen slapped at the spear that had been lowered to stop her from going any further. "Alun ap Grwn, are you blind? I'm no more a boy than you are. Now enough with your nonsense. I'm going to the stables."

The guard gaped at her, then snapped the spear back up. His usually stolid expression was gone, replaced with utter confusion. "Queen Gwenhwyfar, I—didn't recognize—"

She waved the apology off. "Never mind. I'm going for a ride, and I suppose I will need an escort. Send for whoever of the Companions isn't busy, will you, and direct him to the stable. Or better yet, go yourself."

"Ride?" the man replied, looking dazed. "Stable? But, Queen Gwenhwyfar, you can't—"

"I most certainly can," she said sharply. "and I am going to. Now get one of the Companions to—"

"But—there's no one here but Kai and Medraut," the man stammered. "And I'm under orders from the King himself. You're not to be disturbed, and on no account I am not to let you leave—"

The first part of his sentence was lost in the slap to the face that the second part was. She whirled on him. "*What?*" she exclaimed in outrage.

"I'm not to—let you leave—your rooms?" he faltered, as she put one hand to her belt knife and stared at him, eyes blazing with rage.

"We'll see about that!" And with that, she headed off at an angry trot, outpacing him, as he tried to follow her, protesting every step of the way.

She was so angry that she just shut his words out. She headed straight for the King's privy chambers, since it wasn't yet time for the usual audiences, nor for the Companions to gather about that famous round table. Her blood boiled. He had *said* that he understood! How could he—how dared he—

Her chambers were separated from his by the courtyard; she

passed along one side of it, the first time she had actually seen the sun and the open sky in days. Her breath steamed in the cold air; it felt good and clean after all the heat and perfume.

She stormed past the startled guards on his doors, the protesting Alun right behind. The first room, where he would usually have been, sitting at a desk, was empty. There were no maps on the desk, no discarded cloak, and the mosaic floor that imitated the pool of the courtyard outside had been swept immaculately clean.

The second room, where he usually lounged with Kai or others he considered close as kin, was also empty. The cushions were placed neatly on the Roman-style couches. There were no cups and horns waiting on the side table to be collected, no litter of food from breaking fast. And the small council chamber, with the frescos of Hercules defeating a lion, was just as empty. And his bedroom, as small as hers, was not only empty, but cold. Very empty, even of servants.

She turned on the guards, who had followed her in. *"Where is he?"* she shouted.

"G-g-gone, Queen Gw—l"

"I can see that! *Where?*" If he and the Companions had gone off hunting and left before she was awake so he had an excuse to leave her behind—

"Roughly half a day from here, more or less southwards, dear sister."

That was not a voice she wished to hear.

She stiffened as Medraut strolled past the guards, a goblet held negligently in one hand. He took a sip of the contents as she stared at him, uncomprehending. Surely they were not hunting that far afield? And surely there was no need for Arthur to go visiting an ally in this weather—was there?

"Half a day—what does that mean?" she demanded, her stomach

sinking with dread. Because there was *one* reason why they would all have left . . .

"Just what I said. He left this morning to join most of the Companions and the warriors. And his allies, of course." Medraut smiled at her, evidently enjoying every moment of this.

"Warriors—allies—why?" No. Surely not. Surely Arthur would not have—

"The Saxons, of course. The moment they heard he'd married again, they decided to take advantage of it. Just like the last time, when they attacked in the winter. Evidently they did not learn the lesson. Or they heard that Arthur tamed the White Phantom, so now they believe it is safe to harass our border again." His grin widened. "You've been carefully sheltered from all this terrible news so that you wouldn't be upset by it. Arthur was only waiting until he was sure you were breeding to go take the field himself."

Her mouth dropped open. "Wh—*breeding?*" Suddenly the conversation—or lack of it—they'd had last night all made sense. But not in the way that she'd assumed last night.

He thought—

"Of course, we were all sympathy when we learned of your outburst. And we agreed that it was safe enough to leave you now—not to mention that it's very unpleasant to be around a female when she is so . . . temperamental. Women do get so emotional and so irrational when they're breeding." Oh how she hated the snide smile on Medraut's face! She wanted to smash it off . . . her hands clenched and unclenched at her sides. How much of that nonsense he had just spouted had *he* poured into Arthur's ear? Her jaw was clenched so hard that her teeth were actually beginning to hurt, and she forced herself to relax, but her fury at *both* of them did not abate one bit. Of course he had taken the field himself. He hadn't wanted her in the first place. She was only now beginning to realize just how he thought of women in general—that he had never, even with the evidence in front of him, thought of her as a warrior. Certainly he had not thought of her as the equal of one of his Companions. Bronwyn was right; though he had first seen his first wife as a warrior, she had later shown herself to him as a woman, and he had buried the warrior beneath the woman in his mind. He was not a man who could see both. And in her case, he did not want to.

And Medraut? Medraut had encouraged him.

"Here. Drink this, dear sister," Medraut said, handing her the goblet. She almost dashed the contents in his face. But instead, she swallowed them in two gulps, not even tasting them, except to recognize them vaguely as mead. She thrust the cup back at him. "Your women protested that it was too early to tell, but he only smiled, and said, 'Well, whatever else would cause a lady to suddenly demand fletching supplies and sit in her solar to make arrows? I expect her next demands will be for pickled vegetables, and stewed dormice.' And then he laughed and appointed Kai and myself to be in charge of the realm while he was at war." Medraut chuckled. "Such a trusting man. I suppose he thinks he's tacitly grooming me to take Kai's place eventually. But then, he knows that Kai will take excellent care of his queen, given her condition. And I, of course, told him that I would be sure that you had my very particular attention."

"He—*what?*" She was so enraged now that she was dizzy with it. "But I am the queen! I—" She groped blindly for the edge of the table to steady herself. *She* should have been the one left in charge, not Kai, and certainly not Medraut! That she had not—it was an insult past bearing.

"Exactly, dear sister." He laughed. Oh, how she hated that laugh! "You are only the queen. Obviously he couldn't leave a mere woman in charge. That is hardly the Roman way—but you look ill, dear sister."

She held the table with both hands now, the room spinning around her.

"You see, you have exerted yourself entirely too much. Let me help you to your chambers—" He waved off the anxious guards. "No, no, it's quite all right. I can carry her easily."

And indeed, he bent a little and scooped her up as if she had been a child. He was much, much stronger than he looked. And by now, she couldn't even push him away. Her arms and legs didn't seem to want to work at all, and she was so dizzy that she couldn't even get her eyes to focus.

Her head lolled against his shoulder, and she hated, *hated*, the foul, possessive way his arms tightened around her. She tried to speak, but nothing would come out.

Once more she crossed the end of the courtyard, but this time, even though she wanted to squirm out of Medraut's arms and run away, she had to close her eyes against the way the heavens swung wildly about.

The chill air didn't help, and the warmth that enveloped her once they got to her rooms only made things worse. She wanted to scream in protest as he invaded her very bedchamber, but her voice wouldn't work. "Go get her women," Medraut ordered the single servant, as he laid her down on her bed.

"That didn't take long at all."

That was a voice . . . a voice she should know. But it wasn't one of her women. Gwen stared up at Medraut, and at the woman who had come to join him. A woman wearing *her* dress. A woman that was so like her, that Gwen seemed to be looking into a mirror. For a moment she thought, *magic.*

And then her mind finally presented her with the right answer. "Hello, sister mine," Gwenhwyfach said, and giggled, looking down at her. "What? No words of greeting?"

Gwen's throat worked, but nothing came out.

"My potions have always been effective," Medraut replied. "Because I take more care with them than my sister does."

"But your sister has other talents." Gwenhwyfach reached up with a proprietary hand and smoothed Medraut's black hair, and for one moment, his eyes flashed annoyance. She was looking at Gwen, however, and didn't see it. "I have the cart all ready, my love. We only need to roll her up in the blankets and have your man carry her out."

"Good." Medraut reached down and tilted Gwen's chin so she was looking directly at him. "You see, dear sister, I could not take the chance that any woman the High King married actually *might* manage to breed Arthur an heir. I must have put together a dozen plans, depending on how important the woman was. The worst would have been one of the Ladies . . ." He made a sour face.

Gwenhwyfach laughed. "There is no chance one of them would have given up her Power to come here!"

"True enough." Medraut looked down at Gwen, and she wanted to shudder at the expression in his eyes. "But when he decided to marry you, I knew I had the easiest and most elegant—and least risky—solution in my own two hands. *My* Gwen becomes the queen she has always wanted to be and makes sure Arthur dies childless. *You* will be taken away."

His wife interrupted him, glancing with some concern between herself and Gwenwhyfar. "Do you think that anyone will notice that she was wearing those—things—and I am wearing her gown?"

Medraut shook his head. "Only the guards and the servant saw her. Besides, she can always say that she changed her clothing after her spell of illness. I dismissed the servant that dressed her to the kitchens, and no man ever remembers what a woman is wearing."

"Only what she isn't." Gwenhwyfach said mockingly, and Gwen

felt chilled to hear her own laugh coming from her sister's throat. "Oh, I am looking forward to this. You may be sure I will well bewitch the High King, my love. Arthur will have such a greeting when he returns as will make him never want to leave my bed again. I will use every wile your mother ever taught me."

"It would greatly please me if you managed to dispose of him there, my love," Medraut smiled. Incredibly, he was not the least bit disturbed at hearing his own wife describe how she intended to seduce another man! Then again . . .

. . . he was certainly Lot's son in spirit, if not in actuality.

"But if you do not, when the Saxons finally kill the old man, or the Ladies give up and let me spill his blood for the Land, the Old Stag will give way for the Young Stag, and I will be High King. Just as mother promised." His eyes glittered, and inside her, she grew cold with fear. How had she never seen this before? How had she never seen how ruthless he was, how he would do anything, use any tool, to take the High King's throne? Now, of course, it was far too late.

"I'm sure by now you are also wondering, 'But what about the Druids?' Since it was the Merlin who was so very eager to kill me in my cradle." He laughed. "And of course, the Merlin managed to imprint his desires on the entire Druidic Council. I thought about that, too, well in advance of putting my plans in motion. I have been working at this for years. All of the Merlin's cronies have tottered off to the Summer Lands, and I hold the young ones in the palm of my hand." He spread his hands wide. "And now it all comes together. You, the High King's queen, disposed of. The Druids, mine. The Ladies so concerned with fighting the encroachment of the Christ men that they ignore me. My wife in your place. All of it, building the stair that will take me to the highest place in the land."

She was fighting hard now to even stay conscious. Her vision narrowed, darkened. There was a roaring in her ears. She couldn't hear him anymore. Couldn't see him.

So this is death, she thought bitterly.

And then she had no more thoughts at all.

She hadn't expected to wake, so when she did, it was with a shock as great as the blast of cold air that struck her in the face. She struggled to move, to open her eyes, and plunged into despair when she couldn't. Wave after wave of nauseating emotions washed over her. Panic. Terror. A deeper despair. She tried to force calm on herself, tried to get control, only to have fear wrest it away from her. Her ears were still full of a roaring sound, but under that, she heard the clopping of hooves, and her body was bouncing on a hard, flat surface, and rolling about a bit. So she was in that cart Gwenhwyfach had mentioned. She'd been incompletely poisoned. But she still couldn't move. She was being carted off, to be buried alive. The thought of the frozen clods falling on her face, the earth filling her throat, her lungs, choking her—

She thought she would be submersed in terror forever.

But even the terror wore itself out. It ebbed, slowly. And that was when she realized that she *could* open her eyes again. And she could—barely—move her fingers and toes.

When she forced her eyes open, she couldn't see anything but light filtering through a coarse cloth that covered her face. And she was tied firmly hand and foot—tied, in fact, to a pole that ran past her head and feet, so she couldn't bend or kick. But she was awake, and she could move. That counted for something.

And that was when she realized that even if her hands and feet were bound, her mouth was not.

"Help," she croaked, weakly. Then, "Help!" she yelped, louder. *"Help! Help! He—"*

The cart stopped. The cloth covering her face was pulled back, roughly.

"Now, now," said Medraut, making no attempt to hide his gloating. "Surely you don't want to leave my company so soon, Gwen?" He gave her no time to do more than gasp at seeing him. He reached down and wrenched her head back by the hair, stuffing one end of a horn into her mouth. "You'll just need to go back to sleep for now. We have a way yet to go." He let go of her hair and pinched her nose shut, then poured more of that cloyingly sweet mead down the horn. "Drink or drown, my love."

She had no other choice. Choking, coughing, she drank. Some of it got into her lungs, where it burned terribly. As soon as he was sure the drugs were taking hold of her, he pulled the horn out of her mouth and smoothed her hair with a tender hand, wiping the tears of pain and rage from her eyes, and fastidiously cleaning some of the slopped mead from her mouth.

"There we are. That's better, isn't it." His eyes were alight with a strange look of pleasure. "What? You thought I was going to kill you? I told you years ago that you were going to be mine; why would I want to kill you? I only married your sister because she was so like you." He patted her cheek, while she shrank back inwardly in horror. "And now I have you all to myself. Your sister will be so concerned with keeping Arthur happy, she won't have time to worry about what I am doing. Besides, she thinks I am going to throw you in a river or bury you, not that I am taking you off to—well, it doesn't matter where. All that matters is that I prepared it for you years ago. Oh, you don't like me now, I know. But you'll learn to love me. I know you will. You won't be able to help yourself."

He laughed, and pulled the coverings over her head again. And mercifully, the roaring, and the blackness came back, and she was carried away by them and hid inside them.

Chapter Twenty-One

Gwen sat cross-legged on her pallet on the floor, patiently braided her own hairs into a thread. A few threads and she could make a cord. If she had a cord, she might be able to strangle Medraut with it . . .

There was not much else to do. She lived in a small room with a high window in one wall and a mattress heaped with furs on the floor. The floors were stone, the walls were stone, and the timbers of the ceiling could not be reached by any means from the floor. Without a knife, it was not possible to cut up the furs or the canvas cover of the mattress. She was wearing heavy woolen gowns of material too tough to tear and too closely woven to pick apart, without any fastenings or cords. She was barefoot.

The latrine was a heavy stone basin in the corner with a hole much too small to stick anything down. The huge guard that brought her food sloshed a bucket of water down it when he came in.

Medraut had gone to great lengths to make sure that there was nothing in here she could use as a weapon. Her food was served in a grass basket, and she ate it with her fingers; her drink came in a blunted drinking horn that wouldn't serve as a weapon itself and wouldn't smash to give her something with a point or edge. Those were taken away when she was finished, and the guard stayed there until she finished.

This place, whatever it was, must have been built on the Roman style, for the floor was warm, though not nearly as warm as Arthur's palace.

She was not sure how long she had been here. Weeks, certainly. Months . . . probably. For most of the early part of this ordeal, she had been unconscious for long stretches thanks to Medraut's potions.

Medraut visited her from time to time; his visits were irregular, and the only way that she knew one was going to occur was when she began to feel dizzy after eating. He made sure that she couldn't move long before he unlocked her door. She had been completely unsuccessful in detecting whatever he was putting in her food; she'd tried not eating altogether, but eventually hunger drove her to eat. After all it wasn't as if she wanted to die—that was the last thing she wanted. She wanted to get free.

She was pretty certain that on the last several visits, Medraut hadn't touched her, although she knew very well he had done whatever he liked early on. Probably he had found that lying with someone as unresponsive as a corpse was rather unsatisfying. Instead, of late, he had a chair brought and sat in it, talking at her until she lost consciousness. That might actually have not been so bad if he had given her any real information. She knew far more than she wanted to know now about how he had gotten rid of Arthur's sons, how he had hoodwinked Arthur into trusting him, what most of his late childhood had been like—and far, far too much about how he had been certain she was destined for him from the moment he saw her.

But a very, very strange thing also happened when she was drugged—and sometimes, when she was asleep.

Visions—maybe. If visions they were, she could hardly credit them. But if they were not, why on earth would her mind have made such a thing up?

She got glimpses into the life Little Gwen was leading in her place, and at first, everything happened as she would have predicted. Little Gwen absolutely reveled in her place as queen, wallowing in the baths and the preening, gossiping viciously with her ladies and for mischief setting them against each other, ordering gown after sumptuous gown, and entertaining Arthur in her bed with a wanton abandon that made Gwen blush with shame.

But then something happened. A new Arthur began to appear in that bedchamber of nights. An Arthur that *she* had never seen, a man who, despite his years, seemed more vibrant, more alive, than she had ever seen him. And under the charismatic spell of *that* Arthur . . . Little Gwen softened. Gradually, she ceased tormenting her ladies. Gradually, her demeanor took on a cast that Gwen couldn't really identify at first.

And when she did . . . that was when she simply couldn't believe the dreams. Because—if she was right—Arthur was taming the untamable Little Gwen, winning her to him the way he won his men's hearts. And she simply could not believe that anyone as self-centered as Little Gwen could come to care for anyone other than herself.

She'd had another of those dreams last night. It seemed just as impossible as the ones before it. If she didn't know better, she would have thought that Little Gwen was having second thoughts about betraying Arthur.

Impossible.

As she braided, she began to feel the tingling in her lips that signified he had slipped a potion into her again. With a resigned sigh, she thrust the thread she was braiding with the others she had made under the mattress, then stretched out under the furs and waited for the paralysis—and Medraut—to arrive. She stared up at the ceiling and the tiny bit of sky that was all she could see through the window.

She was almost beginning to look forward to this. It made for a change in the endless sameness of her days. She had thought she was bored as Arthur's queen; here she had nothing whatsoever to do except exercise, comb her fingers through her hair, and braid what came out.

At least she was still fit. She did every exercise she could remember, practiced fighting moves even if she didn't have a weapon, stretched and flexed until she was more limber than she had ever been in her life except as a small child. She had learned how to run and tumble in these wretched gowns, even if she couldn't run very far in the tiny cell.

She even practiced that meditation that the Ladies did, though she wasn't very good at it. She prayed a great deal. She recited what she could remember of bardic ballads and epics.

She did that now, waiting for the potion to take effect, staring upward, because when she couldn't move, she really didn't want to be frozen in a position where she had to look at Medraut.

The room began to spin, even though she was lying down. Beneath the furs, she tried, experimentally, to move her arm, and couldn't. So . . . he should be entering at any moment.

This was when she heard the bar on the outside of the door slide aside, and the door scraped open. Footsteps on the stone followed as Medraut entered the room, followed by a servant with a comfortable chair; who placed the chair and washed out the basin with a bucket of water. She could just see Medraut out of the corner of her eye; he made a face, and waved a hand in front of his nose.

"Time for another bath and a new gown, my love," he said. "You'll like that, won't you?"

She felt a little sick inside. Yes, she liked being clean. No, she did not like the fact that it happened while she was unconscious. Not one bit. She would wake up with her hair washed and braided, completely scrubbed, and in a new clean gown. She had no idea who or what was doing this, nor what, if anything, happened besides the washing. What was the most disturbing, perhaps, was the level of detail; her fingers and toes were neatly manicured, the nails trimmed, and even buffed to a soft polish. There were none of the perfumed oils of Arthur's baths, but there was a faintly pleasant scent on her skin afterwards. Any tiny abrasions or bruises were anointed with a balm, and calluses were sanded.

"Well, now, where were we?" Medraut asked, rhetorically, since she couldn't answer. She turned her attention back to the ceiling. In a way, since she was forced to listen to these monologues, she was glad even her expression was frozen. At least he didn't know how revolted she was most of the time by his confidences. And why did he ever think that this would make her care for him?

Maybe because Gwenhwyfach used to hang on his every word?

"Ah, I don't believe I ever told you how Lot told me that I wasn't his." She heard him move a little as he settled himself in the chair. "It was one of those rare moments when he was sulking about being Mother's pander, rather than gloating about it. Possibly his temper was because she was lying with someone he hadn't picked himself, and she wasn't allowing him to watch. So when I interrupted him to show him the results of the sacrifice and blood spell I had done all by myself, he knocked me into a wall and called me 'Arthur's unnatural bastard.'"

At this point, likely, Gwenhwyfach had been cooing with sympathy to him. Oh, how she wished she could stop her ears. The images that his narrative called up made her feel even more ill. Her imagination—given what her visions had shown her of Anna Morgause and her past—created scenes of Medraut's mother disporting herself with a lover all too vividly. And it was hardly that she disapproved of lovemaking—though her own experiences were not inclined to make her crave it herself. It was how Anna Morgause had used it: as a tool, a weapon. Even with Arthur. *Especially* with Arthur.

"I knew better than to move. Lot is entirely unpredictable, and there was no telling how he would react. He glared at me a moment, then stormed off. I went to ask Morgana what he meant." Gwen couldn't turn her head to see his expression, but his tone was casual, as if he were telling a tale about someone else. This had probably hurt him—yes, even him—if it was true. If. There was no telling, with Medraut. Perhaps the reason for his casual tone was that it actually had never happened at all.

"She told me that what Lot had said was entirely true. Even the 'unnatural' part." He chuckled. "She explained it all to me, that Mother was Arthur's half-sister, and that even though the gods themselves often mated with their siblings, or daughter with father and son with mother, small-minded mortals thought this was wrong. A very enlightened woman, is Morgana. None of that really mattered to me, either." His voice took on a faint tone of gloating. Now *this,* this she could believe. Very little mattered to Medraut, so long as he got what he wanted. "All that did matter was that Lot, whom I hated and despised, even at so young an age, was not my father. My real father was the man who was King over Lot, who had the Folk of Annwn as his allies, and the Merlin as his servant. My real father was Arthur, the High King. What Lot intended to be the moment of my humiliation became the moment of my release and elevation. That was the moment that I knew that I was destined for great things. I would either create something unparalleled, or destroy it. Either way, my name would never be forgotten."

She would have shivered at his words if she had been able to move. She believed this, too, believed fervently that Medraut hated Lot and Lot hated him—and that Medraut craved fame or infamy and didn't care which he got, so long as he had it.

"Mother sensed that I had learned the truth and questioned me about it. I told her, but only in Morgana's presence, because I wanted Morgana to know I had told, and I wanted Mother to know that we were together on this." He let out his breath in a long sigh of reminiscence. "Mother was always a little afraid of Morgana, and I didn't know why at the time, but I felt that with Morgana there, she wouldn't dare punish either of us. I found out later, of course, just why Mother feared her. Morgana had pledged herself to the Morrigan when her woman's blood first began to flow."

That meant nothing to her—well, except that if Anna Morgause was wary about this Morrigan, it would be wise to be even more wary. He laughed softly, mockingly. "You're puzzled, of course. You wouldn't know of the Morrigan. She is the Dark of the Moon to Cerridwen's Full Moon. They know her well in Eire, though, and it was a wise woman of Eire that taught our Morgana of her. She is the chooser of the dead, the storm crow, the washer at the ford. She is power and chaos, and she suits our Morgana most perfectly. Even Mother was afraid of the Morrigan's power."

Gwen felt a cold that had nothing to do with the potions or her paralysis. It wasn't wise to mix with the gods, the dark ones in particular. "Lot himself has always left Morgana alone, even though he lusts for her to this day. I often wonder if that wasn't why Morgana pledged herself in the first place."

Well, Gwen couldn't fault Morgana for protecting herself from Lot, whose excesses rivaled those of his wife. But dealing with the dark side of the moon goddess—risky, risky business. Everyone knew there were always two sides to every Power, but dealing even with the bright side of the changeable Goddess of the Moon was a great deal like trying to bargain with the Folk of Annwn. Cerridwen was fickle enough; what was the Morrigan like?

It wasn't wise to put a name to the dark ones, nor to give your name to them, and it was even more foolish to bargain with them. Not unless you wanted them to come for you one day, asking a payment much too high for what you got.

It did rather sound as if that was exactly what Morgana wanted.

"So, Mother didn't argue with Morgana, she didn't even chide her. She just said 'Since you have told him, you might as well have the teaching of him.' And that was what she did." Gwen heard him get up from his chair and walk over to her pallet to peer down at her. The ceiling seemed to move in a slow circle, with his face as the center of it. "Ah, still with me. Good. It is really quite important that you hear this, my love. You need to understand just why it's futile to resist me and important to love me."

He sat back down in his chair, satisfied that she was still listening to him. "Naturally, Morgana told me everything then, not the least of which was how the Merlin had tried to have me killed when I was born. Morgana had seen just this thing in her scrying and had told Mother, so Mother had made certain I was safe by giving birth early. By that, Morgana was as much my mother as she was, if not more. Well! When she told me that, I was all for pledging to the Morrigan myself! Unfortunately, the Morrigan does not accept males." He sighed, theatrically. "Nevertheless, Morgana taught me and kept me safe from my brothers until I could defend myself. Shortly after that, Mother decided that it would be a fine idea to wed Morgana to your father. She had intended him for herself, but her magics were thwarted."

Oh, Gwen remembered that all too well.

"Now I would imagine at this point, you are wondering why Morgana didn't ensnare your father. She was more powerful than mother, and the moon goddesses, bright *and* dark, are goddesses of passion and love. It's a logical question." The chair creaked as Medraut leaned back in it. "The answer is simple enough. She didn't want him. Why would she? He was an old man, more than old enough to be her father." After a pause, he began to laugh, harder and harder, the sound filling up the entire room, battering her ears. After what seemed like far too long, his laughter died down. "Oh, my. That was funny. You should be able to understand her feelings perfectly, my love. After all you *are* married to an old man who is more than old enough to be *your* father."

As Gwen teetered on the edge of unconsciousness, it came to her in a last moment of pure nausea that for once, Medraut was right; she *did* understand Morgana's feelings in that, if in nothing else. She understood them perfectly.

Gwen awoke, as usual, slowly. But as she woke, she was aware almost immediately that she was not where she expected to be.

Scent came to her first, and the scent was of steam and soap, with a touch of rosemary. Then came the sense of hard pressure at her back, not the soft mattress. And there was no weight of furs on her, either.

It was warm, extremely warm. As sensation came back to her fingers, she flexed them, and ran them over the surface she was lying on.

Wood.

There was no wood in her cell except the beams of the ceiling.

She fought against the clinging hold of the potion, struggled to free herself of it, feeling hope begin to stir. She had to see where she was! Finally, she got her eyes open, and looked up at the ceiling above her. It was tiled in blue mosaic. And although it was not tiled in a pattern she recognized, she knew very well what this must be: a Roman bathhouse in a Roman or Roman-styled villa.

She was where she was always groomed while she was unconscious. Only this time, for some reason, she was alone. These rooms echoed dreadfully; if there had been anyone else here, she would have heard the breathing, even if they didn't stir.

So, alone, and somewhere other than her cell. Hope took on strength. By this time, she knew exactly how soon she could move as the potion wore off; she was nearly on fire with impatience, until at last, she was able to sit up.

She had been lying on a wooden bench very near a small soaking pool, smaller than the one she knew in Arthur's villa. This definitely was a Roman bathhouse, for the entire interior was paved in mosaic—blue with scenes of mermaids on the walls, brown with plants on the floor and in the pool. Her hair was still damp and a bit heavy but not soaking, so someone had been drying it before she had been abandoned. She was in a chemise, but not a gown, though there was a clean one nearby.

There were, in fact, a great many things nearby . . . including a knife that someone must have been using to clean and trim her nails. It wasn't a big knife, but it was more of a weapon than she had seen in far too long.

With her eyes fixed on it, she held her breath and listened. There was a lot of commotion going on in the far distance. Shouting. Fighting? Something urgent had interrupted the people grooming her, and kept them occupied long enough for the potion to wear off. If that was fighting, they might even have forgotten her.

At some point, though, someone would realize that they had been gone too long. She had to act, and act quickly.

The first thing she did was to don the gown, slit it up the middle, and use strips she cut from the towels she found to bind the result to her legs like a pair of trews. She followed that by making crude cloth shoes of the remains of the towels. Once, she would have been able to go barefoot in anything but snow. No more. And if she managed to escape, she couldn't afford damaged feet. She braided her hair roughly, tied the end with a bit of scrap, then hunted, quickly for what else might be useful.

She took what was left of the towels, the knife, and the pumice stone she found there, and a dipper, shoving everything but the knife into a small wooden bucket. She didn't have the time or the strength to break up the bench to get a club, but she could swing the bucket to bash someone with, and she had the knife.

The only entrance into this room probably led to the changing room. She eased toward the doorway and peered cautiously through it. The next room, also paved and walled in mosaic like the first, was empty, but unfortunately there was nothing useful there in the way of clothing or a weapon.

There were two more doors into the changing room. She could not afford to take the wrong one, lose time, possibly be trapped in the one with the cold bath in it. She listened again, going over how a bathhouse was laid out in her mind; there would be at least one room that had a cold bath in it, but any sound would be coming from the doorway that led to the rest of the building.

That way. What she wanted was the quickest way outside, one that didn't pass any more rooms. Granted, she didn't have much in the way of resources, but stopping to try to steal anything would only increase the risk of being caught. She moved quickly to the corridor. Here the mosaic continued only on the floor; the walls were plaster, painted with fading scenes of Roman gods and creatures of story.

The cloth wrapped around her feet muffled her footsteps and allowed her to move in complete silence. She listened intently as she moved and kept a sharp watch for places she might be able to hide if anyone came along this corridor. But no doors gave onto it except the one at the end, and the only light came from slit windows high up under the ceiling.

The noise was all coming, so far as she could tell, from the opposite side of the villa. And to her delirious joy, the corridor she was in opened not onto a courtyard but onto a bit of graveled yard surrounded by a laid stone wall. And in the center of the yard was a pile of wood, a chopping block, and an ax, left stuck in the block, as if the user had been interrupted. This was the yard that supplied the hypocaust with wood!

With that in her hand it would take more than two or three men to make her a captive again. She ran out into the yard, seeing the mouth of the furnace in the wall to her right as she did so.

She shoved the knife in the bucket, grabbed the ax, and yanked it out; the wall had been built to keep people out, not in; there was a rough way up it by way of the wood stacked against it, and she took it, flinging herself flat on the top of it to avoid being seen.

The wall was built at the top of a steep slope, with woods at the bottom. It was a long way down to the ground. But this height was nothing she hadn't managed before, so long as she remembered how to fall and tumble. The building she had just left loomed higher than the wall—there was no way to tell what all the ruckus was about. She just hoped it would continue.

Breathing a prayer to Epona, she tipped herself feet-first over the edge, ax in one hand, bucket in the other.

She hit hard enough to hurt but not hard enough to break or sprain her ankles, and she turned the fall into a barely controlled tumble and let the momentum hurtle her down the slope at a pace far faster than she could have run. This came at a cost, of course; stones hidden in the long, rank grasses bruised her ribs as she rolled over them, and she collided abruptly with a tree trunk at the bottom. But still—nothing broke, and she was able to scramble to her feet and duck into the woods.

She felt as if she was on fire with exultation. She was free!

Free, yes. But the trick is to stay free. She paused, panting, to take stock of her situation.

All right, I have no idea of where I am. Or . . . when . . . It could be early spring or autumn. The trees were leafless—

But buds on the branches of the bushes that screened her were greening.

Spring, then. She had been Medraut's captive for most of the winter. She still didn't know where she was, and there was no way to find out quickly. Or slowly, for that matter. Assuming she got away, far away, and encountered farmers or a village, she didn't dare ask anyone, for as soon as it was known that she had escaped, Medraut would have his men out looking for her. *Think, girl.* East was dangerous. South was the Saxons. North was Lot's.

All right. No matter where I am, if I go west, eventually I will come to our lands, or at least the lands of Father's allies. All she had to do was figure out just which way was west.

But first she had to put as much distance between her and that villa as possible, and for that the best answer was to travel directly away from it, no matter *which* direction that was.

Bucket in one hand, ax in the other, she made herself think calmly and gathered all of her scouting skills together.

Then she slipped into the forest like a phantom.

Those scouting skills returned with every step she took, until she was slipping through the woods as silently as any deer and leaving less trace. Perversely, the fact that her feet were wrapped in rags meant that she left almost no footprints, and the few she left were unrecognizable as human. Every time she came to a stream, she waded into it and walked along it for as long as her feet could take the cold. She never went in the same direction twice, either, going upstream on one and downstream on the next. So when she heard the hounds behind her and then heard their baying turn to bafflement, she knew she had bought herself at least a little more time.

But if they got downwind of her, they would find her without finding her trail, so she needed to either get downwind of them or get something between herself and them that could confuse the scent.

She was hoping for a nice swamp, or some other pungent way to break her trail, when she realized that there were some sort of animals in the woods ahead of her, for she heard slow footsteps and the occasionally breaking twigs. She froze as she heard snuffling, then relaxed as she recognized the sound as a herd of deer rather than the vastly more dangerous herd of swine. She altered her course to find them, pushing through more underbrush, until she surmounted the top of a little ridge, crouching to keep from making a "human" silhouette that would spook them.

When she did spy the herd, grazing on twig ends, she realized she had made a mistake, but a fortunate one. Not deer. Goats. This was much, much better than deer. Probably the fighting had driven them away from their usual pasture, and their pungent smell would surely cover her scent, and they should be used to human beings. There were about twenty of them, brown and gray, still shaggy with their winter coats.

Cautiously, she stood up. They looked at her calmly, the sure sign that they were not feral. With a grin, she walked toward them and clucked at them. "Come on," she whispered, making a little shooing motion. "We need to go, you and I. There are dogs coming, and you won't like them any better than I do." The lead goat looked at her with his strange goat eyes, snorted, and stamped his foot. The other goats all looked up at him and stopped eating. He bobbed his head, then led the herd off in the direction she wanted.

They let her get right in among them. She began to wonder after a few moments if this was something more than an ordinary goat herd . . . because not only were they going the way she wanted to, but very soon the leader was taking them at quite a brisk pace, and the rest were not protesting at all, nor trying to stop to graze. He took them to a track that was wide enough that she wasn't being slapped by underbrush and kept them on it. She was able to trot along in the middle of them quite as if they had accepted her as one of them.

Even as she thought that, the leader turned his head over his shoulder and looked at her. There was a green flash as his yellow eyes with their kidney-shaped pupils became laughing green eyes; there was a shiver of Power, and she almost stopped dead in her tracks at the shock. Then they became goat eyes again, and the he-goat continued shoving his way through the underbrush beside the path. She hurried to keep up with them.

The Ceffyl Dwr, she thought to herself. The Water Horses sometimes took on the aspect of other hooved animals than the horse. The green eyes were a good clue as to what they were, and so was the fact that this path they were on was never very far from a stream. As they pressed on, he increased the pace again until they were trotting and she was really stretching her legs. It had be a long time since she'd walked this far. Her legs started to hurt. *Ah, gods, if only he would be a horse so I could ride!*

But she knew that was impossible, for he would be keeping his distance from her because of the iron ax and knife. And she dared not abandon the only weapons she had. But "Thank you!" she called softly. The he-goat bobbed his head but did not look back at her again.

Behind them, the sound of the dogs faded with distance, then died away. If they hadn't lost the trail before she joined the Water Horses, they surely had now.

Her side ached; she pressed her elbow into it and kept up.

He could be taking me to the Otherworld . . .

That was a risk she would have to take. Annwn was a dangerous place for mortals, and the Water Horses were not often known for having kindly natures. There was no telling what else she might meet there, either.

But she thought she could probably keep herself safe as long as she kept her wits about her. At this point—yes, Annwn was much to be preferred over being in Medraut's hands.

The goats pushed on, and she held her aching side and ran with them. Wherever they were going, one thing was sure. It was away from Medraut.

Chapter Twenty-Two

The goats finally stopped in the last blue glow of twilight at the edge of a lake—stopped and then plunged in. They didn't stop, either—nor did they swim. They ducked beneath the still, cool surface with hardly a splash at all and didn't emerge again. Gwen found herself quite alone except for a fluttering in the reeds of birds, and the distant mutter of ducks.

Gwen was not at all surprised at their sudden abandonment. Exhausted, yes, but not surprised. The Ceffyl Dwr, like all the Folk of Annwn, were fickle and quite easily lost interest in the plight of mortals. It was wiser, when you got aid from them, not to count too much on it and never to expect anything further.

So here she was, on the edge of a lake with nothing more than the clothing on her back, the ax, and the contents of her bucket. In the dark, hungry, and with a raging thirst.

All right. Things were not so bad.

Though she was hungry, she had been eating well in captivity; a few days without food would do her no harm, and a single night was negligible. She had water right here at her feet. She could find some place to hide in order to sleep, even in the dark, and if the moon came up, well, all the better. The important thing was that she was free, and the Water Horses had made sure that Medraut would have a wretched time trying to track her. Even though he had hair of hers to do so magically, being so muddled up with the Water Horse magic might well be enough to throw him off the "scent" there, too, for a while.

While she could still see, she bundled the knife in the leftover strips of toweling, then got herself a bucket full of water. The dipper made a fine cup, and she drank until she was sated, then sat down and waited to see what sort of moon would rise.

To her great joy, it was full; the sight of the pale orb lifting slowly above the trees made her breathe a sigh of intense relief. She would easily be able to see now, to get into what was probably the single safest place to sleep unless she found an old den to hide in—tied into the crotch of a tree as far above the ground as she could manage.

The light painted a swath of silver across the lake, and touched the wisps of mist that were just beginning to rise from the waters. In the morning, well, there were a lot of things that she could do to find food. There were edible roots, and if she could manage to make a line, she could certainly fish. The ax was a comfort to have, but it was the sharp little knife that was going to make all the difference to her survival.

She gathered up her things and began to prowl the lake shore, and within moments she found exactly what she needed: an ancient tree, uprooted by a winter storm, lying half in, half out of the water. She explored the trunk, pulling brush that had piled up against it aside, and uncovered a hollow beneath it full of dead leaves blown in by the winds that was just big enough to hold her. She shoved her possessions in as far as they would go and crawled in after, pulling the brush back across the opening. The leaves crackled and gave off a slightly bitter smell, which should further serve to mask her scent.

It appeared that the Water Horses hadn't "abandoned" her after all, since this shelter was no more than fifty paces from where they had left her on the shore.

For the first time since she had stormed into Arthur's chambers, she smiled. Triumph tempered with caution made her spirits rise. She had done it; she had escaped, and although she'd had *some* help in getting away and had certainly benefited by good luck, *she* was the one that had rescued herself. That triumph eased the aches of over-used and too tired muscles, warmed her all over, and, finally, let her ease down into the first real sleep she had had since she left Castell y Cnwclas.

It was the sound of a small wren peeping inquisitively not a foot from her ear that woke her. She knew exactly where she was; a warrior got into that habit of waking with full knowledge fairly quickly, and it wasn't one that was easily lost. The sound of the bird was reassuring. If anyone or anything had been snooping about, that bird would not have been poking through the brush that hid her sleeping spot.

She stayed right where she was, though; she could not afford a single wrong step out here. Her resources were too thin to allow for mistakes, and even though she had a head start on those hunting her, they had the advantage of numbers and mobility. She had no time at all to waste. Everything must be carefully planned.

She needed food; it was too early for berries, finding a cache of nuts was chancy, and she didn't want to wait here to see if she could snare rabbits. Roots were possible, especially those of water plants, but the best idea was to fish. In the spring, fish were hungry. The best use of that toweling was to make a fishing line. She could carve a hook easily enough, and a bit of twig would serve as a bobber. She knew exactly where to dig for grubs and worms. So, unravel a long woof thread from the toweling, make a hook, get bait, fish. That was the first order of the day. Next, try to find a flint or other sparking stone; they were often enough found among the pebbles in streams and lakebeds. She had the ax, so she could make a fire if she could find a piece of flint.

Cautiously, she pushed the brush out of the way and took a careful look around before emerging into the dawn.

By the time the sun was overhead, she was full of fish, she had a hook and line, a flint, and had even found a way to sew the "shoes" together, padding the bottoms for a little more protection. They were only cloth, so they wouldn't last long, but she only needed them to last until she managed a better substitute, or found someone she could trust, or stole something.

With more cooked fish, cress, and some baked cattail and mallow roots in the bottom of her bucket, protected by a bit of cloth, she headed west.

She was very glad now that she had taken the bucket. It was proving as useful as the knife. It now held food, dry tinder, and the flint she had found among the stones at the lakeshore, as well as the rest of her meager belongings. The Water Horses had not made another appearance, and she assumed they had either forgotten her or had given her all the help they were inclined to. So before she left the lake, she had left three nicely cooked fish and some baked cattail roots on a rock beside the water by way of a thank you gift.

As she cautiously threaded her way through the forest, using streams as often as possible to keep her trail broken, she made a mental inventory of things she wanted. Real shoes and real trews were both high on the list, and so was a bow. She tried very hard not to think too much about the fact that she had no idea where she was. She was a scout, and an expert one at that. She knew all of the signs that showed where people were, and the farther she got from Medraut's villa, the more likely it was that it would be safe to approach them.

She also kept her eyes open for anything edible, and she gleaned some early mushrooms and a squirrel's cache of nuts that way.

It was not until she found another good place for a camp, this one a hollowed out but still standing, tree, had set several snares made with more raveled thread from her towels, had eaten and made herself comfortable for the night that she realized something.

Even though this was real hardship and was only going to get harder, she didn't care how long it took to find her way to friends.

For the first time in her life, she was free. There were no demands, no duties she was obliged to perform. She answered to no one out here, and her own skills and her own two hands were enough to keep her fed and safe.

As she restlessly shifted, finding a comfortable position in the hollow she had scooped dry in the rotted wood, the inescapable thought came to her. *What if I never went back?*

She immediately scolded herself for being impractical, if nothing else. She was well enough equipped to stay healthy and fed in the spring and summer, but winter would surely kill her. She did not have enough in the way of protection or hunting gear to survive even a mild winter.

But what if—what if she could find a way to live out here? Never go back to Arthur? And for just one heady moment, she entertained a daydream of complete freedom. Perhaps she could find an old hermit's hut—she wouldn't need much. If she were settled, she could spend her time hunting and tanning the hides of what she caught. She pictured herself making serviceable garments from rabbit hide, then, making a crude bow, bringing down deer . . . living out a life with no obligations to anyone but herself.

She sighed, the fantasy dissolving almost as quickly as she had conceived of it. *I'd go mad.* Although she liked her own company well enough, she knew she was not the sort for a hermit's life.

And aside from all that . . . Gwenhwyfach was masquerading as her, and that could have no good ending, not for Arthur and not for anyone else, either. She had to get back and expose the treacherous bitch. Medraut had had a very long time to plan whatever it was he was going to do, and he probably would not have kidnapped her if his plans weren't close to fruition. She owed Arthur that.

The weight of duty and responsibility descended on her again, as if someone had piled heavy stones on her heart. And she cried, just a little, as she settled in for sleep.

After two days of almost direct westward movement, Gwen relaxed a little, and began to look for signs of human beings. While it was true that Medraut's control extended this far, practically speaking, she didn't think he was all that interested in anything that went past the immediate boundaries of his villa. Medraut was, at heart, disinclined to trust anyone but himself. Governing land required a great deal of work—work he couldn't perform if he wasn't physically present. She had the feeling that the reason he had, as time passed, left her alone for so long, was that was still cultivating his place as one of the King's Companions. The work her father did day to day meant he was always dealing with his chiefs and nobles, sometimes over details as small as the harvest from an individual farm. Medraut couldn't possibly oversee extensive property himself, yet it was work he would never trust to anyone else.

So the villa was probably just a remote hideaway, and one with no village, no farms, nothing outside its walls. And while Medraut could probably force or bully cooperation from those living near the place, it was unlikely he even bothered to try to rule anyone living more than a day's ride away.

She began listening carefully for the distant sounds that would tell her there was human habitation—the crow of a rooster, the sound of a dog barking, the echo of an ax on wood.

But the faint sounds she heard first were nothing so peaceful. They were the metal-on-metal clash of swords, faint, far, but not all that far away . . .

And she didn't even think, she reacted. She ran toward the sounds, aided by the fact that the game trail she was on went in the same direction. Whoever was fighting, the odds were good that one side or the other would be friendly to *her.* The brief pang of regret that her strange idyll of freedom was over was lost in the fierce wash of glee that at last, at long last, she was going to be able to strike back at *someone.*

But as she stopped just before the clearing where four men were being held off by a single, incredibly skillful fighter, she froze in shock for a moment. She *knew* that fighter.

It was Lancelin, with his back up against the trunk of an enormous tree so that they couldn't ring him. And from the look of things, he was tiring. She didn't recognize the four men who were clearly trying to kill him, but they were well-clothed and well-armed, and the odds were good that they were Medraut's.

She assessed all this in no time at all, dropped her bucket, picked her target, and leaped to Lancelin's aid, ax held in both hands as she raced in for a killing stroke before they realized she was there. She aimed not for the body, which might be protected by riveted metal plates inside the jerkin, but for the back of the man's neck, where the helm ended. She couldn't see his neck beneath the hair, but she didn't need to. She knew there was no protection there.

She hit that spot with all her momentum and all her strength.

The ax struck home against bone; the handle shivered in her hands as the axhead severed the spine and went halfway into his neck; it lodged in there, but she had already let go of it and was reaching for the sword his powerless hand had dropped. As if she had practiced the move a hundred thousand times, she snatched it out of midair, and throwing herself into a half spin, slammed the flat of the blade into the belly of the man next to him. She hadn't enough time to hit him with the edge, but she didn't need to; she just needed to buy time for a better attack.

As she had expected, there was metal under the leather, but she knocked the breath out of him and drove him back a little. And the shock and surprise of her appearance had given Lancelin the opening to drive his own sword into the third man's throat. That man went down with a strangled gurgle.

Now the odds were two to two.

The two men left glanced at each other, shocked.

Lancelin and Gwen didn't pause even for a heartbeat. As if they were linked together, they both acted and grabbed the moment of that glance to attack.

And in the time it took to draw a quick breath, the second pair were down—Lancelin's from a thrust into his eye, Gwen's from a deadly and accurate swing at his legs, where he wasn't armored.

There were great advantages to being shorter than your enemy, sometimes; she spun again, this time able to aim, and took him across the back of his legs at the knee.

Her man went down, too shocked to scream, hamstrung. And in the next instant, Gwen stepped on his sword arm, keeping him pinned, while Lance put a foot on his chest and a sword point at his throat. She reached down and wrenched the sword out of his hand.

"Whose men are you?" the Companion panted. "What do you want?"

"Medraut's!" the man gasped. "He sent us to hunt for her—"

Lancelin looked at Gwen, his mouth a thin, grim line. She nodded. They had no way to keep this man prisoner without risking themselves. And to let him go would be suicide. Granted, he was hamstrung, but it was possible he would be found.

And if he wasn't found . . . they would be leaving him to die slowly and painfully. Lancelin thrust the sword home, removing the risk.

Then he collapsed back against the trunk of the tree, spent. Wordlessly, she went back for her precious bucket, emptied the contents out beside him, and went in search of water. He might as well eat the food that was in there; it wouldn't keep much longer.

Water was never very far away here—wherever "here" was. She found a stream quite soon and filled the bucket. When she returned with it, he was no longer alone.

But his company was not human. The horse had a familiar look to it, and she was fairly certain it was of her father's breeding, and it was clearly Lancelin's, since it was nuzzling him as he fed it bits of her baked mallow root. She put the bucket down beside him; he didn't bother with the dipper, just picked the whole thing up and poured the water down his throat. Only after he had drunk half the bucket and poured the rest over his head did he finally say something.

"You are the real Gwenhwyfar," he said, in a tone of weary satisfaction. "You could only be the real one."

"The false one can't fight," she said wryly, sitting on her heels beside him. "She prefers that unpleasant things are all taken care of for her, preferably where she can't see the unpleasantness and can pretend it is not happening. Are you injured?"

"Bruises aplenty. Maybe a cracked rib. Those churls might have had horses somewhere about, though they attacked me afoot when I stopped to let Idris graze for a bit." He tried to stand up and winced.

She got back to her feet. "Stay there. I'll have a look about for

them, but don't hope too much. I don't think Medraut lets too many
of his men have anything as costly as a horse."

A brief look didn't turn up any horses, nor any sign of them. She
wasn't surprised. Even afoot, they'd had plenty of time to get ahead of
her; *they* hadn't needed to stop to fish and cook and try to make some
makeshift equipment for themselves.

When she came back to him, he'd gotten his armor off, and he
looked as if he'd been put in a barrel full of stones and rolled downhill
in it. But he wasn't cut anywhere significant—a shallow gash across
the ribs, a couple across the backs of his hands, and another over one
eye. And careful probing proved that he hadn't actually cracked his
ribs.

So now she asked the question that had been burning on her
tongue. "Were you looking for me?"

He nodded. "When we came back from trouncing the Saxons
with Arthur, the queen—the false one—didn't seem . . . right. She
looked like you, but . . . there were too many things that weren't like
you, at least, not to someone who'd fought beside you." He grimaced.
"This will sound rude—"

"So be rude," she replied. "We've fought together, and more than
once."

"She was too womanly." He glanced at her, apologetically. "I don't
mean that you are not womanly, but she—she was like the king's second wife; she reveled in luxury. You were indifferent to it, at least it
seemed that way to me. She spent hours in the bath, and when she
wasn't in the bath, she was fussing over gowns and hair, and when she
wasn't doing that, she was all over Arthur like a camp whore."

He said that last without thinking, then flushed a deep crimson,
glancing at her. But she just nodded, grimly. "She's my sister," she
replied, around clenched teeth. "Schooled by Anna Morgause and
Morgana, and Anna Morgause was . . . insatiable. Those weren't

just rumors you heard about her legion of lovers, they were facts. We called my sister Gwenhwyfach, 'Little Gwen.' She's married to Medraut."

He blinked at that, and blinked again. "But—"

She snorted. "Oh, Medraut is perfectly happy to have her where she is. He may think he's nothing like Lot, but he has no trouble playing his wife's pander. The only difference is that he does it for power, not pleasure. He has several plans afoot to be named Arthur's successor, and he's using Gwenhwyfach to open the door for him."

Lancelin's mouth made a shocked little "o," then he cleared his throat self-consciously and continued. "I couldn't get anywhere near her, of course. And Arthur . . . well, Arthur was . . . rather pleased . . ." He flushed again. "He said, now and then, that his wife must have missed him a—very great deal."

"Arthur is a man," she said dryly.

He coughed. "Yes, well . . . the thing is, Gildas turned up around Midwinter, and she acted as if she had never seen him before, and when he tried to converse with her, she just turned him away. Arthur wouldn't hear that there was anything wrong, of course . . ." He coughed again. "So Gildas talked to a few of us who knew you. Asked us to try to find out what was going on—if maybe the queen had been possessed or enchanted or—well, then he had another idea. Gwenhwyfar, this sounded mad to me at the time: He asked if maybe it wasn't you at all. He pointed out that the Merlin had enchanted Uther to appear as Ygraine's husband, and that was how Arthur was conceived in the first place. He thought that maybe someone had enchanted another woman to look like you."

She blinked at that, because it was so near the truth. Gildas was great deal more observant, and more clever, than she had thought. "And you thought—"

"I knew something was wrong. That queen wasn't the warrior I knew. Her hands were smooth and fair, and she was . . ." He groped for words. "She was *petty*. Instead of wanting to know about King March's schemes, or what the Saxons were about, or even peaceful things like the state of the harvest, she only seemed to care about gowns and gems and how to be amused. So I watched her, and I saw that she stole away now and again to speak privily with Medraut. I told that to Gildas, who suggested that the next time Medraut went on one of his excursions from court, I should follow him to find out where he went. So I did, and then I went to the Isle of Glass and told him about Medraut's villa. And the next thing I knew, Gildas had rounded up some of his monks and gone trotting off to see what Medraut was up to."

She stared at him for a moment, then began to laugh. Because she could, all too easily, imagine Gildas doing just that, trusting in his god to keep him safe. And then she laughed even harder, because she knew now what had caused the commotion that allowed her escape. It had to have been Gildas pounding on the gate, demanding hospitality, which Medraut would not at all have been willing to give him—but which, he would have known, he had to.

Lancelin looked at her as if he was afraid she had gone mad until she explained why she was laughing. "He must have been the one that distracted everyone so I could get away."

She sketched in something of what her captivity had been like, and her escape. She left out the part about being fairly sure Medraut had amused himself with her unconscious body until that palled on him. It would probably only make him angry, and in the long run . . .

In the long run, there isn't much difference between how I feel about Arthur's using me and how I feel about Medraut doing the same . . . Horrible . . . but true. Which was something Lancelin, who adored Arthur, did not need to know.

"It must have been Gildas, the brave fool." He smiled a little. "I was a day or two behind him, he set off so suddenly, and I am ashamed to say, I stupidly assumed no one would attack someone as well armed and armored as I am." He shook his head ruefully, and a lock of hair fell into his eyes. He brushed it away. "And then you came to the rescue . . . this is a rather inglorious end to the story."

"I don't think—" she began, then abandoned what she was going to say. "We should get away from here. There will be more of those men out looking, and some might come this way too."

He nodded at her ruined gown. "Take what you need from them; I'll get into my armor again."

And there it was, exactly what she had wished for; her pick of trews, tunic, armor, sword, bow. Medraut was fastidious about his person and just as fastidious about the men that served him. The first man she'd downed had bled very little, for she hadn't cut the major blood vessels. She took his armor and shirt, the trews from the first man Lancelin had killed, since he hadn't voided himself when he died and they were unsoiled, and the boots from the last one, which were almost a fit. She made it all into a bundle rather than getting changed; when he looked at her askance, she raised an eyebrow. "I can ride in this, and it will take some time to cut myself out of it; I'd rather put more space between us and Medraut than stop to change."

Without a pause, he nodded, mounted his horse, and offered her a hand. She used it to pull herself up behind him, settled herself over the bare rump of his horse, then put her arms around his waist tightly, so that he wouldn't hesitate to get some speed from Idris. He nudged his horse into a canter, and they were off.

She became increasingly self-conscious as they rode—and conscious of him. The feel of his body under her hands, the smell of him—horse, and clean sweat, a little blood, and what smelled like rosemary in his hair. And she became aware that her body was re-sponding to his in a way it had never responded to Arthur.

It's the fighting, she scolded herself. *I've heard the men talking about it. I've seen them afterwards, they can't get to the camp whores quickly enough. It's the fighting and the fear of death and then the real-ization when it's all over, that you didn't die. That's all.*

But it wasn't all, and she knew it. From the first time she'd seen Lancelin, she had wished, without admitting it to anyone but herself and Bronwyn, that he would look at her not as a fellow warrior but as a woman. That he would give her the kind of glances that men gave Gynath and Cataruna. That he would touch her not with friendly indifference but with pent-up passion.

Which was about as likely to happen as for this horse to sprout wings and fly them to Celliwig. She was a warrior.

And she was Arthur's.

Chapter Twenty-Three

As she was already well aware, riding pillion on the bare rump of a cantering horse was not a comfortable way to ride. Especially not a horse of her father's breeding, which had wide hips and a muscular set of hindquarters.

And she hadn't ridden in—well, a very long time. Months. She'd done her best to stay limber, but by the time Lancelin slowed his mount to a walk, her legs were definitely sore. The horse wasn't any too pleased, either, and she didn't blame him.

"I don't suppose you have a place in mind to camp?" she asked as she tried to adjust her perch on Idris' rump; she hoped she didn't sound as if she were whining. This patch of forest was identical to the one they had been riding through, which still gave her no clue as to their location. "Where are we, anyway?"

"North of Celliwig," he said. "If I hadn't been following Gildas, I'd have come straight from there, and you would not likely have found me at all." He shook his head. "Gildas would say one of his good spirits was watching over you. If you had kept going and no one had stopped you, eventually you might even have reached your own father's lands."

"Well, I am very glad I did find you." She laughed. "It was a good thing for both of us. But now we are going south—"

"We are, and into lands I know. As for camping, yes, I do have a place in mind," he continued. "I've used it before. It's very well concealed. We'll be riding until twilight to get there, though."

"I would rather do that than take any chance of Medraut's men catching us." She said it, and she meant it, but she knew when she finally got off this horse, part of her would regret saying it.

But even as she thought that, he turned the horse's head and sent him down into a ditch or ravine with a tiny thread of a stream running in the bottom of it, a ditch that quickly deepened until the sides were higher than their heads. There he dismounted. "Off," he said. "All three of us need to stop for just a few moments."

The horse proved the truth of this by plunging his nose into the bit of a stream and noisily slurping up water. And as soon as her legs stopped hurting, the running water reminded her that there was something else she needed desperately to do. With a rueful glance at each other, they parted company until the brushwood hid them. She was still not willing to stop long enough to change clothing completely, but since she was going to have to retie everything anyway, she did cut the gown off at the hips and pull on the breeches and the boots. Immediately—and not just because she also relieved herself— she felt better. More like herself.

And there was the added benefit that she had two large pieces of heavy fabric that were likely to come in very useful.

She folded the fabric into a pad she could use under herself and trotted back to the horse and Lancelin. A little stretching left her feeling a lot happier about getting back on that horse. The leg of rabbit Lancelin fished out of a saddlebag and handed to her made her feel happier in general. She made short work of it, as he did the same with another leg.

"I'm going to stop one more time so we can hunt," he told her, as he swung himself up into the saddle, then offered her his hand and let her pull herself up behind him again. "We won't have a chance before dark otherwise, and that was the last of my provisions."

"I hope I can still remember how to use a bow," she said dryly. He laughed and put heels to his mount.

True to his word, in late afternoon, he did stop. Under any other circumstances, Gwen would never even have considered hunting, and not just because there might still be men out looking for them. This was springtime, and unless you were very careful, you'd shoot animals with young and leave orphaned babies to die, which was poor husbandry and land care. But there wasn't a choice.

But luck was with them. He tethered Idris in the brush near a pond, and both of them could hear the quiet quacking of ducks. She nodded him towards the pond, and she headed in the direction of a glare of sunlight through the trees that probably meant a clearing. As she stalked carefully along the edge of a meadow, she heard a tussle in the grass and saw two hares fighting. Now, hares fighting could only be male. And the male hares had no part in anything but the siring of the young ones; they went off and left the does to tend the babies alone. She froze as soon as she saw them, but they were so deep in combat they paid no attention to her. Carefully she stuck one arrow in the ground in front of her, moving as slowly as a leaf in a light breeze. Carefully, she put a second to the bow, and pulled it back to her ear.

She let fly. And without waiting to see if the first arrow hit, snatched up the second and put it to the string.

Hares were not very bright at best, and when fighting over females, they were single-minded as well. The second continued to attack the first for a critical moment after it fell over dead. By the time it realized that something was wrong, and its head came up as it froze with indecision as a few dim thoughts managed to escape from the sex-fight-sex madness that spring brought on, it too was dead.

Feeling utterly triumphant, she collected them, gutted them then and there, cleaned her knife and the arrows with a handful of grass and brought back the cleaned carcasses to where Lancelin had tethered the horse. He was already there, tying a gutted drake to the saddle bow.

He looked up. "Two were fighting over a hen. I shot the loser."

She nodded and held up her prizes. He actually grinned as he tied the carcasses alongside his catch.

As the sun set, it turned everything the color of roses—the greening forest, the sky, the clearings they passed through—and she could not help a feeling of triumph as she thought about all the nights she had seen this same rosy light fill her tiny window. She would swear that somehow she would win herself free, and now she had.

"Are you disappointed?" she asked into Lancelin's back. "That you weren't the one to win me free, like some warrior in a tale?"

He was quiet for a while, although she did not feel his muscles tense, so as she was used to seeing, he must have been carefully considering his words. "While the glory of being your rescuer all alone was a heady fancy, it was never more than that," he said, slowly. "First, of course, I did not know if you were actually held captive by Medraut. Second, if you were, his men are many, and I am one. What I planned to do, I fear, is somewhat less glorious. I was going to skulk about to determine if there was a captive there, and if it was a female, and if so, where she was being held. Then to see how closely guarded she was. Then to see if it was you. After that . . ." He shook his head. "My plans were unformed. Pray remember, so far as anyone knows, *you* are still in Celliwig. My first course of action would have been to free you if I could, but I assumed I would not be able to. And I would have to think who would believe me that I could count on to fight with me."

She began to chuckle. "It appears that Abbot Gildas and his monks were willing and able to put up some sort of fight."

His laughter was deep in his chest, and she felt it vibrate in his muscles. "I owe the Abbot a profound debt of gratitude. I hope no one came to any harm."

She didn't *know*. "I don't think Medraut would dare. Though he follows the Old Ways, still, a holy man is a holy man, and you harm one at your peril."

While they had been speaking, the sun descended below the trees; the sky to the east darkened and filled with stars, while the sky to the west faded into ashes-of-roses. Idris picked up his pace; it appeared the horse knew where they were going.

They had to duck under low-hanging branches, and even though the leaves were barely budding, the trees here were very old, enormous, and thick, enough that it was hard to see. The horse could barely get between them, and his hooves made scarcely a sound on ground with a padding of old leaves that gave off a bitter scent as he picked his way over them. The air was close and warmer than it should have been. Even though Gwen was not Gifted in that way, she felt the Power here, humming along her skin, like the warning before lightning is going to strike nearby.

And then, without any warning, the trees opened up. And before them was a ruin.

It was not, as she had more than half suspected it would be, a henge. It was a small house, a house and not a hut nor a cottage of the sort her people raised, yet it was not Roman nor of any other style that she could identify. The roof had long since vanished, and yet several trees and a litter of smaller branches and a thatch of leaves had somehow fallen across the stone walls to create a new one.

"I have no idea who built this here," Lancelin said quietly. "Some Druid? A Lady? Whoever it was, that person had great power. Even I can feel it, and I have no Gift for Power at all."

"It welcomes us." She felt that, as well. This place was pleased to have them there.

He nodded, then threw his leg over his horse's neck and jumped down, lifting her down before she could dismount herself. "I come here when I need to be away from Arthur and the Companions. I can think, here. I can find myself and know even what I am hiding from myself—"

He broke off what he was going to say and quickly took off Idris' tack. He handed her the saddlebags and took the bucket himself. "There's good dry wood in there, and a hearth, and if they have not broken, some pots. For sleeping, I fashioned a pallet, and, there is good, dry bracken and some old horse blankets. If you can get a fire going, I shall get water."

She was about to ask from where, but he was gone. With a shrug, she went into the one-room stone house and found it was just as he had said it would be. In the last light, she quickly made a fire, using his flint and steel, catching the sparks in a nest of leaf fragments, blowing them into a tiny flame and feeding it with twigs until it was strong enough to take the logs. The bracken was piled in one corner, well sheltered, with the blankets atop it and the pallet tossed atop that. Once the fire was going, she hauled the pallet, which was of more bracken stuffed inside a worn canvas cover, down beside it. As she worked, Lancelin came and went several times, filling some of the pots with water. She took the first of those, skinned and cut up the hares, and put the pot into the side of the fire to stew. He continued to bring in water and wood, and at last he left the full bucket outside with Idris.

With a sigh and a wince, he settled down onto the pallet beside her. Only then did she break the silence. "If I had such a place, I would open it to no one."

He did not look at her; he stared at the fire. The soft light did not touch his eyes, "Not even Arthur?"

The air hummed with Power. This was no place for lies. She touched his hand, and when he finally turned, she gazed into his eyes. "Especially not Arthur."

He caught his breath, and emotions chased across his face too quickly to read. "Then . . . there is no love between you?"

She tried not to feel bitterness as she shook her head. "This is the lot of princes. I knew that one day I might be needed for—some bargain. I was the unwanted part of a bargain for horses," she said, the bitterness coming through anyway. "The Ladies wanted a bride for him who was pledged to the Old Ways. He needed an heir. The land needed one. He gave way, but grudgingly. There is nothing about me, the real me, that Arthur wants. I honor him as the High King. But I do not love him, and he does not love me. He wants a dream of a compliant, complacent woman who will bend like a willow to his will, who will ornament his great hall, greet his guests graciously, bear him heirs, give him bed sport, and never seek to join him in council or battle. That is not me. And he does not want what I am." She could have wept to say it out loud at last. It felt as if she had dropped shackles from her wrists. Somewhere out in the darkness, an early frog sang. "If I had known this, I would never have consented. This is no marriage, it is bondage."

Something that she had never, ever expected to see, flared in his face. "Then the gods be thanked!" he cried, and clasped his hands about her face, and kissed her.

A fire leaped up between them, a fire that began at their lips and swiftly raced to her groin. She moaned and opened her mouth to his even as her own hands drew him to her. His mouth was that of a starving man, it devoured her, as hers devoured his. A hunger she had not known was inside her obliterated all other thoughts except of him. Her hands, with a life of their own, unbuckled his armor; he cast it aside. His hands caressed her breasts, thumbs rubbing her sensitive nipples through the thick cloth, and the fire leaped from her groin to her breasts. She moaned into his mouth and pushed him away just long enough to pull the remains of the gown over her head, discarding it into the darkness. His shirt followed it, and they fell back together onto the canvas pallet, touching, tasting, hands and mouths exploring one another.

His fingers traced the line of her side, and she ached, arching her back as his lips and tongue played with her nipples. Impatient, more than impatient, she pulled down his breeches; hers were already around her knees, and she kicked them off. She parted her legs for him, and he knelt between them, staring down at her, his face alight, his eyes shining.

"I love *you*, Gwenhwyfar," was all he said. Then he was on her, inside her, and the two of them moved to a rhythm all their own, until the fire became a conflagration, and devoured them both.

With their discarded clothing for a pillow, they lay in each other's arms and fed each other bits of hare—which, by some miracle, had not been burned to blackness in the bottom of the pot. She listened to his heart pound and traced her fingers over his chin. He held her as if he would never let her go.

"I think I began to love you when you spoke to me after the battle in the winter," he said, quietly. "But I thought—I thought you were spoken for, maybe. And if you were not, well, you were a warrior, your father's eyes and soon to be his right hand. You were the White Phantom, the legend the Saxons had learned to fear. What could I offer you? I have no land, let alone a kingdom. I have only my status as a Companion. Not even my horse is my own."

Cataruna's husband came to us with less, she wanted to say, but how could she? That was the past, and words would not change it. "So I put you from my mind, and when I thought of you, I told myself to think of you as another warrior. And so I did. Until I saw you as Arthur's bride, so beautiful, so regal, and—" His voice choked a little. "—and I knew what a fool I had been, and you were going to Arthur, and if you did not love him then, you would love him soon."

As you love him? She did not say that either. "He did not want another wife, much less one with my name," she said quietly. "And he especially does not want one like me. He kept me as much a captive as Medraut, even if that captivity was in a cage of gold rather than stone."

There was more, much, much more, that she wanted to say. But these were not things that you said to a lover. *When we lay together, the only thing that kept it from being rape was my consent. And I cannot, and never will, welcome him into my bed. He may come there, but I cannot welcome him, for it is not* me *he wants—any empty vessel would do.*

Or *he thought I was breeding. He stayed only long enough to put a child in me and then could not leave me fast enough.*

"I love *you,*" she said, knowing it to be true.

"But—" he began, his voice rising a little in distress. And she knew what he was going to say. That she was still Arthur's—oh, not necessarily by the laws of *their* gods, but certainly by the law of the land and of the Christian one. That Arthur would never give her up. That they had together betrayed Arthur, just as the second Gwenhwyfar had.

But the second Gwenhwyfar's betrayal was because he loved her. He does not love me. He does not even want me.

And she was not going to lie here and try to counter all those things. Not though Arthur had "betrayed" her—because he surely could not have been so blinded by Gwenhwyfach that he didn't realize she wasn't his wife. Not that Arthur could be persuaded, she was sure, to give her up, so long as he could keep his precious horses.

Instead she stopped his protests with her lips and built the fire anew.

As dawn grayed the sky, she woke, and she knew they should move on, of course. They should leave this place in the first sun of the morning, and they should ride straight to Arthur's villa. She knew it as the thin light of dawn penetrated the trees and filtered gently in through the broken wall of the house. She knew it as she listened to the birds sing, as she lay with her head propped up on one hand, watching him sleep. If they left now, they could pretend to themselves that last night had been a moment's madness, the lust that came after battle. They could pretend to forget all the things that had been said, half said, and unsaid between them. If they left now, it would all be over, and she would go back to her joyless couplings, and he would slake his needs with whatever lady of the court or serving wench was willing.

And that . . . would be unbearable.

She considered her options, looked over what could be done as if she were planning a battle. A battle? No, a war. This would be a campaign. She would need to persuade so many people of so many things. First of all, the Ladies, that she would never, ever bear Arthur an heir because if it had not happened by now, it was never going to. For that matter . . . once she told them of her captivity, it would be obvious that for whatever reason, the fault was with her, for certainly, Medraut would have sired a child on her by now if it had been possible. She would have to open the whole sordid tale to the Ladies and show them what a threat Medraut was to the Old Ways. And maybe Morgana too, though that would be harder. Morgana had done nothing overtly, and even though she had pledged herself to Morrigan of the Dark Moon, that alone did not make her a traitor, either to Arthur, or to the Old Ways. The Goddess had both a Dark and a Shining face, and it was wise to never forget that.

And then . . . she had to expose Medraut and her sister for what they were and what they had done before Arthur himself and his entire court and Companions. Arthur's blood he might be, but he could not be Arthur's heir. She would have to find proof of what he had done. She couldn't do that without still being queen, so . . . persuading Arthur to put her aside would have to wait until Medraut was no longer a threat and Gwenhwyfach was properly dealt with and confined by the Ladies where she could no longer harm anyone.

Then, once that was all sorted out, she had to explain her situation to her sisters. And her father. And, finally, Arthur himself.

She almost groaned at the thought of what it was going to take. It could be a year—more—until she and Lancelin were free to be together. But she was a king's daughter and the wife of the High King, and the good of the land and the people came before her own desires. This land must be made safe from Medraut. A new bride for Arthur must be found—one who could be as compliant and complacent as he desired. Yes, even if she were a follower of the Christ priests. Unlike the Ladies, after knowing Gildas—and after having the Abbot himself come so gallantly to her rescue!—she was by no means convinced that their way was at odds with the Old Ways. Did they, too, not have a Lady that they served? Their god too had died and returned.

Oh, this could take months. A year. A year in which every moment of every day must be spent in cunning, in persuasion . . . And yes, she would do this. This would serve the greatest good for the land and for the King. Even her leaving and making way for another was not entirely selfish.

But she could not . . . she could not face that year, without having a little joy hoarded up for herself. She needed this; she needed this in ways she had not even been able to imagine before last night.

Besides . . . she looked at Lancelin, at the shadows under his eyes, at the deep bruises on his chest and stomach, at the half-healed wounds on arms, shoulders, and hands . . . he needed this too. Not just the love, he needed the rest. Arthur was hard on his Companions, but Lancelin was harder still on himself. How long had it been since he had actually taken the time to heal? Too long, by the look of things.

So they would not be leaving this morning. And not for several more mornings.

She put her head back down on his chest, let the morning light creep across their bodies and warm them, and drifted off to sleep again in its embrace.

She sat, drooping a little, on the pallet. "I can't," she said, quietly but firmly. "I cannot ride today and maybe not tomorrow. I haven't ridden in over a year. My hips feel as if they have been dislocated, and if I get back on Idris today, I am going to be half crippled." *That* was not even a lie—and not much of an exaggeration. "And look at you—" She gestured at him as he stood half clothed in front of her. He was the very image of the Young God to her at that moment— haloed with sunlight, motes of dust drifting about him. She fought back desire that made her body ache and concentrated on winning him. "What if Medraut ambushes us? You are in no fit shape for a fight."

He opened his mouth to protest. She gave him a measuring look.

"Be honest," she warned. This was Gwenhwyfar the warrior, speaking to Lancelin the warrior, and he recognized it as such.

He shut his mouth. Looked at her with longing that made her feel warm inside. He heard the warrior and wanted the warrior-woman. She seized on his hesitation and capitalized on it. "I need rest," she said, plaintively. "So do you. And who is being harmed if we take it?" She watched his hesitation fading.

"What about warning Arthur?" he asked, biting his lip. "Medraut—"

"Medraut dares not make a move against Arthur until he knows where I am and whether I am alive or dead." She had thought about this long and hard; and truly, if there had been danger that Medraut would act, she would be on that wretched horse this moment. "Gwenhwyfach will probably flee when she knows I have escaped, and even if she does not, Medraut does not dare leave her there for fear of what will happen to her when I do appear. I do not think he trusts her because I do not think he trusts anyone. He won't risk her betraying him. Arthur is in no worse danger if we remain here long enough to heal."

"But how do we explain taking so long to return to Celliwig—"

She chuckled. "We were pursued. We were elf-led. We were just plain lost. You were wounded. I was ill or injured. It doesn't matter. There is no one to dispute what we say."

He sighed, and his expression turned wistful. "There is truly no danger to Arthur?"

She bit back a sharp retort. *Are you more in love with Arthur than with me?* It was unfair, unkind . . . and yes, it was somewhat true. The bond that tied him to Arthur was complex. Worship of the office and the man, admiration, friendship, a kinship of spirit . . . yes, it was love. He had loved Arthur long before he had met her. He would love Arthur without regard to Arthur's flaws. And while she could not help but feel more than a little jealous, this was something that men did, felt. They needed this. Perhaps it was the way that they saw the reflection of the gods on earth in their earthly brothers.

Even Gildas' monks felt this same passion for their Abbot.

She had seen this many, many times in her men—mostly for her father, sometimes for their war chiefs, and occasionally for her.

So she could and would feel the pain of jealousy, but it was a foolish, stupid woman who thought to take this from the heart of her man. As well to cut off what made him a man.

"I have seen no visions," she said, patting the pallet, so that he finally sat beside her. "I cannot say for certain. But this is what I am sure of, based on what I know of Medraut and of my sister." The memory of Medraut sitting beside her as she struggled with the haze of his potions made her feel like vomiting. "Medraut talked a great deal to me. Talked *at* me, that is—"

He interrupted her, cupping a hand to her cheek. "Don't think about it," he said urgently, and then kissed her. "As long as Arthur will be safe while we tarry a little —then tarry we will." He kissed her again, this time, lingering, his hand straying from her cheek to her breast. "Now . . . let me drive his shadows from your heart."

The fire rose between them again, and she lost herself in it.

Chapter Twenty-Four

They lingered seven days. Seven days that would have been utterly blissful had they not been overshadowed by the knowledge that these days *would* come to an end, that they would have to return to Arthur and the Companions and pretend that nothing whatsoever had happened between them. If it were not for that, she would have been happier than she had ever been in her life.

Seven days, during which she was more completely herself than she had ever been since her childhood. Seven nights so full of love speech and lovemaking it seemed as if she were packing enough loving moments for a lifetime into those warm, honeyed nights. They confided secrets, revelations, history, and memories, and then between them, they made more.

She learned that he had been raised by one of the Ladies who said she was his guardian; he had no reason to doubt her, since there was not the slightest resemblance between her and him. She had him trained in all the arts of war, then sent him on his way with armor, sword, and horse, giving him directions to Celliwig, when he was twenty. There he became one of Arthur's Companions; not the first,

but soon the closest, for of all of the Companions, Lancelin's educa-
tion most closely matched Arthur's, and they spoke the same language. He had remained the closest until the second Gwenhwyfar;
then the estrangement began. And she could tell it hurt—hurt then,
and still hurt. She did her best to soothe that hurt, but there was no
denying that what she and he had was going to drive another wedge
into the widening breech between him and the High King.

The most ordinary act took on weight and meaning when they
shared it. She laughed more than she had in ten years. But at the end
of the seventh day, he began packing up their things, and although
her throat ached with sudden sorrow to see him do so, she did not
protest. All things had to end; there was even a tiny leavening of relief
that now the dread of ending was over. By now, Medraut knew he
could not recapture her. By now, Gwenhwyfach must know she had
escaped. Gwen and Lancelin needed to find out what both of them
were doing and then put their own campaign into motion. If they
were to have a life together, it would have to begin by giving each
other up for a time. Even though she ached so much she felt as if she
were bleeding from every pore.

So, at dawn on the eighth day, Lancelin saddled Idris and loaded
him with their scant property. Wearing the looted shirt, breeches,
and boots, Gwen helped him. And when everything was ready and
they had led Idris out into the meadow, they turned back for a last
look at the place that neither of them wanted to leave.

She felt a heavy weight of grief settle over her, and a lump
formed in her throat. She fought back tears with every particle of
will and determination that she had mastered over the years, but
her heart felt as if it were going to burst with sorrow. The time
ahead, when she must never look at him, never touch him, never
give a sign of her love, stretched out like a road of ashes that she
would never see the end of. She wanted to throw herself down on

the ground and wail, or grab him and beg him to come with her, far away, anywhere—

But if she did that, if *they* did that . . . it would be the murder of part of themselves. Duty and responsibility had made them what they were. Could they still love each other when they both would have betrayed that? Would they be the same people? And even if they were, knowing that they had forsaken *that*, there must then always be the doubt, the wonder, if they would forsake each other . . .

No, they must endure this. And she must endure it without weeping. She must have let a single sniff escape, though, for in the next moment, he had wrapped his arms around her. She turned her face into his chest and gave herself a single moment of weakness.

"This is the hardest thing I have ever done, to go back to him, after—" Her eyes burned with tears. She blinked them back.

"I know," he murmured into her hair. "And to see you, and not be able to touch you—it will be like death, a thousand times a day. But I will never leave you. Even if all I can do is look at you, I will never leave you. I love you, Gwen."

"Oh, how very touching."

The sarcastic voice, hatefully familiar, cut across the clearing.

She felt as if someone had dropped her into the heart of winter. Her pulse fluttered erratically, and she felt sick as she slowly turned her head.

Just where the path they were going to take began, Medraut stepped out from under the trees, sword held loosely in his hand, wearing a carelessly sardonic expression. Except for one thing. His eyes were furious. Gwen stared at him, mind going numb but her own hand reaching for her sword. With almost the same motion, she and Lancelin drew their weapons and stood side by side, prepared to defend each other.

"How charming," Medraut sneered. But as his eyes rested on Gwen, she clenched her hand on her sword hilt. He was never, ever going to forgive her this. "How delightful. You *love* each other. And how long, I wonder, have you been so enamored? Months? Years? What a lovely couple you make. Don't they, my King?"

To Gwen's horror, Arthur stepped out of the shadows to stand beside him.

And so did an entire half-circle of warriors, all of Medraut's brothers among them. She felt choked; she could scarcely breathe.

Arthur's face was black with rage, but he said nothing. Perhaps he was too furious to speak. And all that Gwen could do was stare, helplessly, all of her plans in ruins at her feet.

There was only one thing she thought she could salvage from the wreckage. *He can't charge us with treason. We never conspired to take his throne. Not like the last wife—*

"So, when were you planning to take the High King's throne along with his wife, Lancelin?" Medraut asked, poisonously, as if he was reading her mind. He smiled at her, his eyes dancing with malice.

"Never." Her heart thrilled with pride at the steadiness of Lancelin's voice. "I never wanted a throne, not Arthur's nor that of any other king."

"Ah, but the wife?" Medraut grinned. But that grin goaded her as nothing else had until now. That hateful grin—she had been forced to suffer it for months, that grin that said *I won, you lost, and there is nothing you can do about it.*

Her mind unfroze as a flash of rage fired it, and in a flash, she assessed the situation. They—well, Lancelin—had one chance to escape this. He was a superb horseman. She had seen him leap into the saddle and ride off at full gallop. If he did that now, no one would be able to stop him. The warriors around them were carrying bows, but they had swords in their hands, not the bows. They were also, some of them, still in a state of shock and disbelief; and many were his friends, and for the moment, they would hesitate to attack him. He could get away as long as *he* didn't hesitate or pause for anything. If he stayed long enough to pull her up behind him, though—

"Lance," she whispered urgently, making sure not to move her lips too much. "Get on Idris and get out of here."

Shock at her words made him glance down at her, though he did not move his head. "But—"

"*Leave me.*" She made it a command. "He's not thinking, and he won't, Old Stag that he is, while the Young Stag stands before him. He'll never listen to anything as long as you stand here. He'll challenge you, and you'll either let him kill you or kill him yourself. There's no other outcome for this."

If he kills Arthur, he'll never be able to look at me again without thinking of that. And if Arthur kills him, I will follow. She heard the breath catch in his throat. He loved Arthur; still loved Arthur. *"Go!"* she hissed. "He won't harm me. He'll lose the Ladies and my father if he does."

Though Arthur might not be able to think at this moment, Lancelin certainly could, and her logic was inescapable. With an inarticulate cry of grief that wrung her heart and made a sob catch in her throat, he leaped into the saddle with a single jump. Idris, well used to what this meant, reared a little and plunged toward an opening in the line. The warriors, caught off guard, or perhaps not really wanting to try to stop him, did not react in time. He flashed between them and was gone.

With a look of contempt at Medraut that should have blasted him on the spot, Gwen tossed down her sword.

And waited for them to take her prisoner.

She paced the tiny, dark hut that they had locked her into. Ironic that they had brought her here, to Glastonbury Abbey. But Abbot

Gildas had interceded again, so she'd heard; she didn't know first hand, of course, since she hadn't been allowed to see anyone but her guards, but that explained why she was here rather than at Arthur's stronghold. That good old man was still honoring their friendship; she hoped he wouldn't lose by it.

The hut walls were not that thick, and the guards gossiped; she heard practically every word they said. Arthur was incoherent with anger. There was no word of Medraut. There was no word of Lancelin either, which she took as a good sign. The guards didn't know what Arthur planned to do with her—

Well, he could *plan* all he wanted to, but that did not alter the law. It was not yet treason for a woman, even a queen, to take a lover. She could, if she chose, even make the argument that she had only done so to give him an heir . . . and between bouts of weeping, she toyed with that idea. But it would be a lie, and she decided against it. She was done with lying to Arthur to save his pride.

They'd brought her a gown. She'd refused to change into it. She had no intention of surrendering her identity as a warrior a second time. She did behave herself honorably, otherwise. She did not rush the guards that brought her food and water and took away the bucket. She did not insult them, nor shout at them, nor demand anything of them. She stood quietly in a corner, let them come and do what they needed to do at dawn and dusk, and spoke only when she was spoken to. And yes, she wept, she had cried until her eyes were sore and dry and her cheeks sore and her nose sore and red with weeping, but she had done so silently. If—*when*—Arthur finally confronted her, she was going to force him to acknowledge what she was. In no small part because that was what Gwenhwyfach was not.

It had been three days. That was a cold sort of comfort. The more time that passed, the more chance there was for her friends to rally to her side. The more time that passed, the farther away Lancelin would get and the more likely that Arthur's anger with him would cool a little. The only thing that worried her was—time was also on Medraut's side.

She had to fight with herself constantly, every waking moment, not to break down completely; this was like the conflict with Medraut in a way, and she dared not show any weakness, not if she was going to be taken seriously. It was worst on waking, for her dreams were full of Lancelin; in her dreams she was back in their sanctuary, held joyfully in his arms, and when she woke to find herself curled in the heap of straw in the mud-walled hut, the pain of disappointment was so bitter she could hardly keep herself from crying out with it.

Lying in the darkness, waiting for sleep, was almost as bad; that was when the doubt and the fear plagued her, dogged her every heartbeat and warned her that, no matter what, *this* had forever poisoned what lay between them. That nothing would ever be the same again. That forced to choose between her and Arthur, Lance would always choose Arthur.

Those thoughts were like knives in her gut. And although those thoughts were worst at night, when she fought for sleep, they were never far away.

So she paced, counting the paces, as she had paced in Medraut's prison. She rehearsed what she was going to say, over and over. How she would react. What she would do—she had to take the offensive; the ground was all Arthur's. She had to force *him* to react to what she said and did, not the other way around. She had to put him on the defensive.

She was rehearsing it all for the hundredth time when she heard the bar holding her in scrape across the door of the hut. The sound made her freeze, for it was neither dawn nor dusk. She turned, slowly, to face the little wooden door.

Two guards stood there, two of the Companions she was not familiar with. "Lady?" one said, hesitantly, peering into what must have been dark to him. His voice was very young. "Lady, you are to come with us—"

"I am Gwenhwyfar," she said, steadily. "Queen perhaps, war chief certainly. Not 'Lady.'"

She stalked out of the darkness of the hut and into the light, her eyes narrowed so that it didn't blind her, her back straight as a staff. "Lead on," she said evenly, taking in her surroundings as soon as her eyes adjusted. The island tor of the Isle of Glass loomed to her right, but it was more distant than she had thought, and all around her were the tents of a camp. This looked like a little farmer's hut, or a shepherd's, that Arthur had commandeered to hold her. So, she was not on the Abbey grounds, after all. Perhaps Arthur had wanted to put some distance between them and the Isle, for fear Gwyn ap Nudd would interfere in some way.

Which was foolish thinking. If Gwyn wanted to interfere, not the breadth of a kingdom would prevent him from doing so.

She eyed the guards; they were young. Very young. Evidently her good behavior had convinced Arthur that he need not put his stoutest warriors over her. They flushed as she looked them over. New armor, new tunics. With whom had they served before joining Arthur? Were they the younger sons of one of his allies? She wondered what they were thinking.

"Well," she said, when they didn't move. "If you are to lead me, then do so, if you please."

They flushed again, and one of them made an abortive gesture in the general direction of the largest tent in the encampment, which was, of course, precisely where she would expect Arthur's tent to be, since the encampment was laid out in the Roman style. She nodded and moved off at a deliberate pace, neither dragging her feet nor rushing. She didn't want these boys to have even a vestige of alarm about them because she had plans of her own.

Two more guards at the tent entrance held the flaps open for her. Just as deliberately she stalked inside and the canvas dropped in place behind her.

Arthur waited for her inside, flanked by Abbot Gildas and his foster brother Kai and two more pairs of guards. And before any of them could move or speak, she took the offensive.

Literally.

She crossed the space between them quickly, while they were still reacting to her presence, and slapped Arthur as hard as she could with the back of her hand. The *crack* shattered the silence and shocked them all speechless. Which was exactly the way she wanted it.

"If I had a gauntlet, it would be at your feet, *husband*," she spat. "How dare you, *how dare you*, take exception to anything *I* have done, when you just spent the last seven months fornicating *with my sister?*"

Arthur's mouth dropped open in sheer shock; his eyes went wide and her handprint reddened on his cheek.

"My *sister*," she repeated, viciously, "Who also happens to be *married to Medraut*. While Medraut held me captive in *his* villa, amused himself with me whenever he chose, and *you didn't even notice the difference.*"

"Wait—" Arthur stammered. "What—"

"Ask Abbot Gildas," she said, crossing her arms over her chest. "He managed to deduce the truth without even having a decent conversation with the bitch. Or ask Lancelin—ah, no, wait, you can't, because you wanted to kill him, so to keep from harming so much as a hair on your head, he was forced to play the coward and flee. Because he knew you'd keep throwing yourself at him in a rage no matter what we said."

Arthur was not a fool; she had taken him by surprise, but he recovered quickly. "What kind of idiot do you take me for with this farcical tale of a sister like enough to you to be your twin?" he began. "And married to Medraut? Lady, you strain the bounds of—"

There was a not-very-polite cough from behind her. "I presume that you will take *my* word as truth?" The Lady Aeronwen said, acerbically.

Arthur's face took on a look of confusion again. Not because he was confused by what the Lady had said—no, it was surely because he was trying to find a diplomatic way to respond.

Aeronwen did not give him time. "I can bring a hundred direct witnesses from Pywll, nay, more," she snapped. "Not to mention an equal number from Lothian. Gwenhwyfar of Pywll has always had a younger sister as like to her as a twin and separated from her by less than a year. So much like her that though the brat's given name was Gwyneth, she got the name Gwenhwyfach, and her true name was almost forgotten."

The number of dropping jaws around the tent far outnumbered those who could keep their countenance in the face of such information.

"Moreover," Aeronwen continued, "The girl was fostered to Anna Morgause and schooled by her and by Morgana in magic. She grew to womanhood in Lot's court and wedded Medraut." She raised an eyebrow. "Yes, Arthur. Your son by Anna Morgause wedded his foster sister, Gwenhwyfar's near twin, who was schooled in the same kind of magic his mother wielded. The same kind of magic that drew you to Anna Morgause's bed in the first place and brought about Medraut." The Lady stepped up past Gwen and stood in nearly the same position. "As to whether she was the one in your bed the last several months, that I cannot say. But it seems logical."

"And you *might* ask yourself—and your men—just where Medraut is now," Gwen said angrily. "Where are *his* men? And you *might* ask yourself just what someone raised by Lot thought he was going to gain by putting his wife in your bed. And you *might—*"

But she got no chance to go further with that thought, for at that moment, there was a commotion outside the tent, and someone else shoved his way in through the tent flaps.

It was Gwalchmai, and beneath the beard and the dirt and blood, he was as white as snow. He clutched his shoulder, where red stained his armor and tunic. "The gods forgive me, Arthur—" he blurted, swaying where he stood. "Medraut—that misborn, misbegotten son of a witch and a demon—Medraut's on the way at the head of a Saxon army."

For one moment, there was no sound in that tent; it was as if the world had stopped dead in shock.

Except, perhaps, for Gwen. There was a part of her that had expected this moment, had known it was coming all along, and nodded in bitter recognition of that. That was why she recovered first and whirled, her gaze stabbing one of the two young warriors who had escorted her here. "You—" she snapped. "Get me armor to fit my frame. *My* armor, if someone brought it here. And a sword. And most importantly, a bow and a horse of my father's breeding—my Rhys or Pryderi, if they are here."

Her voice seemed to jar them all back to life. The young man gaped at her and looked at Arthur. She frowned back over her shoulder at him. "You are going to need every warrior you have, Arthur. I saw your camp; most of your warriors are not here," she said, her tone clipped and precise. Maybe they were all doomed. Maybe they had been doomed from the beginning. But she would still fight right up to the moment that doom fell upon her. "Medraut must have been planning this for a long time. This is not a good ground to fight on; the only advantage you have is that it is equally bad for both sides."

Arthur looked gray, as if the ground had been cut out from under him. So Medraut's treachery cut him deeper than her defection? Well, so be it. That was just one more indication of how little he had thought of her and what she truly was, how little he had valued it. But he had his wits about him enough to see that she was right. "Do as Gwenhwyfar commands," he told the boy, and he turned to Kai. "Muster out the men. Send messengers. Gwalchmai, how many are there?"

"Same as last time." The old man—when had Gwalchmai gotten old?—clutched his shoulder as Kai pushed past him. "It's the full Saxon army, the one that retreated when we confronted them. That encounter was just a feint to test us and get our numbers. Medraut was planning this all along, planning to get you separated from the rest of your force. We're outnumbered, Arthur. Badly."

Arthur grimaced and grew paler. But he straightened, and Gwen saw that, like her, though doom fell upon them, he would fight to the last.

"Maybe not as badly as you think." Gwen's mind was racing. "Let me go to Yniswitrin. I'll see if I can call Gwyn ap Nudd out. You likely won't get fighters out of him, but he might make a passage for yours to come quickly. There's more than one tale of mortal armies passing through Annwn at need, and he *is* one of your Companions and an ally King." Right now . . . she wished profoundly she could be the one to lead those armies here. But the King of Annwn would be the only one who could.

"I'll go with you," the Lady said quickly, before Arthur could say yea or nay. "With two of us, he is less likely to refuse."

Arthur looked for a moment as if he were going to refuse anyway, but then he shrugged. "Whatever can be done, we must do," he said, his face a mask of resignation.

Gwen didn't wait for him to change his mind. She strode out of the tent with the Lady sailing behind her.

There were several horses tethered beside Arthur's tent, and to her intense relief, one of them was her Pryderi, who tossed his head, whickered, and picked up his ears when he scented her. Whoever had appropriated him—well, too bad, he was going to have to find himself another mount. She ran to the picket line, pulled his reins loose, and hauled herself up into his saddle. The stirrups were set too long; she ignored them for now. The day she couldn't sit a horse for a straight run without stirrups would be a sad one indeed. As Aeronwen stood in the path, she rode up next to the Lady, and offered her hand. Aeronwen weighed next to nothing—did the Ladies never eat?—and Gwen was able to pull her up behind with just a little grunt of effort.

As ever, Pryderi responded as if he could read her mind; he danced a little and then leaped into a full gallop, answering her touch on the reins to arrow toward the distant isle, which rose above its perpetual mist as if it truly didn't belong in this world. Behind her, Gwen heard the camp coming to life, shouted orders and the frantic clashing of men getting armored and armed. In her ear, she heard the Lady softly chanting. What she chanted—well, Gwen didn't recognize it at all; it was older than any words she knew. But she felt it, felt the Power in those words, and felt that Power being drawn from somewhere ahead of them. Pryderi's ears swiveled, then pointed ahead again. He had never been disturbed by anything; she had schooled him to that.

They neared the mist, and the mist swelled and billowed out to meet them in a solid wall of white. Pryderi plunged into it without hesitation.

"Slow him," the Lady said in her ear, but she was already reining Pryderi in, lest he make a misstep, go tumbling, and kill them all. He tossed his head with rebellion, for he loved to run, but dropped immediately to a walk. The mist closed around them so thick that it was even hard to see the ground right under Pryderi. It clung to them, chill, damp, carrying with it a scent of water and green things.

Pryderi's hoofbeats sounded muffled, as if he walked on thick moss. Gwen looked about, and up, trying to catch the landmark of Yniswitrin, but there was nothing, nothing but mist—

"Give him his head," the Lady said. "Trust his instincts. If the King of Annwn is inclined to open his door to us—"

"The King of Annwn could not fail to welcome the Lady of the Cauldron Well and the White Apparition." Gwyn ap Nudd's voice came calmly out of the mist ahead of them. Pryderi stopped; the mist swirled a little, then parted, and then Gwyn stepped out of it, putting one hand on Pryderi's bridle. He looked up at Gwen. "So. Arthur needs his men. I can, and will, bring them through the doors of Annwn."

She let out the breath she had been holding at his answer and bowed in the saddle. "Then I thank you, Lord of Annwn."

He shook his head. "Do not thank me," he said, his eyes growing dark and sad; he released Pryderi and turned back into the mist. "I do them no favors, cousin, for I bring them to their deaths."

Chapter Twenty-Five

Gwen wished that she could see Medraut's face. From where she sat on her horse, all she could see was the suit of armor and the blank faceplate of his helmet. There was no doubt it was him, though. The helm already had a golden coronet around it. It seemed he was very confident of victory over Arthur.

It was the first time she'd ever seen him in armor, although she had no doubt that he knew its weight well and knew the use of that sword he had strapped to his side. He had been one of Arthur's Companions, after all, and that wasn't just an honorary title. Medraut might avoid fighting whenever possible, but he clearly was able to give a good accounting of himself when he had to.

But right now, he surely found himself feeling disconcerted. He had come with his army of Saxons at his back expecting to find Arthur and no more than two hundred of his warriors. Instead, he found himself facing Arthur and every fighter that could be persuaded to cross the arcane gates into and out of Annwn to be here. And for Arthur's sake, that had been nearly all of them.

Even Lancelin.

Lancelin had arrived on his own, weary, on an exhausted horse. He had been taken straight to Arthur. She did not know what had transpired between the two men; she had not been privy to any of it, and he had made no attempt to seek her out, for explanations or otherwise. But Lancelin now held the left flank of the army, in his old position, as Kai held the right. Not by word or gesture had he even acknowledged that she was there, and by now, only the bands of her will held the pieces of her heart together. He had chosen. And as she had known he must, he had chosen the King.

The armies faced one another across a watercourse barely large enough to be called a river. The timely arrival of his men had allowed Arthur to move his forces to slightly better ground before Medraut's arrival; this place was called "Camlann," according to the local farmer who had guided Gwen to several good places to position archers.

But Arthur was determined to avoid a battle if he possibly could. He had hoped that a show of force would make Medraut change his mind; hoped that he could strike some sort of bargain with his son.

So now, two armies of nearly equal size faced each other across a tiny river swollen with spring rains.

Medraut's face was hidden behind a faceplate of blackened metal. Arthur wore only the open-faced helm of a Roman soldier that he had worn all his life as a warrior. *And so they are, on the field as in life. Medraut always concealing what he truly is behind a mask. Arthur never concealing anything . . .*

Except he had, of course. He had hidden so many things; his own birth had been concealed, he himself had been hidden until he had come of age to take back his father's kingship. He had hidden the fact that he had sired Medraut, hidden that he had tried to kill the infant. Hidden that he had caused the slaughter of who knew how many others in an effort to get the one he faced now. He had hidden that Medraut was his son . . .

So many things hidden . . .

It was as if they had conspired together to create this very situation, making one bad choice after another. One thing she would not do—she was not going to lay this at the feet of the gods. No, this was all the doing of mortals, people who had made decisions that ranged from ill-advised to evil. Including, if she was to be honest, some of her own.

An envoy approached Arthur's lines, a white pennon tied to his spear. Another, sent from Arthur, met him at the edge of the river. They conferred. Arthur's envoy returned, then came back and planted his pennon at the river's edge.

There was a flurry of activity, and a few moments later, Gwen felt her sleeve being pulled. She turned to see that fresh faced young man from Arthur's entourage. He blushed; he seemed to do that a lot. "You are wanted for the parley, L—warrior," he said, stumbling as he tried not to say "lady." She nodded and left one of her men in charge as she joined Arthur. Who still would not look at her. Well, let him sulk. She gazed defiantly at him before following him down to the river's edge, where Medraut already waited. The tension was intense; faces were strained, and hands hovered near weapons. It would not take much to cause these men to explode into violence.

She tried not to show her surprise to see that Gwenhwyfach waited there too, just behind Medraut. Arthur, however, did not restrain a start at seeing her sister, and, in fact, he finally glanced over at Gwen before looking back at Medraut's wife. Nor was he the only one. If it had not been that one was gowned and coiffed as a queen and the other had her hair bound up and was in armor, it would have been as if they were reflections of each other.

So, all of you who didn't believe me . . . there you are. My dear sister, in the flesh, and looking more the queen than I do.

And that seemed . . . petty. Was there any reason for Gwenhwyfach to have dressed as if for a coronation?

Medraut pulled off his helmet and tucked it under his arm. His
face was utterly unreadable. "Well, Father," he began, just a little too
casually.

But anything he was going to say was interrupted by his wife.

Gwenhwyfach suddenly stormed across the grass between them,
and before Gwen could even think to move or speak, slapped her
so hard across the face that her lip split and she saw stars and tasted
blood.

"You witless loon!" Gwenhwyfach hissed. "Fool! Idiot! All my life
you were first. All my life I was second to you. Finally I was first! Finally *I* was the one that someone loved! And you *ruined* that!"

She seized Gwen's hair and wrenched her head around with
shocking strength. "All he asked was for you to love him and be a
true woman for him! All! And what did you do? You sat for months
in his court and cried for your toy armor and sword like a spoiled
brat! So I gave him what he wanted, and he loved *me!* And you took
that away from me!"

With a wrench, she flung Gwen to her knees. "You are no woman,"
she spat. "You're a half man. He should have been mine!"

Gwen stayed on her knees as her mind raced. Now she knew what
it was that her visions in Medraut's cell had shown her. Little Gwen
had not fallen entranced with Arthur—she had seen a way to take
Gwen's place with a man who wanted what she was. She had probably
been planning to betray Medraut—or at least, put this day off until
Arthur died naturally, thus having her crown in both the present and
future. But Gwen had escaped and spoiled her plan. Finally she rose,
slowly, and looked into her sister's furious eyes. "Well, little sister,"
she said, weighing each word and casting them like weapons. "All my
life you have coveted what I had, even when you didn't truly want

it or were ill-suited to it. You wanted Medraut because you thought I wanted him and would be jealous of your married state, but your husband married you because he could not have me." She wiped away the blood from her lip with the back of her hand. "It must be causing laughter among the gods that my husband saw in you the reflection of what he wanted me to be and was enchanted. You rightly say that *you* were the one Arthur wanted, and not me, though he knew it not. Given that, I believe that the scales are even between us."

Gwenhwyfach went white with fury. But before she or anyone else could say another word—

There was a cry and a flash of light on metal up on the slope, where the two armies had drawn near—dangerously near—one another.

And another great chorus of shouts and the cry of *"Treachery!"* and the parley disintegrated into chaos as fighting erupted on that slope and, in a flash, spread over the entire field.

Screaming warriors charged from both sides and overran where Arthur's party stood. Gwen found herself separated from the rest and trying to beat her way back to her archers as the two armies surged forward and clashed. For a moment, before any real blows were struck, she felt hysterical laughter bubbling up inside her.

And then, as always, her world narrowed to the fighting in front of her, everything blurring into stroke and counterstroke, spin and blow and evasion. The noise was deafening; she shut it out. Once, she caught a glimpse of Lancelin riding through a sea of fighters, striking out on either side with his sword. Once, of Medraut and Arthur, fighting furiously like a pair of stags, oblivious to everything around them. Arthur's skill was greater than Medraut's, but Medraut was younger . . .

But mostly, it was just trying to stay alive, slipping in mud and blood, breathing the stink of spilled guts and voided bowels, with a stitch in her side and a burning gash across her forehead, with her arm growing heavier with every swing, and her heart in bits at her feet.

It all blurred together, until she was fighting in a kind of animal stupor, going on nothing but training and instinct.

And then, it seemed, she woke to find herself alone and without an opponent. And there was nothing more to fight. Somehow she had gotten to the edge of the battlefield, and as she looked about and saw no more enemies, her sword dropped from fingers too tired to hold it. Then she dropped to her knees, legs too weary to keep her upright. Numbly, she looked over the field again and saw nothing standing, nothing moving, nothing but the dead and a mist rolling over the battlefield to hide it. It was a vision of horror and carnage out of the end of some epic tale, one that does not end well for anyone—a tale that ends with all the heroes dead.

Despair overwhelmed her. She threw back her head and howled, sobbed, and keened a wordless lament, and she wasn't even sure who she was weeping for. Arthur? Lancelin?

Herself?

The end of the world?

For surely this was the end, the very end, of the world. After this, what could there be? Death, death, death; nothing left but darkness and death.

She sagged back on her heels, and the tears poured from that void where her heart had been. She had thought she had wept before. It had been nothing to this; the only thought left to her, if thought it could be at all, was that she would sit her forever, and weep forever, until she turned into a weeping stone and poured her waters into the little river that must now run red with blood until the end of time.

"Gwenhwyfar! *Gwenhwyfar!*" Someone was calling her name. Shaking her. Would not let her mourn in peace. Shook her again, harder. Finally, to make it stop, she looked up through eyes so swollen with weeping they were only slits.

And the shock of what she saw, with mist weaving around them both, dried her tears in an instant.

"You—queen—" she gasped.

Arthur's second wife, cloaked and robed like one of Gildas' monks, put back her hood with an impatient hand. There was no doubt; it was the same woman who was supposed to be dead. "Yes, well, queen no longer, but yes, I was Arthur's second wife. Now get up and come with me. We have need of you."

"We—" She shook her head. This was impossible. How had anyone survived? "Who—"

"Come, warrior. I tell you, you are needed for the journey across Anwnn, and Gwyn ap Nudd cannot hold the door forever."

As if she had no will of her own, Gwen got to her feet and yielded to the phantom's urgent tugs on her arm. Though if the second Gwenhwyfar was a phantom, she was an uncommonly strong and solid one. "Where—"

"Gildas persuaded Arthur to put me aside. Melwas's *love* didn't last past being confronted with an army." The queen's voice dripped with contempt, then softened. "Gildas is a good man. I have been . . . doing penance for my sins under his instruction. But Arthur needs us now. Arthur needs all of us now." Her voice cracked a little. "He is dying."

I thought he was already dead . . .

The mist swirled and billowed around them, making it seem as if they moved through a landscape of dream—or nightmare. They picked their way through tangled, motionless bodies and seemed to be heading for the single patch of light in the thickening shadows.

And then the mist parted before them. Lit by torches, Arthur lay on a crude stretcher, his head pillowed on someone's wadded-up tunic, surrounded by a handful of his Companions, all of them with faces contorted with grief. It was obvious to Gwen that no one could survive the terrible wound in his gut; it had been bound up, but from the amount of blood that had soaked the bandages, he could not have much longer.

Kneeling beside him, his hand clutched in both of hers, was Gwenhwyfach.

"And . . . you really are . . . the sister?" he was saying.

Little Gwen bent over his hand, weeping, and nodded.

He sighed. "Then . . . you are the one that I loved most truly, most dearly, and I could never be healed of that sickness of love," he said tenderly. "You are my true queen and ruler of my heart, who knew the desires of mine without my ever needing to speak them." His free hand moved feebly to the bandages, and his breath caught. "Medraut is dead; no one has ever survived a single blow of Caliburn, and I struck him nine times. But his return blow was as deep as mine, and full as fatal. I shall die soon—"

"No!" Little Gwen cried out. "No, no, you can't leave me! I need you! I'm meant to be your queen!"

He could only shake his head a very little, as his Companions wept.

A new figure loomed out of the mist. Gwyn ap Nudd, who nodded to the old queen and Gwen. "Arthur," he said, his voice deep and sonorous. "It is time."

Little Gwen looked up at him as if to protest, but at a single stern look from him, she shut her mouth, muffled her weeping, got up and stood aside. Four shadowy figures came from behind the King of Annwn; they approached the stretcher and took it up. Gwyn ap Nudd gestured to all three women to follow.

"You bear witness," said Gwyn, as the Companions watched, seemingly unable to move. "You see that these three queens, all beloved of Arthur, come to bear him through Annwn to the Isle of Glass."

The Companions stared; Gwen wanted to say something to them, but a power greater than she could deny pulled her after the others.

The mist closed behind them as they approached the riverbank. The shadow warriors put the stretcher gently on a boat that was tied to the bank; Gwyn gestured to the three of them to enter it as well. "I can go no further," Gwyn said. "But the gate is open for you, cousin, and by your bargain with my people, none will harm you in passage." Gwen went to the prow and stood there, facing the river and the mist; Little Gwen again took her place at Arthur's side and held his hand.

"And you, Queen-that-was, you know the way. Yours will be the guiding hand." The old queen took the tiller, and the shadow warriors, which all seemed to have the heads of beasts, stag, wolf, bear and otter, pushed it off.

For a long time, there was only mist and water, the splashing of waves interrupted only by Little Gwen's sobs. Gwen thought she saw vague shadows in the water and in the mist, but they never approached the boat, so she was never entirely sure what she saw. She felt empty and exhausted, as if she had left all of her emotions back there on the riverbank. And then, out of the mist, loomed a small wooden dock with more shadow figures on it, silhouetted by torches.

But these were not Gwyn ap Nudd's beast-men. Somehow, Gwen was unsurprised to see that they were robed in the garb of monks and that Abbot Gildas led them.

A good dozen hands reached for the boat and helped guide it to the dock and make it fast. More of them reached for the stretcher on which Arthur lay. As they lifted him out of the boat, to Gwen's shock, he opened his eyes and raised his hand.

"Wait," he whispered, and he beckoned to her.

She found tears pouring down her cheeks, again. "I—forgive me—" she choked out. "I never meant to harm you. I wanted to protect you from Medraut, and then—I thought you didn't care for me, I thought you would be pleased to see the back of me."

"It is you who should forgive me. I tried to make you—what you were not. I took a warhorse, and tried to fit it to a plow." Pain contorted his face for a moment. "Go, and be yourself again. I release you from—every promise, every duty, everything."

He waved his hand. The monks carried him away with Gwenhwyfach in close attendance, leaving Gwen and the old queen standing on the dock. And in that moment, a blankness came over Gwen, mercifully taking all thoughts with it.

Gwen came back to herself sitting in the Abbey church, with no recollection of how she had gotten there, nor how she had come to be clean of the mud and blood of combat and reclothed in another set of trews and tunic. The old queen was on her knees at the altar in the front of the church, but Gwen could not muster the strength or the will to move. It was dark in here, with only the candles on the altar and a small red lamp for light, but it was also dark beyond the windows. Somehow full night had fallen, not the strange twilight of the mist, while she had sat unaware.

Another blank came over her; this one was probably not as long as the last, for when it passed, Gildas was sitting beside her; he peered at her when she moved her head a little. "Ah," he said. "You are back among us."

She nodded and looked at the altar for the old queen. But she wasn't there.

"Arthur?" she asked, her throat sore and dry, her voice coming out as a hoarse whisper.

"He is gone," the Abbot said, simply. "And . . . so is your sister." He shook his head. "When Arthur died, she went mad. She was like a wild thing. She railed at us, that we had not tried hard enough to save him, that we had stolen her crown and her king." He blinked. "I can truly say that I have never seen such . . . such a strange and fearful sight. She was like one possessed."

Numbly, she shook her head. "Only by her own selfishness."

He sighed. "She attacked my monks, clawing at them like a cat, in a frenzy. If she was not possessed, then surely she was mad."

Gwen blinked. "But you said—she was dead—"

"We managed to repel her and drive her out of the chapel. We found her in the morning at the edge of the lake, drowned. She died within moments of him, we think." He shook his head. "She must have fallen in at some deep point. She must have truly loved him to have been so frenzied."

She decided not to disabuse him of his notion. "Yes," she said slowly. "She did." *Or at least, she loved his crown.*

"Then we will bury them together." He peered into her face. "Come. You should sleep."

"But—"

"The old queen—we call her Sister Blessed now—will hold vigil over them. And we shall have them buried by your Ladies, here, though not in ground consecrated to Christian use. Come." He took her hand and tugged at her. She stood.

And then there was another blank moment, and when she came out of this one, she was lying on a pallet, covered by a wool blanket, in a small wooden hut. The door stood open, and sunlight poured through it.

She was still numb, and her mind . . . wouldn't work. It was almost as if she were under the influence of one of Medraut's potions. Finally she just gave up trying to think at all. She let people lead her about, ate and drank what was put in her hands, did what she was told. She stood at the side of the grave as the monks laid Arthur and Little Gwen in it. That gave her a strange sense of dislocation—she felt a moment of utter terror as she looked at the dead face that was so like her own, could have been her own. For that moment, it seemed as if it were she, not Little Gwen, who was being covered over with earth . . .

But the moment passed, giving way again to numbness.

The numbness, the dullness, persisted. She spent days just sitting in the church or beside the lake, or at the Cauldron Well. If someone gave her something to eat, she ate it; if not, it didn't seem to matter. Nothing seemed to matter; not only her heart was broken, so was her spirit, and she was nothing but a hollow shell where once there had been a warrior with her name.

And so the days passed.

And then, one day she woke, and woke fully, and her mind worked again. She sat up and dressed quickly, feeling almost as if she had been very sick, and now the fever had broken.

Yet once she had dressed, she was at a loss for what to do. She had no idea what was going on beyond the boundaries of the Abbey. Had the Saxons overrun the country at last? Was there any resistance to them at all? Was there anything out there, beyond the deceptive peace of this place, or was it all a chaos of warfare and blood?

At least she could find the old queen, maybe, or Abbot Gildas, or one of the Ladies, and ask some sensible questions.

She ventured out into the morning sunlight, and that was when she saw him riding in along the path that led to the Abbey, looking worn and weary and as broken as she.

"Lancelin?" she faltered.

And although he could not possibly have heard her, he looked up, straight at her.

But his expression did not change. And although he dismounted, tethered a horse that looked as beaten and weary as he, and walked toward her, there was nothing of joy and nothing of love, in his face.

"Gwen," he said, stopping a little too far away from her to have taken her hand. "They told me you were here."

And there it was. That love, if love it really had been, had burned bright and guttered out. When she tried to find it in herself, all she could sense were cinders and ashes and regret. She nodded. "I have been ill," she said, and she released that dead love to fall to pieces in the aching void inside her. "I have heard of nothing since—"

"Ah." The silence hung awkwardly between them. "They never sing of these things, in the tales. Never talk about what happens after everything is over."

She swallowed. "And what does happen?" she asked.

His eyes held the wisdom of terrible sorrow. "Life goes on. Planting and harvest, birth and death, sun and rain. The world does not end for everyone. Just for a few." He sighed. "But you don't want to hear philosophy. The Saxons took a terrible beating, and no, they have not overrun the countryside. There is no High King, and things have broken down into squabbling among all the petty kings again. Most of the Companions are dead. Those that survived have retreated to their estates or taken places in the courts from which they came. Even Celliwig is mostly deserted, except for Kai and the few men that limped home from Camlann. Rumor says that you are dead, you are turned Christian and gone into retreat, or you have followed Arthur into Annwn, where you will both await a day that you are needed."

He shrugged. "I came to see if the fourth rumor was true, that you were here, and if you were, to say farewell."

She stood awkwardly, hands dangling at her sides. Once she would not have been able to stop herself; she would have reached for him, begged him to take that farewell back. Now?

"Then do fare well, Lancelin," she said. *He forgave us,* she wanted to say. But he probably would not believe that. He was the sort that flogged himself relentlessly with his faults. "What we did or did not do changed nothing. Medraut did not conjure up that army out of nothing. He had this planned—for years, I think. If it had not been now, it would have been soon."

Lancelin's lips thinned a moment; then, reluctantly, he nodded. He looked up at the stone tower on top of Yniswitrin. "Do you know," he said at last, his tone too casual, "What it was that caused the fighting to break out?"

"I was too far away to see. Only, there was a shout, and I think someone drew a sword—"

"When your sister struck you, half the men were ready to charge. It only needed an excuse. Someone saw a snake and drew his sword to slay it." He shook his head. "And someone saw the sword drawn and shouted treachery. That is what makes me think you are right. Nothing we did or did not do made any difference. This was a mighty storm, and we were but reeds in its path." He looked back at her. "I am going away. I am not sure where, just yet. Somewhere I can find some peace, I hope."

She closed her eyes against the pain in his. "I hope so too, Lancelin. Fare you well."

She kept them closed for a moment as a single tear forced its way beneath the lid of her right eye and moved down her cheek. If there was still anything, any spark in those ashes, he would see that tear, and he would touch it, or kiss it away, and—

But there was no touch, not of finger nor of lips. And when she opened her eyes again, it was to see his figure riding away, back as straight as a staff, yet head bowed beneath burdens he would not let go. It seemed too cruel that he was haloed by the sunlight of a perfect, peaceful day.

She wiped the tear away herself and walked to the little dock. The mist eddied and billowed over the lake, now showing, now hiding, the farther shore.

"And what will you do now, fair cousin?"

Somehow she was not surprised to find Gwyn standing beside her, though she had heard no one approach.

And that was when she realized what made her feel so hollow and so lost inside, so empty, and so broken. For the first time in her life, she had no direction, no purpose, and no certainty. She was a boat adrift, with no paddle and no tiller. "I don't know," she replied, and she closed her eyes on grief. "There seems no place and no need for me now."

He considered that in silence. "Have your hands lost their skill with blade and bow?" he said, finally.

"I don't—I don't think so." Yes, she did have that. And in the chaos that would come now, there would surely be a use for such skills. "But who would take me? I betrayed Arthur—"

"Those who are well aware you did nothing of the sort?" Gwyn replied. He put his hands on her shoulders and turned her to face inland. "Look there. That peaceful Abbey of the Christ followers. The Saxons too follow that path and will leave them in peace, but there are those who will not, who will hear tales of wealth and think it is the wealth of gold and silver, and not of wisdom. They will need a strong hand to help protect them. And look there." He turned her a little, aiming her at that hidden place that held the School of the Ladies and the Cauldron Well. "The Old Ways will die unless someone finds a way to hide them among the New. And the old queen, who is now called Sister Blessed, she would do that if she knew it was needed, for it was the Ladies who welcomed her as well as the Abbot. Or—" And now he turned her to face the mist. "—Or you can join my folk in Annwn. You will not be the first to join us, nor the last. And there is use for you there, as well. Or you can go into the wilderness and make a hermitage for yourself. Or return to your father and serve him and your sisters. Many choices are yours, more than most have now."

He turned her to face him. "You have work, cousin. But you will have to make it for yourself. You no longer serve anyone for the moment; you are your own master."

So there it was. *Be careful what you ask for—it might be what you get.* Hadn't she longed for just that in the days after she had escaped from Medraut? She was her own master.

Her mind stirred, moved again, turning like an old mill wheel too long left idle. Not her father; he had done well enough this long without her, and she could prove a liability, even a danger. There were men, like King March, who would hear of her being there and want to take and conquer her just to be known as the man who "owned" Gwenhwyfar. She would not bring that down on those she loved.

And not a hermitlike existence either. That would drive her mad.

But here . . .

Gwyn had said that he thought there was a purpose for her, past being a mere warrior. The Folk of Annwn had answered to her call. The Ladies themselves came out to defend her.

Abbot Gildas called her friend.

She *could* be the bridge between the old and new. She was, perhaps, the only one who had all the skills and all the friends, to do so. She could not make Arthur's dream of one kingdom come true in this lifetime, but she could plant the seeds for it to grow when the time was right.

A lightness began to trickle into that emptiness inside her. "There is much that can be done here," she said slowly.

Gwyn nodded. "Yes, there is."

She took a deep breath and felt her spirit come back to life. "Then it is time to start doing it."

Afterword

I think every fantasy writer decides at one point or another to tackle "the matter of Britain," otherwise known as the legend of King Arthur. The genesis of my own stab at this came when I was looking into Welsh legends and came upon the curious Triad of "The Three Guineveres." Triad 56 of the Trioedd Ynys Prydein, translated as "The Triads of the Island of Britain," lists the "Three Great Queens" of Arthur's court.

Three Great Queens of Arthur's Court:
Gwennhwyfar daughter of Cywryd Gwent,
And Gwenhwyfar daughter of Gwythyr son of Greidawl,
And Gwenhwyfar daughter of (G)ogfran the Giant.
[Trans. By Rachel Bromwich]

Well that certainly piqued my curiosity, as did the mention of yet another "Guinevere," the "False Guinevere" or Gwenhwyfach, translated as "Little" or "Lesser" Guinevere. She is often said to be the bastard daughter of King LLuedd Ogrfan Gawr, or Ogrfan the Giant, born on the same day as her sister.

Yet another triad, Triad 53, describes the "Three Harmful Blows" of Britain and states that the third was when Gwenhwyfach struck Gwenhwyfar and caused the battle of Camlann.

And last of all I found this extremely interesting item in my researches, three stanzas found by Jenny Rowland: *"in the margin of the Dingestow 8 copy of Ymddiddan Arthur a'r Eryr (Aberysywyth, National Library of Wales, MS 5268, p. 461)."*

[Gwenhwyfar speaks:]
Arthur fab Uthr of the long sword
I will say to you ?now/sadly the truth:
there is a master over every strong one.
[Arthur speaks:]
Gwenhwyfar you are ?Gwenh[w]yfach.
I have never been healed of love-sickness for you.
Medrawd is dead. I myself almost.
A surgeon has never seen a scar
where Caledfwlch [Excaliber] struck once:
I have struck Medrawd nine times."

Now when you add in all the times that Guinevere seems to have been kidnapped, wandered away, run off with someone (not usually Lancelot!) and otherwise had any number of wild excursions, this seems a rather too active life for any one woman. Then you look at the places where she is childless, has one son, twin sons, and wonder which is true. And finally looking at how she supposedly died—where she is buried with Arthur or somewhere else, is killed by Arthur after running off with Melwas, gets married (by force or willingly) to Mordred, becomes a nun, or dies of a broken heart after Kai kills her son (or sons), I began to form a picture in my mind of not one, but three queens by that name.

Now I am not even going to pretend to be a Welsh/Celtic scholar, and I freely admit I made most of this up out of the little bits and pieces I found above. In my mind, I fastened on the third Guinevere, and I could easily see a scrappy fighter, much younger than Arthur, reluctantly wedded to a king quite old enough to be her father, as part of a bargain and power play—but who, schooled early on in the discipline and duty of princes, intended to make the best of it she could. And since the road to hell is paved with good intentions . . .

Therein lies the tale. I hope you enjoyed it.